Russell's

DERRICK

ISBN 10: 1721220054

ISBN 13: 978-1721220052

THE SECOND INSTALLMENT OF GAVIN NOLAN'S BIOGRAPHY

BY
RUSSELL

EDITED BY
THERESA SNYDER

ACKNOWLEDGEMENTS

I WOULD LIKE TO THANK THERESA FOR USING HER AMAZING EDITING SKILLS. WITHOUT HER TALENT, I DON'T BELIEVE MR. WILLIAMSON WOULD HAVE SHARED HIS STORY FOR ALL OF YOU.

Catch a preview of

Russell's

QUINN

The Final Installment

of the Gavin Nolan Series

at the end of the book...

DERRICK

To Missy & Jeff

DERRICK

"As performers we are merchants of morality."

—Erving Goffman

DERRICK

Prologue

Alarmed, the woman's eyes opened. Her nerves twitched slightly, as if an electric shock rattled her body.

Instantly, an eerie darkness consumed her, and an unusual stillness blanketed her surroundings.

Where am I?

With her instinctual medical training, she began immediately diagnosing her own condition: blurry vision, raspy breath, citrus acidic taste at the back of her throat, and weak muscles. The signs were a tell-all. She had been drugged. Most likely either clonazepam or estazolam.

As her thick braids fell in front of her eyes, she realized that her body was hanging in midair. Above her, a rope bound her hands. The burning strain in her deltoids ached deep into her lower back.

The air was unusually frigid. Her entire body was trembling. She looked down and realized she was completely naked.

Who took off my clothes? Her mind raced with a fresh wave of panic.

All she could remember was getting home from a run in the cold rain of a late November day that had chilled her to the core. Since the presentation of her dissertation was only days away, she relieved the building stress with those exhilarating runs. They were especially liberating knowing that she had to head back to the university lab. Entering the darkened house, she had sworn she'd left the light on. She recalled a quick shadow slipping just behind her in her peripheral vision. She'd felt a sudden blow to her head. She'd fallen against the wooden banister—

What day is it?

The presentation was on Saturday. Did she miss it? A sense of dread engulfed her, then fear. All the seemingly endless months and years of planning her project, all the meetings with that arrogant, dimwitted professor, all those countless hours in the lab…it would all be for nothing. Most importantly, all the sacrifices she'd made with her family, spending so much time away from her daughter—and well, her husband too—would be just a waste.

In the inky darkness, a slight shift of movement awakened her senses.

She was not alone. Attempting to say something, nothing came out except a low groan from her lips. The large figure—a man, no doubt—stopped for a moment. Did he hear her? See her?

Tilting her head slightly, more of her thick dark braids fell to the right side of her face. As her eyes were adjusting to the murkiness, she detected a figure near a square object. A red light blinked incessantly, and with her cloudy vision, it seemed like a floating, pulsating blob. Turning away, a sudden surge of vertigo overwhelmed her and she forced her eyes shut.

As she opened her eyes again, the woman saw a faint light seeping from under the cracks of a doorway on the other side of the space. It looked like long skeletal fingers creeping closer to her.

Footsteps approached her. Suddenly, a smooth gloved hand aggressively grabbed her ankle.

"Hey," she attempted weakly. Instead it sounded more like "Haammph."

Below her, the figure worked quickly, tying a rope tightly around first her left ankle, then the right. She wanted nothing more than to kick him as hard as she could, but the drug inhibited her, and her noodle-like legs hung uselessly. As the man worked rapidly, his broad shoulders made him look bulky next to her thin legs. His jerking movements triggered the scent of sour urine that rose from her own skin and stung her nose, and a tear dripped from her eye. Once he finished, he scooted back and moved his head to and fro. Was he on his knees? She couldn't tell from her angle.

The sound of stone scraped along the floor.

The woman concluded that escape was improbable, and her

heart began to race despite the coma-inducing toxin pumping through her bloodstream. A mumbled whimper came to her lips.

Standing up, the man straightened to his full height. His dark clothing constricted tighter against his fit frame, and she could feel his gaze upon her. Was he admiring her? Shaking a braid out of her left eye, she saw that his face seemed unusually dark, but his white skin was visible around the perimeter of his oval face. His chin was rough, scruffy with hair. Was that a beard? Either way, his face was covered in…makeup? She wasn't sure. Suddenly, he turned away from her and disappeared farther into the shadows.

She looked up at her hands, which tingled from the loss of circulation due to the wiry rope. Over the moldy, dusty scent of the room, a faint whiff of fresh popcorn drifted into her nose. Her stomach rumbled. Then the feeling dissipated quickly.

Unexpectedly, the rope around her hands clenched tighter. Her body was being hoisted farther in the air, and the fiery ache in her shoulders screamed, causing her to moan softly. As her body inched higher, the ropes around her ankles tightened. She was being stretched out. Soon, she heard a series of pops emanating within her; her spinal cord was cracking. A rippling shockwave of pain crashed through her hips as the pressure intensified.

On the final yank, the dim light on the other side of the room disappeared. The man stopped pulling on the rope. Oddly, the darkness comforted her as it wrapped around her snuggly.

The man's footsteps came closer. His overwhelming pine-scented cologne wafted over her. She could see his shadowy figure at her waist. Being this close, she could make him out more clearly, but she had a difficult time staying focused. Against the dark makeup, a pearly white-toothed grin materialized on his darkened face. It was similar to that of the Cheshire cat in Alice's Wonderland, yet it was more malicious—a demonic smirk.

Casually, he grabbed her by the waist, causing another pop. His other hand forced itself savagely between the narrow of her legs and opened them wide.

No, not like this, her mind screamed. *Not again.*

But instead of saying this, she could only produce a series of grunts like that of a dying animal. From behind her, she heard scraping metal. The sound of mournful instrumental music rose up in the black space then, almost covering the metallic scraping. The long notes and disconsolate tempo seemed familiar to her...But from what? As the music became louder, the man's gloved fingers slid inside of her slit all too painfully and aggressively. Within seconds, he'd inserted a cold metallic tip inside of her, scratching her inner flesh.

Her muffled cry went unanswered.

With a quick motion, the man reached behind him and produced an object in his hand. Even as the soft light from under the crack appeared again, it glimmered. He slapped it directly on her abdomen, took out a roll of tape, and went about taping the device to her. His gloved hand slowly rubbed the area around the tape and inched up to her breasts. The fiendish grin widened on the man's face. Painfully, he pinched her nipples hard.

His heavy breaths indicated his sinister enjoyment.

"Hmm, my dark beauty," he whispered, "you were one of the best."

His voice was hauntingly familiar. *From where?*

As he lowered his hands, the music stopped, and a muffled narrator spoke in a dull intonation, sounding just as dreary and foreboding as the music. While she couldn't understand exactly what was being said, the distorted monologue was oddly familiar, indicating a stark, serious message. It suddenly dawned on her that other people had to be there too, in that light.

"Hea...heal," she began breathlessly, attempting to sound out help.

The man snorted out a quick laugh and stepped away. She could make out his shadowy figure stepping near the blinking red light. She now saw that the flashing light came from a glowing digital timer; it was set for two minutes.

Shaking her head, she moaned, "Peese...dawwnt...gawd."

The timer began to count backwards: *1:59, 1:58, 1:57...*

The man pulled out a long knife, and she felt the tug of the rope rippling above her. The coarse metal tip edged itself deeper inside.

Instantaneously, the rope snapped.

Her hands fell in front of her. At the same moment, she gargled out a scream as the long, sharp-tipped object slid swiftly inside of her. She felt the warm blood running over the cool skin of her inner legs. Her own weight drove the metal piece deeper, and she soon tasted blood at the back of her throat. The white-hot pain ripped through her, making her body quiver. Instinctively, she determined that the object had already punctured her lungs, which made it more difficult to breathe. The red liquid streaming out of her meant a quick bleed-out.

The woman did not want to die. Especially not like this.

Images of her daughter came to her mind—sweet brown eyes, a big grin with two missing baby teeth, soft brown skin—and tears streamed down the woman's face. Horrifically, she understood the impending grave circumstance: she would never see her daughter again, would never see her finish first grade, would never see her graduate from college, would never see her get married—

1:01, 1:00, 0:59...

Her toes now touched the gritty floor, slipping on her own blood.

From the shadows, the man appeared in front of her and stared at her. He seemed pleased with himself. Leaning closer to her, his radiant jade-colored eyes hungrily consumed her misery. And that devilish smile widened. This close, she could see the layers of a pattern in his dark makeup, much like that of camouflage. Like when she was in the military, when she had to be covert for certain training exercises. Although she never used it in the field, she recognized it.

"If you are lucky, he'll find out who you were, then I'll be waiting for him," the man said, his voice low. Leaning even closer, his warm lips pressed tightly against her ear. "Good night, my sweet."

The man kissed her gently even as she tried to resist. As he inched away from her, she could see that her own blood smeared his lips. His pink tongue licked it away.

Stepping backwards, the man disappeared into the murky shadows.

...0:36, 0:35, 0:34...

"Naw...naw," she cried out to no one.

The mumbling narrator's voice and contemptuous music covered her cries. The damn blinking red light only stared at her and counted down each second.

How she wanted to hug her daughter one last time.

...0:25, 0:24, 0:23...

Closing her eyes, the woman could no longer feel her legs. Too much blood lost. She no longer felt any pain, and it did not matter anymore. She could feel herself succumbing to the nothingness.

The last image in her mind was her sweet little girl playing in the fall leaves mere days before. She could still hear her daughter's lilting giggles as the auburn and orange leaves danced around her small body. She could almost smell the fresh autumn wind. And she could feel her child's small warm hand in her own.

Love you, baby. See you again one day.

...0:09, 0:08, 0:07...

A brief flash of light engulfed her, causing her to open her eyes. An intense radiant heat consumed her bare body. The woman even smelled her flesh cooking like burnt bacon in a frying pan. And for a very brief moment, she sensed her body floating through the air.

She welcomed the quick death.

PART I
JANICE

*"All dreamers and sleepwalkers must pay the price,
and even the invisible victim is responsible for the fate of all."*
—*Ralph Ellison*

*"Last night you didn't call,
Had me worried all night long,
Why you keep doing me wrong?"*
—*Leela James*

DERRICK

ONE

A burst of shouts, cheers, and whistles thundered throughout the packed sports bar. Large flat-screen TVs hanging from the ceiling displayed the Bears game. For the most part, all eyes were thoroughly engaged in the spectacle. All around, a sea of blue and orange jerseys, t-shirts, and accessories blanketed the crowd. The crackling chatter of the sportscasters' overly embellished commentaries reverberated against the speakers, while in the background the low echoes of spectators at Soldier Field hummed like busy wasps. Above it all, the people in the bar continued to speak amongst each other over the noises, adding to the soup of distorted noises.

Since he had been seeing Chad, Gavin understood quickly how much of a football fan he was, even more of a diehard Bears fan. When Gavin arrived, Chad had already anchored a round high-top table with no chairs near the largest TV. They stood around the table, the crowd pressing up against them. Gavin enjoyed being at the bars, watching Chad intently scrutinize the game. Truthfully, Gavin never really enjoyed the sport, but Chad's admiration for it made him even more attractive.

"Goddammit! Catch the ball!" Chad shouted at the screen next to Gavin. A chorus of boos instantly erupted, drowning out some of Chad's words. The replay showed a thick player running toward the end zone for a pass, his fingers just touching the ball before it fell to the ground.

Behind Gavin, a few guys wearing tight Bears jerseys shouted as well, sloshing their beer around and splashing some on Gavin. He took a step to the side and bumped into Chad's friend, Gordon. Gordon had wedged himself purposely between Gavin and Chad, and he glared at Gavin much like a snake ready to attack.

"What the fuck," Gordon hissed.

Suddenly, Chad turned his head toward Gavin and shouted, "Can you believe that idiot?"

The burly guy next to Gavin answered, "Asshole should of caught it!"

"Hampton sucks this season!" Chad returned and turned his attention back to the screen.

Chad had persuaded Gavin to meet Gordon tonight. He was Chad's longtime friend since high school. After hearing the various stories about Gordon and his promiscuous lifestyle, Gavin almost wanted to bow out. And, after meeting the little man in the tight black jeans and low-cut purple tank top, he could only wonder how other men found him attractive.

A few weeks ago, Chad had introduced Gavin to his family. Chad casually told him it wasn't the first time he'd brought a boyfriend home. Even though Gavin was on edge, Chad's mother made him feel more relaxed, while his father kept a tighter lip. His mother was a principal for an elementary school, and his father worked as an accountant at a small firm in the city. While Chad helped his mother in the kitchen with the prime rib, his father was too preoccupied talking about Chad's career to ask Gavin anything about being a cop. In between, one of Chad's sisters and her new boyfriend popped in, which seemed to ease the awkward tension a bit. Last week, his mother invited them over for an early Thanksgiving dinner, which was a good sign. According to Chad, of course.

Before that, Chad had introduced him to several friends, which consisted mainly of other gay and lesbian couples. Naming Gavin the *cop boyfriend*, all of Chad's friends readily received Gavin into the fold. They were fascinated about his job of course, and Gavin had to deflect many of their probing questions. What made him feel even more at ease was that they accepted Gavin and Chad's PDA as they held hands and kissed each other on the cheek. Gavin's unease was dissipating. Yet being in public with Chad seemed to be the challenge.

Something he had yet to confess to Chad.

Chad had been trying to get Gordon to meet up with them for weeks, but Gordon would always cancel at the last minute, postponing it or making up senseless excuses. Now that Gavin had finally met him, he found him to be much more reserved than Chad's other friends. In Gavin's peripheral vision, Gordon looked sour and standoffish as he crossed his arms over his narrow chest.

At that moment, the game went to a commercial break, and the sound of the TVs were switched off. Thunderous beats of an up-tempo electronic dance track pulsated throughout the place, bringing the atmosphere into magical life. Some were already dancing in tight spaces throughout the bar. Others were fixated on checking everyone else out or fighting through the crowd to get a smoke. Some fell into conversations with friends or strangers. Near the exposed brick two-story wall, shirtless bartenders with painted Bears symbols on their chests worked behind the light-up bar, while waiters in tight blue shorts and sleeveless Bears t-shirts ran around, hurriedly taking orders.

Skirting around the table, Chad slipped his thick arm around Gavin's waist and kissed him on the cheek briefly with a smile. His recently grown goatee caressed Gavin's skin.

"Ready for another round, boys?" Chad was already reaching for Gavin's empty bottle.

"Sure thang, sweetie," Gordon replied in a syrupy tone with an exaggerated grin. The dark mascara, blue eye shadow, and light rouge made his long, gaunt face look Egyptian in the darkened bar.

"Be right back."

Gavin squeezed Chad's hand as he walked away. Staring after him, he thought Chad looked especially good tonight. His dark chino pants hugged his firm, round ass nicely. Gavin's feelings had intensified for his lover over the weeks, probably due to meeting his family and friends. Chad was helping him discover a whole new lifestyle that he was beginning to admire more and more. Watching Chad disappear into the crowd, Gavin's eyes scanned the bar and soaked up the scenery.

All the while, Chad had been asking to meet Gavin's brother and his friends. A part of him held back. What would Evan think about his brother being gay? As far as friends, he didn't know how they would react. In the last few months, he had been hiding this new life from everyone else. Perhaps it was selfish, but he didn't want to somehow spoil it.

Soon. One day soon, he thought.

Gordon straightened his posture and pulled out a tattered

phone. His long fingers danced over the screen.

Clearing his throat, Gavin leaned over and asked, "Why do you hate me?"

The man stopped typing and eyed him up and down menacingly. "I don't hate you. You're just fucking annoying."

Well. Blunt, aren't we? "Why do you say that?" Gavin wished for a beer at that very moment.

"Since you came around, I haven't seen much of *my* Chad."

Your Chad? "I apologize for taking up so much of his time," Gavin said sardonically.

"He can do whatever he wants. I don't tell him not to see his friends." Gordon rolled his eyes toward the dance floor. For a few moments, the energetic techno music surrounded them as they remained silent. Looking over his shoulder, Gavin spotted Chad by the sight of his newly sculpted high-top haircut, shaved on the sides.

Then Gordon shouted over the music, "Chad told me you were married once."

"Yeah, once," Gavin returned and glanced at him. His eyes gravitated toward a group of women in Bears outfits who were hanging all over each other.

"How long was the marriage?"

"Too long."

He inquired indignantly, "How come?"

Gavin chose his wording carefully; he somehow didn't trust Chad's friend. "She had a boyfriend."

Gordon didn't look surprised. Again, another wave of music grew louder between them as the crowd appeared to be gathering around, reclaiming their spots for the game.

"First you like the pussy, now you like the cocks. That it?" His voice lowered to a deep baritone.

"What's your point?" Gavin asked him.

Abruptly, Gordon leaned on the table toward him. The sickeningly sweet smell of cheap perfume wafted into Gavin's nose.

"Listen, Chad's my best friend," he stated vehemently. "Been through a fuckin' lot."

"I gathered—"

"Cop or no cop," Gordon interrupted, "don't fuck over Chad." He leaned in within inches of Gavin's face and added, "or you're gonna deal with me, mothafucka."

Dramatically, Gordon resumed his position, grinning. He was probably pleased with himself.

Got it, Gavin thought.

At that same moment, Chad appeared with their drinks: one beer for himself and one for Gavin, and an apple martini for Gordon, who squealed in delight. Just as before, the EDM was switched off and the game was back on. For a few minutes, Gavin stared at the television, watching Chad and the crowd shout at it. Gordon coquettishly slid closer to Chad, touching his arm and whispering something into his ear. Slugging back his beer, Gavin felt like the third wheel on his own date.

"I know that slut!" Gordon shouted and hopped off his stool. "Going to say hi to her. Bitch owes me a favor."

"Sure," Chad said, smiling as he let his friend kiss him on the cheek. Chad squeezed himself closer to Gavin, and his warm hand found Gavin's lower waist, which felt comforting.

"Don't you like this place?" Chad shouted in his ear. "Having a good time with Gordon?"

"Sure, having a great time," Gavin returned, finishing off his beer.

"Liar!" Chad chuckled at him.

"No really, I am." Gavin looked into Chad's dark brown eyes.

"Let me guess," Chad said. "He said, 'don't mess with my friend' or something like that, right?"

"Not exactly." Gavin shifted closer to Chad.

"Relax," Chad answered. "Gordon hates *everyone* the first time, don't worry. He's just like that."

"Good to know," Gavin replied.

Loud sounds echoed through the room, and Chad's eyes went to the screen.

"Yeah, throw the damn thing!" Chad shouted while the people around them cheered.

Glancing around, Gavin spotted Gordon at the table of women. His body was animated as his thin arms flew about in the air and his head jostled back and forth. While three of them were seemingly interested in what Gordon had to say, the other two were busy tasting each other's lipstick to even care.

"Since you met some of my friends already," Chad said, standing straight. He looked even larger in his tight black Henley shirt—almost like a linebacker himself. "When do I get to meet yours?"

Before Gavin could answer, his phone vibrated.

"Wait on that," Gavin teased, looking down at his phone. It was Derrick. "Got to take this."

Chad's smirk soured slightly.

Gavin inched toward the bathrooms at the very back of the bar. As he looked at the TV screen, a commercial came on and the music pumped out.

*****

Turning his back to the crowd in the narrow hallway, Gavin called Derrick back.

"You rang?" Gavin stated simply.

"Seen the news?" He sounded out of breath.

"Um… no," he replied. Pressing his hand against his other ear, he said, "Looking now."

Pivoting on his heel, he turned to look at a nearby TV. On it, Lisa Deurne, the same reporter who'd interviewed him some time ago, was standing in a crowded neighborhood. Her brown coat was pulled tight around her body, a hat sitting snug over her long blond hair, which flowed out as she spoke into a mic. Small white puffs of her breath appeared in the cold night air. The bottom of the screen read *Breaking News: Large Explosion Near S. 55th Street.* As the cameraman followed her, Deurne ducked past the fire trucks and stood in a clear shot of a building still on fire. At the peak of the building, elongated licks of fire shot out of the top windows while firemen aggressively sprayed water at it. Enormous billows of gray smoke cascaded out of the bottom into the surrounding area, causing a foggy atmosphere and eventually disappearing into the night sky. Within the haze, just behind the reporter, the red and blue lights of the emergency vehicles appeared like dusty stars in a creamy cloud nebula.

"The fire's at Opus Theater." Derrick's connection was breaking slightly.

"I know the place." He'd gone there from time to time to watch documentaries when he was in grad school. He and his ex-wife, Emily, had their first date there. Bitterly, he commented, "We don't do fires."

Derrick gave a quick snort. "G, you're fuckin' hilarious!"

"What does this have to do with us?" Gavin turned away from the TV, took a couple steps down the hallway, and leaned against the wall.

On the other end, Derrick asked, "Where are you? It's loud."

A fit man in a Bears muscle shirt passed him closely, smelling faintly of whiskey and spicy cologne. He gave Gavin a wink, nodding toward the bathroom as he rubbed his crotch.

"At a bar, watching the game."

"Football? Thought you didn't like that shit," Derrick replied.

"Why are you calling?" he asked, ignoring his partner's question.

"No choice…" Derrick's voice faded out, and then came back, "…all have to go down. Priority. Creighton's orders. I'm about ten minutes away from the scene."

Fuck you, Quinn! "Since when has he started doing that?" Gavin said.

"He's the asshole boss," Derrick returned quickly. "Better get here quick. Shit looks crazy down here."

"Fine," he grumbled. "Be there when I get there."

"Hey," he added, "Creighton specifically requested us. Well *you,* really."

"Why?" *The asshole could have texted me.*

"Don't know, man. Maybe you're the fucking poster child for the department," Derrick rebutted. "And dress warm. Cold as a bitch tonight."

The phone went dead.

The beefy man came out of the bathroom and gave Gavin a sultry smile. He leaned toward Gavin and whispered, "Call me." His hot, sour breath cascaded over Gavin's cheek as he slipped a paper into his hand and then disappeared into the crowd. Opening it, Gavin read: *Love to bottom for you. Doug.* Doug's number followed the quickly scrawled message. As Gavin looked back, he noticed a bunch of good-looking guys whistling and patting the beefy man on the back.

Fortunately, this was a good way to get out of the rest of the night and having to make forced conversation with Gordon.

Gavin approached the table, where Chad's warring interests in Gordon's story and the football game forced his eyes to spring back and forth like a tennis match. Gordon's deep voice carried over the sounds of the bar, and Gavin could hear the end of the story.

"Finally, the motherfucka has the nerve to tell me that my stilettoes were not high enough." Gordon placed his hand over his chest. Leaning closer to Chad, who seemed more intent on the game than hearing about stilettoes., Gordon added, "So I says to that asshole that I ain't going be his queen that night. And walked away. Know what happened?" He took in a melodramatic breath, hoping Chad would look. "That stud chased after me, bought me drinks, and then we went back to his place."

"Then what?" Chad asked, as if on cue.

Gordon grabbed his arm dramatically and said, "Once we got to his place, he starts gettin' all over me. I'm like, into it. Then…then he takes off his pants. Oh lordy! That white boy had the tiniest itty-bittiest little dick I've ever seen. I pull on my dress and tell him to use a pair of tweezers to jerk off with, 'cause I ain't gonna have it. Then I walked out."

Gordon erupted in laughter while Chad joined in with what sounded like a forced polite chuckle before sipping the last of his beer.

"What did I miss?" Gavin asked evenly.

"Shit, the story about my last date," Gordon said, eyeing Gavin's groin. "That's all. White boys think they're the shit, when really they ain't got nothing in the basement, honey."

Before Gavin could reply, Chad stepped toward him and wrapped an arm around his waist.

"Important call?" Chad said into his ear.

"Yeah," Gavin returned, looking at him. "I have to go."

"Something big?"

"Think so." Gavin gave him a half-smile.

"Don't worry, honey," Gordon interrupted with an amused grin. "I got my *boy*."

"Yeah, don't worry," Chad returned. "I'll take an Uber."

"Thanks." Gavin was already putting on his coat, remembering that his gloves and hat were in the car. Then he said to Gordon, as politely as possible, "Pleasure to meet you."

"Pleasure is all mine." Gordon leaned over and air-kissed each of Gavin's cheeks. He then added, "Sure we'll see more of each other."

Regrettably. Gavin nodded.

"Hey," Chad said softly in his ear. "What about me?"

Gavin leaned over and kissed Chad's soft lips tenderly. Chad reached around his lower back and squeezed him tightly. He was still getting used to the public displays of affection. Whispering in Chad's ear that he would call him later, Gavin left the two behind.

As he exited the bar, the electric beat pulsated from the speakers once again, and he could hear the windows thumping from the deep bass. The sharp cold wind knocked him in the face, causing an intense chilliness to sweep throughout his body.

The long night was about to get much longer.

TWO

As he shifted the Mustang into a lower gear, Gavin eased onto 57th Street, away from South Lake Shore Drive. The road was nearly desolate. Stopping at the signal, he glanced over at the Museum of Science and Industry, bathed in the majestic glow of coppery light. It was a monument to the park once known as White City from the 1893 World's Fair. Its ornate features echoed a bourgeoning Chicago at the turn of the century, where the stockyards, steel plants, and commerce gave the city its roots. Despite the great fire that swept all of the other buildings, the museum survived and proved to be a test of time. Amidst the beckoning light, the creeping shadows and the dark hidden park surrounded the place, as if the haunting blackness wanted to consume the building for one last time.

Easing on the gas, he shifted the car into gear, past spirals of steam coming from various manholes. No one was walking outside (no one dared to at this hour). The temperature read a balmy seven degrees. Inching his way closer, he could not help but think of White City's infamous deadly secret. Less than a mile from the World's Fair, a Dr. H.H. Holmes had built a special house of horrors and hunted the grounds of the fair, preying upon the naïve out-of-towners new to the city, offering them a place to stay and then eventually murdering them. Herman Mudgett—Holmes' real name—was caught and sentenced for killing at least eighty people. However, the police never actually obtained an accurate body count since the house burnt down at the time of his arrest. Looking through the darkened streets, Gavin wondered if Mudgett's presence was still around, attempting to lure the helpless back with him.

Perhaps Holmes was watching him now.

Despite the dark history, Hyde Park was a hip, urban community with its own unique vibe and people. Many affluent city councilmen and councilwomen, lawyers, and business owners resided here. Its bohemian influence could be seen in the surrounding area with the various coffee shops, boutique clothing stores, and artisan workshops. Rarely did he come down this way, but he always enjoyed the area. Yet, when he worked on the far South Side, this area was never a stop, just a quick pass through.

Maybe Chad and I should come down here one time, he thought. *Eat at some place.*

Turning right off 57th and nearing the town center, Gavin could see the flashing lights of a squad car barricading the street. Sluggishly moving forward, he noticed several residents were bundled up and heading out of their doors in the same direction. Plumes of white mist cascaded from their mouths as they walked quickly up the street. Within moments, a young cadet put one of her gloved hands up. Gavin pressed his badge to the window and she nodded and flagged him through. As he gingerly passed, her attention turned to the car behind him. She yelled at the driver to back it up.

About two blocks away, he parked his car in a nearby alley. After tightening the buttons around the collar of his black bridge coat, wrapping the gray plaid scarf around his neck, and slipping his gloves on, he got out of the car and followed the crowd. Their eerie enthusiasm over the explosion seemed too surreal. A frigid knife of wind pierced him quickly, making him squeeze his shoulders tighter and force his hands deeper in his pockets. Approaching the barricade, he flashed his badge again and ambled toward the chaos, snaking his way around the vehicles.

Several ambulances were already on the scene, the paramedics treating some people inside the warm cabs. Nearby, he could see two uniformed officers sitting in the back of one and sucking on oxygen masks. Both of their faces were blackened with residue. About a hundred feet away, one of the ambulances came to life with full sirens and began to move out. Through the window, Gavin caught a glimpse of an older black man on the stretcher as the EMT worked around his body, adding more tubing to his arm. Once it was out of the way, Gavin witnessed the gravity of the explosion.

The Opus Theater was a gouged-out smoldering shell of a building, resembling a nefarious beast defeated at the hands of a mob of local villagers. Its massive first-floor entrance breathed out the last of the smoke, the toothy marquee scarred with black soot. Above, its blackened window-eyes stared down upon the people menacingly. As Gavin ambled closer, avoiding the other officers, a gripping scent of chemicals, fabric, and noxious gas filtered into his nostrils, then wafted away with the wind. Next to the theater, a pair of smaller sibling buildings, a shoe business and a comic magazine shop, were scarred and smoldering as well. Even from here, Gavin could make out the shattered glass sparkling grimly against the siren lights.

As he had seen on the news, the fire trucks clustered near the front of the buildings. The crews were already wrapping up their gear, and one was lowering its long ladder. Firemen dashed from the trucks into the dark façade of the building, being swallowed up by the dying beast. Other men tugged on the thick gray hoses that were haphazardly tossed around on the street. Already, pockets of ice were forming on the standing water and small icicles began to grow from the edges of the building. Gavin carefully stepped over the hoses, which reminded him of ripped-out intestines from the gut of the savage beast, and tried to get out of the firemen's way.

Hastily, a fireman rushed past him and knocked him slightly. Grunting an apology, the man kept talking into his radio and rounded one of the trucks. The smell of smoke invaded Gavin's nostrils once again.

From behind him, Derrick shouted, "About time you fucking got here."

Turning around to face his partner, Gavin said, "Solider Field was a nightmare."

"Excuses, goddamn excuses," Derrick returned. His hat looked uncomfortably tight against his head. "Where were you?"

"A place," he answered vaguely. "And you?"

"At home with the kids alone. Let Maria get out of the house for a little bit." Derrick rubbed his thick gloved hands together.

"Do the kids listen to their dad?" Gavin noticed the spectators pointing at the light smoke emitting from the upper windows of the theater.

"They were fine," he admitted. "Vero sleeps so much, doesn't cry."

"You tell me that a lot."

"Well, my son is the shit." He gave a sour face as his eyes darted around the area. "I'm not too familiar with Hyde Park."

"I used to come here in grad school to see some

documentaries." Gavin read the marquee title: *On the High Tides of Global Warming.*

"All I know is that Obama's house is a few blocks away from here." Derrick sounded excited.

"Have you been by it?"

"Once or twice," Derrick said, nodding his head. "Think he's going to sell it when he's done?"

"Probably," Gavin said honestly. Getting to the point, he finally asked, "Do you know what's going on with this?"

"The uniforms tell me that there are five dead on the inside." Derrick's eyes scanned the building. "One in the lobby, two in the theater, and two in the back. Four others were rushed off to the hospital, not critical but with severe burns, and about two dozen lightly injured."

"Jesus." Gavin shook his head. "That's a body count."

Nodding toward the other side of the scene, Derrick said simply, "That shit gets too old."

A group of local news vans were huddled together about half a block away. Gavin saw Creighton talking with them, nodding his head and speaking rapidly into the microphones shoved in his face. Even in his tan overcoat, his features were rigid and poignant.

"He's a show-off." Derrick's comment lingered in the air.

Gavin glanced back at the theater. "Why the hell are we here?"

"Not fuckin' sure." Derrick appeared even bulkier in his thick navy-blue jacket.

"Did you get to talk to him?" Gavin asked, seeing the equally pissed-off expression on Derrick's face.

"Yeah. For a minute before he was pulled away. Said that we just have to do our thing." He paused. "Bullshit."

"I don't see anyone else from the station." Gavin's eyes were scanning for any face that was recognizable. "These uniforms are under Captain Leger."

"Who's he?" Derrick craned his head, looking around.

"Complete dick."

"Worse than Creighton? That can't be possible."

"Worked with him indirectly," Gavin explained. "When I was with Santiago. Enrique and I were on a major drug bust near here. We were ready to proceed, had back-up, court subpoenas, everything in order. Heard that he whined all the way to Commissioner Ronin, saying the bust was in his district and they wanted to take it. *Asshole* Leger stepped in three hours before the takedown and forced the arrest. And of course took the credit."

Derrick shot a glance over at Gavin. "That ain't right. A bust is a bust. Everyone wins."

"You'd think so," Gavin replied, hearing the disappointment in his own voice. "Enrique was pissed that day. Of course, they screwed up the bust. Got number two in the gang, not number one—the guy we were initially after."

Gavin later found out the thugs went back on the street due to lack of evidence; the drugs had gone missing after the bust. How Leger still had a job was beyond Gavin's comprehension.

"I don't get that." Derrick shifted slightly in his stance. He nodded his head toward a young fireman approaching him. "Ah, here's someone who wants to help us."

The fireman introduced himself as Rodger Delanie. He looked no more than nineteen at the oldest, but his thick shoulders were that of a serious bodybuilder.

"I didn't bring the right shoes to go in there," Gavin returned.

"Well, I think he's got a pair in his hands for you," Derrick commented, pointing down at the oversized black galoshes. "Got to look the goddamn part."

Gavin laughed loudly and caught some stares from people near the ambulances. Quickly, he and Derrick slipped the galoshes over their shoes. The monstrous boots on his legs were just one reason he hated fire investigations.

"They are expecting you in the back," the man said. "Be careful of the debris. There's still some smoldering in a few spots. Please follow me."

Not saying a word, Gavin let the husky firefighter lead the way into the mouth of the beast.

*****

"This your first fire, Delanie?" Gavin asked the young man. The toxic smell of the fire hit him directly, forcing him to breathe through his mouth. He could taste the bitter chemicals dancing off his tongue.

"No, Detective." Delanie's baritone voice echoed off the

burnt walls. "But this is my first one where people died."

"Sorry," Derrick responded empathetically.

Pointing toward a tarped black body that lay near another set of doors, Derrick tugged at Gavin's arm to show him. The yellow tags marked a square number five, and a team of CSI people were already taking pictures of the area. Near them, a battery-operated light filled the tight space. Although heavily waterlogged, the tight concession lobby remained fairly intact. However, the long scars of fire marked the door frames and stretched along the ceiling. The squishing sound of the wet carpet, the clicks of the camera, and the murmurs of conversations bounced off the once ornate walls.

Delanie pushed open the theater doors. The place was filled with creeping shadows, yet pockets of battery-operated light pushed it back into the far corners. The area where the screen had once been was completely burned, exposing the seared back wall. Tendrils of long scorch marks snaked their way across the walls, and the heavy velvet curtains hung in crispy shreds from the ceiling. Once again, Delanie advised them to watch their step, nodding at the fallen materials in the aisle.

"Where were you when I called?" Derrick queried softly enough for only Gavin to hear. "It was loud."

"You already asked me that," he deflected, glancing back at Derrick.

"With that someone, huh?" Derrick smiled.

"Who, what?" Gavin avoided looking at him. "No... Yes."

"Who's this secret lady?"

"What do you mean?"

"I know you got someone, Gavin." Derrick's mischievous tone hummed in his ear. "Those sudden phone calls, taking a night off on a Saturday, quick glances for texts. Or should I say, sexting..."

Why are you bringing this up now, D? "Alright, I get it." Gavin could feel his face redden.

Delanie, who was a couple of steps ahead, seemed oblivious to their conversation as he spoke into his walkie-talkie.

"Naw, man, I'm glad you are seeing someone," Derrick replied. "Especially after what happened."

"Suppose."

"When I am going to meet her? Maybe you, me, Maria—"

"Soon, okay? Soon," he interrupted.

"Look at that." Derrick pointed over to the front rows.

At the fourth and fifth rows in the dead center, several more CSI members were photographing two burnt corpses. The explosion blew back the bodies into a crumpled position on the chairs. *Hopefully they had a quick death.* Gavin stayed silent.

Moving on, they reached the exit door near the front of the theater. Another warning from Delanie informed them of the rubble and potential structural damage in the next section. Briefly looking back, Gavin heard the crackling of radios, like eerie ghostly crickets fluttering in the distance. In the opposite direction, three firemen were still containing some smoldering chairs.

"Shit," Derrick muttered, tapping Gavin's shoulder. He nodded up.

The once ornate ceiling now had entire sections missing. Squinting slightly, Gavin could see the dark night sky.

Once they passed the doorway, a series of portable lights cascaded over the area. Gavin was unable to decipher the debris, the contents of which were haphazardly pushed away from the clear epicenter near the opposite end of the room. Up above, about a third of the ceiling had disintegrated, leaving a huge hole. The cold wind invaded the space, dissipating the soot scent slightly. More CSI team members sifted diligently, gathering debris in clear evidence bags and marking each spot with photographs and red markers. Near the apparent epicenter of the blast, several firemen were discussing the area, pointing at spots.

"Have to get back to my captain," the young fireman said. "Need anything else, just let me know."

"Thanks," Gavin replied.

"Where the fuck do we begin?" Derrick grumbled.

"You can begin by bringing back that hottie," Susan said behind them.

Gavin turned to find the doctor kneeling near a shriveled, burnt corpse. Her scalpel gingerly poked and prodded the body's seared skull.

"Isn't he too young for you?" Derrick returned with a snarky grin.

Gavin stated, "I didn't see your van."

"Came through the back." She looked up at him and then at Derrick. She added, "As long he's eighteen-plus, no laws broken, baby."

Shaking his head, Derrick snickered. One of the CSI team, an annoyed-looking woman whose gray hair probably came directly from her stressful job, shot him a glance.

Standing up and ripping off her plastic gloves, Susan said, "No offense, love you guys, but what the hell are you doing here?"

"Creighton's orders," Derrick answered first. His midnight eyes darted over the scene.

"Really?" Susan's eyebrow raised. "Thought this was under Leger's jurisdiction. His people are a bunch of assholes. You guys actually respect other departments."

"Is that a compliment?" Derrick stepped toward the corpse, looking down at it.

"Only for Mr. Sexy here," Susan cooed and winked at Gavin.

"Gonna do a brother like that?" Derrick quipped.

"Can you tell us at least what we are dealing with?" Gavin said, exasperated with both of them.

"Alright, I'll go through this quickly." She pulled the collar of her bright red parka closer to her neck. "You noticed the first three bodies out in the theater, right? From a quick observation, the two in the theater seats were killed by the explosion. Their necks snapped from the blast. Probably died instantly. The one in the lobby was knocked down and died of smoke inhalation. There were a few people in here, maybe she was run over."

"Why's this body here?" Derrick commented, pointing down.

"Two to be exact, honey," she said quickly.

"Can you be more specific?" Gavin felt a sudden chill throughout him.

"This one on the floor," she said, pulling out another pair of gloves, "might pique your interest more, Williamson."

"Let's see." Derrick grinned.

"The victim, probably in his late twenties." Susan knelt near the corpse. "White male was shot at close range in the back of his skull." Her long finger inched close to the exit wound near the base of the skull.

"Do you know if this is the crime area?" Gavin glanced over the smoldering debris.

"Can't say for sure. Not in my paygrade," she confessed as she stood back up. "CSI guys will have to confirm that. On the wrists and legs, I saw the remnants of tape that had been binding the victim."

"Maybe he was dragged in here and shot," Derrick concluded and gave a side glance over at Gavin. "Why then the explosion?"

"Save that question for the fire marshal," Susan replied, grabbing her kit off the ground. "Come. We're going to look at the final victim."

While following Derrick, Susan walked through a narrow path in the rubble toward the center of the room. On the floor, a thin burnt body lay twisted against some objects.

"We have a female victim." Susan kneeled, opened her kit, and retrieved a long scalpel. "This one's special. I can't say conclusively she was the nearest to the explosion, but indications of the severity of burned tissue can only lead to that assumption. See here and here."

Gavin followed the point of the instrument. The feet of the victim were severely contorted, almost snapped off. He craned his neck slightly over Susan's shoulder and could see the bone sticking out at the ankle, which was charred.

"Here on her wrists," Susan's scalpel barely touched the surface, "I believe to be some residual evidence of rope. The intensity of the fire made the rope bond with her flesh. I can safely say that she was nude. Any clothing would have fused into her upper dermal region."

"You believe that our victim was naked and tied up?" Derrick queried as he skirted carefully around the corpse and circumvented Susan for a better view.

"Can't say for sure until I get her back," she said.

Leaning over Susan's shoulder, Gavin noticed a hole about the size of a small baseball in the shoulder blade.

"What caused that?" He pointed it out.

Glancing up toward him, she replied, "Good question. Right now, I don't know what created such a separation at that point. Obvious signs of a shooting can be ruled out because there are no exit wounds. When I get her back, I'll have a better answer for you. Sorry."

"Don't be," Derrick said. "From the remains, can you give a description so we can narrow down the search?"

"Yeah." As she stood up, Gavin and Derrick followed suit.

"From the width of the hips, she would be in her late twenties, possibly early thirties. By her facial features and width of her eyes, I would say she's African American." Sighing slightly, she added, "She was athletic, very lean. That's why most of the flesh burned off her quickly and the fire consumed the muscle tissue. That's all I can give you right now."

"Thanks."

"Still," Susan said, "I'm not sure why you are here."

"That's the question of the hour," Derrick answered.

"Love to stay and chat with you boys, but I got a shit-ton to do." Susan licked her pink lips and pulled her scarlet hat farther down on her head. "My new assistant, Fernando, is coming with a stretcher shortly. And it's getting fucking cold."

"Fernando?" Derrick asked, shifting his stance. "What happened to Chris?"

"Asshole quit," she replied bitterly. Subtly nodding her head, Susan said, "Maybe she can help you."

Looking over in that direction, Gavin saw Evelyn Lopez step through the doorway, talking to someone behind her. Her ash-colored jacket hugged her frame tightly, and her cream wool hat was snug against her hair. Soon, a tall man with a thick gray mustache and wearing a fire helmet appeared, nodding his head. The stern look on her face meant an intense conversation between them. What struck Gavin the most, she was not in uniform.

The fire was getting much more complicated.

THREE

Trepidation overshadowed Evelyn's fine features while she spoke to the fairly tall fire marshal. They navigated their way toward Gavin and Derrick, and when they were within earshot, Gavin heard the marshal reveal that the current fire was similar to the other ones. Evelyn simply nodded her head. At that point, she introduced him as Captain Thomas, and Gavin accepted the man's firm, quick handshake. The crackles of the captain's radio indicated that Thomas was needed for some detailing work nearby.

"Detective Lopez," he said finally in a thick, smoky tone. "Give me fifteen and we can go over the blast." He left them and ambled off through the rubble to the other side of the space.

"Detective Lopez?" Derrick queried with a slight grin. "Why didn't you tell us? Congrats."

Not making eye contact with either of them, she replied, "Um…I didn't want to make it a big deal."

"We can talk more about that later," Gavin interrupted prudently. "Why are we here, Evelyn?"

"I, um, I requested you." Whether it was from the cold or her nervousness, her shaky voice was almost a whisper.

"How?" A sudden rush of interest tingled within him.

"I called Creighton." Her dark eyes darted past him, as if she were distracted.

Instantly, the smile slid off Derrick's face, and a surprised, almost pissed-off expression replaced it. Clearing his throat, he raised his voice. "There are certain channels you must go through. You can't just do shit like this."

At least we are in agreement. Before Gavin could speak, Evelyn jumped in. "I understand that, Derrick. I didn't have a choice…"

"There's always a choice," Gavin snapped, replying before Derrick could speak. "You could've called us. You could've walked us through the case."

Evelyn bit on her lower lip. "It's not that simple. Captain Leger was, *is*, being... being *unagreeable* with my suggestions."

"What about your training, Detective?" Derrick asked.

Rolling her eyes, Evelyn stated bitterly, "He's the main problem."

"Is he not supporting the training?" Gavin began.

"No," she said, and then finally looked into his eyes. "He's a complete idiot. I feel I'm on a path of failure, not success. The training, the cases, and the paperwork. Now this case, *I've* been doing the majority of the work. And it's getting bigger than I can handle."

Sounds familiar. Gavin asked, "What's Leger's response?"

"He told me"—she paused for a second, gathering her words—"he said, 'if you want to be a good detective, sometimes you have to hit bumps in the road.' When I insisted on having another detective train me, Leger told me, and I quote, 'grow a fucking pair.'"

"What the fuck?" Derrick commented. "Who's your partner?"

Looking down at the ground, she replied, "Voss."

"Is he here somewhere?" Gavin glanced around.

"Yeah."

"Does he know we're here?" Derrick's voice lowered slightly.

"We'll see. I haven't seen him in the last fifteen, twenty minutes." She too began to scan the area. Suddenly, she muttered, "Shit. Here he comes."

*****

Emerging from the shadows of the theater, a long stick-figure of a man walked steadily toward them, letting his arms flap to his sides. Oblivious of his surroundings, the man's stride increased as his open tan overcoat fluttered behind like decaying moth's wings. As he got closer, the orange spotlights highlighted the man's alarmingly gaunt face, the reddened cheeks and piercing blue eyes a clear sign of absolute anger washing over him.

"What the fuck is going on here, Lopez?" Voss' cracked voice was hollow. Stepping over some waterlogged boxes, he turned his head slightly and coughed heavily into his hand.

You should get that checked, Gavin thought. Before Evelyn could answer, Gavin said, "I'm Nolan, and this is my partner—"

"Nolan?" Voss' long veiny hand rubbed at the salty white stubble on his cheeks.

"Same one," Derrick returned, standing straighter. "What's it to you?"

"Are you his personal bodyguard or something?" Voss critically evaluated Derrick.

"His partner, asshole," Derrick returned.

Lopez said, "this is Derrick William—"

"Guess you need a bodyguard after all," Voss cut her off. Taking a step toward Gavin, he questioned, "are you the cop that got tied up by that crazy goddamn homo a couple of months ago?"

"Why the hell do you care?" Gavin replied as a pop of anger pulsated just under his skin.

"Just want to know if you're the same guy." Voss took another step, just in front of Evelyn.

"Maybe."

"Double checking." A snarky grin appeared on his face, exposing tobacco-stained teeth. Then he added, "'Cause I made a bet on you that you weren't gonna make it."

Gavin stepped forward, feeling his hand ball up. "I'm happy you lost."

"I'm not," he said lowly, smiling wider.

"You son of a bitch," Derrick growled and took a step toward the scarecrow.

Instantly, Evelyn forced her way between Voss and Derrick and Gavin. "Alright, gentlemen, can we pull up our pants and stop measuring our dicks?"

Gavin stared at Voss and said, "We're here because of Creighton."

"Creighton? That goddamn dickhead?" Voss seemed taken aback. Then he looked at Evelyn. "Did you know about this?"

"Sounds like"—Derrick took another step toward Voss— "*you* can't handle the case. And *you* need our assistance."

"Bullshit!" Voss exclaimed. His words echoed, which made a couple of CSI members crane their heads their way. Looking at Evelyn, he said, "Do you believe this? They think I can't train you and solve a case."

"Guess not," Gavin replied.

"Was this *your* doing?" He pointed his finger at Evelyn.

"Aren't you the same Voss," Gavin queried, "who screwed up the big coke bust some years ago and let the dealer go free? Because the key witness got shot on your protection detail? Because you were, um, taking a proverbial shit."

Voss' cheeks reddened even more.

"What a fucking screw-up," Gavin added, half-laughing.

"That wasn't my fault, you prick," he hissed, only inches from Gavin's face. Then his smirk widened and he said, "How do you remember that? Maybe your Daddy told you that bedtime story." He paused. "At least I won that bet on *him*."

With rage, Gavin took a swing at Voss and clocked the thin man across his nose. Voss stumbled back, almost tripping over some waterlogged debris. His surly grin widened, and he returned, "Guess I touched a nerve, you little cunt."

"Hey, Voss, I didn't…" Evelyn bent over to help Voss. Instead, he shook her away like a pesky gnat.

"You're so fucked," Voss growled loudly as he wiped a trickle of blood from his lip.

"I think you're the one who's fucked." Derrick puffed up even larger and stepped toward Voss.

"Derrick," Gavin stated, pulling his partner by his arm. He already regretted hitting Voss.

"Fuck you both, and fuck you, Lopez," Voss spat out. He turned and began walking away as he shouted, "I'm not takin' this shit, so FUCK this!"

Within moments, both Voss and his loud cursing disappeared into the shadows.

"Sorry, guys," Evelyn sighed. "That's just how he is."

Stepping toward Evelyn, Derrick stated sincerely, "If you are dealing with that cocksucker, then we apologize."

"Yeah. Sorry about that." Gavin felt his anger subside. "We'll do whatever it takes to help you."

"No, no. I actually wanted to hit him myself, but you beat me to it." A small smile crept onto her face. Nodding toward Thomas, she said, "We have some work to do."

Derrick suggested they meet with Thomas who, with his men,

had been watching the event unfold. Taking quick glances toward the shadows, somehow Gavin knew they were not finished with Voss by any means.

*****

As they approached the huddle of firemen with Captain Thomas leading the conversation, the epicenter of the blast was quite evident. The force of the blast had blown the majority of the debris far away. Glancing back, Gavin noticed where Susan was preparing the woman's body for transport a good hundred yards away. As they walked through the makeshift aisle, he could feel pockets of heat still brewing in the rubble.

When they were within a couple of yards of the group, Evelyn said, "Gavin and Derrick, I will catch you up with the case soon. Please listen to what we are talking about. With fresh ears and eyes, you'll see things that I may have missed."

"Is Thomas good to work with?" Derrick asked as he haphazardly pushed some wood pieces to the side with his foot.

"Very." She pulled her coat tighter so it didn't hit any charred debris. "While he was not on the first scene, he caught up quick from the last one."

"Is this the third fire?" Gavin queried, looking at her.

"Yes."

"How did you know that this would be your guy?"

"Thomas calls him an arsonist." Evelyn ignored his question. "I think this arsonist is more than just an arsonist."

"How did you know this was your arsonist?" Derrick asked, repeating Gavin's question.

"He calls in the explosion before it happens," she stated simply.

Derrick gave Gavin a side glance.

She quickly added, "Really, I want to talk about this. But we need to process this one first. I promise I'll catch you up."

"Detective Lopez," Thomas spoke up as he dismissed his group. Then to Gavin, "I take it you and Voss are not seeing the same picture on this investigation."

"Not particularly," he replied with a faint grin.

"Well, he's not exactly the most receptive individual on the team," Thomas commented. Pulling out a laser pointer, he directed a flash of red dot around the white spot. "The point of explosion is right about here. From the severity of the damage and the blast zone, my men concluded this bomb had a component of nitroglycerin, as found in the last explosion. I would say it was a high density blend of materials to create more heat. The scorch marks along the perimeter of the circle indicate the immediate cooling of the explosion.

"The arsonist wanted to be noticed. And to be bigger, even greater than before. The shockwave of the explosion, which has no accessible oxygen like a window or door, was larger. It's why the ceiling is ripped open and there's severe cracks in the adjacent wall."

"If the bomb has more oxygen, the fire dissipates quicker and more easily," Derrick added. "So to speak."

"Know a little something about explosives?" Thomas replied.

"Not my area of expertise, but some," Derrick said solemnly. "Was in the marines. Two tours in Afghanistan."

"Afghan, huh?" Thomas's tone carried a hint of despair, then he regained focus. "My men and I are gathering up the fragments to reassemble the bomb itself. But it seems the same as the last one."

"Can you briefly explain what we could be looking at?" Gavin chimed in.

"In itself, a simplistic bomb at its best." Thomas clasped his hands behind his back. "It would be like a cylinder, or two. Fairly tall, up to two feet. Not especially heavy, lightweight material like copper or aluminum. Easily transportable. Quick to set up. The timer has been simple, which we will most likely see in this one."

"Explain why this one is different," Evelyn commented.

"The arsonist has a specific way of setting up the timer." Thomas's deep voice echoed despite the other crackling noises around them. "He likes to use an L-delay switch."

"A set-up-and-run," Derrick added. Glancing over at Gavin, he explained, "We used those pretty much all the time. Simple ones were set with X amount of minutes, and then you run like hell."

"Yes," Thomas replied. "This guy likes to use one model with a remote start."

"Would this guy like to watch the fire?" Gavin noticed that Evelyn looked preoccupied with her thoughts. "I mean, would he enjoy the moment of the fire?"

"In most cases, arsonists enjoy watching their own work," the marshal replied. "That's how they usually get caught."

"In this case," Evelyn returned, "I don't believe he enjoys it. He has a different motive."

"Either way," Thomas said matter-of-factly, "the arsonist is getting bigger and louder, if you will. I should have a preliminary report for you by tomorrow. I'll give you as many details as possible."

"We'll be in touch," Gavin said.

Before Thomas turned to leave, Derrick asked, "Did I offend you, talking about Afghanistan?"

"No, Detective," the marshal returned austerely. "My son served and died there. He stepped on an IED two years ago. He was only nineteen."

"I'm so sorry," Derrick said.

Nodding his head, the fire marshal said his goodbyes and headed to a nearby door that led to the alley.

For the rest of the night, and despite the falling temperatures, they split up and tackled the scene as best they could. Derrick was lost in his own mechanical duties, speaking with the CSI team about gathering evidence and shifting through the debris himself. At the same time, Evelyn excused herself and interviewed possible witnesses who were waiting in a nearby shop. Gavin absorbed the gravity of the situation, walking through the explosion and thinking solely about the naked female victim. Why would the killer go through so much trouble to cover up the intended target? The other victims were just collateral damage to the explosion.

Later, when he finally got home, he climbed into the shower to warm up and attempted to scrub off the reeking scent of smoke, chemicals, and death from his skin.

Still, Evelyn's words echoed in his mind: *The arsonist is more than an arsonist.*

FOUR

Sitting at the granite island in the open kitchen, Gavin positioned himself to look down upon the busy streets below. With barely five hours of sleep, he was amazingly alert. He shifted on the stool and reached for the glass of orange juice, his arms aching slightly from the quick workout earlier. He needed to clear his head before he and Derrick sat down with Evelyn this morning. Although there was hardly anyone at the gym, he'd hoped to catch Chad at his usual five-thirty time slot. Maybe to apologize again for leaving so early last night. But Chad didn't show up.

As he scanned his emails on his laptop, he found that Evelyn had diligently sent zip files about the arson cases. The time stamp read two thirty-three that morning. Hopefully she'd gotten enough sleep. By her haggard, distant stare last night and Voss' outburst, Gavin realized the complexity of the case was building.

As he downloaded the files, his phone lit up with a text from Chad: *Can you let me up?* Once the file was complete, he closed his laptop, slid it into his bag, and went over to buzz Chad in. Moments later, he heard a soft knock at the door and opened it. Chad stood with two cups of coffee. He smelled of fresh wintery air.

"Morning," Chad said softly with a wide smile. "You always greet everyone half naked?"

"Depends on who it is." Gavin backed up and let him in. Chad carefully lowered his saddle bag onto the floor with a quiet thud, taking off his jacket and putting it over a nearby chair.

"Just how you like it." Chad handed him one of the coffees. "Strongest coffee with three shots of espresso."

"Thanks, you didn't have to." Gavin took it, leaning against

47

the couch. "Was hoping to catch you at the gym."

"Gordon coerced me into staying out a little longer." Chad moved closer, placing his hand on the narrow of Gavin's back and pressing their bodies together. "He's a bad influence."

"I bet," Gavin returned casually before taking a sip of coffee. "Tasty. Isn't my place a little out of your way for the morning? I mean, since you didn't go to the gym."

"Caught me, Detective," Chad smiled and leaned over to kiss him. "I came here with a different motive."

Subtly, Chad slipped his hand beneath the waistband of Gavin's pants and lightly caressed his bare buttocks. An excitement rose within Gavin as their tongues tangoed passionately and tightly. Gavin slid his hand over Chad's cotton button-down shirt, feeling the contours of his hard muscles and stopping on the narrow of his collar. His fingers obediently began to undo the top button. In a quick, smooth motion, Chad took their coffees and placed them on the nearby table. Then his thick lips found their way to Gavin's clavicles before traveling down to his chest. Within moments, they'd stripped off their clothes, and Chad had Gavin bent over the couch, entering him savagely.

Gavin could get used to mornings like these.

*****

Gavin arrived at the small interview room a half hour late. Evelyn and Derrick were waiting.

"You're late," Evelyn said.

"I like your hair," Gavin returned with a smile. "Didn't get to see it under that hat last night."

"Ass-kisser," Derrick said under his breath. He sat up straighter, his crisp white button-down tightening against his barreled chest.

Unintentionally, Evelyn touched her shorter, asymmetrical-cut midnight hair. "I wanted something cleaner, something that felt Japanese inspired."

"Nice," he replied, pulling out his laptop. "Did I miss anything? Is Voss going to be joining us?"

"Waiting on you," Evelyn replied. "And Voss won't be here. Texted me that he can't make it."

Or doesn't want to. Gavin was relieved. Relaxed, even. He glanced over at Derrick, who shrugged his thick shoulders.

"The asshole ain't here. I'm done with his shit already," Derrick declared, pretending to wipe his hands clean.

"Aren't we direct this morning?" Gavin smiled at him.

"Actually, we were talking about how nice it was that Creighton supplied us with this room," Derrick said sardonically. "He's going to set up Evelyn a desk near us to spread out her junk."

"Alright then." Evelyn ignored the banter. "I know I sent each of you my case files. I doubt either of you had a chance to look them over. We can open the first packet to the initial report, then I can—"

"Stop there," Gavin interrupted, holding up his hand.

"I was about to present," she began. Her eyes darted back and forth to the mirrored wall.

"Evelyn," Gavin said calmly with a smile. "It's just us. Okay?"

"Not interested in the dog-and-pony show," Derrick added, leaning onto the table and propping his arms on his elbows. "That shit gets old."

Gavin added, "Don't get us wrong. You're going to have to do it. And *we'll* help you."

"But..." She trailed off.

"No." Gavin needed her to open up and be more relaxed. "Just tell it how you saw it. Then we'll discuss last night."

"In your own words," Derrick said softly.

Nodding her head, she let out a heavy breath and rested her arms on the table.

"Less than a month in," Evelyn began, "I quickly understood how Voss was as a trainer. For the most part, he thought I was his personal secretary, not his partner. And how he was as a cop— childish, whiny, overbearing and needy. Around the beginning of September, we were finishing up a serial robbery case. Just a kid holding up drugstores in the area—not the smartest kid. We caught him out on the street trying to hock the stolen goods right outside of his house. Of course, Voss said that's how cases should be.

"Right after that, as we had the suspect apprehended and booked, Leger assigned us a fire in an abandoned house on 63rd and South Ashland. A body was discovered in the basement of the building. On patrol, I never had to deal with a fire case. When we got to the scene, most of the building was under control and we were allowed access. Voss barreled ahead of me, told me he had done stuff like this before. He even said, 'it'll be a dead-end case, kid.' When I went down to the basement and saw the body... something was not right."

"What do you mean?" Derrick queried, taking a sip of his water.

"Let me back up for a second." Evelyn stared at them as her fingers played with a paperclip. "The coroner, Fred Watson, had already examined the body and said to Voss that it had been purposely dumped in the spot. He pointed out the fire-infused rope strands on the body's hands and ankles. Victim was a female, late teens, early twenties, thin, around five-one. No ID on her. Even now. A Jane Doe. During the autopsy, he found a trace of hallucinatory drugs in her bloodstream and evidence of needle marks in her arms. But what struck me as odd was that the body had been positioned on its back against the farthest wall."

"What about the fire itself?" Gavin asked, leaning back in his chair.

"The fire inspector on the scene claimed there were no clear signs of what caused the explosion." Evelyn glanced over at Gavin. "He only concluded that some type of accelerate was used to start the fire. Most likely gas."

"No explosive device like last night?" Derrick shifted in his chair.

"No," Evelyn simply said.

"What did Voss think?" Gavin took a sip of his now cold coffee.

Sighing, she replied, "He thought that I was off. He still believed it was a homeless person who wanted to kill herself."

"What the hell?" Derrick was aghast.

She continued, "I didn't think it was possible. I found it unusual for a homeless person or junkie to go into an abandoned house, tie herself up, and then set fire to herself. Definitely not a suicide. After last June with you guys, I knew this was a homicide. After some hefty persuading, I talked Voss into doing door-to-door interviews. Unfortunately, many people were too scared to come to the door. Most of them seemed to be at work or else refused to answer. I came across this young group of kids who were playing, and I asked if they knew anything about the house. A girl around thirteen said that she remembered someone lived there a couple years ago for a short time. Another person, an elderly woman, said that she used to know the previous owner, but that person had already died.

"The case went dead. No leads. Nothing." She shook her head slowly, disappointed. "About six weeks went by, and the middle of October came. Leger had us—well, me—on a series of B and E's in Hyde Park. Some guy was breaking into people's houses while they were there, tying them up, assaulting the women, and leaving with their valuables. We couldn't get a real fix on the guy."

Gavin scrunched up his eyebrows in thought. He looked at Derrick, who motioned for Evelyn to continue.

"Anyway, a warehouse was called in on 37th and Damian. You know that area, a nice family-oriented neighborhood," she said, giving a grim half-smile. "Two bodies were discovered in the facility. When we arrived on the scene, the fire was still smoldering and under control. That's when I met Captain Thomas, who was on the scene. Of course, Voss went up to him, ranting on about unsafe conditions and whatnot. That man doesn't have a filter."

Derrick shot a glance over at Gavin.

"When we finally got in, Watson was right there again. He was examining a corpse that was in a different section of the warehouse. Not where the actual explosion had been. From the supported evidence, the victim—a homeless man, Sam Conrad, late fifties—was recently released from a mental care unit. His Medicare ran out, and without any family, the hospital released him. Watson directed our attention to the other victim. The victim was a female once again, this time late twenties, Caucasian, around five-five.

"Without Voss nearby, Thomas pointed out the ignition area, similar to last night." Her eyes darted toward Derrick. "In the report, it was half as much explosive material. Yet this one caused the largest fire due to the empty older warehouse, which ignited the walls faster."

"CSI has it detailed, correct?" Derrick was writing a note to himself.

"Yeah," she confirmed. "Back to the victim. The placement of the body was weird."

"How so?" Gavin leaned forward on the table.

"It wasn't thrown back as far. Like where last night's body was found, near the blast zone. Thomas later spoke with me. He said it was impossible for a body not to have some measurable distance from the explosive device. The impact force would throw a person twice as far."

"Do you believe the body was weighted down?" Gavin asked.

"Yes," Evelyn replied confidently. "But the evidence doesn't suggest that. She was tied up; there were residual fiber remnants. Watson performed the tox screen, and he found the same drug as the one in the other victim." She paused. "Oh sorry, the victim's name was Donna Gable. Lived near Oak Park, single, zero friends. Her work told us she had some issues, was actually written up a couple of times. She did have an ex-boyfriend, Eric Holtz. He shut up quick when Voss questioned him."

"Think this Holtz guy did it?" Derrick stretched out his arms and cupped his hands behind his head.

"No, but Voss thought so," she replied rather rancorously. "Yes. Holtz has a record, drug possession, but that's it. Voss did such a piss-poor job."

"Another cold end?" Gavin seemed perplexed.

"Well, not exactly." Evelyn looked at both of them. "See, I didn't realize it until two weeks later that the person who was doing this, *this arsonist…*" She trailed off as she reached for her laptop. "I sent you the recording as well. On the night of the warehouse fire, the suspect called it. Here… listen"

The atmosphere of the room became unusually still. Then, the audio recording filled the air.

"Nine-one-one. What's your emergency?" the operator said.

"There's going to be a fire," the distorted voice crackled ominously. *"On 3789 Damian Avenue."*

"How do you know about this, sir? What's your name?" the operator asked, concerned.

"Come, or she'll die too," the voice replied.

"Sir, I'm sending emergency vehicles," the operator began.

"More will drop until he figures it out," he snapped viciously.

The call ended abruptly.

"Play that again," Gavin demanded.

They listened a second time, and the synthetized, ghoulish voice lingered in the air.

"Shit, shit, shit." Derrick sat straight up, mesmerized as well. "What does he mean by 'more will drop until he figures it out'?"

Shaking her head, Evelyn replied, "Honestly, no clue. Last night, at seven thirty-seven, when the documentary began, the same message came through nine-one-one. Exact same message. Listen." Her fingers clicked on the buttons, and soon a similar conversation took place, ending with *"more will drop until he figures it out."*

"You're both upset at me for calling Creighton. I had no choice," she stated. "Voss is treating this like an open-and-shut case. I think he'll fuck this whole thing up." She paused. "I think this arsonist is far from over."

Derrick stood up and opened a case file, pulling out the first fire victim. "How do you know that the first crime was his?"

"Because last week, after some prying and pleading from Leger for assistance, I got nine-one-one calls from the house fire." She stared at Derrick with a somber expression. "He placed a call for that one as well."

"You're correct, Evelyn, this guy isn't an arsonist," Gavin surmised.

Looking down at her phone, she said, "Shit, we're supposed to meet Dr. Hobbert for the autopsy in half an hour."

*****

The open pen of the precinct reverberated with the noise of conversations, phones, and the hustle of detectives, officers, and witnesses busy about their work. As Gavin snaked his way around a group of uniformed officers coming out of their shift meeting, he saw that Creighton's blinds were down in his office, but the door was wide open. Gavin inhaled a deep breath and knocked on the glass.

"What?" Creighton answered in a heavy tone. His back was to Gavin.

"Can I speak with you, Captain?" He took a step inside.

"Yeah. Sure." Creighton's rigid posture exposed the deep valley in the center of his thick back.

"Privately."

"Close the fucking door then, Nolan."

Gavin shut the door most of the way, leaving it open a crack, and sidestepped several boxes of archived case files. On the floor, several files were stacked haphazardly. Then, he noticed how Creighton was feverishly digging through a box on his desk. His look of concentration seemed so focused. Behind the desk, the once neat binders on the back bookcase were lying randomly, some opened and stacked precariously. Creighton was such an orderly person. Everything in its place. This just seemed off.

"Well?" Not looking up, Creighton's fingers crawled through the file papers quickly.

"About Lopez." His voice sounded hesitant, even to himself. "And her case."

"You mean *your* fucking case now," he corrected.

"I don't. We don't mind helping, but—"

"Who the hell said that you are helping?" That made Creighton stop and pen Gavin with a hard look.

"The case is another district, and I feel—"

"Who gives a shit, Nolan?" He raised his voice slightly, almost angrily. "Lopez called us for help. And goddammit, we're going to. Don't fucking worry about Leger. I got that taken care of."

"How?"

"Not your concern," he stated. "Ronin and I believe that *you* can handle this case much better without that pussy, Voss." He paused, giving a half grin. "Leger's pissed you fucking punched Voss too. You didn't make his happy fucking list."

"Voss is off the case?" Gavin asked.

"For all intents and purposes, yes."

"And Lopez?"

"You, Williamson, and Lopez are running the case now." Turning back to the box, his attention returned to the files. "I'm arranging a transfer for her into our district."

Gavin replied, "Didn't know you had that kind of pull?"

Stopping once again, Creighton glared at Gavin and said, "Are you fucking questioning my status, Nolan?"

What the hell is wrong with you, Quinn? "No," he said, pointing at the boxes. "Seems like you are busy with something else other than a case."

Creighton shifted his stance and faced Gavin, his trimmed slightly gray beard framing his chiseled face. "It's called administrative work, Detective Nolan," he stated sarcastically. "Something that Ronin requested me to do. Is that fucking okay?

Should I have your fucking approval on what I do every fucking day?"

Feeling taken aback, Gavin returned, "We should talk about it more."

"What's to talk about?" His eyes pierced Gavin. Then he added, "Besides, I gave you a key, remember? Come on over and we can talk all you fucking want."

Looking at the cracked door, he noticed a couple of uniforms standing near it. He felt a flush of redness on his cheeks.

"Oh wait, you don't have time anymore. You've got your new boy toy," Creighton interjected quickly. "Guess he's your new fuck buddy."

"How do you know about him?" Gavin felt slightly nervous. He had been trying to keep Chad under the radar at work. But Derrick noticed it. And Quinn noticed it—

"Does it fucking matter?" Creighton said and then returned to the files. "If you are done, get the fuck out. I'm busy."

At the same moment, Derrick texted him: *Where the hell are you?*

Hastily, Gavin walked out of the office, leaving the door open. Quinn always had a way of getting to him, and he was pissed. He rushed to meet Evelyn and Derrick in the parking lot. Still, something was going on with Quinn.

Fuck him. I don't have time for his petty bullshit.

FIVE

Gavin eased into the passenger seat of the car, ignoring any remarks from Derrick. Evelyn was already nestled into the backseat, right behind Derrick. Once his door closed, Derrick shifted the car into gear and headed it toward the street.

He called his favorite IT specialist, Mylo, who had done such superb work in the past on Gavin's cases—especially with finding information on Vincent earlier that year. As soon as Mylo answered, Gavin gave him a brief backstory on last night's bombing and then instructed him to search the camera feed around the theater at the time of the explosion.

"Sounds like a simple job," Mylo stated.

Quickly, Gavin got him up to speed on the nine-one-one calls. "I'll send you the recordings so you can analyze them."

"That might take a little more time," Mylo said hesitantly. "Have to check the voice software system, contact the nine-one-one office, and check data encryption. Things like that."

"I'll contact nine-one-one about the recordings as well," Gavin reiterated. "If you get any blowback, let me know. I'll get Creighton on them."

"Shit," Mylo replied. "Must be a big one."

"Probably." Gavin glanced over at Evelyn, who was talking with Derrick. Her eyes were staring out the window, and she seemed slightly more relaxed than last evening.

Immediately after Gavin disconnected from Mylo, he emailed the supervisor on the nine-one-one desk, who happened to be a good friend, and briefly explained the request of the recording. Of course he copied Creighton, making sure his callous accusations did not haunt him later. At that point, he looked up and discovered they were near UIC campus, just passing Greektown.

"No, they never found out who the perpetrators were," she answered Derrick, looking down at her laptop.

"What perpetrators?" Gavin asked.

"Derrick was asking about the missing weapons in lockup," Evelyn answered. "Back in August, a large sting operation happened near Blue Island, which uncovered a huge illegal weapons supply. It took a good year to set up the takedown, what I heard. They finally got a break because the suspect, an arms dealer from Eastern Europe, was supposed to be in Chicago to make a final deal with a notorious South Side gang."

"Yeah, I remember," Gavin said, and he glanced over at Derrick. "You showed me the clip of Jesse Jackson leading a huge protest through the city about keeping the neighborhoods safe."

"Yes. Evelyn, explain what happened next." Derrick concentrated on the road, turning on the windshield wipers to bat at the large snowflakes that had started falling.

"Literally, it was my sixth day at the precinct." She looked up at Gavin. "The bust happened in Leger's district. When I walked in that day, half of the weapons had disappeared from lockup. Leger was on a rampage, and the entire station was on lockdown. FBI, IA, Homeland Security, and the rest of the alphabet swooped in. A goddamn mess. I was just interviewed about it last week."

"I didn't hear anything about that in the news, or even the rumor mill. Did you?" Gavin asked Derrick.

"You shouldn't have," Evelyn commented. "Ronin came in himself and personally put the lid on speaking to the press and any other officers about it. Should have known even then how Leger was... is. He's just bad."

"Had an experience like that," Derrick said softly. "Things like that are red flags, Evelyn."

Evelyn nodded and leaned back into the seat. Derrick carefully switched lanes from behind a slow-moving delivery truck and navigated the car toward the ME's office. A slight vibration came from Gavin's phone, and he looked down.

Thanks for this AM, Chad texted.

A nice surprise, Gavin typed backed.

Want to continue later tonight? Chad responded.

My place?

Of course. Chad added several emojis at the end.

Smiling and looking ahead, he saw they were only a few blocks from Susan's office.

*****

Appearing to be exasperated, Susan briefly greeted them in the doorway of the examination room. With her hair back, she looked as exhausted as Evelyn had the previous night, but she ushered them through the double doors. Her white lab coat fluttered lightly behind her as she guided them to the nearest table by the cadaver coolers.

On the other tables, bodies were covered in a white sheets, their toes marked with a single manila tag. However, she left the burnt body exposed. As he approached the corpse, the harsh white light illuminated the seared flesh, the grisly distortion of the body, and the lingering lasting scream on the mouth. The combination of antiseptic sterile air and rotting singed flesh formed a sour taste in the back of Gavin's throat. Nonetheless, he could not help but stare at the burnt flesh.

Sneaking around Derrick to the head of the table, Susan busily threw on a pair of latex gloves and donned a pair of clear visors. Underneath them, her light sapphire eyeshadow magnified her stunning doe-brown eyes. It seemed to offset the serious distress on the rest of her face.

"Time is money, right?" she announced sarcastically. "I've got bodies lining up to be examined. Can I start?"

"Yes, please," Derrick answered, placing his hands on his hips and edging his way opposite Gavin, who stood to the left of Susan. Evelyn anchored a spot at the end of the table with a notepad in hand.

"Gentlemen and lady," she said loudly, "upon first initial examination, as dictated in my report, we have an African-American woman, five-six, athletic in nature. You can see in the contour of her facial structure. The muscle mass in her legs and arms indicate a strong woman, probably a cyclist or even a runner, like my vanilla latte next to me." Susan winked at Gavin. "About ninety percent of her upper and lower epidermal layers were scorched beyond recognition. Even the subcutaneous tissue was severely damaged. If she had survived, she would have suffered for a short amount of time. The chances of recovery from the extent of the burn would have been unlikely. This beauty's definitely one for the records."

"Was she still alive when the explosion happened?" Derrick's baritone voice filled the quiet space.

"Normally, determination within the rigidity of the muscles would be seen," she replied, pointing at the arms and legs. "The intensity of the explosion melted most of her muscle tissue. Thus, the fire consumed the flesh quickly. With her light frame, I would have expected her corpse to be flung back into the wall."

"Have you an ID on her yet?" Evelyn spoke up.

"Yes, I was able to get a decent x-ray of her teeth." Susan turned slightly, reached for a folder, and handed it to Derrick, who tucked it under his arm. "Meet Mrs. Janice Carlton."

Instantly, Evelyn turned and started toward the exit.

"Where are you going?" Susan questioned, her tone making it clear she was offended.

"We need to notify the family," Evelyn said, glancing over at Gavin.

"We'll notify after we are done with Susan," Gavin commented. "Resume please."

"But..." Evelyn looked dumbfounded.

"Evelyn," Derrick said, "it will take a lot longer to notify her family. The victim's not going anywhere. The more we learn about how she died, the better job we can do catching this son of a bitch."

Nicely put. Gavin nodded toward Derrick, who seemed more relaxed. Looking down, he could not help to stare at the eyeless, blackened sockets in the dead woman's skull.

Saying nothing, Evelyn resumed her position and bit her lower lip.

"As I pointed out," Susan stated. She reached over again to the table and showed a stainless steel dish of thread. "The nylon rope was embedded in her flesh. I removed most of the material and sent it off to CSI. The remainder here," she pointed with her finger, "clearly shows the thin material most likely torn into her wrists and ankles."

"Could that be the reason why her ankles were almost torn off?" Derrick pointed to them.

"No, I can't say conclusively." Her eyes scanned each of them. "If I had to make an assumption, I'd say she was weighed down. I took the liberty of performing a tox screen. In my opinion, she probably was tied up after she was drugged. I'll know the results in a couple of days." Sidestepping closer to Gavin, she gestured for him to move, which he did. A scent of lavender drifted into his nose over the grisly smell of the corpse.

"There's a puncture wound on the left upper breast area," she said, leaning over the corpse as her fingers touched the wound. "A hole of about six point nine centimeters. Unlike the other victim at the theater, the white male, it is not a gunshot wound—I found something all of you would find more interesting. Excuse me."

With both hands on the dead center of the corpse, Susan's fingers slid inside a slit in the chest, and with some force, she opened the upper torso like a child's picture book. In Gavin's peripheral vision, Evelyn put a hand to her mouth while Derrick leaned closer to better see the corpse's insides.

"I reassembled the organs for you," she stated as her fingers began to probe the dull pink fleshy organs. "Please look at her lungs. Typically, lung tissue would be scarred with smoke inhalation then eventually the heat itself. She has very little at the top here and there, which means she died just seconds before the fire. It wasn't the fire that killed this beautiful black angel. Upon removal of the organs, I could see that an object had penetrated her internally. It created a long distinct shape with the same diameter throughout her organs."

Susan's gloved hands casually moved the organs to the side to reveal a long distinctive open wound, which poked out of the liver, ran along some intestines, and continued through the left lung.

"The point of origin began here," Susan said softly. "It entered her body through the victim's vagina."

"Wait, back up. What do you mean by 'object'?" Evelyn asked, not really looking at the corpse.

"From my estimation, a long cylindrical object pierced her organs from the lower to the upper regions of her body. I would estimate the object to be at least twice in length of her body."

"The victim was skewered?" Derrick surmised.

"Yes, it indicates that." Susan flipped the ribcage back into place, which made a sickening crunchy tone. "A substance was found on the outside of her vagina. I sent the residue to CSI."

"Was she alive?" Evelyn asked, looking at Susan and then glancing over at Gavin.

"By the amount of coagulated blood around her sexual organs," Susan replied, "I will have to say yes."

For a brief moment, only the hum of the overhead lights occupied the space. Finally Susan said, as she turned to a different med table, "I have something else for you too."

"This didn't occur with the other two victims?" Gavin questioned Evelyn.

"No," she answered. "Dr. Watson's reports did not show any piercing of the body."

"Fred?" Susan perked up with a smile as she removed a pair of gloves and scooted around Derrick.

"Yeah, why?"

"Shit, that boy and I go back." Susan's airy tone was refreshing. Still, her back was to them as she was digging through some bags on a nearby table.

"Like in the naughty way?" Derrick commented, winking at Gavin.

"Fuck no," she replied solemnly. "He's married. Been married over twenty years, God bless. He's one of the few good ones around here. Taught me a lot."

"Would you mind giving him a call for us?" Gavin clasped his hands behind his back.

Turning back around with an evidence bag, Susan retorted, "For you, sexy, anything." Then she handed the bag to Evelyn, who timidly took it.

"Giving presents out now?" Derrick shifted in his stance.

"Only the good kind." Susan quickly replaced her gloves. Leaning over, she stuck out her chest more, allowing the long slit in her shirt to reveal more of her breasts. "About here on the upper part of her abdominal area, I found a couple of pieces of plastic infused into her flesh. The ones in that bag."

Gavin glanced at the jagged black pieces. "What are they?"

"Beats the hell out of me," she replied. "Maybe you can figure it out."

Evelyn held it up and out. "It looks like pieces of a weird puzzle."

"Did you find any more fragments?" Derrick asked.

"No, I probed around." Her gloved fingers carefully touched the corpse's stomach.

"From what you stated," Derrick said, "the victim had something attached to her body, was skewered alive, and set on fire."

"In a roundabout way, yes." Susan smiled and went around Derrick.

"Perhaps," Derrick said, gesturing with his hands, "the killer is hanging the victim above the object? I mean, it would explain the bound hands. But why the feet?"

"And why was the body then thrown across the room?" Evelyn questioned.

"We have nothing to prove that, D," Gavin stated humbly. Yet he thought his partner might be right.

"Our guy," Derrick added, now walking around the table. "I am assuming we all agree that the suspect is a man, right? A man would have to have the strength to hoist this woman, who is about one thirty in weight, in midair, so he could set up his bomb."

"He didn't do it to the other two, though," Evelyn interjected.

"No, but he's metamorphosing, changing his game," Gavin returned. "Normally, an arsonist is consumed with fire and its potential damage. You're right, Evelyn, this guy is not an arsonist."

"Maybe the explosions are only a distraction," Derrick commented.

Evelyn nodded. "Maybe. I was distracted by seeing only the fire itself."

"No, not all," Gavin began.

"Alright," Susan said abruptly, putting both of her hands up. "Would love to hear more about the case. And if there is anything I can do for you, I'm more than happy. But I gots work to do."

"Got the message, sister," Derrick replied, already sidestepping around the table and walking out of the room.

"Sorry, Dr. Hobbert," Evelyn returned.

Crinkling her nose, she said, "Girl, don't call me that—unless I'm around a gorgeous man." Her eyes darted at Gavin. "You're with handsome over here. Call me Susan."

With a small smile, Evelyn said, "Fine, Susan." She paused. "By the way, if you lean any more, your girls are going to fall out of that coat."

"I sure hope so," the doctor responded cheerfully, adjusting her blouse slightly. "A real hot paramedic is due for a delivery.

Twenty-something, tight back. Mmm, mmm. See if I can get some of that brown ass."

Pivoting on her heels, Evelyn walked away and stifled a snicker. Gavin began to follow her out the door.

"Wait, Gavin," Susan said in a lower tone.

The sincere smile dropped from Susan's face as she eagle-eyed the swinging door when Evelyn disappeared around the corner. Digging into her pocket, she thrust a folded piece of paper into his palm. Her warm dark hand made his hand into a fist, hanging on to it for a minute.

"I was going to give this to you last night," she said, "but too many people were watching us."

"This will be the last time," Gavin stated and slipped it into his front pocket.

"Better be." She paused nervously. "I can get into a shitload of trouble. The last time. Okay?"

Nodding, he said softly, "Thank you. I appreciate it."

"And you went to Harrold Street Pharmacy, right?" Her eyes darted toward the doorway. "Only filled it with Lila Chang, okay."

"Yes, yes. Don't worry." He half-smiled.

"Don't give me those sassy blue eyes," she said. "Gavin, you need to see a doctor. A real doctor. If your back hurts so much…"

"Not all the time, just here and there." Gavin chewed down the lie. "You're a fantastic friend."

Licking her thick auburn lips, Susan stepped closer. "I understand that asshole Vincent fucked you up hard. I get it. But if the pain persists…" She paused. "Look, I treat the dead, not the living. Period."

Quickly, he kissed her cheek. "Don't worry," he whispered.

She wrapped her arms around his shoulders and gave him a quick squeeze. Instantly, she released him and stepped back, pretending to flatten her lab coat.

"Get the hell out of here, before I do more than a feel-up." She winked before she turned away and occupied herself with the nearby table. Shortly after, Fernando walked in, and she began snapping off orders to get the other corpse underway.

Gavin hated to lie to Susan about the so-called back pain. For the most part, he gingerly used the pain meds, taking half doses for the worsening headaches. The migraines subsided slightly when he took the medicine, which allowed him to work. Realistically, he could not have any prescribed medications after a traumatic incident. Quinn would not hesitate to bench Gavin for an indefinite period of time, until he had a doctor's approval to resume work.

"Susan blowing you kisses?" Derrick mused as he buttoned up his coat.

"Jealous?" Gavin returned immediately.

"Hell no." Derrick shook his head. "God knows where that pussy's been."

"Hola?" Evelyn spoke up. She already had her wool hat snug on her head. "Woman here? See? Jesus Christ, guys."

Evelyn began walking as Gavin and Derrick followed her.

Derrick smirked. "While you were playing doctor, Evelyn already called the family, who was notified earlier this morning. Carlton's husband is driving back from St. Louis from a conference."

"And I spoke with CSI," Evelyn stated as she pushed open the double doors. "They are sending all pictures related to cylindrical objects. God only knows how many that could be."

"Have to start somewhere, right?"

When they arrived back at the precinct a half hour later, Creighton was nowhere to be seen. For the remainder of the day, they divided work accordingly.

Evelyn went through witness testimonies to see if anyone saw anything before the event. Taking a break from the stacks of witness reports, she even took the initiative to speak with CSI. Instead of them trying to sift through all the pictures of cylindrical objects, she wanted them to narrow down the possibilities.

Relentlessly, Derrick began to gather initial information on Janice Carlton and combed the DMV records and other municipal outlets. When exhausting the basic resources, he then shifted his attention on Captain Thomas's initial report on the theater's explosion. While they had not yet re-constructed the explosive device, he determined that he should learn more about the mechanism. "It would give a hint to the killer's personality," he finally commented.

At the same time, Gavin assisted Evelyn in diving into the hundred logged witness statements. Even in the first couple of reports, witnesses saw no one else in the theater. Several Good Samaritans dashed into the blaze to help rescue the three dozen people watching the documentary. Yet no witnesses—neither store owners, employees, nor people on the street—reported any suspicious activity in the alley or around the building. Looking up at the burnt faces, Gavin studied the eerie grimace that unified the victims' last moments before the blaze had consumed their bodies.

Still, Susan's analysis suggested that Carlton was deceased just moments before the explosion. *Why hadn't anyone heard her scream? Why would this guy go through this extraordinary effort to kill Carlton?* Each woman had been drugged before the fire, as if the killer did not necessarily want to inflict pain. The damaging fire was a clear indication in each moment, and the bodies were near the source of the explosion. Purposely. *Why did he go through so much trouble in burning the place down?* The day concluded with endless pictures of ruins. Yet his thoughts still wound up on a single question:

Why poor Janice Carlton?

SIX

The next morning, the activity of the station flourished in a somewhat chaotic harmony. Overnight, as the snow subsided, the increase of stupidity ensued through an unprecedented amount of break-ins and even looting, in both residential and commercial properties. Even now, the late-night uniform officers were present as the new batch were heading out onto the streets. As people passed through the hallway, Derrick squared up his back against the industrial gray wall and seemed unusually lost in thought.

"Do you want Evelyn to do the questioning?" Derrick queried, sipping the notoriously shitty vending machine coffee.

"She could lead it," Gavin replied. "We'll jump in as necessary."

Saying nothing, his eyes followed a new rookie officer behind a training officer who was instructing her on the tasks of the day. Derrick scrunched his lips slightly and wiped at his tired eyes.

"What's wrong?" Gavin leaned his shoulder against the doorframe nearby.

"This case bothers me." Derrick stood straight. "Not sure why we took over on this."

"Creighton insisted." Hearing his own words, it did not sound convincing.

"Don't know, just seems like we butted into someone else's shit," Derrick said. He glanced over at Gavin. "Not that I mind pissing off Voss, that dumb fuck. It just doesn't feel so…simple."

"Think I know what you mean." Gavin felt his phone vibrate from a text message in his pocket and ignored it.

"I've seen some shady shit before." Derrick's deep voice lowered slightly. "When I was a training sergeant, I knew there was a certain system and protocol you had to follow."

"Didn't know that you trained soldiers?" Gavin leaned against the wall. He was fascinated by Derrick. Rarely did he speak about his time in the military.

"Yeah, it was a great job. Should have stayed at it," he replied. "But I could easily weed out the bad from the great. And those who fell between accepted my commands. And orders came from the top. The trickle down military bullshit. Like here. Evelyn didn't get the right training from the start. That's what makes me nervous."

"Maybe Creighton wants us to train Evelyn properly," Gavin returned. "Set her up for success."

Looking away and toward the double doors, he replied, "If that's the case, G, the asshole could have told us. Or at least give us a heads-up anyways."

"Yeah, but—"

"Here she comes with the husband." Derrick nodded his head and stepped away from the wall.

Through the glass doors, a rather tall, athletic black man in a dark, distressed leather coat entered, and Evelyn guided him over. A short heavyset black man wearing a cheap suit walked just behind her. Derrick plastered a small smile on his face while Gavin stood at attention. Evelyn introduced Janice's husband, Curtis Carlton, who shook their hands. At the same moment, the other man, an Alan Carlton, who was a cousin, gave a card to Gavin that read he was a tax attorney. The men slid into the interview room, as did Evelyn.

As Gavin entered the room, Derrick followed him and mumbled, "Fucking attorneys."

*****

Curtis Carlton slumped into the chair, letting his long dangling arms rest on the table. His eyes appeared swollen and red from exhaustion. At that point, Alan Carlton placed a hand on his shoulder with a seemingly brave smile and mumbled something into his ear. Soon, Curtis sat slightly straighter and looked up at Gavin.

"As I stated to Detective Lopez here," Curtis said immediately. "I'll share what I know, but I was away on a business trip. I just don't understand why, even how, she was murdered."

Murdered? What did you tell Carlton yesterday? Gavin gave a stern look over at Evelyn, who deflected it.

Evelyn asked, "Why were you out of town, Mr. Carlton?"

"Short business trip," Curtis replied softly. "I work sales for a small gourmet food supply company up in Skokie. My sales area reaches from South Chicago, all through the rest of Southern Illinois, to the eastern part of Missouri."

"That's a large area to cover," Derrick, who continued to stand against the wall just behind Evelyn, stated.

"Yes it is, Detective Williamson. The pay's alright and the commission's decent."

"May we have a list of your contacts during the visit?" Evelyn spoke up.

"I don't see why that's called for," Alan interrupted. "Curtis's wife was killed here in Chicago. Are you suggesting that he killed his wife?"

"No, we are not implying anything," Gavin returned, shifting in his chair. He stared at Curtis. "It's just standard procedure."

Before Alan could say anything, Curtis replied, "Yes, I can provide that information."

"As soon as you can," Evelyn quickly replied. "You told me that your daughter was not with Janice this weekend, but with your mother. Why would that be?"

"Neesha usually went over to my mother's house," he said casually. "My mom helps us with her."

Evelyn opened a file in front of her and said, "Our records show that Mrs. Carlton has not been employed for the last year—"

"Why would your wife bring your daughter over to your mother's frequently?" Derrick interrupted. "We assumed she was a stay-at-home mother."

Shaking his head, he said, "No, she was working on her dissertation."

"In what?" Gavin was intrigued.

"Chemistry. Biomolecular chemical engineering," he said bitterly. "In fact, she was supposed to, ah, present her findings this coming week. That's why my schedule worked for her, so she could concentrate. And Neesha could spend time away."

"Obtaining a PhD takes a lot of time and dedication," Gavin remarked.

"Yes, yes it does," he answered, nodding his head. He no longer wore a look of grief, but of seriousness.

"Can you provide a list of names from the university?" Evelyn's automatic questions seemed to throw off the atmosphere.

"I suggest you don't," Alan said softly to Curtis.

"Stop it," he hissed at the cousin. Then he looked at Gavin. "Sure. Anything."

Alan sat more rigid in his chair, turning slightly away from Curtis.

"You don't know about her whereabouts these last few days." Derrick's question sounded more like a statement.

"Correct." Curtis's long slender fingers drummed the surface of the table.

"When was the last phone call from your wife, Mr. Carlton?" Evelyn leaned forward.

"Not sure," he replied. "Think it was early Thursday morning."

"So you had no contact with your wife between Thursday morning and the time of her death on Monday evening?" Evelyn interjected.

"Any particular reason you didn't speak to your wife all that time?" Derrick added. In Gavin's peripheral vision, he saw Evelyn purse her lips slightly.

"No, we just didn't talk that much." Curtis shrugged his shoulders sluggishly. "Her project was important to her. And she likes, or liked, her space. Always did."

"Was it challenging to have a wife who was determined and driven?" Gavin suggested, noticing beads of sweat forming on the husband's thick dark hairline.

"Are you asking if Curtis was jealous of Janice's education?" Alan questioned. His dark eyes glared at Gavin. "Curtis loves, loved Janice. He would never do anything to harm her."

"We are not implying anything, Mr. Carlton," Gavin replied to Alan. He turned to Curtis and questioned: "Why didn't you fill out a missing person's report if you hadn't heard from her for several days?"

"You don't have to answer these questions, Curtis." Alan began to stand. "We came here in full cooperation to find out who murdered his wife. Now you are basically accusing him of some sort of crime."

Curtis did not move. His fingers tapped faster, and a stern look fell over his mocha-colored face. Somehow, Gavin knew that the husband was not saying everything.

"Will you take a seat, Mr. Carlton?" Evelyn gestured to Alan. "This is an informal meeting."

"Curtis, we should leave." The cousin ignored her and stepped back from the table. "They already have their own conclusions—"

"Alan, stop being an asshole," Curtis said loudly, which seemed to shock even Derrick. "I didn't ask you to come with me—"

"Yeah, but you need help now, man," the pudgy man started.

"I can finish this." Curtis then looked at Alan. "They're here to help me. Help Neesha. To find who… who actually killed Janice."

Shaking his head, Alan's eyes shot daggers at each of them. Gavin chose to ignore him and concentrated on Curtis, who seemed bereaved again. Finally, Alan huffed away, telling Curtis he would meet him outside.

*****

For a few minutes, Curtis composed himself, staring at the table and letting his tears fall onto it. Briefly, Evelyn left the room and then returned with a box of tissues, handing several to the grieving man. In a kind gesture, Derrick took the place of Alan next to Curtis and put a hand on his shoulder, asking him if he was ready to continue. Gavin saw only a man who had lost his wife—not a killer. After he drank some water, Curtis nodded his head to Derrick and affirmed that he was ready to continue.

"What can you tell us about your wife, Mr. Carlton?" Gavin's soft voice seemed loud in the quiet room.

"Janice was a complicated woman," he answered.

"Can you elaborate?" Evelyn's voice seemed less abrasive.

"I mean, she was such a loner," he softly stated. "I actually met Janice through a blind date. One of my buddies set us up. I remember how beautiful she was, how we just hit it off, how we had the same interests. It just seemed too good to be true. We hit it hard and fast. And then we were married a year later."

"That's quick," Derrick commented.

"Yes, it was, even for me." Curtis's tone seemed distant and listless. "When we moved in together, I realized then how Janice was as a person. What other people saw was absolutely different from what she was like at home. On the outside, with friends and family, she appeared to be perfect, outgoing and high-spirited. At home she was serious, a demanding perfectionist, and blatantly rude. For the first couple of months, I thought I was doing things the wrong way. Even together, she would go days without speaking to me. I'd have conversations about my day with her, and I would get short replies like 'okay,' 'sure,' 'hell no'—stuff like that."

"Her not talking to you since Thursday was just normal?" Gavin asked.

"Yes." Curtis looked at Gavin. "When she had Neesha, you'd think that she'd change. No, having a child was a complete inconvenience for her. *I* was the one doing most of the work, getting Neesha dressed, feeding her, getting her to bed. With her in school, it was hell, man.

"See, Janice completely absorbed herself in her studies. Staying at Northwest until late in the evening and going back right away in the morning. Or when she was home, she would be on her computer, reading or just ignoring me and Neesha. I tried to be interested in her project. Instead she talked down to me, explaining it to me like a child and making fun of me if I didn't know what she was talking about. Fucking frustrating. Sorry."

"Don't worry," Derrick replied.

"I knew," Curtis continued contemptuously, "at least Neesha would be taken care of if she went to Grandma's house. To make it worse, I earned the money for the house. Janice felt my sales job was a menial position. She often complained about how little money I earned."

"Didn't the college give her a stipend?" Gavin asked.

"Yes," he rebutted quickly, looking at Gavin. "But she used that money for strictly her personal use. *Her* groceries, *her* books, *her* clothes. Not for me, not for Neesha."

A self-sustained individual in a marriage? Gavin pondered.

"Graduate school has fierce competition," Evelyn stated. "Do you think that one of her colleagues may have harmed her?"

"No," he replied. "I met a handful of her friends. They are literally in their own universes. The conversation was a struggle. Then again, they never really talked to me."

"Do you think she was having an affair?"

"What? No." His tone sounded defensive. "No. She wasn't like that. We were just not—she is… was, just not that—"

"Intimate?" Lopez added, leaning on the table.

"Right," Curtis replied. "I mean, that was a huge part of our problem. When she entered her doctorate program four years ago, she put, uh, our alone time on the back burner. If we didn't have Neesha before she was accepted, I could swear we'd never done it before."

"The sexual side of your marriage was non-existent?" Gavin asked politely.

Curtis began tapping at the table again. For a few minutes, he was silent. Finally he said, "Janice was like that from the start."

"How so?" Lopez inquired softly.

"Don't get me wrong. She is... was, fine as hell," he commented. "Always took care of her body, running, working out all the time. Another obsession. When I met her, she'd just come back from serving overseas."

"She was in the military." Derrick glanced over at Gavin and then asked Curtis, "Do you know where?"

"She never really talked about it," he said. "I never brought it up. I do know that's how she got her undergrad degree." Curtis's fingers drummed more. "Fight and learn, she said." He paused for a moment, and his eyes met Gavin's. "We didn't have that much sex; she was always hesitant about it. When we dated, she refused to go beyond kissing. She told me that she had a horrible experience once. Our wedding night was the first time we had sex."

Gavin saw Curtis bite his inner cheek. He leaned forward and asked, "Mr. Carlton, where were you on the night of your wife's death?"

Curtis's eyes went down to his open palms. Only the soft hum of the heater filled the room.

"We can pull your phone records," Gavin stated.

Evelyn shifted slightly in her chair and said, "Listen, Mr. Carlton, we are trying to be reasonable here."

"Mr. Carlton," Derrick said, leaning in close, "you were seeing someone on the side. Because I bet jerking off got old fast."

Curtis glanced over at Derrick with a bewildered look, still saying nothing.

Thanks, D. You picked up my scent. Gavin added, "You found someone else to take care of your needs."

"Yes, I did," Curtis replied in a low voice. "Years of not

getting anything. Plus, her shutting me out of her life more and more. Neesha was growing older. I just met someone online. A nice woman."

"Were you with her on that night?"

Curtis's eyes were watering up again. "Yes, yes I was."

"Alan didn't know?" Lopez asked.

"No, no one knew. I hid it." He sighed heavily. "Actually, I was planning to divorce Janice and take sole custody of Neesha."

"We are going to need her name," Evelyn said harshly.

"Just to clarify your whereabouts," Derrick added and gave Evelyn a quick look.

Curtis agreed and said, "Please keep her out of this."

"We'll try," Gavin returned empathetically. "Mr. Carlton, is there anyone you can think of who would harm Janice?"

"No, no one I know of." He shook his head. "She could kick anyone's ass."

"Was Janice any different the last couple of weeks?" Gavin queried.

"Not that I can remember," he said, tapping his finger.

"Around your house? In the neighborhood?"

Gavin could see the man thinking, attempting to hold back his tears. "Well, one thing. Sorta odd."

"Everything is something," Gavin said.

"About a month ago, she was unusually nervous when I got home." Curtis sat straight in his chair. "Never seen her like that. She was pacing by the window while Neesha was watching TV. I asked her what was wrong, thinking it was about her school stuff. Her eyes were wide. She was just shaking her head. She finally said that she was being followed. Of course I got nervous for her. I wanted to call the police because she stays on campus so late. She shook her head and yelled at me. Told me that it'd be useless. I don't know, man, but she didn't sleep that night and for a couple nights afterwards."

"Did you ever report it?" Evelyn asked.

Derrick shot her another glance. He reiterated, "Did it ever happen again?"

"No, not all," he replied. Restlessly, he shifted in his chair and checked his watch. "She didn't bring it up again."

"Mr. Carlton, can we have access to your wife's computer?" Evelyn questioned.

"Fine with me. I have nothing to hide. Anymore." Before he was about to get up, he asked, "So, what happened to my wife? The police officers lacked details."

Thinking a moment, Gavin answered, "She was found in a theater explosion near the University of Chicago's campus."

A look of disbelief came over his face. "I don't know why she would be down there. She hated that school for turning her down for the PhD program. Called them a bunch of 'pompous dickheads.'" Then he looked at Lopez. "Sorry, I couldn't take the army out of her."

"No offense taken." Evelyn sat back.

"She wouldn't have any connections in that area?" Derrick interjected.

"No. She hated Hyde Park. Then again, she hated a lot of things." He stood up. "I just hope you can find whoever did this. Sorry, I have to go. I, uh, I have an appointment with the funeral home to make arrangements."

Once Curtis left the room, Derrick immediately left as well. Gavin helped Evelyn gather her things and walked her over to their desks.

His thoughts went back to Janice not being very motherly. Looking up at both the charred remains and DMV pictures, he wondered what her last thoughts were before death.

Did she really think that lowly of her own daughter?

SEVEN

A half hour later, Derrick had finished hanging up a couple of pictures of Janice Carlton's body on the whiteboard. Gavin was about to type up the report on the interview when Evelyn approached Derrick with a stern face.

"Next time, don't make me look like that asshole cop," Evelyn said.

"Not sure what you're talkin' about." Derrick wrote a quick note near one of the pictures.

"That interrupting bullshit," she stated. She stepped close to Derrick, forcing him to stop writing.

"Evelyn, your line of questioning was rudimentary. I had to stop the witness from bolting," he replied. "You've got a lot to learn."

"Stop the macho shit," she fumed.

At that point, Derrick's smile slipped off his face as he faced her. "Better watch what the fuck you say to me, Detective."

Stepping over, Gavin interjected, "Evelyn, you brought us on. Obviously, Voss was not doing his job at all. You were writing the reports and interviewing the people. I get it. Derrick gets it. We get it."

She looked at Gavin and pointed at Derrick, who glared down at her. She started, "His bullshit—"

"On a case like this," Gavin interrupted, ignoring her, "you need to learn when to ask the basic questions, and when you need to listen. It's not like being on the street, where you get the facts and split. As a detective, it doesn't work that way. Especially with a grieving husband."

Subtly, stretching her neck, she said, "It was rude, Derrick."

"We work as a team," Derrick said. "You, G, and me, now. What happens in the interview room, or speaking to someone about the case, you have to listen. Usually, people will tell you more without asking too much. Get it?"

"We are a team now," Gavin agreed. Nearby, he could see a couple of uniforms looking their way. "As a rule, Derrick and I like to discuss immediately. Get impressions. So we can get a direction. Right now, we have nothing."

"Are you blaming me for that?" she replied defensively.

"No, I blame Voss," Gavin returned.

Taking a deep breath, Evelyn eyed him and Derrick. She finger-combed her hair out of her eyes and leaned against the desk, setting the files down.

"Sorry," she said to Derrick.

"No problem," he returned.

Gavin asked, "What's your impression of Curtis Carlton?"

"Not our killer. He was too interested in his girlfriend." She pulled out a piece of paper. "It's a LaToya Harris. She has a St. Louis address but a Chicago number."

"Must have been a lot of business trips down there," Derrick commented. "I'll give Ms. Harris a call."

Evelyn handed him the paper.

"What else?" Gavin folded his arms.

"He was genuinely sad," she replied. "Either guilt or loss, not sure either way."

"What about you, D?"

"From a husband's POV, Janice was obsessive," he indicated. "She had her own routine. Nothing else mattered. Not even her daughter."

"Also, she wouldn't speak to him for days on end." Evelyn perked up. "That's really odd for any relationship. I couldn't imagine not talking to my girlfriend for a period of time."

"I could use a vacation once in a while," Derrick mused with a slight grin. "You're right. And he just accepted that part of her. Don't know. Sounds odd."

"He was justifying his affair," Gavin surmised. He said to Derrick, "Maybe when you have a chat with the mistress, you should ask if she had contact with Janice."

"Maybe a stalker? Wants Mr. C all to herself?" Derrick nodded, thoughtful. "Perhaps."

Holding up her phone, Evelyn stated, "Well, Curtis is pretty prompt. I have a list of her school contacts. And he should be dropping her laptop off later this afternoon."

"Cooperating, that's good," Derrick stated.

"What struck me," Gavin returned, ambling toward the whiteboard with Janice's DMV picture on it. "If Janice was such an independent person, why was she upset that one night?"

"Maybe she saw something that she shouldn't have?" Evelyn suggested.

"No, I don't get that sense," Gavin replied. "Maybe you ought to contact the school list. See if her personality matches what the husband says. Ask them if they knew anything about that day."

Nodding her head, she said, "Trigger their memory?"

"Listen to them," Derrick advised. "I'll go with you."

"Good," Gavin stated. "While we were interviewing Carlton, CSI sent us pictures of possible objects. I'll go over them so they can start testing for blood."

At the same moment, his phone vibrated. Looking down, he saw a text from Chad, who thanked him for last night's passion.

"Bootie call?" Derrick changed the subject. His voice was a better tempo, a little more upbeat after the tension with Evelyn.

"Mmm, Mr. Nolan, are you keeping a secret lover?" Evelyn teased, finally smiling. Then she excused herself to use the bathroom without waiting for an answer.

"Maybe," Gavin finally said to Derrick, who was grabbing his coat.

"You know, you should come by the house," Derrick suggested. "Maria would like to meet her."

It's not a her. "You told Maria?"

"Of course," Derrick said simply. A large grin fell over his face.

Derrick received a call just then and began talking on the phone. Gavin was bewildered. Would he really have told Maria? A nervousness floated within him. Was he ready to share Chad yet?

*****

77

Over the next couple of days, Gavin began to dig into Evelyn's reports and interviews with witnesses on the last two cases. He needed to see what more she had missed. Clearly, her line of questioning was fundamental at best, while Voss used accusatory, blunt questions. Digging deeper, he came across the interview with Eric Holtz, the second victim's ex-boyfriend. Evelyn's basic line of questioning did not allow for an open conversation: *Where were you? Can anyone vouch for your presence? When was the last time you saw...?*

As he read through other interviews, Gavin discovered Voss's lack of support was obviously evident where Evelyn noted she had initiated the interviews. She even wrote a blatant note at the end of each report: *Voss walked out of interview halfway through.* Gavin decided he would have to go back and re-interview. He just had to figure out how to delicately explain it to Evelyn.

At the same time, Evelyn's mood shifted from complacent to apparently subdued. The lack of evidence was taking its toll on the case, which was almost dead if anything. With the fire at the Opus Theater already days behind them, the chances of getting any more eye witness testimony seemed unlikely.

After canvassing the campus, Derrick and Evelyn returned to discuss their findings about Janice Carlton. Janice's advisor, Dr. Rebecca Parks, was surprised by her death, saddened even, and claimed how brilliant and perseverant her student had been. Janice's academic record was spotless, and she'd received high credits and recommendations from the college. When Janice didn't show up for her dissertation, Dr. Parks had set a contingent date for Janice to re-present her findings. Most importantly, the advisor disclosed how she'd set up a position for Janice as a chemist with a large pharmaceutical company near Dallas, Texas. With a follow-up call, Derrick was able to confirm that she would have been starting in mid-January with a prestigious position and large salary.

Gavin surmised that Curtis did not know about that.

When Derrick interviewed several fellow graduate colleagues, their comments showed their complete shock about Janice's death, and how she would be sorely missed. They thought she had a positive attitude and was extremely dedicated to the discipline. Janice was well-respected by the college community. One of her friends, a Beatrice Walters, explained how much Janice's studies were for her daughter. In fact, Beatrice stated that Janice *"gushed over Neesha,"* something that contradicted Curtis Carlton's statement. When Derrick asked about any mood changes or change in behavior, they claimed that Janice was always in control, focused, and steady. Rarely did she sway from her good-natured demeanor.

In the midst of their findings, Creighton's indirect demands through group emails for results escalated. While Gavin answered most of them, Evelyn seemed more perturbed after reading them. He suggested to her not to take Creighton's brash comments personally, but his words did little. Last evening after she'd left, Derrick stated softly, "She's got to figure it out on her own, G. She's a goddamn pistol. She just needs to learn patience. Something that you can't teach her."

Perhaps Derrick was correct.

Gavin could not help her situation any more than he could control her attitude. He would have to speak with her soon, before she said something out of context. Something that she would regret later.

Needless to say, by the end of the night, the case was coming up short. Derrick sensed it as well. When he spoke with CSI, they'd yet to find any conclusive evidence of a long cylindrical spear from the scene that tested positive for Janice's DNA. The only shimmer of hope came from Susan's tox screen, which reported a heavy dose of clonazepam in her blood steam.

The following morning while Gavin was getting ready for work, Evelyn called him, explaining she had to meet Creighton at the commissioner's office. She then added, "Didn't want to burden you with more bullshit."

"Evelyn," Gavin said, "we'd back you one hundred and ten percent."

"But Captain Creighton—" she began.

"Don't ever worry about him," Gavin insisted. "When he wants something, he takes it. His eyes are on you."

"I'll tell you the outcome when I come in," she replied weakly and hung up.

At the same moment, he received a call from Eric Holtz.

"You the detective on Donna's case now?" he asked roughly.

"Yeah," Gavin replied, slipping on his jacket. "Would you mind answering some questions?"

"Naw, man," he said, his voice low. Loud mechanical noises

echoed in the background. "Can you meet me at work?"

"No problem," Gavin replied. "Text me the address."

"One thing though," he said.

"Yeah," Gavin said, grabbing his case.

"That asshole cop, Voss, I think. He ain't coming with," he stated bitterly.

"No. Not at all."

"Fine. Meet you later. Have to get back to work." With that, Eric hung up.

It would be best to interview Eric without Evelyn around. If the guy felt that way about Voss, Gavin could only imagine what it would be like if he saw Evelyn again. Immediately he texted Derrick about the meeting.

*****

Gavin entered the precinct through the back door, hoping not to catch a glimpse of Evelyn or Quinn. Walking quickly, he scooted past the locker room area, then the vending machines, and past the alley kitchenette near the breakroom. Even the sounds of idle chitchat from others seemed to annoy him today. In the bull pen, a group of uniformed policewomen and several detectives stood or sat around their desks. For a brief moment, the typical cacophony of obnoxious noises had been substituted by pleasant voices.

In the center of the group, Derrick's thick back was to him, speaking to a group of officers, nodding his head. A genuine smile filled his face as he rested his hand on Detective Rodriguez's shoulder. After the alderman case, Rodriguez and Derrick had become good friends, talking about their kids and such. He saw Gavin coming toward him, and his smile increased.

As he rounded the corner, Gavin saw Maria in the center of the group. Her short stature and fine delicate features stood out amongst the uniformed and plainclothes men and women. Yet, their attention was on the tightly wrapped light pink blanket in her arms. Casually, she glanced over to see Gavin approaching them, and a sincere smile caressed her thin, lightly glossed lips.

"Maria," Gavin said finally. "What brings you here?"

Leaning over with the baby in her arms, she gave Gavin a brief and tight hug.

"Good to see you too," she replied. A couple of the officers started saying their goodbyes to her, giving her brief hugs before leaving for their shifts. The other detectives shook hands with Derrick and headed out.

"I don't mind seeing you, because I hardly ever get to," he returned and glanced over at Derrick.

"Maria needs the car today," he returned, smiling.

"May I?" Gavin held out his arms for the baby.

"Of course," she replied and freely handed the baby over.

The little girl was light in his arms and nestled against his chest, slumbering away. Her beautiful skin tone reflected Derrick's rich color, while her fine facial features resembled Maria's. The fresh scent of the child wafted into his nose pleasantly over the undertaking musk and chlorine of the station.

"She's adorable," Gavin commented. He said to Maria, "I'm glad she got your looks."

"Eat shit, G."

Hitting Derrick's shoulder, Maria said, "Hush. Don't swear in front of her."

Defensively, Derrick said, "The kid's barely two months old. Like she can repeat words."

"When she comes to you when she's three and tells you to 'eat shit,' then I'll be the one laughing." Maria pulled on her long dark moss coat, which consumed her tiny frame. "Anyway, Gavin, I was dropping off idiot over here…"

"I'm standing right here," Derrick began.

"And I saw the girls in the office. They waved for me to come in," she replied. Then she eyed Gavin, smiling. "You're a natural."

"Thanks. Last time I held a newborn was my little brother." Gavin hugged the baby tighter, feeling the comfort and warmness. "Yeah, suppose you can't do a drive-by without showing her off."

"Nope," Derrick said with conviction. "We better get going to our appointment."

Handing over the child, Gavin replied, "Yeah. I suppose."

"Are you coming to Thanksgiving at our house?" Maria asked nonchalantly as she fussed with putting the child in the car seat.

Surprised and looking at Derrick, he replied, "I wasn't aware of one."

Maria stopped and stood straight up. Despite her small frame, the expression of annoyance that flashed across her eyes was intimidating, Gavin had to admit. "You mean you didn't ask him, Derrick?"

"I was getting to it," Derrick stumbled. He shrugged his shoulders to Gavin. "Really, I was."

"I don't want to impose on a holiday," Gavin began.

"Gavin," Maria spoke firmly without letting her husband speak. "I'd like you to come to Thanksgiving at our house. It'll be fun. We have plenty of food, trust me."

"What about your family? I don't want to bother them," Gavin began quickly.

"Ah, what's another two? Right now, there's about twenty or so coming," Maria stated. "Not sure what you and your brother do, but we'd like it if you came and enjoyed it at our house."

Flattered, he said, "Can I get back to you on that?"

Maria stepped toward Gavin. "Even if you want to bring your *mamacita*, no problem. Please come."

I can't say no. "What do you mean?" Gavin gave Derrick a suspicious look.

"Fine, I'll accept that as a yes," Maria stated, smiling. She put her arm through the car seat quickly.

"Guess you're coming to dinner," Derrick stated. He gave Maria a quick peck on her rosy cheek.

"Suppose so," Gavin said, not realizing he had accepted the invitation.

Within a few moments, Maria Williamson left the station with several waves from the other officers. For the first time, Gavin realized how much of an impact Derrick made at the station.

PART 2
DONNA

"Was it hard? I hope she didn't die hard.'
Sethe shook her head. 'Soft as cream. Being alive was the hard part.'"
—Toni Morrison

"All alone still, not a thing in my name
Ain't got nothin', runnin' from love
Only know fear…"
—SZA

DERRICK

EIGHT

By midmorning, Derrick pulled the unmarked car into the tight parking lot. The window front read *Jerry's Garage*. The faded *r* and *y* made the building seem much more rundown. Its three garage doors were closed tightly next to it, boasting a mosaic of endless smudges, streaks of oil, and grime. Because the garage was so small, the surrounding apartment buildings dwarfed it into a cubby hole on the block. The peeling paint near the corners and the bent roof line were accentuated by the pure snow caps lining the exterior.

"Feels rather South Side," Derrick commented dryly, grabbing his gloves from the back-seat.

"Think I'll pass on the coffee," Gavin replied as he opened the door.

On the side of the building, near the third garage door, three bulky men in thick coats were talking loudly. The men discussed the approaching weekend football games. Near the wall, one of the men leaned against a late model Dodge Charger on cinder blocks.

As Derrick approached them, the huskier man with the darkest skin tone casually eyed them. Immediately, they stopped talking but continued to puff at their cigarettes. Between the cigarettes and frigid air, the billowing smoke enshrouded the men.

"Eric Holtz?" Derrick asked them.

"Not us, man," the husky man stated. The other two rolled their eyes.

"Can you tell us where he is then?" Gavin stood straighter, staring down the younger man, who fidgeted with his lighter.

"Mothafucka's inside," the youngest one replied defensively and flicked his cigarette butt into a small gray icy snowbank.

Derrick turned toward the stained windows, and Gavin followed him, listening to their footsteps crunch on the poorly salted asphalt driveway. Behind him, one of the men said, "Aw, shit. Mr. K's gonna fuck Eric's ass up this time. Told him no mo' goddamn cops at the shop." They snickered amongst themselves.

Inside the claustrophobic reception area, the smell of gas, rubber, an underlying musk, and stale air invaded Gavin's senses, making him not want to swallow. Looking near the grimy maroon desk, he saw the bathroom door was half opened, exposing a dark, rusty stained sink. Nearby, a single coffeemaker coated in a rich brown crust sat on top of a haphazardly placed table in the corner. Above it, an old TV played a morning talk show at a barely audible volume. Against the sweaty windows were four plastic tattered orange chairs, upon one of which a thin elderly black gentleman sat patiently, doing a crossword puzzle.

"May I help you, gentlemen?" a tall, squarely built man with a large potbelly asked. Behind his glasses, the man's eyes pierced them even while his fingers danced off a keyboard in front of him.

"We were wondering if we could speak to Eric Holtz?" Derrick queried innocently, flashing his badge indiscreetly.

"In trouble again," the man said. He wore a scratched name badge that read *David, Manager*.

"No," Gavin replied. "I just spoke with him. He's helping us on a current case."

"Helping? Huh. That's goddamn new." Suspiciously, the manager stopped typing on the computer. "Don't waste his time. Got a backlog of work."

"It won't take long," Derrick said.

"Fine." The man sauntered through the nearby door.

When the door opened, the vibrations of hip-hop music instantly vibrated off the small space. Derrick gave Gavin a brief shrug and a smug face. The manager could be heard shouting for Eric over the noise. Behind the dirty windows, Gavin saw a shorter, thin man look up from the hood of the old Honda. Within a few minutes, Eric was in the waiting room, wiping his oil-laced hands on his dirty uniform.

"Promised Mr. Langdon here his car will be fixed in an hour," the man said to Derrick.

Nodding, Derrick half-turned and said to the waiting elderly man, "Don't worry, sir, it'll be just a moment."

Eric went through the side door and walked past them

without a word. Gavin followed him out into the cold. The manager yelled out, "Any later than ten minutes, I'll dock your pay, Eric."

*****

Eric made a beeline for the three men near the garage. Their conversation currently consisted of Gavin and Derrick's presence as the men pointed at them and gave them snarly stares. Derrick approached the group and broke them immediately, telling them that Eric needed some privacy. Begrudgingly, the men dissipated and slipped back through an exterior side door back into the garage.

Already, the man was lighting up a cigarette. He shoved his free hand into his overalls, pressing his strong arms against his body, seemingly unaffected by the chilly wind.

"Your co-workers?" Derrick nodded toward the door.

From here, Gavin noticed the larger man staring out the window with a look of contempt and bitter anger.

"They all good." Eric exhaled a dragon breath of smoke. "They ain't no trouble."

"I wasn't saying that," Derrick began.

"Eric, like I told you on the phone," Gavin stepped toward the man. "We want to ask you some follow-up questions about your girlfriend, Donna Gable."

"Ex-girlfriend," he returned, eyeing Derrick distrustfully.

"Whatever. We want to hear it from you," Derrick returned, glancing over at Gavin. His thick gloved hands were shoved deep in the pockets of his long black coat.

"I told that asshole cop everythin' I knew." Eric stood straighter, which made his uniform tight against his muscular frame.

"You mean Detective Lopez?" Gavin asked.

"Naw, man, tha' thin white fucker."

"Detective Voss?" Derrick queried.

"Yeah, man, he was a goddamn mothafucka." Once he put out the cigarette butt, he clasped his hands under his armpits. The cold was getting to him. "Hauled me away in a cop car and asked me a bunch of questions. Fuck, man, I was at my little nephew's birthday party too."

When Gavin asked Eric what Voss had asked about, Eric described getting roughed up by a couple of other white cops and then told to confess about Donna's murder. He finally said, "That fucker had a printed statement and wanted me to sign it."

"Why didn't you?" Derrick said softly.

"'Cause I didn't do nothin'!" he said loudly.

On the narrow street, a couple of school buses passed by, filled with young students.

"Would you mind talking to us a little bit about Donna?" Gavin shifted slightly.

Grimacing, he grunted out, "Awright."

"How did you and Donna get along?" Derrick questioned. His body leaned against the car as his eyes scanned the area.

"Dated for a while. Maybe eight, nine months."

"You make it sound like that was a long time," Gavin commented.

"Fuck, it is—was—for me," he replied. He cupped his hands to his mouth and then said, "It was on, then off, then on."

"Was the last time you saw her on or off?"

"We had a fight." Eric's chocolate eyes looked down at the pavement for a moment and then at Gavin. "It was my fault."

"So it was off."

"Yeah."

"What was it about?" Derrick inquired.

"You know, a fight."

"How was it your fault?" Gavin took a step toward him. "Seeing someone else?"

"Naw, man, nothing like dat."

"Did you get rough with her?" Derrick said, standing straighter. "Your arms look pretty big for a small guy. Like beating up girls for fun?"

"Fuck you." He was about to turn and walk away.

Derrick sidestepped to block Eric's path. "Hey, did you beat up Donna and then kill her?"

Glancing over at Gavin, he seemed enraged. His light cocoa-colored cheeks flushed red. Eric replied heatedly to him, "What da fuck's he talkin' 'bout?"

"I mean," Derrick continued, leaning toward the man like a giant. "Did you have another girlfriend on the side? Someone else you got to beat up, kill, set on fire—"

"Man, I don't know any of that shit!" Eric interrupted

heatedly. "Didn't kill no one!"

"Where were you last Monday night?" Gavin asked simply. In his peripheral vision, he noticed that all of the men were watching them from the garage window and talking to themselves.

"At home, goddammit!" Eric's deep voice was guttural.

"Home?" Derrick returned. "Really? You got to do better than that."

"Yeah, at home," he said insolently, moving closer to Derrick.

"With who?"

Eric was shaking, either from the cold or rage—Gavin couldn't tell. The small man stood his ground, looking like he wanted to lunge at Derrick.

"My daddy," he finally said. "He's got cancer. Hospice."

Looking down at the man, Gavin could see the grief in his watery eyes.

Derrick stepped back and said, "Sorry man, just doing my job."

"Well, fuck you." Eric stepped past him.

"Eric, another woman died the other night. Like Donna," Gavin stated.

Eric was about ten feet away from the door when he stopped. He looked back at Gavin and said, "You lyin'."

"No, it's the truth."

Eric's face changed slightly, then his expression saddened more. "Do you think I'm a suspect?"

"No, we just want to talk to you about Donna."

For a moment, only the busy street filled the noise between them. "Let me talk to my boss. Give me a sec."

*****

"Hope he talks fast, my balls are shrinking," Derrick whined, wrapping his thick arms around his jacket.

Smirking, Gavin checked his texts, seeing one from Evelyn: *Creighton and Leger are going at it. No Voss. Feels awkward. Tell you later.* Quinn never backed down from any fight. To him, Evelyn was a coveted item in his arsenal. Shaking his head slightly, he frowned.

"What's up?" Derrick asked.

"Eric's coming back," Gavin returned, shoving his gloved hands into his pockets.

Another thin lit cigarette hung from the man's lips as the faux fur collar of his pleather jacket practically engulfed his neck.

"Mr. Watson told me he's gonna dock my pay," he grunted. "Fuck him."

Nice boss. "So, what did you want to tell us about Donna Gable?" Gavin stated simply.

Eric smoked quickly, sending plumes of white mist blowing around them. Behind him, several window shades of the apartment building were open. Several younger children pressed their pecan-colored faces against the glass, letting their hot breath create a series of misty-shaped amoebas.

"I met Donna at a party," Eric began abruptly, staring off toward the street. "She was different from any girl I knew before. She… I don't know, was cool. Cool in the way that she wasn't takin' any of my lines, you know. Like how da other bitches do, how I get pussy. She thought I was a dumbass and laughed it off. Shit, she was hot. Her eyes so dark, they made me melt. My boy Trey got me hooked up wit' her. Unlike other girls, who gave me some fucking play right away, she was different. Strong, tougha than the rest. Tried all my moves, man, but she didn't go for it. When she left, Trey thought she was too good for me. Gave me some shit for it. Before Donna left, I gave her my number. Thought for sure she'd text me or, fuck, sext me, man."

He paused for a moment, seemingly lost in thought. "'Bout a week later, I was hangin' out with my bro, T-Dawg, the fat-ass one in there. Donna texted me. I was like, no shit. I called her, worked some lines on her. She stopped me an' said, 'Don't be usin' lame-ass shit on me. Just be real.' So I asked her to come out and chill or somethin'. She said fine. I met her at Ol' Henry's, where we all hang out at, ya know. That night, she was lookin' fine as hell too. She had some wine, I had some Courvoisier. We talked. Ya know, I never fuckin' talked to no girl like I did wit' her. She just listened. I talked 'bout my momma dyin', me takin' care of my little sisters, my old man. Yah, she was like magic. When I took her back ta her place, she didn't let me in. Thought I was gonna get somethin', but she held back. She kissed me 'n went inside."

"When was this?" Derrick asked.

"'Bout May, I think," he replied. "We dated for a few weeks. We kissed heavy 'n rubbed all over each other. She liked rubbing. I'd take my shirt off, flex, ya know, then I'd touch her shirt... she'd freeze. Just fuckin' stopped, man."

"Why do you think that is?" Gavin shifted on the tire, smelling the faint scent of the dumpster with tagged signs over it.

"Shit, I thought I gots a virgin," he replied and glanced over at Gavin. He commented, "Would be real nice, right?"

"Anyway," Derrick interrupted. "Go on."

"Right, right. She said dat she just wanted to take her time. I was thinkin' she was all into God, ya know. Don't get me wrong, there's nothing like lovin' the Lord. No, she wasn't. Her apartment was plain. Orderly. But one night, we fucked. It was a hot June night, 'n we got sweaty. Dat night I fucked her all night long. And her pussy tasted so sweet—"

"Alright, I get the picture," Gavin jumped in, looking over at Derrick, who grinned slightly.

"Saw each other for two months," he said. His voice lowered. "Thought things were goin' good. Shit, this was da longest time I been wit' a girl. Ever, man. Usually, I get one or two girls ridin' the E-train, ya know. Wit' Donna, it was different. I didn't do any messin' on the side. God's truth. I *respected* her."

"Were you falling for Donna?" Gavin queried innocently.

"Yeah, man," Eric replied honestly. "I was. Hard, too. Had her meet my family. Was goin' ta talk her inta livin' wit' me. My paw lik'd her, put a smile on his face. He thought I did right."

"Did you ever meet her family?" Derrick shifted slightly. "Did she ever talk about any friends?"

"Naw, she said, like, her family wasn't around no more. Her parents died when she was young, 'n she was in foster homes." He cleared his throat. "She said dat she was in the army, or something like that."

"Which one?" Derrick asked.

Shrugging his shoulders, he replied, "Not sure, man. But I didn't push it tho'."

"Why did you break up?"

Eric reached into his coat, fished for another cigarette, lit it, and inhaled a third of it.

Looking up into the windows, Gavin noticed the children

were gone, yet a frosted edge of their smeared faces remained, like a faceless specter listening to their conversation.

"See, I wasn't cheatin' on *her.*" His voice was bitter. "Donna was steppin' out on me."

Gavin straightened his posture. "How did you find out?"

"We did things, went out, bullshit like that," he stated. "Mainly, we went back ta her crib for some fuckin'. One night, late August, she didn't want no more fuckin'. I'm like, Donna, what gives. She just fuckin' changed. She was al' menstrual like. She said nothin' 'n just left. Didn't see her for a week. Then she called me up, all friendly like. She was up and down, man. That's how da next months was. Just didn't know which Donna I'd be gettin' each day. Two weeks 'fore we called it quits, I see her phone... she was gettin' a bunch of missed calls."

"Who were they from?" Derrick asked.

"Don't know, caller ID blocked 'em." Eric fished out another cigarette and lit it. "I asked her 'bout it."

"What did Donna say?" Gavin inquired.

"Not what she said, see," Eric replied. "She just didn't say nothin'. Bitches do dat, get calls 'n not say who. Clear fuckin' sign, man. She said I was makin' up shit, 'n I was lyin'. Almost got into a real fight. Almost hit her, 'n she kicked me out."

"Who ended the relationship?"

"Donna," he said mournfully. "Felt real bad, real bad 'bout it, too. Called her, went by her place, everythin'. She didn't want nothin' to do wit' me. Took it too hard. I started drinkin' heavy. Shit, almost lost my job here. Didn't hear nothin' from her 'til she called me a week 'fore she died."

"Do you think she wanted to get back with you?" Derrick stated, stepping toward Eric.

"Naw, not at all," he said, lowering his head and becoming interested in his lit cigarette. "She texted me, said she wanted ta see me. She sounded different."

"Nervous? Scared?" Gavin shifted his position, trying and failing to keep warm.

"Yah, scared," he said. "I met her at this small shithole restaurant. Near her apartment. She was sittin' at a table, lookin' out the window. Looked like she hadn't been sleepin'."

"What happened next?"

"She didn't see me come in," he continued. "I sat down 'n she nearly jumped out of her skin. Thought she was playin'. She was shaky, twitchy 'n shit. I thought she was on somethin', ya know. I know she didn't do drugs though." Eric pivoted slightly toward Gavin and stared directly into his eyes. "She told me she was wrong 'bout breakin' up, said sorry 'n shit. Wanted us ta be together. I'd already started seein' 'nother girl." He paused and gave Gavin a small, sad smile. "Part of me, man, wanted ta say yes. But her phone kept ringin' 'n she wouldn't answer it. I grabbed her phone. Still no ID. Of course I got mad. If, I mean, I took her back, Donna'd be here." He trailed off.

"Eric," Gavin began sympathetically.

"I was angry 'n told her ta fuck off," he said. "She started cryin'. I got louder 'n got kicked out. Why that asshole cop thought I done it. I was just a fuckin' dawg."

Gavin remembered Evelyn's side note about the restaurant owner witnessing the argument.

Eric wiped his eyes with the back of his hand. "Maybe if I listened to her, maybe if I took her back…"

"You could not have predicted what would happen to her, okay?" Derrick stated as he put a hand on Eric's shoulder.

Eric attempted to control his sob and looked over at the garage door.

"Is there anything else you can remember about the last time you saw her?" Gavin asked.

"Yeah, I do." He caught his breath. "Don't know, it sounds kinda dumb."

"Anything might help."

"When I left da place, I passed a large black truck, tinted windows 'n shit. A Ford. Ain't no dealer car, ya know? Those fuckin' thangs are pimped out." Eric looked past Gavin toward the glass windows. "Hey, shit, gots ta get back ta work. Need my check."

"One more thing, Eric," Gavin said. "Did she ever mention she was being followed?"

Eric seemed caught off guard for a second, but said simply, "No, man."

Gavin gave Eric his card and asked him to call if he remembered anything. Eric shoved the card into the inside of his jacket and hustled back to the garage.

DERRICK

NINE

Slouching in the passenger seat, Derrick stared out the window while he cryptically spoke with Maria. Rarely did Gavin take the wheel, and today, the traffic heading back to the station was thick as he navigated the sedan slowly down the Kennedy Expressway. Ahead of them, the very tops of the towering buildings evaporated in the low-hanging swirling clouds, making them look chewed off. Once Derrick got off the phone, he asked Gavin about his thoughts on Eric Holtz.

"Sounded like the boyfriend really cared for Donna. He was broken up about her death. You don't seem convinced though." Gavin quickly switched lanes to the Division Street exit, jerking the car between two semi-trucks and causing a series of horns to blast off.

"No, I am," Derrick replied. "It's the bullshit Voss did. That's what pisses me off."

"Voss wanting to convict the boyfriend without evidence?" His eyes spied another opening in the next lane.

"No, a fucking white cop rattling a young black man." Derrick glanced over at Gavin. "The city has too many race issues as is. A dickhead cop thinking he can be judge and jury is just pure bullshit. Voss makes us all look bad. Especially black cops. There's too much violence on the street. In our communities. How can we protect those who need protecting when white asshole cops are beating black suspects?"

"Surprised that Holtz didn't sue, or go to the press even." Gavin aggressively pushed the car into the exit lane, checking quickly for passing cars that honked around the nose of the vehicle.

"Ain't the point," Derrick returned. "Voss's actions are

unacceptable. Sick thing, Holtz can't do a damn thing. His record of drug dealing taints his credibility."

"We should do something," Gavin stated. "Go to Creighton and tell him what he—"

"Fuck the captain," Derrick interrupted angrily. "Creighton is always about Creighton. That's all."

True, very true. "Maybe we can—"

"Sorry, G," Derrick said, holding up his hand. "Thought being a cop, I could make a difference. But all that same old bullshit never goes away."

Gavin absorbed the gravity of Derrick's words. Exiting off the highway and onto Division, going under the viaduct, they were quickly approaching the precinct. For a long moment, they did not speak. Then, Gavin eased the car to a stop at a light. Off to the left, he observed several homeless huts set up in the shadowy depths under the bridge behind the chain-link fence. With the temperatures dipping down to dangerous levels, he hoped they would be seeking shelter soon.

"Sorry about Maria this morning," Derrick said unexpectedly. "She's very persistent."

"No biggie. I don't see enough of her," he replied. "Maria was fine. Your daughter's cute too."

Smiling, Derrick said, "Thanks. But, seriously, you're more than welcome to come to dinner. Bring your honey."

Finding the first available space, Gavin quickly parked behind the station. As his partner reached for the door handle, Gavin said, "Wait a minute, Derrick." A sheen of sweat layered his hands. "I want to tell you something."

"Derrick? Must be important if you use my full name."

"It's about my *honey*," he began, glancing back at the closed exit door.

"She's ugly?" he quipped.

"No..."

"She's married?" Derrick added quickly.

"No, not like that. I..." Gavin felt his heart race.

"Shit, you already got her pregnant," Derrick began with a shit-eating grin.

"She's a man," Gavin blurted out. He felt his lungs collapse in his chest.

Derrick reclined back in the seat, yet he didn't necessarily look shocked. His dark eyes shifted from Gavin to the snowy brick wall ahead of them.

"I've been seeing a man, for a while," Gavin continued, and he sensed his trepidation easing slightly. Hearing his own words relaxed him, though he could not fathom where Derrick's thoughts lay. He then added, "You actually met him. Once."

"You mean that black guy in the hospital?" Derrick responded casually.

"You remember Chad?" Gavin was taken back.

"Hmm. Chad, huh?" he said softly and then looked at Gavin. "You don't have that many friends, Gavin."

"True." Gavin glanced in the rearview mirror at the back door.

"What does Evan think?" Derrick asked.

"Haven't quite gotten around to telling him," Gavin answered truthfully.

"Am I the only one you told?" Derrick's eyes darted between the wall and Gavin.

"Yes."

"Hmm. I'm truly flattered, man." A small grin formed on his face. "Have you always been attracted to men?"

"Not really…" Gavin shrugged his shoulders. Instantaneously, flashes of being with John in the warehouse many years ago flickered through his mind.

"Even with Emily? Did she know?"

"No, but that doesn't matter," Gavin simply stated.

"I always thought there was something going on with you." He gave Gavin a side glance. "Like someone else was in your life."

Gavin said, "No. It was one of the true reasons why we divorced. Something I recently came to terms with."

For a moment, an awkward silence fell between them. Each passing second, Gavin thought it was a mistake. *Maybe I shouldn't have told him. What if he thinks less of me?*

"Good for you," Derrick finally said, and looked him in the eye.

"What?" Gavin was in disbelief.

"Emily was a bitch. No offense." His low voice was compassionate. "It's about time you found someone who takes care of you. Respects you. It's hard to find, man."

"Will your family be offended if I bring another man?" Gavin asked.

"G, Maria's little sister brings over new girlfriends every other month." Derrick shifted in his seat, getting ready to open the door. "Besides, Gavin, love shouldn't have boundaries. Man and a woman, woman and a woman, man and a man... as long as you are happy. That's all I care about."

With a seemingly approving smile, Derrick left the car, uttering expletives about his hatred of the cold, and dashed into the station. Gavin remained.

He was actually happy. Glancing at himself in the mirror, he wondered if those were tears forming in his eyes. Despondently, a dark voice whispered in the background, *Could Derrick have known about Quinn all this time?* But Gavin told himself that wasn't possible.

Or was it?

*****

About midafternoon, Gavin completed an initial report of Eric Holtz's conversation. Curiously, he found himself glancing up at the whiteboard, studying Donna Gable's crumpled and burnt body. Both Donna and Janice had extreme personalities: ultra-independent, averse to sexual activity, controlling in their relationships. While their significant others acquiesced to their eccentric demands, their relentless love masked the women's natures. Still, the victims were absolutely different, and their attractiveness—fine lines, high cheekbones, and exquisite lips—were undeniable. Each of them had unprecedented beauty, even in their DMV pictures: Janice's thick glorious pinned-back braids and Donna's light, flawless expression. At the same time, their eyes spoke a different story: hiding, distant and, dare he say, cold.

Why did the killer choose these women? The lingering question hung in the back of his mind.

In front of him, Derrick placed the receiver back on its cradle and wrote some quick notes on a pad. Shaking his head slightly, he yawned into a cupped hand.

"Go, D. Leave, really," Gavin stated.

"Nah," he replied and reclined in his chair. "Maria's got the car."

"Take the unmarked. Not like anyone uses it that much."

"Contacted Donna Gable's former employer," he said, ignoring Gavin's suggestion. "Sounds like she was a model employee. She was on time. Never had a bad day. Did her work. Never complained about her job."

"Get any co-workers' numbers?"

"Yeah, gave me a couple of extensions." Derrick lifted up his notepad. "For the most part, she was quiet and a hard worker. Never went out with any of her co-workers. Never went to the seasonal office picnic or holiday parties. One said she always claimed to have other plans. A couple thought she was depressed. They all miss her, were all shocked by her death."

"From Evelyn's report," Gavin remarked, "Donna's employer didn't want to answer any questions about her."

"Well, G." Derrick gave him a little smirk. "In a roundabout way, I asked the supervisor if any police had contacted her. She said that a rude detective called, asking to see Donna's employee record. Of course, she couldn't give it out. He got upset and hung up."

"Are you surprised?" Gavin stood up.

"Fucking Voss," Derrick grunted.

"Want some coffee?"

At that same moment, Creighton sauntered through the double glass doors. He already had his overcoat off and folded in his arm. Several policemen were approaching him with questions, but he waved them off. Gavin could see that he was looking directly at him.

"Nolan! Williamson!" he shouted out. "My office! Now!"

With that, Derrick craned his neck and glanced over at Gavin. "Shit," he growled.

Gavin said nothing. Even from this distance, Creighton seemed peppy, barking off orders to others as he went to his office. A quiet rumble ensued throughout the bull pen as Gavin and Derrick followed Creighton, the other detectives telling them they were in deep shit. They were probably right.

*****

Moments later, Gavin acquiesced to sitting in the incommodious olive-green leather chair in front of Creighton's desk.

Just behind him, Derrick decided to lean against the doorframe, looking as if he were ready to bolt at any given moment. His large arms were folded tightly against his chest, which made it appear even bulkier.

Creighton busied himself, checking his computer. He remained standing as he leaned over the chair. An overzealous smile painted his face and accentuated his piercing light eyes. Oddly, he hummed softly in the tight space and tapped his fingers gently against the keyboard. Next to the desk near Gavin, five different case boxes were stacked neatly, the year *2003* printed on their sides. That was about the time Creighton became a lieutenant and worked some major cases.

"Perfect." Creighton's voice was bubbly, even excited. "Had to check one thing. Can you make sure the door is closed, Williamson."

Derrick obeyed. The door pinged shut.

"You may be aware that I had a meeting downtown, concerning Detective Lopez," he stated. Placing his hands on his hips, he appeared much like a conqueror. "I met with Captain Leger, a couple of people from the union, and Commissioner Ronin. Voss was a no-show."

Gavin said nothing.

"I have good news," he continued. "Detective Lopez will be a permanent detective in our precinct."

"How did that go over with Leger?" Derrick queried suspiciously.

"That asshole and I do not necessarily see eye to eye all the time." Creighton looked over at Derrick with a syrupy smile. "He's very possessive of his people, which is always harmful. Once he obtains a good piece for his collection, he snatches it. Hides it. Keeps it all to himself."

Sounds too familiar. "How does this relate to Evelyn?" Gavin asked matter-of-factly.

"That's also his goddamn weakness." The smile widened on his face. "Voss made him look like a fucking idiot. I'm sure you boys read the reports submitted by Voss. Right?"

"We were just discussing that," Derrick confessed, giving Gavin a side glance.

"Good. What did you think of them?"

"Sloppy. Missing details. Too many holes in the interviews," Derrick said.

"And you, Nolan?"

"Voss was pointing fingers at nothing," he stated.

"Exactly," Creighton replied. "I pointed that out to Ronin. That Voss was doing a shitty job on a high-profile case. Plus, he was bringing Lopez down as a new training detective."

"Did Ronin accept that?" Derrick asked.

"Bet your ass he did!" Creighton exclaimed cheerfully. "Fucking put Leger on the spot. Of course, Leger couldn't defend Voss. And then it got a little ugly. Ronin made the final decision to have Lopez placed here. With you two."

"What does that mean?" Gavin sat straighter in the chair.

"Nolan, you are taking the lead on this one again," Creighton said. He leaned against his desk. "Williamson, you will assist Nolan in training Lopez on procedures."

"We work as a team, Captain," Derrick returned, sounding bitter.

"Of course you do," Creighton replied sardonically. "I know that. It's just for show. Both of you will train Lopez. And both of you will work on the case."

"What about Lopez?"

"She's still on it with you guys, or until I find her a partner," Creighton stated. His smile was obnoxiously large.

"How did Evelyn take that?" Gavin questioned.

"She accepted it," Creighton said, and then to Derrick, "Look, it's only on paper. But in the end, this could mean a promotion for you, Williamson."

Derrick said nothing, sighing heavily. Gavin noticed Derrick pull himself up straighter.

"And one more thing," Creighton added. His smile was fading. "This case has to be thoroughly investigated. There are multiple deaths surrounding the victims. The media is sniffing around for answers. Ronin wants results. So I need reports each day. Even if you haven't discovered anything new. Sum up your day's findings. I need those goddamn reports."

He paused and stood up. "Williamson, given your history, I know that you can train Lopez properly. Because you play by the book."

"Hope everyone else does the same too," Derrick returned. "Anything else, Captain?"

"No, not for you." Creighton then turned to Gavin. "You stay for a moment."

Pivoting on his heel, Derrick quickly escaped and left the door slightly ajar. The inharmonious clatter of the bull pen rushed in, making Gavin feel slightly more at ease. The nearest desks were unfortunately empty and not much traffic passed the door—signs of a shift change occurring.

Quinn scooted nearer to Gavin. Habitually, he checked his phone and laid it haphazardly on his papers.

"Yes?" Gavin said impatiently.

"I also talked about you to Ronin," Creighton said.

"For what reason?" Gavin shifted in his chair.

"How valuable you are to the CPD, and the precinct." Casually, Quinn clasped his hands on his lap, hunching over. His chest hair poked out subtly from the top of his button-down.

"What did he say?"

"He agreed." Creighton licked his lips. "After being kidnapped and then killing the suspect, he admired how quickly you recovered and came back on the job. He says that's true dedication."

"How does this help me?"

Leaning toward Gavin, Quinn put a warm hand on his leg. "It puts his mind at ease."

Quinn's heavy hand gripped his thigh tightly. That familiar look befell Quinn's face—the subtle look of lust in those moments, in their secret moments together, before he would—

What is he thinking? We are at work. Moving his leg from under his grip, Gavin stretched and then stood up.

"How does that work for me?" Gavin's nervousness echoed in his words.

"Call it potential." Quinn stood up as well, taking a step closer to him and leaning in. His voice was soft. "Even, dare I say, an investment."

"Investment?" Gavin was backed against the shelf. From this view, no one could see into the office.

"Your career." Quinn came within inches of his face. "So much going for you."

Quinn placed a hand on Gavin's chest; the radiant heat was

intense. A subdued hint of whiskey floated from Quinn's breath.

"As in, a promotion?"

"Yes," he said, staring into Gavin's eyes. His hand slid down Gavin's shirt slowly. "I feel like you can get to the next level. To lieutenant."

"What about Derrick?" Gavin's eyes were at the open door as he felt Quinn's body press against his.

"He'll get your job. He gets the benefits too." Quinn's hand settled on Gavin's crotch. "Except you're getting the full package."

"Quinn," Gavin began, unexpectedly feeling his desire grow.

Quinn whispered in his ear, "After this case, you'll be on a good road to success." His fingers fumbled silently with Gavin's zipper, and soon they slid inside, playing with Gavin's hardening manhood. "Feels like you're all excited by that."

Gavin glanced over at the door and heard a couple of uniforms just outside.

"Quinn, not here," Gavin whispered. "Not now."

"But why?" Quinn's hot breath was on his neck. Soon, his fingers crawled around the front slit and touched his cock. "Mmm. Don't you like the danger?"

For a lingering second, the pleasure was engulfing Gavin. With a slight yank, Quinn pulled out the tip of his cock into the open, and his eyes darted down. Quinn rolled his fingers aggressively around Gavin's thickened tip and eased out a little more of his cock. Beads of sweat began to form on the back of Gavin's neck and rolled down his shirt. Quinn pressed his body harder against him, and Gavin could feel his captain's erection pressing through his pants' leg. His head jerked up. He could swear that he'd heard a knock on the door, and he pushed Quinn away. Quickly, Gavin zipped up his pants and glanced over, seeing no one there.

"What the fuck, Gavin," Quinn sounded back gruffly.

"No, never here," Gavin replied back simply. "Those are *your* rules."

A devious grin took hold of Quinn's lips. An outline of his hardened cock was clearly visible in his tight gray suit pants.

"Fuck the rules sometimes," he returned.

"What the hell's been wrong with you lately?" Gavin stepped toward the door. "The other day you were an asshole. Today, you're like this. What the hell?"

He stood straighter, looking more serious. "Nothing's wrong with me. You should stop blaming me for your own fucking problems, asshole."

At the same moment, Quinn's phone began to ring. He glared at Gavin for several rings until he answered it, angrily. As Quinn turned his back, Gavin walked out the door.

With his heart beating nearly out of his chest, Gavin desperately hoped no one had seen them.

*****

Emerging from the restroom, Gavin calmed himself down. Quinn's blatant intentions in the open had driven him into a frenzy. Part of him wanted to storm back into the office and confront Quinn immediately. But he knew it would create an unnecessary scene. Something Gavin could not afford doing.

Yet.

Ambling toward his desk, Gavin caught brief glances of Quinn shuffling around his office. A new case box was on the desk, and he was plucking through it randomly. Gavin did not have time for that man's games. He had to do his job—

Call it an investment…

—and no longer be distracted. Looking at the whiteboard, he realized the case was becoming even more complicated. The reports he would have to submit, the training they would have to do with Lopez. The constant invisible eye from Quinn over their shoulders would be ever present. And, Quinn had added his own personal agenda into the mix.

His desire to be a cop was dwindling. Being a lieutenant would require more work and hours overseeing the department. And he'd have to work with people who already distrusted him… Was it really worth it?

"Pissed off too?" Derrick commented. He was leaning against his desk.

"You could say that," Gavin returned. The tension ran in him and made him remain standing.

"I tried Evelyn, but she hasn't responded."

"Wouldn't blame her."

"No, no fucking way." Derrick shook his head. "I got out of

the service to get away from bullshit like this."

Fucking Quinn. "Suppose we have to keep a couple of steps ahead of him."

"We have shit, G." Derrick stood up and took a step toward the door.

I know. "Just have to keep digging."

Turning slightly, Derrick's face was stern and cold. "Do our goddamn job right. And train Evelyn too. Just doesn't seem right."

"Derrick, go home," Gavin finally said.

Derrick didn't argue that time. He straightened up his desk somewhat and then slipped on his coat. His large bulky frame stood straight as his dark eyes seemed to burn a hole in Quinn's direction. Before he left, he leaned close to Gavin and whispered, "Never worry about what you told me. I can always keep a secret."

"Thanks, that means a lot," Gavin replied, noticing the other desks around them were empty.

Derrick grinned. "Doesn't mean you get out of Thanksgiving."

"No, not at all," Gavin replied with a half-smile.

With a coy wink, Derrick turned and walked away. Gavin heard a couple people compliment him on how beautiful his daughter was as he walked to the door. As Derrick shook their hands or touched their shoulders, a soft sincerity washed over his face.

TEN

For the remainder of the day, Gavin tried to focus on the case. The dull, familiar ache in the back of his head signified another migraine was slowly forming. Cupping some ibuprofen, he dry-swallowed the gel caps and acquiesced on waiting to take the last of the stronger pills that were at home.

He'd taken several side glances at Quinn's office. The door was shut, the captain's shadowy figure silhouetted against the closed blinds. Nevertheless, his mind kept gravitating to Quinn. Their tumultuous relationship was taking its toll as those heated, passionate moments rapidly flashed in his mind. Quinn's erratic behavior was becoming more noticeable. Even other detectives and uniformed officers were witnessing his bouts of anger and disruptive fits lately. His move on Gavin in the office was the final straw.

Shaking his head slightly, an onset of guilt blossomed when he began to think of Chad and their new relationship. How could he be truly with Chad when his mind was on another person? Chad was giving himself wholly to him, while he was restraining himself. Gavin dared not repeat what he did with Emily, hiding another lover on the side. He would have to tell Chad about Quinn—it was only fair.

Not yet. Soon.

Next to him, his phone vibrated. The caller ID displayed Susan's name, and he answered.

"Hey babe," she cooed back. "Love that sultry voice."

"Is this a social call?" He leaned back in his chair.

"No, unfortunately." A rustling of papers crackled in the background. "I may or may not have some more information for you about burn victims. Had a little spare time today to call Fred Watson." She paused. "You know, that man has got a Soul Train voice. Mmm-mmm, I could listen to him for hours talking about his kids. So, so fine."

"Anyway," Gavin urged her.

"Right," she stated. "I was wondering if he found any plastic pieces on the other two victims. Turns out that he did."

Gavin was alert and looked over the whiteboard. "Why weren't they on the report then?"

"When he arrived on the scene, CSI was already tagging evidence. Fred handed those pieces over to them. He forwarded me the evidence number bags. Just sent it to your email."

After refreshing his webpage, Susan's email popped up. "Got it."

"Good. You'll have to get them from CSI holding."

Finally, a small break. "Yeah, thanks."

"One more thing," she continued. "I asked for his opinion on whether the victims were still alive before the fire because he was the first pathologist on the case. He claimed the first unknown victim had injured lung tissue from smoke inhalation. He could not conclusively determine if the drug in her system caused her death."

"So he determined the cause of death was fire."

"Correct, very good," she said. "He concluded the second victim died before the explosion. A similar small amount of injured tissue on the lungs as well. He didn't state it on his report because—"

"Not conclusive evidence," Gavin finished. "The victims were alive when the explosion happened."

"Exactly. Whoever is doing this wants the women to suffer horribly." More rustling papers in the background. "Shit, baby, I got a call coming in. Have to take it."

"Thanks, Susan."

"No problem. Just keep being sexy," she mused and hung up.

Opening up the email, he clicked on the evidence bags. Within moments, he requested for the items to be shipped to the station and any pictures related to them. Since it was already around six, most of the station was cleared out. Quinn's light remained on.

All he could imagine was how terrified the women must have been seeing the arsonist set up the explosive device in front of them.

*****

The next day, an intense freezing wind whipped and snapped

at Gavin's coat, forcing him to bury his face into his collar. He picked up the pace as he walked toward the main office of the Chicago Fire Inspection Bureau. The weather was supposed to dip down to the single digits today despite the bright sun in the sky, while the wind chill would reach down to minus twenty-five. It was unusual to have such cold weather in Chicago in early November. Opening the door, he spotted Evelyn in the empty reception area.

"Morning," she said, standing straighter. "Glad you had nothing planned today."

"Wouldn't be anywhere else," he replied sarcastically. Warm air slowly defrosted his skin in the tight space.

"Right?" She had already unbuttoned her coat. "Derrick is already here."

"Yep. Got his text." Opening his dark, long coat, he embraced the warmth and shook off the cold.

The white sterile walls, hard red chairs, faux plants, and cheap speckled white linoleum flooring made the waiting area look institutionalized. On a thin red rack near the entrance doors, pamphlets about fire prevention, inspections, and safety materials were neatly in their assigned slots.

"Think anyone is going to greet us?" Evelyn asked, draping her coat over her arm.

"Evelyn," Gavin said. "I'm sorry you had to endure Creighton yesterday."

A faint smile caressed her pink lips. "No, you shouldn't apologize. I did it. I caused the problem." She paused. "Actually, Creighton wasn't that bad."

"Don't have to lie," he began.

"Seriously, Creighton had my back," she replied softly. "He made no-show Voss and Leger look like complete idiots in front of the commissioner. He was—is—good at defending me. And himself. Plus, he plugged you and Derrick too." She paused. "I'm a big girl. Really, I get my place. I'm new. Need to learn. Might as well learn from the best, right?"

Smiling, he returned, "But that isn't the point."

"As Derrick pointed out," she returned, "protocol."

Soon the double doors opened, and a young blond fireman wearing a CFD long-sleeved t-shirt greeted them. His thick arms expanded the shirt while his stocky frame tapered at his waist. Within moments, they followed him down a long equally sterile white corridor.

"By the way," Gavin asked causally. "How's Enrique?"

"Don't know. He's acting all weird," she returned. "The last time I talked to him, about a week ago, I told him I'd be working with you guys. Thought he'd be happy. Instead, he was kind of a prick."

The fireman gave her a side glance with a grin.

"How so?" Gavin's curiosity was piqued.

"Sorry. Forget it." Shaking her head, she returned, "Never mind. Some other time, we'll talk about it."

With that, they walked the rest of the short distance in silence.

*****

The fireman led Gavin and Evelyn into a partially open garage that made up the entire length of the building. More sterile white walls surrounded the area, and the exposed ceiling above with its iron braces, duct work, and crisscrossed plumbing were all a glaring bright white. Both ends of the space had two-story garage doors, and the sounds of their heels and muted conversations echoed as they navigated around two parked fire inspector vehicles. On the opposite cement wall, several racks housed a variety of axes, crowbars, and other equipment that looked more like modern art pieces against the bright white than functional tools.

On the opposite side in the center, Gavin noticed Derrick and Captain Michael Thomas speaking with each other. A couple of other men in jeans and CFD t-shirts were nearby, leaning on a worktable and drinking coffee. Even from here, Gavin could see Thomas pointing at several dark pieces on a white table, a number tag attached to each piece. Next to it, on another smaller table, several pieces of the same type of material had also been laid out.

"Evelyn," Thomas said as they approached. A faint smile caressed the man's lips, making his caterpillar mustache wiggle. "Pleasure as always."

"Same to you," she replied, accepting his hand for a handshake.

"Captain," Gavin stated and offered a hand.

"Detective Nolan. Hate to bring you here on a Saturday."

"Call me Gavin," he said simply. "No problem."

Thomas introduced the other firemen from their nearby district. Next to him, a thinner man who appeared to be in his late fifties was introduced as Thomas's assistant, Greg Olsen.

"Gavin," Derrick began, "Captain Thomas was just going over the pieces that were recovered from the theater fire."

"Yes," Michael stated. His voice was rough and scratchy, as if he were getting over a cold. "I didn't want to start until all of you were present."

"Fair enough," Gavin said, watching the assistant boot up the computer monitor near them.

"We just re-assembled the explosive device late yesterday," the captain stated. "Thought it would be imperative to your investigation to understand how this device works."

"It's ready, Captain," Greg said.

Evelyn took a couple of steps toward the table. Derrick and Gavin followed suit. Thomas chose to stand at the end and cleared his throat slightly. Under the disinfectant odor of the building, a faint smoky scent lingered in the air.

"We extracted about eighty-nine percent of the materials from the theater explosion," Thomas began. "Even though we do not have all the pieces, there is a distinct pattern to the arsonist's assembly of the device." He pointed to the dead center at a contorted round black object. "That would be the timer device. As I indicated earlier, it seems that the L-switch is a standard piece that could be found in any store, really. The timer is self-automated."

"Some explosives," Derrick added, "can be operated remotely. A normalized method."

"Correct," the captain replied. "Most arsonists use a remote detonator. They typically like to watch the destruction from a safe distance."

"So why does it make this device different?" Gavin questioned.

"When you have a timer, the person has a limited time to get out of there." The captain turned to Greg and asked for a pair of gloves.

Nodding, the man got off his stool and went over to a nearby workbench.

"It's more dangerous," Derrick added, keeping his eyes on the burnt objects. Then he looked at Gavin and added, "Probably this guy's sick motivation, in my opinion."

Evelyn leaned over and craned her head to look at the burnt objects.

"I agree," Thomas stated. "Unless you know how to disable the device, time plays against you. It's the reason many criminals use such devices. They want complete destruction, including human lives. It makes our job more challenging to find these types of bastards."

A moment later, Greg handed over the box of gloves to Gavin, and each of them donned a pair.

"Two things that make the device distinctive," Thomas stated. He shifted slightly and opened a program on a nearby laptop, and the screen came to life. A graph appeared, describing chemical components in a mountain range of percentages. "When we tested the materials, the ratio of explosive materials—nitroglycerin to carbon, and organic paste—was highly concentrated. Because of the closed area, the higher amount of packed oxygen caused an even more intense explosion. The blast radius, as you may recall from the scene, had an epicenter of twelve feet."

"The victim was approximately twenty-five feet away," Evelyn pointed out.

"Yes," he replied. "Theoretically, the body should have cleared a good forty feet of distance. Or into the far opposite wall." He changed the screen. "This simulated account shows what should have happened."

The screen displayed a square box on the left and a graphic of a skeleton-like person near the device. A bright flash simulated the detonation, and the digital body flew into the air, landing a good distance away.

"For all intents and purposes," Thomas continued, "it's the body that surprises all of us. The physics don't seem to add up."

"It proves that Susan was correct about the injuries on the victim's ankles and wrists," Derrick stated and glanced over at Gavin and then Evelyn. "She was held down."

"Do you find that similar to the warehouse fire?" Gavin asked as he watched the simulation repeat.

"No," the captain replied. "Her body was found where it should have landed according to the chemical weight of the explosive."

"Was the chemical compound the same too?" Derrick asked, straightening his hunched posture.

"Yes, we also went back over those pieces." Thomas nodded at the other table. "Same composition. Less potency."

"What about the house?" Evelyn shifted her stance.

"Honestly, don't know," he replied gravely. "I will have to find evidence from the site and compare it this week." Looking at Gavin, he added, "My gut says it would be the same though."

"Why?" Evelyn looked up, the strands of her long jet-black hair falling to the side of her face.

"Because, Evelyn," he said frankly, "an arsonist has a signature. It's how he operates the explosive, how he knows to create the right damage and take control of the fire itself. This person is becoming more brazen."

"Show them the other piece," Derrick said to Thomas.

"Right." The captain walked over to a smaller table and retrieved a metal tray. "When you sift through a burnt-out building, it's imperative to search each piece, much like an archeologist does in any excavation. Actually, Tony, over there"—he pointed at the stocky fireman, who raised his hand in acknowledgement—"found each one."

Ambling back toward them, he gave Gavin the small tray. On it, two sets of blue, green, and red wires were intertwined carefully and tightly. Both were slightly singed at the edges. With his gloved hand, Gavin picked one up and handed it over to Evelyn while he took the other.

"They're braided," Evelyn said softly.

"Exactly," Derrick said.

"Every arsonist has a signature," Thomas explained. "The one marked B is from the theater. The one marked A is from the warehouse. This is his signature."

"Our guy is definitely intelligent," Derrick stated. "If someone wants to disable the explosive device, there's no slack to cut any of the wires. A greater risk the bomb will explode."

Derrick held the embedded wires in his thick fingers and brought them closer. A perplexed look flashed over his face before he shook his head and set it back down on the tray. A slight grimace remained on his lips.

"The tight wires indicate precision in his work." Thomas leaned back on the other table and crossed his arms. "The arsonist is making sure the devices cannot be disassembled or disarmed. He wants full destruction."

"Do you believe that the next bomb will be larger?" Gavin inquired.

"Most likely," Thomas said gravely. "Not just in property damage, but in human lives."

*****

When they reconvened in the small lobby of the building, Thomas informed them that if he found any more prudent evidence, he would share the details. Saying their goodbyes, the fire inspector and his assistant disappeared behind the double doors.

Derrick checked his phone. "Didn't take too long."

"Thomas's rather efficient," Evelyn commented as she wrapped a bright poppy-colored scarf around her neck.

"That he is," Gavin concurred. He said to Derrick, "What are your thoughts?"

"Our guy is definitely not an arsonist," he replied quickly. "Typically, he would stick around and watch the event. See it unfold."

"Isn't it true in most cases that arsonists are often younger, and not necessarily the brightest ones in the class?" Evelyn said.

"Yes, they want attention," Derrick confirmed. "Others do it for the insurance money."

"The amount of explosive compound and braided wiring," Gavin jumped in, "suggest that our guy is more sophisticated, more complex." He recapped Susan's conversation with Watson to them.

"G, this guy is brutal." Derrick's concerned look was evident. "Seems like we are several steps behind."

"It was me," Evelyn started. "It's my fault."

"No," Gavin said, reassuring her. "Monday, you start re-reading your reports again with a clear head. See if you need to re-interview anyone. Not all, but ones you feel may have been holding back information. Either Derrick or I will tag along."

"Alright." She took a big breath and said, "I noticed something in your interview with Eric Dalton. Read the report this morning. He said Donna was in the military. Didn't Curtis Carlton say that Janice served as well?"

"Not sure if that's anything significant," Derrick retorted.

"Maybe, or maybe not." Evelyn stared at Derrick. "I want to be thorough."

"Fine," Derrick said. "But you'll have to go through proper channels and get their military files. I can show you on Monday."

Smiling, Evelyn brushed back a loose piece of hair.

"What Thomas said about Janice's body not moving in the explosion and Susan's autopsy," Derrick started, "proves that she was held down. I'll get a request for CSI to give us samples on those probable objects."

Nice. "When you do," Gavin responded, "copy Creighton on it. That way they'll get their shit done faster. You know how he and CSI don't get along." He looked at Evelyn. "Sometimes, *only* sometimes, Creighton is good for a couple of things."

"I'll follow up also with Thomas about the actual compound," Derrick continued. "Maybe where our guy gets his explosives and where it's shipped might get us somewhere."

"Alright, we're getting a plan," Gavin replied with a brief smile. "Since we all agree wholeheartedly that this guy is really a savage killer, I'm just wondering about the locations. Of all the places he could destroy, why those places?"

"Maybe they were familiar places to him?" Evelyn suggested.

"He's evolving. He's becoming much more menacing," Gavin stated.

"You're suggesting the explosions are a distraction," Derrick said, more a statement than a question.

"Possibly," Gavin said simply. "If it turns out to be nothing, then I just wasted a day of research. Nothing more."

Evelyn only nodded.

Again, Derrick took out his phone and smiled. "Is that about it, G?"

"Plans today?" Gavin buttoned up his coat and slipped on his gloves.

"Yeah, her brother is having a birthday party tonight." A large smile crossed his face. "Lots of tequila."

"Hope it's the good shit," Evelyn commented.

"Always is." He snorted out a laugh.

"See you later, have fun," Gavin said as they headed toward the door.

They all went their separate ways. Gavin headed back to the station and quickly wrote up a report about Thomas's findings, including a brief plan of action for next week. He had to be three steps ahead of Quinn now.

Later that night, Gavin and Chad went out to a quaint Italian restaurant where the clams in white sauce were exceptional. Over a couple of glasses of wine, they talked about their week, or rather Chad talked. Gavin did not mind being engaged in Chad's world. Eventually, they went back to Gavin's apartment, where they made love on the couch, in the shower, and finally in his bed. As Gavin drifted off to sleep with Chad's soothing warm skin against his, his thoughts led him back to the case.

A house, a warehouse, and a movie theater. What will be next?

ELEVEN

A slight rumbling in his stomach forced Gavin to glance over at the time. Closing in on eleven a.m. Monday, he finished the follow-up report from the meeting with Captain Thomas. Late Saturday night, Creighton deemed it necessary to be more detailed as they progressed in the case. Fucking Quinn.

Since Gavin had woken up that morning, a nagging headache hung at the base of his head and seemed to slow him down. Opening the near drawer, he shook out several aspirins and drank the last of his water. Craning his neck toward Creighton's closed office, he hit send on the report and got back to his work. These arduous tasks unnecessarily outweighed any potential progress he could make on the case. Should he become a lieutenant, the paperwork would only worsen. How could he find a killer when he was nailed to a desk all goddamn day?

Near him, Evelyn got his attention, which was a nice break from staring at the computer screen. Briefly, she explained that she intended to re-interview the restaurant owner where Donna Gable and Eric Holtz had their argument. She'd recognized the small gaps in the conversation where she could have interviewed possible employees. When she suggested returning back to the neighborhood on Ashland and knocking on some doors to jar some memories about the house fire, Gavin agreed it was a good idea.

Derrick rounded the corner then and made a beeline toward them. His long black coat flapped behind him and brushed against other desks along the way. He was unsettled and in a rush. Earlier, Derrick had texted Gavin that their daughter was running a high temperature. With her nursing background, Maria's astute detection meant a trip to an emergency room.

"Hey guys," he said, breathing heavily.

"How's the baby?" Evelyn had a concerned look on her face.

"Fine, now," he said, exasperated. "Still has a high temp. The doctor thinks she might have an ear infection. But Maria isn't convinced. Already called our regular doctor and made an appointment for later."

"Hope nothing serious," Gavin returned.

Shaking his head slightly, he replied, "M."

"Hey, keep your coat on," Evelyn stated as she stood up. "Please."

"Where are we going?"

"A little talk with some nice people," she mused.

Shrugging his thick shoulders, he looked at Gavin. "Guess I came just in time." Then he looked at her and said, "As long as we stop and get some lunch."

"Yes, sir," she quipped. Her laptop bag was over her shoulder. "Do you mind driving the first round?"

"Sure, why not," he said. Then to Gavin, he added, "Guess we'll talk later."

"Only a text away," Gavin answered.

Evelyn followed Derrick toward the back of the station. They disappeared behind a group of uniformed officers who were getting ready for afternoon line-up.

******

A few minutes later, Gavin began his search into the buildings. He focused on the most recent fire: The Opus Theater. Within minutes, a Google search produced several articles and tidbits of its history on his laptop screen.

He skimmed the articles and discovered the movie theater had once been a showpiece landmark, but soon became a forgotten relic of the past. It opened in 1898 and became a pinnacle for the affluent. With the onset of the Great Depression, it closed its doors and didn't reopen until the early fifties to be converted into a movie theater. It had its ups and downs for a few decades then was forced to close again in the summer of '02 due to poor management. That fall, the University of Chicago took full ownership, using it strictly for academic purposes to showcase forthcoming documentaries and educational films.

A 2007 university article Gavin found reported on fundraising pledges to restore the theater to its old grandeur of long ago, yet no follow-up information could be found about the event. Then, last year, the university posted a letter on their website which stated, *"Poor maintenance and lack of proper management has further pushed low attendance levels of the fine theatre. Staff, alumni, and students will indubitably miss the campus perk."* After that, a handful of letters had surfaced about the theater from university professors, administration, and the student body urging to re-appeal the decision. Needless to say, the voice of the few did not uphold the bureaucratic decision. Thus, before the next school year began, it was closed again and placed on the market.

Digging deeper in the history of the theater through the police database, Gavin uncovered a series of complaints from the nineties to 2001. Then, after U of C took over, several reports returned from 2003 to 2006. The complaints from local residents and business owners stated issues with the films being shown at the theater. They also mentioned lewd behavior of theater patrons and some blatant exposure. Looking at *Tribune* movie listings for that time period, Gavin saw that the movies were either bad B-rated horror movies or documentaries. Yet, no follow-up from any police official took place.

"Odd," he whispered, brushing back his chestnut-colored hair with his fingers.

Gavin swiftly picked up the phone and dialed the university. After a few minutes of being shuffled from department to department, he finally landed at the school of fine arts. Speaking with a stern receptionist who seemed disinterested in his call, he firmly stated that he was the investigating detective looking into the fire. The woman informed him that Dr. Kimberly Saunders had been out for the past two weeks at seminars on the West Coast. But she assured him in an exasperated tone that she would pass on his message as soon as the doctor returned.

As he moved aside the file, his phone rang. It was Mylo.

"Took you long enough," Gavin quipped.

"Yeah, sorry about that, Nolan," Mylo returned, sounding exhausted. "Been busy with other people's bullshit lately."

"Thought I was your favorite?"

"Captain Creighton has been making me his errand boy," he

stated bitterly. "Like I have nothing else to do. The asshole."

Looking over at the closed office door, Gavin asked, "What kind of errands?"

"Looking for old case records." He paused. "Shouldn't be telling you. He'll have my ass."

"Don't worry about him. It won't go past me."

"Better not," he replied. Mylo blew his nose loudly. "Working from home. Caught a flu bug or something. Called because I don't have any good news for you. The calls made by your suspect were most likely used on a burner cell. Untraceable. The devices were purchased at locations across the city. I sent it to you."

Damn. "Thanks."

"But," he added, slightly more upbeat, "the IT super over at nine-one-one is a good friend of mine; she'll be able to trace the call immediately. That way the call can be pinged on the nearest cell tower. If it comes in again."

Not if, but when. "Alright."

"Little more," he continued. "Your suspect prerecorded that message. I went through and scrubbed for any ambient noises or street sounds. Nothing. Clean. Probably created in a studio, or with some filtering software. Honestly, you can buy that shit anywhere. The time lapse is about eighteen point three seconds. My friend believes that'll be enough time to ping off a tower."

"How soon would we be able to track the location?" Gavin leaned on his desk.

"Within three minutes of the call. Enough time for the suspect to escape," Mylo said. "Sorry I couldn't help you more."

"No, it's all good. But hang tight," Gavin returned. "I may have something for you shortly."

With that, Gavin said goodbye. Stretching his neck from side to side, he felt the soreness in his deltoids and chest from his heavy-lifting workout earlier. He stared up at the conical lights, lost in thought. The recorded message meant the killer had a plan.

How long ago had he conceived it?

******

The afternoon pressed on with no word yet from Derrick or Evelyn, so Gavin exhaustively searched for information on the warehouse on Damian.

It was an old building, built right after World War II. It had been empty for nearly twenty years, and based on police reports, various break-ins and disturbances had been common occurrences at one point. A local nearby gang claimed it briefly for its headquarters, only to be busted shortly after. Still, Gavin sensed that the warehouse had something important for the killer. Of all the warehouses in Chicago, *he* chose this spot.

In the mid-nineties, a new set of owners from Sanford and Pierce Realty Group had purchased the location. Evelyn left a note about the ownership, along with an office number, and claimed to have left a message. Since they'd purchased the place, it looked as if the crime had minimized. There were very few incidents from 1997 to now, except for minor reports of homeless people and some gang tagging on the exterior.

Gavin called Sanford and Pierce Realty and was greeted by an overly cheerful receptionist. Quickly, he inquired about the warehouse and gave the address. She then asked about potential rental property, which seemed to be a standard selling pitch, and he insisted on speaking to one of the owners. At that point, she informed him that he would be speaking with Mr. Pierce.

While he was on hold, Gavin googled the realty company. On the screen, an impressive background of Chicago's skyline anchored the logo above the skyscrapers. Clicking on the "Company founders" tab, he found a recent photo of two men sitting next to each other in a bright wood-paneled room. Each looked to be in their early sixties. The taller, thinner man appeared more genuine, with a graceful smile and a hint of pride in his dark eyes. The other man, shorter and thicker in stature, looked more stiff and reclusive as he forced a smile.

"Detective Nolan," a low, gargling voice greeted over the phone.

"Yes, I am. Is this Mr. Pierce?" Gavin had his notepad ready.

"Mitchell Pierce," he answered.

"My name is Detective Gavin Nolan with—"

"Yes, Beatrice already informed me of your credentials," the man gruffly replied.

Guess I interrupted your day. Looking up at the whiteboard, Gavin asked, "Can you tell me more about your property, a warehouse on Damian?"

"It's commercially run property." He cleared his voice. "We've owned it since 1996. My partner, Donald Sanford, decided to divide up the huge space and attract small businesses to use the location for their needs. With the recession between oh-eight and ten, a lot of businesses had to sever leases. These days, attracting new businesses has been more challenging. To say the least."

"Why that location?"

"At the time," he responded instantly, "Chicago was going through a resurgence for investors. With many people heading back to the city, new locations opened up on the near southwest side. Like many forward thinking members of the community, our goal was to bring large business back to Chicago. And, of course, to increase property value and quality in the same process."

"The gentrification proved to be slower than anticipated," Gavin surmised.

"Yes, the resurgence," Pierce corrected him. "It was, and still is, a slow-moving process."

"Were there any businesses in the warehouse at the time of the fire?"

"Only one. However, it was on the other side of the building." Gavin heard a faint voice in the background. "Thank goodness for them that they were in the process of moving facilities."

"Moving out of the property?"

"Yes. We made a decision to sell off that property. To cut our losses." He paused. "Currently, we are doing some light renovations to make it more appealing for potential buyers."

Convenient that the fire happened, hmm? "Are you able to recoup some loss through insurance claims?"

"Why does that concern you, Detective?" A spark of defensiveness peppered his words.

"To your knowledge, the warehouse was completely empty?" he asked instead with a smile, knowing that he could trigger the man easily.

"Yes, it was," he confirmed.

"Any problems with break-ins and such?"

"Yes. The last two years, more break-ins occurred." A shuffle of movement fluttered faintly in the background. "Vagrants entering in and out at all times. I'm sure you would be able to pull the numerous complaints."

"I will," Gavin replied casually. "A homeless person died in that fire as well."

"Yes, such a shame." Pierce's tone was patronizingly unconvincing. Then he added, "And that young lady as well."

"We believe the perpetrator, who caused the fire, intentionally committed murder," Gavin stated.

"Are you saying that he may be after one of us?" Pierce asked.

Interesting question to ask. "Probably not," Gavin returned honestly. "Our suspect seems to have other motives."

"What can I do to help you, Detective?" He covered the phone and spoke to someone in a low tone.

"I would like a list," Gavin responded, "of all the businesses, contacts, and records of anyone in contact with that warehouse since you owned it. Please email it to me." He rattled off his email address.

"Very well. It's a comprehensive list. My assistant will gather the information for you," Pierce said matter-of-factly. "Anything else, Detective?"

"No," he returned. "But I'll be in touch if I have any more questions, Mr. Pierce."

*****

When it was close to five thirty, Gavin took off his glasses and rubbed his eyes, feeling the strain from staring at the computer. In the last hour, the realty group had sent over an extensive Excel spreadsheet that listed nearly one hundred businesses that had leased space. An owner and partners were listed for each business, for a total of nearly six hundred names. Overwhelmed, he leaned back in his chair and dry-swallowed a couple more ibuprofens. The lingering headache impeded his ability to concentrate on the list. As he glanced around wearily, he saw that most of the desks around him were empty and the front area had quieted down.

As he stood up to stretch his legs, Evelyn called.

"Hey, I was going to call you," he said, leaning against the desk.

"Ah, you miss us already," she replied. Gavin heard the distorted grainy sounds of traffic and could tell he was on speaker.

"We talked to the restaurant owner this afternoon, and he confirmed the argument between Donna Gable and Eric Holtz."

"What we would expect," Derrick piped in.

"Keep your eyes on the road," Evelyn said to Derrick. Gavin smirked. "We were able to talk with staff. The waitress, Maria Carrera, remembered Gable specifically."

"Sounded like Gable was a frequent flyer at that nasty dump," Derrick added.

"Yes, Carrera said Gable ate alone all the time." Evelyn's voice faded slightly. "Ate at the same table right next to the windows near the front entrance. They even waited for it if it was occupied and other tables were open."

"Habitual?" Gavin queried.

"No shit," Derrick stated firmly. "Confirms her erratic behavior."

"What do you mean?" Gavin folded his arms.

"Carrera said that she was moody," Evelyn jumped in. "Around the time of her death, she came in every day. Nervous. Jittery. Sorta like what Holtz mentioned. Carrera asked her if she was okay. Gable ignored her."

"Gets better," Derrick said.

"Yeah," Evelyn spoke up. In the background, a series of muffled horns blasted off. "Derrick spoke with a dishwasher who may have also noticed that black truck."

"May have?" Gavin questioned.

"It's a long shot," Derrick stated. "The kid, no more than seventeen, recalled he saw a similar black truck on the street a couple of times. Only when Gable was there. Then it was gone afterwards." He sighed. "Now, G, how many times did this happen? Can't say. But to me, man, I think the kid was a little strung out."

"Not exactly reliable." Gavin stood up and looked at Donna's face on the whiteboard.

"Point taken." Evelyn's voice sounded deflated.

Quickly, Gavin recapped his conversation with the university, Mylo's findings, and Sanford and Pierce.

When he finished, Derrick stated, "Hey, Creighton said we could get some support if we needed it, right?"

"Yeah," Gavin said, though he wasn't really sure about that.

"A good person in processing may help us on that list."

Derrick paused. "Mary Liminski. Great gal. You'll love her. In fact, I'll text her shortly and see if she's on shift tomorrow."

"Alright, fine." Gavin looked down at his notes about the house. "Evelyn? Did you ever find out who owned the house in the first fire?"

"Yeah. Name was Roslyn Henderson. She died several years ago. Didn't follow up any further than that."

"Good enough." Gavin scribbled the name down on a nearby pad. "Anything else?"

"Nah," Derrick answered.

With that, Gavin told them to enjoy their evening and hung up. As he typed up a quick report from the day's search, his thoughts went back to Donna Gable. The poor woman had been alone and afraid, and she was being stalked, most likely by their suspect. Still, it could not be a simple coincidence that Donna Gable was picked out of the crowd. Much less Janice Carlton.

He sent his report to Creighton and stared at the whiteboard yet again. The burnt corpse of the unidentified first victim seemed to stare right back at him.

The only question on his mind in that moment was:

Why you?

TWELVE

Sliding into the precinct a little after nine, Gavin regretted the extra push at the gym. This morning, he'd actually woken up refreshed, and the headache no longer ravaged his brain. Chad's text message to meet him for a workout was all too tempting. How he loved staring at Chad lifting weights, seeing his muscles bulge and veins pop through a tight shirt and loose shorts draping his dark tree trunk legs. But while he enjoyed watching his lover, the longer-than-usual run had left him exhausted.

As he sidestepped the morning lineup and glided his way toward the open bull pen, he sipped his lukewarm coffee. It was pungent in his mouth, and he threw it in the nearest garbage can. His phone vibrated with a text from Derrick: *We're waiting.*

Sometimes Derrick was too impatient.

Overnight, a small snow squall had left a couple of inches on the ground and made the commute absolute hell in the city. No matter—the typical cacophony of muttered conversations, typing, and printers reverberated in the open space and rang in his ears. Catching a glimpse up ahead, he saw Derrick and Evelyn perched near their desks like hungry vultures in anticipation of another meal. Next to Evelyn, a squatter policewoman with pinned-up canary-yellow hair was talking, holding her phone up and pointing at it. When he got within earshot, he heard the woman say, "Oh, yeah. My Courtney is twelve now. She thinks that she's a teenager. But, oh, she's not."

"Can't believe your kids are that old already," Derrick said.

"Yeah, Williamson," she replied. "Enjoy your little ones now. 'Cause when they get larger, oh, they get a mouth."

Evelyn snickered slightly and sipped on her coffee. Immediately, she noticed him coming toward them.

"Gavin," Evelyn stated. "How was the drive in?"

Before he could respond, her phone rang and she walked off to the side to answer it.

Derrick returned snidely, "What drive? He lives only a goddamn mile and a half away."

Lowering his bag onto his desk, Gavin ignored him and extended out a hand. "You must be Officer Liminski."

"Yes, I am." She shook his hand with a firm grip. "Oh gosh, sorry, we never really met. I used to work second shift before. Now, I got first shift."

Her crisp northern Wisconsin accent reminded him of the movie *Fargo*.

"Good for you," he said, taking off his jacket.

"Already briefed Mary on the case," Derrick said and stood up.

Mary shifted her stance slightly and nodded toward the whiteboard. "Oh, bad. Such a shame," she commented sadly. "They were pretty."

"That's why we need your help." Before he left last night, Gavin had printed off the Excel spreadsheet. He grabbed the copy and handed it to the officer. "Here's a list of businesses from the second fire."

Her fingers thumbed through it briefly. "What am I looking for?" she asked Derrick.

"G?"

"Well, I'm not exactly sure," Gavin admitted. "Our suspect used that location for a specific reason."

"Yah, okay." She looked at the paper.

"Mary is great at finding whatever you need," Derrick responded. "She helped on the alderman case a couple years back. Indirectly."

"That too was a long list." She smiled briefly. "I'll do what it takes to get this guy."

"Good. There has to be something in that list to clue us in on why the killer targeted that spot." Gavin looked over at Derrick.

"Thanks again, Mary." Derrick hovered over her.

"Oh yah. It sure beats filing violation reports," she said. "That gets old real fast, right?"

******

Soon, Officer Mary Liminski said her goodbyes with a smile

on her face, scooted away with her paper, and disappeared around the corner.

"How do you know her?" Gavin asked. He turned on his desktop computer.

"During the alderman case, Mary called me directly." Derrick walked around to his desk. "Mylo was driving her fucking crazy. So I let her vent. Actually, she helped me—us—find the right accounts to nail those assholes to the ground."

"Why didn't you ever tell me?"

"Thought I did," he replied casually. "But I have good news."

"Really?" Gavin glanced over at Evelyn, who was still on the phone.

"CSI finally found a murder weapon that matched the wounds Susan found on Janice Carlton." He pointed to his computer screen. "It's a rod. Aluminum coating. About seven and a half feet in length and three inches in diameter."

On the screen, the charred, bent rod lay on a stainless steel table with an evidence tag, number thirty-five, wrapped on the end.

"That's a weapon," Gavin stated.

"No shit," Derrick replied. Gavin stepped closer to him, catching a subtle waft of sandalwood cologne.

"What you guys looking at?" Evelyn stepped over to them and looked at the screen. "That'd hurt."

"Probably did," Derrick answered.

Leaning over quickly, Evelyn grabbed a small envelope and handed it to Gavin. "This came for you earlier."

Recognizing the envelope from evidence, Gavin ripped it open. Out slid another clear envelope marked EVIDENCE. Inside was a small burnt chip in a plastic bag.

"What's that?" Derrick queried.

"What Watson found on Janice Carlton," Gavin returned as he handed it over to Derrick. Evelyn craned her head to look at it as well.

Taking a step toward his desk, Gavin grabbed the other piece. "Sorta looks like the other one."

"Looks like a puzzle," Evelyn stated.

Gavin held the piece up to the light. He could detect a slight smoothness to the object. Just like the one in Derrick's hand.

"Maybe the explosion ripped whatever this is into pieces,"

Derrick commented. "It seems like they each belong together."

"But don't," Evelyn finished. "Do you think the suspect planted something on the victims?"

Shaking his head, Derrick answered, "For what purpose?"

Looking over at the whiteboard, Gavin still did not have an answer.

*****

Within a half an hour, Derrick and Evelyn headed out to the Ashland neighborhood. They planned on canvassing the neighborhood with the hope that someone would remember anything about the house's former owners or the fire. When Evelyn had been on the phone earlier, she was confirming a possible witness who lived across the street. On the way down, Derrick would contact Mylo about searching for a black truck near the Opus Theater.

Performing a quick Google search on Roslyn Henderson, Gavin pulled up an obituary notice that stated she had passed away seven years ago. A surviving daughter, Lynette Denton, was listed. Utilizing the police database, he found that her name was associated with Billie Denton, who was currently serving year one of a fifteen-year sentence for armed robbery. Denton's address popped up several times, indicating signs of domestic abuse. Dialing a number listed through the DMV, he reached a recorded message that provided an alternative number.

After the third ring, a woman with a guttural, stern voice answered the phone. In the background, sounds of children, a loud television, and hip-hop music echoed, almost drowning out anything else. Telling him to hold on, she poorly muffled the receiver, yelling at the kids to turn down the television. When he introduced himself, she interrupted by telling him that her husband, Billie Denton, was downstate, and if he needed questions answered then he should call them. Dismissing her, he inquired about her mother. Defensively, she turned cool—even suspicious—on the other end, asking him what he wanted.

"I'm wondering about her house," Gavin prefaced. "Why did she sell it?"

"Please call me Mrs. Henderson. I don't go by Denton no more," she said in angst. "Momma got emphysema. Smoked all her life. Three packs a day. Solid too. Told her to quit, 'specially 'round my kids, when they were babies. We always fought over that."

"She couldn't keep up with the house anymore?"

"Naw," she said. "It was me. I couldn't keep up with it. Stubborn ol' lady. Momma wanted to live in it as long as she could. Didn't want to go into any state home. She come up and lived with me. For nine months. Until I had to put her into the hospital. She died after. Sometimes it feels like just yesterday." Her voice saddened slightly. "Why you askin' 'bout her?"

"Well, there was a fire at your mother's house a month or so ago," he returned. Then he added, "A body was discovered there."

"I heard too." She was blunt. "What about it?"

"I'm wondering who your mother was in contact with to sell the house," he prompted. "It could help in the investigation."

For a brief moment, she shuffled on the other side. The sound of heavy breathing issued, and then a slamming door.

"Had to move to 'nother room." Her breath was raspy. "My momma never did anythin' with the house. *I* did it all. Sorta met him too."

"Who, the buyer?" Gavin sat straight in his chair. "Do you remember anything about him?"

"Well, not him 'xactly," she corrected. "Some otha person who represented the buyer. Get me?"

"Do you remember the agency?"

"Oh, lordy, no," she replied, sighing. "That's a long time ago."

"Tell me what you remember." Gavin wrote down a note: *A third party?*

At that point, Lynette Henderson described how sick her mother had become, and that she eventually had to be on oxygen all the time. She knew her mother could no longer live alone, so she brought her home. Because of this, she could not take care of her mother's house and decided it'd be best to sell it. The agent informed her that houses in her mother's area were not moving on the market. But all of a sudden, the agent called her in a month about a potential buyer who wanted to purchase the house, sight unseen. Lynette understood that her mother's house was in terrible shape and that the home inspector would find many flaws. The buyer didn't even go through with the inspection, however. Less than three weeks later, the house was sold.

"Did your agent handle all the paperwork?" Gavin leaned

onto his desk.

"Naw, I got rid of it when Momma died." She sounded disappointed. Then she added quickly, "While I was talkin', I was lookin' for his card. I try to keep my shit, I mean papers, in a good pile." There was a ruffling of paper in the background. "There it is. My agent was Phil Brussen, a good guy. We now go to the same church." She gave the agent's number.

"Thanks, Ms. Henderson."

"One more thing." She cleared her throat. "I did keep track of Momma's house. Her friends kept me in the loop. Lots of old people on that block now. Oldens lookin' after each other. Her friend, Mabel Dickenson, called me from time to time. After the sale, the house stood empty a long time. 'Bout two or three years ago, she told me someone moved into the house. Middle of the night too. 'Cause the truck woke her up. Couple a big white guys unloading stuff."

"Do you know how long they were there?" Another note on his pad: *Movers?*

"Don't know," she admitted. "Billie and me weren't gettin' along. I did call her 'round the holidays. Told me she was happy the new people weren't there anymore. Mabel heard all sorts of strange noises in the middle of the night coming from Momma's house."

"Think she'd be willing to talk to me?"

"Sorry, Detective, Mabel died a year ago," she answered. "Cancer, bad too. Went quick. Praise Jesus."

Gavin thanked her for her help and told her to call him if she remembered anything else.

After leaving a message for Brussen, the agent called back about fifteen minutes later. Gavin explained his interest in the Henderson house, and the agent indicated that he knew both the older and younger Mrs. Henderson because they all went to the same church. When the older Mrs. Henderson was getting ill, the daughter approached him about selling the house. Because the younger Henderson was occupied with her sick mother, children, and awful husband, he helped her through the selling process. He even offered to clean up the house to make it somewhat presentable, despite the poor condition it had been in.

"Couple of months ago, I saw in the news about the fire in the house," Brussen finally said. "They discovered a body. Is that true?"

"I am not at liberty to confirm the details, Mr. Brussen." Gavin's tone reflected a serious cop attitude. "But a body was discovered at the location. Any help from you would be greatly appreciated."

"Oh my goodness." Mr. Brussen cleared his voice. "What can I do to assist you, Detective?"

"What do you recall about the buyer?"

For a second, there was a brief silence.

"Sorry," he replied, sounding deflated. "I never interacted with the buyer per se. It was all done through faxes, emails, and the closing paperwork."

Interesting. "Can you send over the closing paperwork for the Henderson house?"

"Absolutely, but it will take some time. Two days at the most." He then added proudly, "I store all copies of my closings."

Thanking the agent for his time, Gavin gave him the fax number to the station and said his goodbye.

Standing up, a resurgence of energy flowed through him. Perhaps it was a break. A university getting rid of the management company, a warehouse with multiple business units, and a house that someone desperately wanted. What could the connection be? Looking over the whiteboard, Gavin noted that the locations didn't hold any distinctive pattern. Why those spots? What was the killer trying to show them?

Casually, he glanced over at Creighton's empty office, glad he wasn't there today. He texted Derrick to ask any neighbors about strange noises and a moving truck two years ago.

Why? Derrick responded.

Have a feeling, he texted back. *Will explain later.*

After writing up a couple of reports, Gavin headed toward Officer Mary Liminski's cubicle. He would help her make some necessary calls as well.

******

"That was goddamn amazing," Chad whispered, wrapping his thick arm around Gavin's waist. Gavin had just rolled off of him and now lay on his back, his manhood still pulsating from the rigorous activity.

Never had Gavin imagined lying in bed with a man and not

worrying about any consequences. A thin layer of sweat caressed his skin as Chad pressed his body harder against him. Gavin's fingers moved along the curvature of Chad's chiseled back and danced softly off his silky dark skin. The smell of Chad's hair wafted subtly, a fine leathery scent that electrified him.

"Guess you should tell me that you're going away more often," Gavin replied softly. Chad had mentioned he had a conference to attend in Rio de Janeiro right after Thanksgiving. Gavin would have loved to go with him, if the case weren't so consuming.

"Maybe." Chad's warm breath cascaded over Gavin's bare chest. "I'll get you a souvenir."

"Would you be wearing it?" Gavin mused softly.

Chad pinched his stomach playfully. "You're naughty, Mr. Nolan."

In that moment, Rufus jumped onto the bed near Gavin and began to nestle in the corner.

"I think your cat is beginning to like having me around," he commented.

"So is the owner," Gavin returned. Looking up at the ceiling, he said seriously, "Chad."

"Yes?"

"I would like you to meet my mother," he said, and his heart raced.

Chad moved quickly, propping himself up with his elbow and looking down at Gavin. Even in the soft shadows, Chad looked both surprised and pleased.

"Really? This Sunday?" Chad kissed Gavin's chest. He then added, "Every Sunday morning like clockwork, you go visit your mom. I don't question it."

"No, let's wait until Thanksgiving," he returned.

"Perfect, baby," Chad replied as his hand cupped Gavin's jaw tenderly. "You protect your mother. You love her too much to see her hurt. I was just waiting until you were ready to share her with me."

Strangely, Gavin's eyes teared up. Chad told the truth. After Vincent had sent that man to her room, Gavin felt even more protective.

"Thanks for understanding," he replied, feeling a tear fall

from the corner of his eye.

"Detective Nolan," he stated. "You are a hard man to know."

"Why do you say that?"

"Because I'm just now meeting your family."

"I don't have many friends," Gavin admitted.

"Aren't I one?"

"That and more." Looking at him in the dim light, Gavin touched his face, outlining his jawline carefully. "I don't know what's happening here. But I'm enjoying it."

"Me too."

Chad leaned closer and kissed Gavin passionately. Gavin's aching cock began to awaken as Chad's lips slowly slid down his cheek, onto his neck, and then to his shoulder. Chad shifted his body lower and eased his way down Gavin's body. The sensation of his lover's mouth against his skin made him tremble.

Chad engulfed Gavin's manhood then, slurping and sucking it aggressively, and soon his wet mouth gingerly slipped down between the crevice of Gavin's buttocks, his tongue licking him there. After a couple of minutes, Chad inserted his thick, hardened cock into Gavin, spreading his legs wider while he yanked mercilessly on Gavin's manhood. As Chad's thrusting became rougher, so did the pulling. Gavin grasped Chad's thick arms and breathed heavily, feeling the bed shake. As Chad let out a heavy groan, signifying his climax, so too did Gavin, spurting his seed all over his own chest.

Collapsing on top of him and dripping in sweat, Chad kissed him once more. Gavin wrapped his arms tight around Chad's thick back, never wanting to let him go.

Perhaps it was then, Gavin realized he was falling in love with Chad.

PART III

RHONDA

"I had only to move my fingers a little and jab them into the soft tissues, gouge away his sight

and give him more agony than he was giving me..."

–Octavia E. Butler

"I got a question for ya

See I already know the answer

But still I wanna ask you

Would you lie?"

–Mary J. Blige

DERRICK

THIRTEEN

An explosion had ripped through the Merchant Mart.

Arriving on the scene, Gavin headed past the line of news cameras as reporters shouted out questions. A sense of panic already filled Chicago in the wake. Earlier that morning, having just come back from the gym, Gavin happened to turn on the local station for background noise. When he emerged from the shower, he glanced over on the screen. From a helicopter shot, elongated amber licks of flames spread from the building's windows as dense black smoke billowed out. The caption below the newscaster simply read: *Chicago under terrorist attack?*

Walking up to the window in his towel, the black cloud could be seen from his apartment. At the same moment, his phone vibrated. Creighton had texted: *Nolan, Williamson & Lopez. It's your guy again. Get your asses here ASAP.*

Walking onto Kinzie Street, Gavin sidestepped several EMT responders. The gathering crowds formed at the edge of the perimeters behind CPD barricades, and uniformed police were holding them back. Most of the spectators watched in awe, seeing the billowing smoke rise in the air. Gavin looked down at his phone; it was twenty minutes after eight. Derrick had texted him that he was already on the scene and had instructed one of Captain Thomas's men to escort him up.

Paradoxically, the sunlight seemed to enhance the chaos. Several ambulances were lined up, treating dozens of people for smoke inhalation and lacerations. Hearing their words, Gavin gathered that they were shocked by the sudden explosion and had run out of the building. Some were sobbing into their phones, telling their loved ones that they were okay. Patiently and efficiently, the seven EMT workers danced around them, attempting to treat as many as possible. One ambulance lit up, and the barricade broke. Inside the truck, Gavin saw a woman lying still as a medic gave her CPR.

He increased his pace toward the building. The tendrils of hoses slithered on the ground, and the water was already freezing. Ahead of him, the fire trucks were parked haphazardly on the street, sitting as close to the river front as the drivers could get them. Concurrently, half a dozen firemen and firewomen ran into the building's side entrance. Their radios squawked against their chests, a voice informing them that the fire was finally being contained. Approaching a truck, Gavin flashed his badge and asked for Captain Thomas. Within seconds, Thomas's assistant, Greg, appeared and told him to follow.

As they hurriedly entered the building, Greg briefly informed Gavin that the explosion occurred on the nineteenth floor, in the southeast part of the structure. Already, a hallway had been sectioned off from the public, and two service elevators were in use. A half dozen police officers were posted along the way, blocking any potential onlookers. About halfway down the hall, one elevator door opened, and Gavin saw a man on a stretcher. The EMTs were rushing out the door as the man groaned in pain. The bandages on his legs and left side seeped with blood.

Moments later, they stepped inside the elevator along with five more firemen. The rancid smell of soot, smoke, and dampness filled Gavin's nose, forcing him to breathe through his mouth. The radios crackled once more. If he'd heard right, the voice on the other end reported two more dead bodies on the twentieth floor. Already, Gavin's trepidation was clutching his stomach. After a quick ride up, the elevators opened to another equally chaotic hallway.

He received a text from Evelyn: *Coming up LaSalle. Should be there in 10.*

Text us when you arrive. Someone'll bring you up, he responded back.

Following the men to the left, Gavin already saw a makeshift wall in place. The cool draft of the outside blanketed him, while oncoming firemen scooted around the wall. In a small enclave, he noticed Derrick, who was on his phone. His midnight wool hat was tight on his head, and his thick dark coat made his body look immense. Gavin thanked Greg for guiding him up.

"No problem," Greg said. "We are checking the flooring and the structure to make sure they are intact for safety. Once it is all cleared, Captain Thomas will want to meet with you." Soon, he turned and slipped behind the makeshift wall, joining the other firemen and firewomen.

Approaching Derrick with a feigned smile, Gavin overheard his partner say, "Alright, Mylo. No. No. You're fine. Anything that can help us." With that, Derrick disconnected the call.

"Morning," Gavin said. "I would have brought coffee, but…"

"I'd be peeing like a motherfucka," Derrick returned, craning his neck and trying to catch a glimpse at the wall. "Mylo said his program didn't work as well as he planned. It pinged off two towers. Nothing more."

"Same message?" Gavin queried. Two firemen emerged from the wall, passed them, and walked quickly down the hallway.

"Yeah," Derrick returned, shaking his head. "One body was discovered in the space. So far, they found three more bodies on the next floor. As of right now, nine people have not been accounted for. Most of the people got out."

"It's like a war zone down there," Gavin said.

"Seems our guy picked a time right before the building was completely full," Derrick said. "The death toll would have been higher."

Gavin wondered if the killer specifically had this time in mind. Out loud he said, "He wants the attention."

Derrick's dark eyes glanced over at Gavin, and the grin on his lips slipped away.

Moments later, Greg emerged from behind the wall and waved both Gavin and Derrick over. Derrick took the lead and sauntered toward him without a word. Gavin could sense his partner being much more tense than usual.

As he followed Derrick and Greg behind the wall, evidence of the fire's wrath became quite clear. Extended scorch marks had hideously etched themselves into the walls. Even in the smoldering destruction, the frigid air enveloped him and forced him to dig his hands deeper into his pockets. As they walked, several firemen were returning from the site. Their conversations stopped immediately once they saw them approach. Only the muted sounds of the radios chirped in the narrow space. Making a quick left, they entered what would have been a reception space. Gavin's eyes widened as he absorbed the blatant destruction.

The blackened space was still smoldering despite the water dripping from the ceilings and the standing puddles. The cold temperatures caused several icicles to form along the scorched open ceiling. The rays of sunlight hit the damage at such an angle as to make the drifting smoke appear like sheer velvet fabric dissipating in the breeze. Ahead of them, several of the windows had been blown out. Some of the wall, including bricks and timber, hung haphazardly around the edges. Past the destruction, Gavin saw the other side of the river at Chicago's skyline.

"Jesus fucking Christ," Derrick muttered near him.

Gingerly, Gavin walked further into the space while Derrick ambled toward the left. The space itself was massive. Unknown materials were melted in boxes scattered all over the floor, racks sat twisted near the side walls, and pockets of smoke trailed out of file cabinets nearby. Much like the sounds of snapping bones, each step on the rubble and glass echoed in his ear. He could only imagine what this space had been used for. Any evidence of actual logos or box labels were clearly destroyed. The killer wanted this place to be wiped off the map.

"Be careful, Detective," a fireman near him said. He raked out a smoldering pile, and then nodded at the exposed windowless pockets. "Until it's cleared, I wouldn't step over there yet."

"Got it," Gavin replied.

"G!" Derrick called out loudly.

Turning around, Gavin saw that the epicenter was clearly marked where Captain Thomas, Greg, and several other firefighters stood pointing at the floor and above at the gaping hole. To the very left of that, Derrick knelt. It was difficult to see what he was examining.

Approaching him, Gavin saw an elongated crumpled body, scorched from the blaze. As he stepped closer, the drifting scent of burnt flesh hit him. Bending over, he asked, "Our body?"

"Yeah," Derrick answered solemnly. "From where Thomas is standing, it looks like it traveled nearly twenty-five feet."

"Look." Gavin bent over and pointed at the hands and feet.

"They were bound."

"Bet we'll find a similar rod as before," Derrick stated and glanced up at Gavin.

Gavin's phone vibrated. Evelyn's text stated that she was down below. Standing up, Gavin walked over to a nearby fireman and asked him to escort her up. Agreeing, the young man skirted the debris and made his way down the hallway.

"Holy shit." Derrick stood and stared up at the ceiling.

Gavin glanced up. The floor above had a large gaping hole. Even from here, the activity around the hole was evident as people peered back down at them.

"The explosive was massive," Gavin stated.

"As Thomas predicted."

In that same moment, Greg called them over near Captain Thomas. Avoiding some of the debris, Derrick said, "Soon as CSI guys come up, I'll have them comb through and bag up any pertinent evidence."

"Hoping Susan is on her way up," Gavin returned.

"Detectives," Captain Thomas spoke as they came closer. The seriousness of his expression made his gaunt face more rigid and stern.

"What do you have, Captain?" Derrick said immediately, shaking the men's hands out of habit.

As Gavin also shook their hands, the hacking sounds of axes and the scraping of metal reverberated in the open space as the cleanup continued.

"We can clearly see that the point of the explosive device is here." Thomas raised his voice over the background noise. Near his feet, he aimed a laser pointer at the deep hole in the floorboards. "While it did not rupture the floorboards, the explosion was directed up and out." He gestured with his hands like a flight attendant to illustrate the explosive wave. "And to the sides."

Looking up, Gavin spotted a couple of firemen near the hole and asked, "Why didn't the ceiling collapse?"

"Good question," he answered. "These two floors and even the one below are blocked off. Currently, we're having men checking stability. Then you'll be able to conduct your investigation."

"Very good," Derrick stated. "The blast did considerable damage. We're not falling through the floorboards, are we?"

"I believe the structure of the market and the embedded brick walls withstood the blast," he stated, taking a step toward the charred center. "As we discussed on Saturday, the compound must be similar. Here and here." Gavin watched the laser circled several long licks of white marks. "The intensity of heat created the markings of an extreme burn. Most likely over fifteen hundred degrees, if not more. The arsonist used more product in the device. As soon as my men begin the recovery process, I will have a better working knowledge of it."

"Would you assume it'd be the same style as before?" Derrick shifted slightly.

"In matters like these," he replied, "I try not to make any assumptions."

"Very well," Gavin stated before Derrick could say anything. "Let us know what you find out as soon as possible."

"Sure. One last thing though," Thomas added. "Had the arsonist not called this one in, the damage and possible death toll would have been greater."

Captain Thomas assured them he would send an early report once they salvaged the bomb fragments. Then he turned and marched off with Greg just behind him, their radios continuing to crackle. Shortly after, Evelyn wandered in with a look of disbelief at the destruction. Behind her, several CSI members began to enter the scene. Excusing himself, Derrick made a beeline for them. Before Evelyn could utter a word, Gavin briefed her on what had happened thus far.

Susan appeared around the corner with her med case in hand. A sour look was painted on her face as she gingerly stepped over the debris.

Right behind her, Fernando attempted to push a gurney through the tight hallway. A couple of firemen squeezed their cumbersome uniformed bodies through scraping their equipment against the walls. Naturally, Susan barked out orders to the lanky Hispanic man to hurry up.

Approaching her, Gavin said, "Welcome to the party, Dr. Hobbert."

"Forgot to bring my marshmallows," she replied bitterly. Her eyes scanned the location and pinpointed the body immediately. To Derrick she said, "Hey handsome, can you help out my guy with getting the cart over here?"

Rolling his eyes, Derrick muttered back, "You shouldn't hire scrawny interns," he stated, annoyed. But he marched over toward the struggling young man.

"Susan," Evelyn said softly behind Gavin.

"I didn't just get here. FYI." Susan walked toward the corpse. Gavin and Evelyn followed her. "I did brief exams of the three bodies already down on ground level. One died due to blunt force trauma, probably a blow to the head from a falling beam. One died of smoke inhalation and had signs of suffocation. And the last one simply had a heart attack. Probably trying to escape down the stairwell and the stress was too much."

"Nasty," Evelyn commented softly.

"Not especially," Susan responded. Her eyes darted around the space. "Given the destruction, I wouldn't be surprised to have a morgue full of bodies, honestly."

"I have a lot to ask," Gavin began before Susan could say anything more.

"Everybody's on the goddamn priority list." Her hostile tone bit back as she hastily walked through the debris.

"Susan," he said, grabbing her arm and stopping her. "This guy is sending a clear message now. We need as much information as you can possibly give." He paused and looked into her eyes. "Please."

Sighing and closing the top button of her coat, she glanced over at Evelyn and then back to him. "Bat those baby blues at me one more time, and I'm going to have to spank you." She then stated, "You said please. So fine."

Walking quickly over to the body, Susan knelt down and put on a pair of latex gloves. Gavin looked at Evelyn, who'd buried her face in her jacket in an effort to escape the harsh bitter wind. In that same moment, Derrick caught up with them. His eyes were darting back and forth from the body before them and the CSI members gathering evidence.

"With an initial observation," Susan said as she poked and prodded the dense blackened skin of the corpse with a scalpel, "the victim is a woman. By the narrow of her hips and pelvic structure, I would gauge her to be in her late twenties. I would guess she does not have children, otherwise the separation would be indicative. From her facial bone structure, I would say that she is possibly

Hispanic. She's no more than five foot one."

"Tiny," Evelyn commented, craning her head slightly over Susan's shoulder.

"She should have flown out the windows," Derrick surmised and looked over at Gavin.

"Anyway," Susan went on, sounding annoyed that she'd been interrupted. She dug the scalpel into the gaping hole in the victim's upper left chest area. "The object seems to be the same size as the last one. I suspect the internal organs will be damaged and seared from the metal pole. Again, her arms were tied up and her feet were bound. Look at this."

With the scalpel and tweezers, she pulled off a thread of some sort. Reaching over, she placed it in a small evidence bag. "The cord was not charred or burnt off like last time. That's weird. Maybe CSI can get some DNA you."

She handed the bag over to Derrick, who held it in front of his face. "Why is that weird?"

Shaking her head, she replied, "Given the blast and high temperatures of the fire, they should be melted off. So to speak. I ain't no chemist though."

"Can you tell if she was still alive when the bomb went off?" Gavin queried.

"Honestly," Susan looked up at him, "not at this point. I'll make a note."

"Basically, this one matches the other two," Derrick replied.

"Essentially, yes," Susan stated. "Once I get her back, I'll run dental records."

Susan moved back slightly as her assistant squatted near the corpse and rolled the body toward her. Even then, a large whiff of death and burnt flesh engulfed them. Gavin turned his head away for fresh air.

"Um, Dr. Hobbert," the assistant said sheepishly.

"What?" Susan retorted, irritated.

Gavin craned his neck and saw the corpse's back. In the center, a silvery object was attached to her flesh.

"What's that?" Evelyn queried, stepping closer.

"That's something new," Susan stated. She pulled another tweezers from her box and carefully separated the disk from the flesh. She placed it into a bag and handed it to Gavin.

Holding it up, Gavin observed the metallic glints on the round object. The edges were singed and the surface was blackened, but it was pretty much intact.

"Would that be the plastic pieces, like we found on the other bodies?" Evelyn stated.

"Looks like a CD to me," Susan said. "If I remember correctly, the object from the second victim had that same smooth surface."

"Our killer has something to show us," Derrick returned.

"BODY! BODY!" The shout came from above.

Everyone turned around and looked up into the gaping hole, where a young fireman stood.

"Fuck me," Susan muttered, shaking her head. She quickly stood up and ripped off her gloves. She barked at the assistant to bag up the victim. Then she looked at each of them with a grimace and said, "Sorry, more work calls."

At the same time, a young, fit firewoman walked up to them and said, "You Nolan?"

"Yes," he said, still holding the seared CD.

"Captain Creighton wants to meet with all of you." Her sweet voice took on an authoritative tone. "Follow me."

With that, Derrick shrugged his shoulders and walked behind the woman. Evelyn followed suit. Gavin took one quick glance at the body. In the dead center, the victim's back was not as burnt. The killer had been wanting to speak to them all this time.

But what about?

FOURTEEN

Proceeding back into the warmth of the building, Gavin could feel his cheeks thawing out. The firewoman turned left at the end of the hallway and then down a narrow corridor. On each side, the loft spaces undergoing renovations were covered by plastic tarps, with construction tools and materials and paint buckets visible through the glass windows. The firewoman stopped and pointed inside an opened door to a different office. Like himself, neither Evelyn nor Derrick spoke a word as they entered the office. A makeshift emergency headquarters with storage had been created where CSI people occupied one part, storing their equipment, and firemen occupied another area. People from both groups sipped from to-go cups of coffee, warming themselves. The chatter in the space assaulted Gavin's ears as they described their accounts of the fire.

In the far corner, in front of the floor-to-ceiling windows, Creighton stood with his back to them. Even in his dark brown overcoat, his rigid posture and stance seemed commanding as he spoke on the phone. When he saw them, he casually flagged them over with a hand.

"Yes, yes, yes." Creighton's voice was unusually calm. "I will."

Below, the street remained in a state of chaos. The fire trucks were already wrapping up their equipment, ambulances were cut down to three, and people scurried around the vehicles like scattering vermin. Still, the pending crowd tripled, and more uniformed officers tightly secured the barricades.

"Alright, Nolan," Creighton's deep voice announced. "Fill me in on what the fuck's going on."

Giving a side glance first to a disgruntled-looking Derrick, and then to Evelyn, who seemed lost in her thoughts, Gavin gave a brief summary of the situation.

"Same scenario. Shit." Creighton sighed heavily and asked Derrick, "What do you think?"

"The killer has been wanting to say something for a while," he said plainly. "He just gave himself an audience."

"What about the CD?" Creighton asked Evelyn.

"We'll send it to Mylo," Evelyn stated. "See if he can get anything off it."

"Tell him that all other work is non-priority," he said to Gavin.

"Including yours?" Gavin queried. In his peripheral vision, Derrick's eyebrows raised slightly.

Pursing his lips, Creighton's light eyes flashed a hint of anger. "Make sure he concentrates on whatever the fuck *you* need."

"What about the other bodies?" Evelyn asked.

"Found two on the twentieth, one in a stairwell, two on nineteen," he continued. He added, "And not your goddamn concern. Bringing Robinson and Franklin on it. They're light on cases."

"Captain," Derrick said, "this guy's becoming dangerous."

"I agree," Creighton replied. "Right now, the media is calling this a terrorist bombing."

At those words, a couple of firemen looked over, concerned.

"Can't have a city-wide panic either. I'll tell them it was a faulty gas pipe. Or some bullshit." Creighton's voice boomed, making the others in the room look their way.

"That's not exactly the truth," Evelyn remarked.

"Lopez, it fuckin' isn't," Creighton began.

"We can't let the killer receive the credit," Gavin interrupted.

"Correct, Nolan." A slight smirk came to Creighton's lips. "This sick fuck wants attention. And I'm not going to give it to him."

Derrick nodded in agreement.

"I listened to the nine-one-one call," he said and looked at Derrick. "Let's all try to keep that tight. A fucking shitstorm is going to happen if it gets leaked. Got it?"

Looking at both Evelyn and Derrick, Gavin replied, "Honestly, it seems like the suspect's two steps ahead of us."

Creighton said nothing for a second as his eyes looked down below at the street. Quickly, they flickered back to Gavin with a stern look. He adjusted his coat and declared, "I'm going to talk to the goddamn press. See if I can get the assholes off your backs."

"Thanks," Evelyn said timidly.

"Don't fucking thank me yet, Lopez," he retorted almost vehemently as he took a step toward them. His eyes rested back on Gavin with a slightly coy smirk. "If the suspect is two steps ahead of you, I highly goddamn suggest that you get your asses in gear to get three fucking steps ahead of *him*. Before the son of a bitch gets real fucking creative."

Abruptly, Creighton left the room, colliding into people unapologetically along the way.

******

Hours passed and the day crept into the early parts of the afternoon. The crowds around the building slowly dissipated while the news teams remained camped out in their vehicles. As promised, Creighton diverted the suspicion of a terrorist bombing to a fatal gas explosion and blamed the cause on faulty equipment. By ten o'clock, the majority of the firemen had gone back to their stations. Captain Thomas and his men lingered around for a while, traveling in packs through the destruction. For the most part, they did not bother Gavin, Derrick, or Evelyn. However, five more bodies were discovered in the debris. Including their not yet identified victim, the total count was eleven dead.

The killer had made his mark.

During this time, Evelyn took a uniformed officer with her to the security desk. The officer went through the tapes to look for any signs of the suspect while she interviewed guards and inspected possible entries. At the same time, Derrick worked with the CSI team closely, understanding what could be evidence and attempting to find a similar pole. Meanwhile, Gavin painstakingly interviewed several of the building managers about any suspicious individuals, ID badges being lost, unusual packages and whatnot. Each of them kept rendezvousing at the explosion site to do recaps. Despite the newly hung tarps on the holes, the frigid air was dipping down and freezing the debris, making work impossible for the CSI team.

Exhausted and starving, Gavin stepped into the warm hallway and called Mary.

"Oh, Detective Nolan," she said merrily. "I only covered the first twenty lines of the list. I can't say I'm making good progress."

"That's okay. It's a big list." Looking over at the temporary wall, he asked, "Can you just switch gears for a couple of hours?"

"Of course. What you got for me?"

"Dig into public records on Merchant Mart," he stated. "More specifically, businesses and owners on the eighteenth to twentieth levels?"

"Easy-peasy." Her voice was crisp and airy. "Anything else?"

"That's it for now. I'll call with any developments," he told her before hanging up. It was good timing, because just then Mylo rang.

"What's this disc in a bag?" Mylo's gargled voice sounded perturbed.

"It was on our current victim," Gavin replied.

"That's nasty," he replied.

"Can you see what's on that?"

"Hmm, not really my specialty," he retorted stubbornly. "I do know someone who can help. If you don't mind me bringing in someone not on the force."

"Whatever it takes. Who is it?"

"My sister," he stated.

Somehow Gavin could not picture what Mylo's sister would look like. In any case, he reminded Mylo to have her sign the necessary non-disclosure forms in order to assist on the case. With that, Gavin hung up.

At around two o'clock, Derrick, Evelyn, and Gavin decided to call it quits at the site and head back to the station. They had enough reports to write to keep them occupied for the rest of the afternoon. Sitting behind his desk finally, still not feeling any warmer, his mind gravitated to the actions of the killer. He kept the victims alive, called in the explosion moments before, and now, he was leaving CDs.

Somehow he had a feeling the victims were not so random after all.

FIFTEEN

The next morning, the blustering, snowy wind snapped at the back door of the station. Gavin pulled the door shut with force, keeping more snow from entering the already frigid hallway. A procession of damp slushy mats filled the empty narrow corridor as a savage blizzard was again ravaging the city, forcing many of the schools to close, causing massive cancellations at both airports, and creating icy stretches on the roads. The intensity of a storm never truly delayed Chicago though; it persevered despite the weather conditions.

Shaking off the snow from his jacket, the unusual quietness and a series of empty desks welcomed him in the bull pen. Oddly, he enjoyed the peace for the time being. Exhaustion lingered on from yesterday's events, which created a returning dull headache this morning. He needed to concentrate, so he'd brought a prescribed pill with him for reassurance. Regrettably, Gavin had a mountain of reports to read through from CSI and the fire department.

Evelyn still had not reported in and Derrick had texted that he was running behind. With the state of traffic, Gavin wasn't surprised.

However, Susan had received an identity confirmation and sent him the information just before he'd left the apartment. At least a name was attached to the body now: Rhonda Sills.

As he rounded the corner, near the inlet of vending machines, he discovered Detectives Matthews and Diaz standing around the recently acquired coffee-maker, which had been set up only steps away from the horrific vendor coffee.

"Your case's making headlines," Diaz surmised sardonically.

"Not my choice," he replied with a feigned smile.

"Yeah, we know," replied Matthews. The spidery wrinkles

around his eyes made him appear older than fifty. "Why didn't you ask us to help?"

On the alderman case, they'd helped in rounding up Masterson's prostitutes. While their leads led to no evidence, their support was extremely helpful. Shrugging his shoulders, Gavin returned, "Not my call."

Under his breath, Diaz grumbled about Creighton, calling him *Captain Asshole.*

"Come, let's talk," Mathews replied as they began walking to their desks. Their position was adjacent to Creighton's office, which was dark and closed.

Behind him, he could hear Derrick say, "What's up, boys?"

"Hey Williamson, how the hell are you?" Dias asked, clasping his small hand into Derrick's thick one. "Saw the baby the other day. Thank God she got her mother's looks."

"Fuck off," Derrick replied almost too gleefully. "What's going on here? A family meeting?"

"Not really," Mathews said, not looking up from his desk. His chubby fingers danced over some files until he finally said, "Ah, here."

Casually, Gavin took the file from Mathews and opened it. On the inside, a crime photo showed a smoldering house sandwiched between several smaller houses. "The fire about a year ago out in Hanover Park?" Gavin asked.

Dias folded his thin arms over a shallow chest, nodded his head, and leaned against his desk. "Yeah, yeah."

"Overheard that your victims are tied up and then set ablaze. Right?" Mathews pointed at the file. "Made me think of this one."

Without saying a word, Gavin flipped to the next page. A charred body was lying in the middle of what had been the kitchen. Derrick craned his neck to steal a look at the page.

"It's a burnt corpse," Derrick stated, sounding unsure.

"Maybe it's nothing, just odd," Mathews admitted. "When Dias and I arrived on the scene, the fire department had most of the blaze already extinguished. A fucking fireball. The victim was Greta Mueller, seventy-four, lived alone. A neighbor reported the fire. When we spoke with the neighbor, he said that she had no family, not many friends, kept to herself. Real private."

"When the body went to the coroner," Dias interjected, "it

appeared that Mueller had been tied up. No clear evidence of a B and E or robbery. The severity of the fire practically burnt most of the house down to the ground."

Gavin flipped through some more photos. He saw charred furniture and household items that looked like deformed shadows, scaly midnight shingles littering the ground, and a photo of the entire house, which had collapsed in on itself. He asked, "Do you believe that someone set the fire?"

"Yes," Mathews said. "We couldn't prove it though. No traces of accelerant."

"What did the fire inspector say?" Derrick queried and took the file from Gavin, flipping through the pictures.

"A gas explosion," Diaz said. "Mueller had an electric stove. Maybe the furnace pilot went out. They could not determine exactly."

Gavin looked over at Derrick, saying nothing.

"Get this," Diaz lowered his voice. "We talked to a neighbor. He swore he remembered she had a visitor at her house a couple of days before the fire. He only remembered because he heard shouting come from the house late at night. And he noticed a large truck start up and peel out of the driveway."

"Happen to know the color?" Gavin queried.

"What the report says," Matthews answered. "Black."

Gavin looked over at Derrick, who said, "Why didn't Schaumburg Police investigate this?"

"Lazy bastards. Maybe they were too busy holding each other's dicks." Mathews shrugged his shoulder. "Don't know."

"Can we have this for a while?" Gavin asked, holding the file.

"Hell, it's yours now," Mathews chided. "One less unsolved case on our desk is fine with us."

"Thanks." Derrick turned and walked toward their desks. Gavin left to let Dias and Mathews finish up their work.

Gavin approached his partner. "What do you think of that?"

Derrick lost his smile and replied, "G, seems like we are working cases that others don't want to do. Tired of cleaning up other people's bullshit."

"Guess so." He put the file on the corner of his desk. "Think we should go talk to Robinson? See if he needs help on the victims."

"Fuck no, we got our own shit to do," he proclaimed. "I just got off the phone with Sills' super at her apartment building. Got access to her apartment."

Gavin put on his jacket as he walked toward the glass doors. The windows were being pummeled with snowflakes. He pulled out his phone and texted Evelyn the address. She replied back: *Be there shortly. Traffic sucks.*

Gavin and Derrick got into the car. Whether Derrick wanted to admit it or not, a similar fire had happened a year ago. And a black truck had been spotted.

Too many coincidences could easily become a pattern.

******

Sliding into the apartment building's narrow entrance, Gavin attempted to close the door against the howling wind, but a building snow drift blocked it. Stomping his feet, he buzzed the manager button to the right. Within moments, a nearby door opened. A woman who looked to be in her late fifties and wearing an oversized Cubs sweatshirt over her small frame approached the glass door.

Suspiciously, she eyed Gavin and yelled through the glass, "You the detective I spoke to?" Her light eyes, the whites of which were webbed with red spidery lines, pierced him.

"No, I'm his partner, Detective Nolan," he yelled back, producing his badge.

"Fine," she grumbled and let him in.

The corridor was as narrow as the small entrance, smelling of disinfectant, mold, and curry. Taking a step around her, he peered into the nearby room. The cramped office was disorganized: a small desk filled with loose papers piled in several stacks, a computer monitor covered in an array of Post-it notes, a bulletin board covered with invoices, and a low pleather-covered office chair surrounded by boxes of unknown items.

"I'm giving this to you," she stated and handed him a key. "How soon can I have the apartment back?" she asked, her tone irksome.

Glad you care about your tenants. "Depends on the investigation," Gavin began.

"The residency waiting list is long." A gruff, sour expression fell over her wrinkly face. "I have someone interested in the place now."

"Should be no more than a week," Gavin lied, trying to change the subject. "Can you tell me anything about Ms. Sills?"

"A model tenant. Unlike the other goddamn tenants here," she complained, chewing the inside of her cheek. Distracted, the woman glanced down the long hallway. "She paid her rent on time. Rarely saw her. Heard she worked only night shifts."

"Any friends you know of?" he continued. "Boyfriends?"

Soon, the elevator doors opened and a young black man in scrubs and a heavy overcoat came sliding out. His expression turned to one of surprise when he saw the woman, and he quickly put on his headphones. Putting her hands on the narrow of her hips, she scolded the man for not paying his rent. The young man eyed Gavin and then muttered something about paying by the end of next week. Before the woman could chastise him more, he quickly slipped into the wintery wonderland.

"Asshole interns," she commented, shaking her head. "Work a thousand hours. Study the other half of the time. Claim to have no money, and don't pay my goddamn rent. They can still pay for their expensive shitty cappuccinos and lattes at ten bucks a pop. Christ."

"Any of them Sills's friends?" Gavin asked, becoming agitated with the woman.

"Listen," she replied sarcastically. "Do I look like I care who goes in and out of here? We've got a locked entrance."

Anybody can break into that. Looking up, he saw that security cameras were posted at the entrance and pointed up. "Mind if I get the tapes on those?"

The woman briefly laughed. "Ain't going to do you any good. The cameras broke down six months ago. Haven't had enough time to replace them."

"False security, allowing predators on your site," Gavin stated.

A foul look surfaced on her face. "Do you need anything else? I'm late for my other job as is."

"No, but I will be in touch," Gavin said.

With that, the woman grabbed an oversized parka off a nearby hook and forcibly zipped it up. Opening the door, she gave Gavin a bitter frown, threw the hood over her head, and escaped into the wintry landscape. Almost knocking into Derrick, she passed him and kept her head down as she disappeared around the corner. Gavin's partner came lumbering into the entrance.

"Fuck, I hate snow," Derrick grumbled behind him. He stomped his feet to remove the built up snow. "Who the hell was that?"

"Grumpy old bitch," Gavin muttered.

"Whoa, guess she's not getting a Christmas card from you?" As he pulled off his gloves, Derrick was already scanning the hallway with a look of disgust. "Thank God there's an elevator in this dump. Didn't want to walk up flights of stairs."

Sills lived on the eleventh floor of the residence complex. They shoved themselves in the tight space of the elevator for the ride up.

*****

The dim light cast huge shadows over the sparsely decorated interior of the small studio apartment. As Gavin stepped forward, a small, scrawny calico cat emerged from under the chair. Immediately, it meowed repeatedly, rubbed Gavin's calves, and stared up at him. He scooped up the cat, which did not resist and erupted in rumbling purrs.

"You've made a friend," Derrick cooed behind Gavin, smiling.

"Poor thing," he said softly, scratching her under the chin. "Looks like she hasn't been looked after for a while."

Flicking on the nearby light, Gavin walked into Sills's efficiency apartment, which was probably less than four hundred square feet. On the immediate right wall, a clunky oversized flower-printed futon took up the majority of the tight space. Above it hung a large painting of a sunny beach. A small table was parked by the only window, with a single industrialized light suspended over it. The twin dining chairs with matching floral coverings appeared to have come from a flea market due to their worn condition. On the opposite wall, there was a makeshift kitchen area with a two-door cabinet, a half-sized fridge, and an electric stove. In the corner, a large yellow wardrobe was nestled near the window at an angle. Unlike the grimy apartment building, Sills' space was refreshing, bright, and melodious.

Derrick took a side step toward the only other door in the tight space. "Well, this is definitely for a single person," he commented.

"There, there, shhh," Gavin cooed softly to the cat, who eagerly head-butted his hand. "Let's see if I can get you anything to eat."

"Hey," Derrick said from behind him.

Pivoting on his heels, Gavin glanced back. Derrick pointed at several metal sliding locks and deadbolts that had been installed on the door. As he twisted each knob into place, several soft clicks sounded in the quiet air.

"Think you can buy that at Home Depot?" Gavin remarked, placing the cat down on the floor.

"Probably the deadbolts, but not sure about these full bar locks." Derrick unlatched each of them. "Seen these types of locks on panic rooms and high security areas. Some serious shit here."

"Probably why you didn't escape, huh?" Gavin said to the calico cat as the animal pawed at his legs.

"Not a place where many friends visited?" Derrick added.

"Probably not for a while." Gavin opened the cabinets quickly and searched for some cat food.

"The bathroom looks absolutely untouched," Derrick said as he poked his head out the door. "Clean, and very orderly."

"Someone must have seen her before she was taken." Gavin pushed some pasta packages aside and found a single can of cat food. He looked down again and smiled. "You're not starving today."

"Two seats at the dining table, by the window," Derrick stated. "She liked her solitude."

Gavin scooped some food into a small bowl and set it down. The cat ran straight to the bowl and hungrily ate.

"Look at this," Derrick said. On a small bookshelf near the futon, a line of classic books on philosophy were neatly placed in order. "Nietzsche, Kant, Plato. Deep reader?"

Saying nothing, Gavin ambled over to the bathroom. The tiny space was clean, with the feminine touches of a floral shower curtain and pink towels. He opened the medicine cabinet. Between the bottom shelf for contacts and the top shelf of toothpaste and creams, a small drug store filled the middle shelf: Ritalin, risperidone, aripiprazole, olanzapine, quetiapine, and ziprasidone were just a few among the others. He grabbed one and stepped out of the tiny room.

"She had some issues." Gavin held up the prescription for Derrick to see. "I remember when Emily prescribed similar meds to her patients. In low doses. Each of these are pretty heavy. Riley Simmons. Her doctor, I imagine."

"Guess we'll have to go talk with the doctor," Derrick replied. He had squatted down to look at the bed. "This is interesting."

"What?"

Derrick lifted the cover. "Look at how the bedsheets are tucked in. Square neat. Tight." He pulled at them.

"Okay, I'll bite."

"Military standard," he answered. Standing straight, Derrick reached for a small key near the door. "Hmm, I guess I'm going to check her mail, huh?"

He headed out of the apartment.

Casually, Gavin moved the window curtain and watched the large snowflakes hit the thin elongated window with a soft thump. The hazy, nearly white-out view overlooked the hospital campus and the southern tip of downtown. Gavin imagined Sills brewing a cup of coffee, reading one of her theoretical books, and glancing up on occasion. Perhaps even the cat joined her on the table or her lap to keep her cozy.

Sills lived in solitude. No one shared her space.

Gavin did a quick search of Sills's apartment for a phone, laptop, or any device. He figured that she did not take it along with her and stored it there. Within five minutes, in the second dresser drawer amongst her minimal clothing, he found a laptop. Sitting at the table, the cat jumped effortlessly on the bed and stared at him. Once it came to life, he discovered that Sills did not have any passcodes on it. He realized she was not worried about any cyber-protection as he opened several files on her desktop.

The door opened and Evelyn walked in casually. She spotted the cat and slowly walked toward it. "You're adorable," she said softly. "What a charming place."

"Hello, stranger," Gavin greeted, not looking up from the files containing Sills's past schoolwork. "You like the place? The neighborhood's for shit, parking sucks ass, and the landlord's a bitch. Can't have everything, I suppose."

"Look who I found?" Derrick's thunderous voice startled the cat as he stepped in.

"What you got?" Evelyn ignored Derrick and walked over to Gavin, craning her head at the laptop.

"Nothing major," Gavin returned, standing up. "Easy to get in, no passcodes. Guess Sills had nothing to hide."

"Did you get into emails?" She took off her thick navy-blue hat, shaking her hair slightly from the snow.

"No, but you can." Gavin allowed Evelyn to take over. While he enjoyed digging into someone's world, she needed the practice in finding evidence. To Derrick, he asked, "Anything interesting in her mail?"

"Looks like she paid her bills on time," Derrick reported as he handed the mail over to Gavin, who then leafed quickly through it. "Very little debt. Couple of travel magazines."

"Not surprised," Evelyn said as she kept her eyes on the computer screen. "The décor reflects her need to be far away."

"What kept her here?" Derrick said softly. "From the amount, it's about two weeks of mail."

"Maybe the suspect took her sooner," Gavin stated. "Wait." He pulled out his phone and dialed Susan.

On the fourth ring, she answered, "Oh lover boy, I was just about to call you."

"Perfect. I'm going to put you on speaker." He clicked the button. "Susan?"

"Yep." She sounded annoyed. "Are all of you together?"

"Hey, Doctor," Evelyn chimed in.

"Suze," Derrick said simply as he continued looking through the mail.

"Hate it when you call me that," Susan chided. She cleared her throat loudly, causing a brief static on the line.

"What do you have for us?" Gavin leaned against the wardrobe.

"On the initial autopsy," she explained, "what I told you at the site. The wound is consistent with the other victims, the hands and rope were tied with the same type of rope, and the majority of her epidermal skin was destroyed from the intense heat."

"What about her inner organs?" Derrick asked.

"Well, that's interesting." There was a shuffle of paperwork.

"Can you clarify?" Gavin queried.

Stopping, Evelyn looked over, brushing strands of hair out of her eyes.

"From her pelvis, through her major organs, and into her lung, the spherical object created damage to the tissue." Her voice was stern and loud. "As with Carlton, her body was nearly well done throughout. But Sills' body did not react the same. In my best assessment, and from various tissue samples, especially on the back where the CD was discovered, I can positively say Sills' body was frozen at some point."

"Frozen?" Evelyn asked with a look of disgust.

"Are you sure about this?" Gavin stood up straight.

"About ninety percent," she returned.

"One more thing, Susan," Derrick said loudly. "Can you give us an actual time of death?"

"I can give you an approximate time," she replied. "With frozen corpses, time of death is not actually precise."

"Thanks, Susan," Gavin said.

"Next time, sexy," she said, "you're going to be in my foursome." She hung up the phone.

With that, Gavin knew the killer was planning the order of kills. If that was the case, he already had eyes on the next victim.

But who?

Beyond the door, the sound of two distinct voices came toward them. Gavin heard the murmuring of a woman and a man with snippets of laughter in between. Soon, a door slammed shut, and there was nothing.

"Christ," Derrick said, folding his arms across his chest. "He knew her."

"Huh?" Evelyn asked, her face puzzled.

"Our guy knew Sills," Gavin reiterated to her. "I think you're right, D. If Sills was frozen, he must have taken her at least three weeks ago. Susan will prove that."

"Before Janice Carlton?" Evelyn did not seem convinced.

"Yes," Derrick stated.

"Somehow each of the women, including Sills, knew our guy," Gavin stated boldly.

"If that's the case," she said, "how?"

"When we figure out that question," Derrick answered, "then we'll know why he was after them."

"What did you find out in her emails?" Gavin nodded at the laptop.

Derrick left the mail on the bed and began to search the wardrobe next to Gavin.

"Think I found two people," Evelyn said. "A Molly Barker. Seems like a friend. Here's her last email five days ago: 'Rhonda, honey, please, please call me. I'm worried sick. You're not picking up your phone. Last time you did this, it was a week. It's been over fifteen days now. I'm worried. Please, please call me. M.'"

"Who's the other?" Derrick inquired as he shifted her clothes around.

"The other comes from an Ann Ziegler. Her boss. The last one dated exactly one week ago." Evelyn paused. "It says: 'Rhonda, I can no longer keep you on staff. After many discussions about your frequent and habitual absence from work and not returning my phone calls, I am forced to terminate your employment. Please understand I need to rely on people in order to operate patient care consistently. Since you have been on board, your tardiness and absenteeism have put the team in a jeopardizing situation more than once. I do hope you find the necessary treatment. Regards.'"

"Missing for a week. Absent from work," Gavin surmised. "Seems like Sills had a serious problem. Explains the slew of meds."

"Think I know why she never picked up." Derrick pulled out a phone from a jacket hanging in the wardrobe, looked down at it, and said, "It was completely dead."

"Sills was taken from here." Gavin stood straighter. *Perhaps like the others.*

"Calling CSI now. They'll have to process the place," Derrick stated authoritatively and scooted into the hallway.

Evelyn was about to stand up.

"Hey," Gavin stated. "Can you forward those emails from the friend? Then email her from your account. Ask her if she can talk to us. Leave our numbers. Don't give her any details yet."

"Fine," she said. Then she added, "Her employer leaves her number as part of her signature for emails. Would you like me to call her directly?"

"Yes, could you?"

"Perfect."

Gavin took a couple of steps toward the bathroom. He grabbed one of the prescription bottles.

The killer had been here. Gavin glanced around the apartment. Why had Sills let him in? Given the bolts on the door, had she been coerced into opening it?

Gavin scooped up the cat and locked her in the bathroom for the time being.

He had to protect the only thing Sills ever loved.

SIXTEEN

About a half hour later, Gavin stepped outside the apartment. When the two CSI members came in the lack of space felt claustrophobic. Their conversation and footsteps sounded loudly through the cracked door. The way the sound carried through the still hallway made it apparent that the other tenants would have noticed any struggle in Rhonda's apartment.

Reaching the end of the dimly lit hallway, he looked out at the snowy street below. The sluggish traffic barely crawled forward. He watched the commuters struggle for a few more moments before he called Riley Simmons, Rhonda's doctor. Gavin left a message, hoping the doctor would call back in a timely manner. Staring at the prescription bottle in his cupped hand, he texted Susan: *Did you check Sills' blood for any drugs?*

Even during the day, the corridor was dim. The suspect would have had to drug Sills in order to move her. Instinctively, Gavin knew the suspect would not change his method of attack.

Just as he was about to turn from the window, the precinct's general number rang.

"Detective Nolan," he said.

"Oh, hey there." Mary's whimsical charm wafted over the phone.

Half smiling, he said, "What can I do you for, Mary?"

"Thank God I put my snow tires on in time. I just buzzed on through the streets like nothing." She slurped her drink on the other end. "If you don't have a set, you should really thinking about buying some."

"I'll take it under advisement," Gavin commented.

"I've got something for you." A series of clicks could be heard. "The place where that awful fire happened yesterday was actually one huge space. It was owned, or rather leased, through one company.

Oh, ya wanna guess?"

"Sanford and Pierce Realty?" Gavin felt his heart race.

"Exactly," she said proudly.

A lead. "Do you know who the owners were or the business name?"

"Not yet," she said. "There was no pertinent information available."

"What about the other list?" Gavin shifted slightly to see Evelyn outside in the hallway, talking on the phone.

Sighing heavily, she replied, "I'm about a fifth done. Nothing is out of the ordinary."

"Don't give up, keep going," he returned.

"Oh, no, much better than filing stupid traffic tickets," she said. "Have a great day."

After hanging up with her, Gavin called Sanford and Pierce Realty and requested to speak with Sanford. Moments later, the receptionist replied that he was in an all-day meeting. Hanging up, he thought that if the Merchant Mart and the warehouse were leased by them—

He called Mary back immediately.

"Oh, hey," she said. "Something wrong?"

"No, not at all," he said. "Find out about the ownership on the Opus Theater. My gut says that S and P Realty is involved."

"I was wondering if you were going to ask," she said proudly. "I'll get on it."

While Derrick supervised the CSI team, Gavin and Evelyn knocked on other apartment doors for the next hour. The majority of people did not answer the door. A handful who did answer had no clue who Rhonda Sills was or looked like. Exhausted, they regrouped in the apartment after the CSI team finished. Evelyn decided to take Sills' cat because she couldn't live with the thought of handing it over to a shelter. Tenderly, she scooped it into her thick scarf and held it in her arms like a child. As she walked away, she was telling the cat that she would be going to a good home. Once Evelyn left, Derrick turned to Gavin and asked to leave.

Shrugging as he put his coat back on, Gavin just replied, "I'm not your boss, D. Go."

"I promised Maria a date night tonight," he replied, pulling his wool hat tight against his head. With a coy smile, he said. "Sun, rain, or even goddamn snow, it's going to happen."

"Well, hope you have a good night then." Gavin slipped on his gloves. Then he added, "If you're gonna love, wear the glove. Unless you want number three, Dad."

Derrick snorted out a quick laugh and gave him the finger. Stepping into the wintery mix, his partner rounded the corner and disappeared. Gavin headed back home.

At least Gavin could have a beer while writing up the report and process the day.

******

Around seven that night, he finished up the report at his kitchen counter and closed his laptop. After sliding off his stool, he ambled toward the window. Already the storm was moving over Lake Michigan, and the heavy snow tapering off. Still, a few flurries danced madly in the light of the streetlamps, which were decorated in holiday décor and swaying violently to and fro.

This would be his first Christmas in his apartment. Perhaps he would decorate it too. And get a small live tree. He always enjoyed live trees. They reminded him of long-ago times with his father, mother, and young brother. The coming holiday actually felt positive. The stress of the divorce and Emily had weighed too heavily on him before, making it difficult to truly celebrate. This year, he would be able to spend it with his lover.

A smile crept onto his face.

Chad didn't call yet. They were supposed to have dinner tonight. Turning around, he reached for his phone. It rang at the same time.

"Hello," he began joyfully, half expecting to hear Chad's voice.

"Is this Detective Nolan?" a woman asked in a raspy voice.

"Yes, may I ask who this is?"

"Dr. Riley Simmons," she answered immediately. "I am Rhonda Sills' psychiatrist. You wanted to speak to me about her."

"Yes, I was wondering if you could provide me with some information on Rhonda," he explained.

"Detective," she returned sardonically, "it is a doctor-patient confidentiality. So what I have to say—"

"Dr. Simmons," he interrupted, "Rhonda Sills passed away two days ago. I left that note specifically with your answering service."

"Passed away?" The doctor's voice turned shaky.

Gavin heard a choke of a sob in the background.

"Doctor?"

"Um, yes," she said lowly. "Are you sure it's Rhonda Sills?"

"Yes, I'm positive." Gavin leaned against his granite countertop. Hearing other people grieve over the death of loved ones never was easy.

"Did she, um, take her own life?" the doctor asked.

"No, she didn't commit suicide," he said. "Why do you ask that?"

"Rhonda had frequent suicidal tendencies." She paused, seemingly catching her breath.

"No," he stated. "Unfortunately, we discovered her body."

"Where? How?" The doctor sounded alarmed.

"I would like not to discuss that over the phone," he said. "Could I meet you tomorrow?"

"Oh, Rhonda, Rhonda," she replied mournfully. He heard a slight sniffle on her end. "Sorry, I'm at a funeral of a close family member in L.A. I'll be back in Chicago late Friday evening. I can meet you at my office on Saturday morning. Say around twelve? My last session ends at eleven forty-five."

"Yes, that would be fine," Gavin said quietly.

Dr. Simmons gave him her office address, which was near Oak Park. With a sob, the doctor hung up.

The woman had seemed overly shaken by Sills' death, or was it the funeral she was attending? Did she care about all of her patients that much? Or just Rhonda?

The door buzzer rang. Gavin went over to the security camera and saw Chad on the screen. A smile returned to his face. Moments later, Chad was at his door, holding a pizza and a six-pack of imported beer.

"Thought we were going out?" Gavin asked, giving him a kiss and smelling the fresh chilly air all over his skin.

Shaking off his snowy jacket and dropping his gym bag near the door, he replied, "Not in this weather."

"Did you have a good day?" Gavin asked, taking the pizza box and beer.

"My exciting world of data processing would bore you," Chad said sarcastically.

"Probably better than mine." Casually, he turned and walked over to the counter.

"That bad, huh?"

"Want to watch a movie or something?" Gavin ignored him. The incredible aroma of the food made his stomach growl.

"Or something," Chad said softly.

"I mean, I can look at On Demand..." Gavin began.

From behind, Chad wrapped his thick arms around Gavin's waist, placing his warm lips on Gavin's neck. A soft whisper came to his ear, "Well, I'm cold. I need some heat."

Kissing the back of his neck, Chad's thick hands were already under Gavin's shirt, rubbing his body. Gavin leaned forward slightly on the cool granite and felt his lover touch him tenderly as his excitement began to grow. In one smooth motion, Chad undid Gavin's belt and opened his pants, sliding them down to the floor. Soon, his lover stripped him of his shirt and trailed his wet kisses down the curvature of his back. With some gentle force, Chad parted his legs, and his thick hands spread open his cheeks. Within moments, Chad's warm, wet tongue explored his crevice hungrily and savagely, occasionally sucking on Gavin's dangling balls. Gavin leaned forward on the countertop, pressing his stiff manhood on the hard surface. He glanced over at the window, watching himself being conquered by his lover. Quickly, Chad removed his shirt and then buried his face in Gavin's buttocks. Closing his eyes, the electric tremors of excitement flooded Gavin moments later as Chad slid his thick beast inside of him.

Eventually, they would get to the pizza.

SEVENTEEN

"Thought I would never have to come here again," Derrick remarked as his eyes drifted over the modern sterile façade of Chicago Hospital. Earlier that morning, Evelyn indicated through a text that she had set up a meeting with Sills' former employer.

"Why's that?" Gavin eased the unmarked car into a line of cars waiting for the packed parking lot.

"My dad," he replied cryptically.

Since they'd left the station, Derrick had been acting unusually subdued. Assuming he didn't get enough sleep, Gavin kept glancing over at him. His partner was not himself, lost in his own world.

"Why?" Gavin asked softly.

Slowly turning his head toward him, Derrick answered simply, "He died here."

"I didn't know." Gavin pulled forward and reached for a ticket. The cold wind cascaded inside the car.

"I don't talk about it much," he stated, staring ahead. "Maria gets upset at me because I don't talk about him or my family much."

"May I ask what your father died from?" Gavin steered the car toward the ascending ramp.

"Lung cancer," he said. "He wasn't a smoker. He used to work in a steel mill and had long shifts. I don't really remember too much of him. He left early in the morning, came home late. He was always so tired. It turned out the factory he worked at had a major asbestos issue. Momma said Daddy used to say it snowed in the middle of the day when the heat was just right."

"How old were you when he died?" Gavin inquired, slowing the car down.

"Close to ten," he said. "After he died, Momma worked a lot more. Never really saw her then either. We had to move after he died. Couldn't afford the apartment anymore and went into a real small place. On 107th. Not a good place then, and not a good place now. I had to share a room with my brother, and Momma and my sister shared one together."

"How old were your brother and sister?"

"Albert, named after Momma's father, was seventeen," he responded distantly. "And my sister, Esther, was fourteen. Albert didn't help much and was never around. Got into trouble most of the time. I thought it was great because I had my own room. Esther had some bad habits herself. She thought she was better than us. Saying that she didn't belong at home. Saying she wanted to be on her own. She and Momma got into it a lot. Think Esther always hated me because she always had to watch me. I kept my nose to the ground. I didn't know anybody in that part of town. I did have a cousin, but he was sixteen. I walked to school by myself, past the drunks, past the hookers and past the dealers. I just got used to it, I guess.

"When I turned twelve," Derrick continued. "Albert died. He overdosed on heroin. I was too young to see the signs. I guess I was oblivious to it. Of course, Momma was devastated, and I was the only one to console her. Esther pretended she didn't care. We buried him next to Dad. To this day, I think Momma was the toughest woman alive, losing a husband and a child. And she persevered."

"What about Esther?" Gavin inquired casually. He found a parking spot on the sixth level and eased the car between a German import and a small compact car.

"Hmm, Esther got worse," he stated disdainfully. "Had a lot of boyfriends. Some with gang tats. Some just drunk or high on whatever. And some were just motherfuckers. She'd bring them around when Momma was at work. When they came over, I would put on my headphones, listen to music, and do my homework. I didn't want to hear them fucking. Nasty shit. One time, when Momma was at work, one of Esther's boyfriends got into some street problem with another gang. I was outside 'cause it was a July day, and I was talking with friends. They were on the stoop. Some car came rolling past and opened fire. I hit the cement straight away. Esther did too. I couldn't hear the screaming because of the gunfire. But my friend was hit in the stomach, almost died, and her boyfriend had six new holes in his chest. The first time I saw real death."

"Jesus, D. That's hardcore." Gavin could not imagine seeing that at such an early age. "Did your mother find out about that?" Gavin stirred in his seat, popping the car into park.

"Oh yeah," Derrick said, nodding his head. "Boy, she was pissed. She whooped Esther's ass into the next block when she got home. Think half the building and the entire neighborhood heard them yelling that night. Even my headphones couldn't block that out. The landlord kicked us out three days later."

"Shit," Gavin retorted softly.

"Yep, hood life." A brief, gloomy frown appeared on Derrick's lips and then disappeared. He seemed like he didn't want to move.

Looking down at his phone, Gavin read the text from Evelyn: *Where are you? I'm waiting up on eight.*

Just got here. Be up there soon, he responded back.

"Funny thing," Derrick said as he opened the door, "my sister was pregnant by the dead guy. Momma threw another shit fit. She even told her to get an abortion. But Esther was stubborn and thought it was meant to be."

"She kept the child?" Gavin was already out of the car.

"Of course," he said bitterly. "Alfonso Albert. My first nephew. After I left the house at eighteen, she continued to get pregnant. She was proud to be working the government system, as she said."

"What did your mother say about it?" Gavin flanked Derrick's right side as they approached the elevators.

"Momma didn't want nothing to do with her kids," Derrick said. He pressed the button. "She loved them. But she was not going to be Esther's daycare service. Momma kicked her out of the house when number three came. Said she put food on the table for me, not for her welfare kids."

"Take it there's a few daddies?" Gavin hugged himself to block the cold air.

"My sister serviced more men than a reverend at a Sunday church mass," he replied.

"Being a little blunt, D?"

"No, just hate the bitch." Derrick turned to Gavin and added sourly, "One of the many reasons why I stopped speaking to her."

I wonder what the others were. Slowly, the elevator doors slid shut.

*****

They found Evelyn waiting in the very center of the hallway. The floor was dedicated to conference rooms and the administration wing of the hospital. Yet the antiseptic scent drifted in the air like a sterile perfume. Evelyn looked impatient as she tapped at her phone. Her slick dark navy-blue pants suit complemented her thin frame while she moved out of the way for a group of nurses passing by her.

"Ann Ziegler is a real *puta*," she commented lowly. Automatically, she headed toward the nearest closed door. "They're in here."

"They?" Gavin questioned as he followed Evelyn's quick stride. Derrick's soft clicks were right behind him.

Entering the small conference room, they were met by two women sitting in front of the small thin windows that exposed the bright sunny city behind them. At the end of the narrow pine table, a short, thin man preoccupied himself with some paperwork to his right and a laptop in front of him. He gave them a brief glance before looking back down. Immediately, the two women stood up. The first one, a shorter and huskier version of Evelyn, approached him and extended a hand. "I'm Ann Ziegler."

Gavin introduced himself and Derrick behind him. Ann's small cold hand was firm and confident. The other woman, who had a thicker frame and a pretentious smile plastered on her face, introduced herself as Rose Tessler, the HR director. Ann introduced the gentleman as Dr. Dennis Freman, Assistant Chief of Staff, who said nothing.

Interrupting your day, are we, Doctor?

"Thank you for meeting with us," Evelyn said. Already, a pad of paper and pen lay before her.

"Detective Lopez," Ziegler replied sternly, "you stated that we had to meet in a timely manner."

"I apologize for the immediacy of the matter," Gavin interjected. "Currently, we are working on a sensitive case that involves Ms. Rhonda Sills."

"Her body was found in a Merchant Mart fire a couple of days ago," Derrick added. He placed his thick forearms on the table and folded his fingers together.

"That big fire on the news?" Tessler spoke up, appearing to be shocked.

"The very one."

Glancing over at Derrick, Gavin noticed his partner's intense stare boring into the two women. He could sense how much Derrick disliked them. At that point, Dr. Freman stopped typing, took off his wire-rim glasses, and sat straighter in his chair. While Tessler's face hinted at some remorse, Ziegler remained unfazed.

We have their full attention. Thanks, D.

"We are looking for any occurrences or issues she may have had leading to her last days working here," Gavin stated.

"I'm not sure what I can tell you about her," Ziegler answered automatically.

"Can you describe her behavior in the last few weeks?" Derrick rebutted aggressively.

Looking down, Tessler slid a file over to Ziegler.

"When I hired her, she began with a lot of potential." Ziegler tapped the file in front her. "Sills exhibited thorough patient care and follow-up treatment. Because of her extraordinary bedside manner, she scored well above others in service and care for the patients on a weekly basis."

"How long was she employed here?" Lopez inquired casually.

"Five years and four months," Tessler said firmly.

"Then why did you terminate her?"

Tessler gave a glance over at Ziegler, but it was Ziegler who answered. "Three consecutive days of no-shows without a call-in."

"Was this typical behavior for your star nurse?" Derrick chided.

"Rhonda had an issue," Ziegler admitted.

"For the last several months," Tessler explained with a slow monotone voice, like she was speaking to a group of school children, "Ms. Sills had been coached and counseled several times. They centered on tardy issues and absenteeism."

"She would just show up when she wanted to?" Evelyn questioned.

"No, I write the schedules and the nurses know their hours. It's how it always worked," Ziegler said. "The last year, Rhonda struggled keeping her schedule straight."

"How so?" Gavin asked.

"When she was hired, she had such a nice personality toward the patients," Ziegler admitted. "For three and a half years in a row, she received the Best Patient Care award. She had the highest ratings." She paused. "But then after the last year or so, she progressively slipped."

"How would she react when you confronted her about the issue?"

Evelyn asked, sitting straighter in her chair.

"Rhonda was dismissive," Ziegler replied. "She promised that she would change. She said that she was just going through some things, etcetera. For a week or two it would be fine. Then she would start up again. One nurse even caught her giving the wrong dosage of meds to a patient."

"Did you write her up then?" Gavin queried, looking over at Dr. Freman for any reactions.

"No," Ziegler stated. "I did pull her into Rose's office and suggest she take some days off. Rest. Then come back. Start fresh."

"Did she?"

"Yes," Tessler answered. "When I observed her on the floor, she appeared back to normal."

"What happened next?" Evelyn interjected.

"About June, she began to come in late, or leave halfway through her shift," Ziegler stated, sounding rehearsed. "I approached her once again in Rose's office. She gave some apologies, but her work only deteriorated after that. She would not complete her paperwork. She stopped helping others in final checkups."

"Did she ever indicate any personal issues?" Gavin asked Ziegler.

A forced grin pierced Ziegler's thick lips. "All of my staff are unique individuals. I take extra pride in nurturing and respecting the privacy of my staff's lives. The nurse must be professional at all times."

"So the answer is no?" Derrick stated rather than questioned.

"That being said," Ziegler ignored Derrick's comment, "as I indicated, Rhonda was a great person when I initially hired her. Rarely, she would speak about her private life. She came on the floor and performed her duties superbly. Then, this last year, she seemed to all but fall apart. Privately, I pulled her into my office and asked her about any family issues. She remained closed off."

"What about other staff? Did she have any friends?" Evelyn asked.

"Unlike my other staffers, she was a loner." Ziegler's stone face began to hint toward compassion. "She came to the holiday parties and picnics, but she kept her distance."

She's not giving anything. Gavin shifted in his seat, then said: "We noticed that she had a lot of heavy medications in her cabinet. As a health care professional, would you have been concerned that a staff member was taking drugs and helping patients?"

Both Tessler and Ziegler gave each other a quick glance toward Dr. Freman, who still seemed to appear disinterested.

Tessler cleared her throat and stated, "Her prescription dosages are… were, acceptable levels to perform her duties on a daily basis."

"In essence," Derrick returned, "Sills was great when she had her drugs, but off of them she was a train wreck. Is this why her erratic behavior began?"

"Detective Williamson," Tessler answered and stiffened her back. "Many of our staff members take various levels of medications for many different medical reasons. The staff are constantly screened for illegal and even legal substance abuse."

"Sounds like you had an issue with this," Evelyn spoke up. She pulled a copy of the email from her pad of paper. "According to your email, Sills' behavior finally went too far. What does this mean?"

A moment of awkward silence fell over the room.

Clearing his voice, Dr. Freman spoke. "The nurse in question had a reputation for having irreconcilable differences with various members of the staff. Rhonda had accused male staff members of making sexual advances toward her. She even claimed that several of her co-workers were stealing prescription drugs and selling them, ah… outside. Frankly, her claims had irrevocable effects on departmental procedures and policies over the last several months."

"Did you ever follow up on these accusations, Doctor?" Derrick asked.

"Of course we did," Tessler replied stoically. "We did internal investigations on the matter. No proof had been discovered."

"That doesn't say much," Derrick commented.

"We assure the well-being of our patients, *and* our staff," Ziegler responded quickly. "We take every matter seriously."

"Not seriously enough," Gavin replied. "Somehow Sills was murdered. It looks convenient for you as well."

Dr. Freman stood up and said, "Detective, I believe our friendly discourse is now at a close. Should you want to speak with Mrs. Ziegler or myself again, our team of attorneys will be present." Then he turned and walked out of the room. In unison, Tessler and Ziegler stood up and said their goodbyes.

Once they left, Derrick turned to Gavin. "You know how to fucking piss off the right people."

"Raw talent," Gavin quipped, giving him a wink.

According to her boss, Sills had a knack for spreading rumors and innuendoes. However, she was a good nurse and well liked amongst her patients. No matter, much like Gable and Carlton, she had changed in the last year. They had all changed in those last months.

Maybe the suspect was making his presence known to them.

*****

A steady flow of people entering and exiting through the obscenely pretentious lobby area made it necessary for Gavin, Derrick, and Evelyn to locate themselves off to the side near the pristine waiting area. The beams of sunlight gleamed through the tinted two-story floor-to-ceiling windows and created obtuse prisms on the sterile white marble floor. The sounds of bell pings, rushed footsteps, and muted conversations rang in Gavin's ears. Next to him, Evelyn casually sidestepped an oncoming family and gave a genuine smile to the young girl holding her mother's hand as the mother was being escorted in a wheelchair. As they passed, the mother's frightened expression did not quell the child's concern as they moved toward the inner corridors of the hospital.

"Where do you want to go from here?" Evelyn asked, somewhat impatiently.

"We need to follow up on Ziegler's claim about Sills' behavior," Gavin replied. He turned toward Derrick and asked, "Would you mind if you two stay here and question some of the staff?"

"Not at all," Derrick replied. "Besides, I don't like how Ziegler or Tessler handled Sills."

"I agree," Evelyn returned. "They were throwing her under the bus."

"Good," Gavin said. "Glad you picked up on that."

"Doubt if we'll get to speak with Dr. Douchebag," Derrick commented, grimacing.

"Try to stay clear of him," Gavin instructed cautiously. He then looked at Evelyn. "We are running an investigation. If they give you any slack, or any just cause for not speaking with any staff member, tell them that we can hold them for—"

"Interfering with a case, or even hiding potential evidence," she answered.

Gavin smiled slightly. "Guess I don't have to tell you much."

"Not exactly," she conceded. Looking over her shoulder, she said, "Since we are going to be here for a while, I'm going to grab some coffee and a muffin. I'm starving. Want anything, Derrick?"

"No, ma'am," he said, unbuttoning his jacket.

"Fine," Evelyn said and walked away.

"She's getting better," Derrick returned.

"Little steps, D," Gavin answered. "With the fire on Tuesday, I forgot to ask you, when you went back to the house on Ashland, did any of the neighbors report anything?"

"Shit, forgot," Derrick uttered. "Yeah and no. Lots of elderly people who keep to themselves. Some of them barely opened their doors for us, scared maybe. But one elderly man who lives in the apartments across the street says he saw people in the house. Couldn't say when though. Another woman claimed to see lights on several times. She also said gangs used it for their drugs, and we got a scolding to do better police work."

"Nothing concrete." Gavin's tone expressed his disappointment.

"Why?" Derrick returned as his eyes scanned the area.

"Nothing really," he said, shrugging his shoulders.

"What were you gentlemen talking about?" Evelyn was already back, sipping on a coffee. In her free hand was a clear plastic container holding a cranberry muffin.

"Gentlemen?" Derrick put a hand to his chest. "Hear that, G?"

"Yeah, on that note," Gavin pulled up his coat collar, "I'm heading back to the station. You two play nice. Call me if something comes up."

"Yes, Uncle Gavin," Evelyn mused with a syrupy smile.

Derrick snorted out a quick laugh.

Pivoting on his heel, he headed out of the lobby and caught a sitting cab just at the end of the main entrance. As he pulled away from the hospital, his thoughts went back to Derrick's story. The immense scale of the hospital would frighten any young kid, especially if he had a sick parent. Gavin shook his head slightly. He could not even imagine the pain Derrick had endured as a child.

A pain that never really goes away.

.

EIGHTEEN

Stretching, Gavin stood up and decided to walk away from the numerous emails, recaps, and reports on the fire. They all indicated the same outcome: no clear evidence to connect the suspect with any of the locations. CSI was unable to obtain even a half-fingerprint from the wires of the bomb used at the theater. Susan's final autopsy report supplied no further evidence to catch the suspect. So far, Mylo had not yet returned his calls about the discovered CD.

He walked toward the whiteboard to find Rhonda Sills' DMV picture staring back at him. Her light skin, slightly flattened nose, and widened eyes indicated Mayan descent, and her other fine features appeared subtly beautiful. Her beauty equated that of Carlton and Gable. Still, the lack of luster in her exquisite dark eyes showed undefined sadness. Looking at the picture next to her, Gavin thought that her crumpled burnt body against the blackened debris truly made her alone.

Even in death.

Glancing over at Creighton's dark office, he folded his arms across his chest and took in a deep breath. Four bodies. Fifteen casualties in the wake of the explosions. Four women—one still unknown—with different backgrounds, and all murdered in the same manner. Convinced now, Gavin realized these women were no longer random victims.

What the hell is the connection?

Gavin caught a glimpse of a thick packet on Derrick's desk sitting dead center. On the top fax page was a message in scratchy handwriting: *Gavin, here are the real estate papers you requested. Any more questions, call me. Phil Brussen.*

He grabbed the packet and skimmed through the pages until he reached what he was hoping to find.

"Sanford and Pierce Realty," he whispered. His heart quickened. He picked up his phone and called Mary Liminski. She answered happily, and then apologized for not getting further on the other list.

"You just caught me heading out," she continued. "I was about to leave and pick up my son."

"Have a question for you," he stated quickly. "It's about the Merchant Mart location."

"Well, did you get my email?" Her voice sounded more curious. "'Cause I sent it to you around one yesterday."

While she spoke, Gavin went to his emails again and scrolled through them. In the middle of a pack of recopied CSI reports, he discovered her email. "Found it," he said. "Sorry I missed it."

"Aw, Nolan, you had a lot going on. I should've called you." She paused. "The suite area where the fire took place was leased under Sanford and Pierce Realty. I attached a map of the location."

Clicking on the PDF document, he saw a series of highlighted rectangular boxes indicating the space where the explosion occurred. Suite 1943 was the epicenter.

"I couldn't find a name or owner per se of the leased area," she explained. "But the amount of leased business property is quite measurable, especially for a downtown location. I figured it out to be roughly seventy-five thousand square feet. I know how expensive the city is, and its rates, ya know. To have that much business space on prime location would be astronomical."

Enhancing the image, he found that Mary was correct. *So much space. But for what?*

"Well, I had a little time to spare," she added. "I called into the property manager office of the Merchant Mart and asked for any further information on the lease. The woman, who was rather rude, claimed it was used as a commercial distribution area."

"You just impressed me," he replied.

"Thanks," she replied. "I just try to follow up. I wish we had more luck on the warehouse."

"No, I think you are getting somewhere with this." He looked over the images of the fire. "Mary, instead of looking at the entire warehouse, try to locate the businesses where the fire was concentrated. That might narrow it down."

At that point, Mary indicated that she would do so first thing in the morning. Once he hung up, he then sent her a follow-up email of pictures of the warehouse. He typed simply: *Looking at the East side of the building, Mary. Thanks for your hard work.*

******

Minutes later, he was on the phone with Sanford and Pierce Realty Group. The same receptionist indicated that Sanford and Pierce were in meetings all day and could not be disturbed. Without becoming too upset, Gavin stressed to her that if either of the real estate brokers would prefer not to be arrested for tampering with or covering up evidence in an ongoing case, they should call him immediately.

Gavin had just come back from refilling his water when Mylo called him back. "You rang?" His voice was groggy.

"What's wrong?" Gavin asked. "You're not your usual happy self."

"I've—*we've*—been having trouble restoring the CD." Mylo took a sip of something.

"Issues? Clarify, please."

"The fire melted more of the disk than I suspected." He sounded distant, like he was on speakerphone. "My sister retrieved some still images. No complete footage yet."

"Is that good?"

"Well, they are, um…" He stopped. "They are a lot to handle for my sister. Even the small breaks of semi-pixelated images have been disturbing. I mean, *we* are used to it. Not my sister."

"If that is going to be the case, then pull her off of it," Gavin returned.

"Easier said than done," he responded. "Her skill at retrieving damaged data is stellar. I hope by tomorrow, I should have something for you."

"Fair enough." Gavin leaned back in his chair. "Wondering if you can help with something else."

"Sure, I could use a little break." Gavin heard clicks of the keyboard in the background.

"I'll text you the last victim's address," he stated. "Can you go back through security footage surrounding her building? ATMs?

Traffic? You know the drill. About three to five weeks ago?"

"Huge span." He paused. "What am I looking for?"

"This might be a long shot," he admitted. "A black truck."

"Model? Make? Year?"

"Mylo, if I knew," Gavin began.

"Got it. Vague enough for me," he interrupted. "I'm on it."

******

About a half an hour later, Gavin was sifting through some of the CSI pictures to identify the possible pole. As clear as the pictures had been, a developing headache was making the images slightly blurry. Lowering his glasses, he rubbed his eyes. Just as he set them on the desk his phone rang. The caller ID read a three-one-two area code. He picked it up.

"Hello, Detective Nolan. My name is Larry Hewittson." The man's deep voice made him sound like a chronic smoker. "I represent Sanford and Pierce Realty Group."

"How may I help you?" Gavin sat straight up in his chair.

"From my understanding," he stated assertively, "you would like to speak with Mr. Pierce and Mr. Sanford concerning some leased property."

"Correct." His voice morphed into a no-bullshit policeman tone. "They are prime locations of my murder investigations."

"As their counsel," Hewittson stated too confidently, "I have to say that public records can suffice for any possible points to your investigation."

Fucking lawyers. Gavin drummed his fingers and retorted, "It would benefit Sanford to cooperate with the police department in order to shed some light on new evidence."

"Again," the lawyer seemed to dismiss Gavin, "I do not see any benefit for my clients to come down to the police station to be interviewed."

"We can come to them," Gavin suggested, exacerbated by the lawyer. "Unless they are hiding something from us, in which case I can easily obtain a search warrant and request their office records."

"Hold on." A slight *click* could be heard, as if Gavin were being muted.

He leaned back in his chair, placing a hand on the back of his neck and massaging it gently. He rolled his head from side to side, the rhythmic pace seemed to ease the tension.

"Detective?" The lawyer was back on the line. "We have you scheduled for ten o'clock Monday morning at their main location on Wabash."

"I'll pencil them in, Mr. Hewittson," Gavin returned sarcastically and then hung up.

Whenever someone requested a lawyer, it usually meant that the truth was being buried. He only wondered what the realty company was hiding. Four women still had no clear connection, yet the murder locations had a similar factor. It was no longer a coincidence.

NINETEEN

Late in the afternoon, Derrick and Evelyn finally returned from the hospital, and they appeared as exhausted as Gavin. Plopping the thick jacket onto his chair, Derrick excused himself to take a "much-needed goddamn piss" and sauntered away. Along the way, he nodded to and even shook hands with other officers and detectives. Gavin admired how well-liked Derrick was in the precinct.

"You look pissed off," Gavin commented to Evelyn, who sluggishly took off her long jacket.

"Felt like a waste of time," she stated. Her cheeks were slightly flushed. "I'll let Derrick explain more."

"And you won't?" Gavin returned as he leaned back slightly.

"No, no. What struck me the most about listening to the staff," Evelyn replied, "was how Sills had been a great nurse. The patients adored her. Plain and simple. Despite whatever troubles with the others, she was very good at her job."

"Opposite of Ziegler's opinion." Gavin swung his chair slightly to face her.

"Don't get me wrong," she continued, pulling out her phone. "One said she was acting more 'kooky' than usual. I asked her to define that. Sills was extra paranoid. The other nurses knew that she was taking meds. But they all thought she'd stopped."

"Wonder why she was still on the floor," he said.

"I wondered that too," Derrick answered just behind him, plopping into his chair.

"Hey, I have to call back Molly Barker," she said simply. "Sills' friend. Didn't hear my phone ring on the way back." Evelyn sat down, crossing her long legs and punching in numbers quickly.

Before he let Derrick explain himself, Gavin filled him in on

180

the high points of his afternoon.

"And for the past couple of hours," Gavin conceded, "I have been scrolling through any public record of each location, searching for phone records, gas bills. Whatever would have a name attached to the places."

"Nothing?" Derrick asked. He leaned against the desk and collapsed his arms across it.

"Seems as if all the information was—"

"Scrubbed," Derrick finished.

"Yes." Gavin gave him a quizzical look. "How would you know about that?"

"Something about this whole thing is just off," Derrick said, shaking his head slightly. His midnight eyes scanned the whiteboard. "Seems awfully convenient for someone to be so clean. The suspect is picking off these women without leaving any trace. Now we have three locations that are tied to one real estate firm."

"Exactly," Gavin said. "Plus, the suspect knows how to create a device. Maybe killing the women in a fire carries some religious undertones."

"Hmm, I don't think so," Derrick returned, scrunching his lips. "If it was religious, we'd have seen some biblical quotes, cross symbols, things like that. Think it's more of a purification?"

"How so?"

"Unlike an arsonist who admires the fire, he uses it to cleanse his own conscience." Derrick swung his chair and pointed at the crime scenes. "The explosive device means he wants an ultimate washing. No matter the collateral damage."

"He ensures it by staking them on a pole," Gavin said gravely. "In the killer's mind, what could they be so guilty of?"

After a moment, Derrick said, "These women are not so random."

My thoughts exactly, D. "How can you be sure?" Gavin stood up.

Evelyn finished on the phone and approached Gavin. "You think all of the women knew the suspect?"

"You were listening this whole time," Derrick stated.

"When you have five brothers and four sisters in a small house," she replied with a slight smile, "it's hard not to eavesdrop. Call it an investigative skill. Or multitasking."

"We just don't have any proof to link any of the victims to each other." Gavin's tone was authoritative yet reasonable.

"We're not looking at the right spot," Derrick replied as his eyes fell on Gavin.

"Maybe I should comb through each of the women's histories again," Evelyn suggested.

"Better yet," Gavin said, "give Mylo a call. He can work some magic."

"Fine."

"You were right about the locations, G." Derrick's baritone voice seemed loud. With a grin, he added, "Think I might help on the utilities part."

"Let me guess, you have a friend," Gavin stated and winked at Evelyn, who had a blank expression.

"Yep, she was a great first class corporal," Derrick said proudly. "Trained hard, willing to put up with my bullshit—"

"From your army days?" Evelyn queried.

"Marines," he stated flatly as he took out his phone. "Let me see if I can get some more info."

Evelyn interjected, "Well, since Derrick's doing that, we have to go visit someone. Grab your jacket."

"Fine. Are you driving?" Gavin leaned over to grab his coat.

Her coat was slung over her shoulder, she gestured Derrick for the keys to the unmarked car. Derrick was already on the phone with his friend, talking about some memories. His face lit up as he spoke. Waving bye to him, Evelyn snatched up the keys and headed out.

Gavin slipped on his jacket, happy to leave the station.

*****

Entering into the modest-sized apartment, Gavin could see that Molly Barker lived meagerly: an oversized davenport covered in a floral bedsheet, a thick stuffed chair stuck out in the open, and a small chipped white dining table hugging the corner. Shoved in the corner near the small flat screen TV were two large bins opened with what looked like boys' toys and books. The open galley kitchen was clean, void of any unnecessary items. A hint of lilac scent caught his nose as the short, frumpy woman stepped aside to let them in.

Humbly, Molly offered Gavin and Evelyn a seat on the couch as she sat on the edge of the chair. A lingering sadness draped over Molly's round face through her swollen red eyes. Above, Gavin heard faint footsteps, noises of a television, and soft murmuring.

"I just don't understand how this could happen to Rhonda," Molly said quietly. Her fingers played with the small crucifix around her neck.

"We are trying to figure out Ms. Sills' whereabouts before she disappeared," Evelyn said gently. "How well did you know her?"

"I met Rhonda at school a few years back," Barker stated. "We were in the nursing program, the accelerated one down at Robert Morris. Met her there. There was something about her that I liked. I barely had enough money to survive, much less go to school and work. And she saw it. Sometimes she paid for lunches when we hung out between classes. Rhonda never really complained about money. Always a bargain hunter. Wanted the cheapest things. Sometimes I would go with her to thrift shops and she would pick out the most hideous, cheapest items to wear. Somehow, they fit her though."

"Did she have a lot of other friends?" Evelyn queried.

"Not that I know of." Molly sat straighter in her chair. "We got along fine. Many of my friends couldn't tolerate her mood swings, but I thought that was just Rhonda being Rhonda."

"What do you mean?" Gavin asked.

"Rhonda was different." Molly's green eyes shot over at Gavin briefly and then drifted away toward the window. "When we would go to restaurants, Rhonda insisted that we sit against a wall, preferably a booth near the windows. She stared out into the streets. She refused to eat off china and used only paper plates or takeout containers. Rhonda thought the dishes were filled with germs. When she met me, she would come, no matter rain, shine, snow, hot or cold, always in this hideously ugly wool overcoat that she'd never take off."

"She was quirky," Evelyn commented, casually glancing over at Gavin.

"Quirky? No," Molly replied, surprised. "My friends thought she was rude and obnoxious. Eventually, I stopped having her meet with any of them, and we would just do things on our own."

"Was she more comfortable then?"

"Yes, more relaxed."

"You must be a good friend," Evelyn stated. "But she lived down in the city, and you're here."

"I had to leave the city when I was pregnant, right after nursing school." The woman fidgeted with the cuticles on her bitten fingertips. "My ex-boyfriend didn't care about Devin or myself. I just couldn't raise a child in the city."

"You only have one?" Evelyn leaned toward Molly.

"No, I have two. Cody doesn't have the same father," she stated simply. "Another jerk who left."

"Sorry." Evelyn leaned closer to her.

"Not really, I'm glad they're gone." Molly straightened herself. "Actually, Rhonda helped me a lot. She was here whenever she had some time off. Didn't mind taking the train late at night. She loves, I mean loved," she paused, "my kids like they were her own. Sometimes, I didn't have to pay for a sitter. She would watch the kids while I worked some nights."

Substituting for something she could never have. "Did she talk about her own family much?" Gavin pursued.

"No." Fidgeting with the cross, Molly gave Gavin a timid look. "I mean, once she talked about her mother. She had her mother's middle name. Rhonda told me she went crazy and was locked up someplace out east. Boston... not sure, really. Never talked about her father. Her mother told her that he was a real good-looking Spanish man. No sisters or brothers I knew of. Think it was just her. Alone."

"Did she ever have a boyfriend?" Evelyn asked softly.

A small grin crept to her face. "No, Detective. She didn't."

"What is it?" Gavin questioned.

"Rhonda liked girls."

Evelyn looked over at Gavin and restated the question: "Did she have any girlfriends?"

Shaking her head as her stringy, mousy brown curls batted about, Molly answered, "I don't know. She gave up on men entirely after the military. She said that she never wanted anything to do with them. Rhonda protected me from her lifestyle. Not sure why. She never introduced me to anyone. She said that she could never make them last."

"Why do you think that?" Gavin leaned forward and propped

his elbows on his knees.

"Detectives, Rhonda had some issues. I know that." Molly clasped her hands into her lap. "I may be only a nurse, but I saw the signs of someone who was suffering from a mental disorder. My younger brother had major bouts of depression, before bi-polar could be properly treated. When he was seventeen, he hanged himself in the bathroom because his girlfriend dumped him before the prom. I found his body." She paused. "I suppose I liked Rhonda because I saw that she had an issue. Maybe I was trying to help her." Her eyes began to tear up.

Gavin said, "We are going to ask a difficult question, but we have to do our job."

Molly nodded as she dabbed the corners of her eyes.

"Would you know anyone who would harm Ms. Sills?"

"I knew you were going to ask that," she stated softly. "I really thought long and hard about this, because I want to help you."

"Thank you, Ms. Barker," Evelyn acknowledged, putting a hand on the woman's knee.

A brief, confident smile came to her face. "I do remember in the last few weeks that she was acting rather odd. I mean *more* odd than usual."

"How so?"

"About two months ago, she suddenly stopped coming here to see me and the kids," the woman responded. "I asked her why. Rhonda answered in her cryptic fashion, 'Just can't.' I pushed her about it, but she hung up the phone. Then she stopped answering her cell phone. I mean, she'd only call back after I left three messages in a row."

"Was this normal?"

"No, actually. When I called, Rhonda knew to answer. Many times I explained that to her. She knew about my brother. The last couple of weeks, it was hard to reach her."

"In your email, you claimed that Sills disappeared more than once."

A sad and distant look fell over Barker's face. "Yes, Rhonda couldn't fully cope with stress. Sometimes, she would be off the radar for two, maybe three days tops. I knew she would call. Never knew where she went. Or if she went anywhere. Then Rhonda would contact me. About end of August, she disappeared for an entire week. Gone. I checked the hospitals, called the police stations, reported her missing. And then she appeared. She said that she needed some alone time."

"That must have been a scary situation," Gavin empathized.

"Yes, it was." Barker glanced down at her phone.

"Are we keeping you?" Evelyn asked as she shifted slightly.

"No, my father has the kids, but he's older and not as mobile. Just don't like leaving them with him for too long." Then she turned to Gavin and said, "I know how important this is."

Gavin asked, "Do you know if anyone had access to Sills' apartment?"

"No, not at all. I didn't have a key…" She stopped mid-sentence and suddenly spurted out, "Oh my gosh, Ms. Penelope. Is she okay?"

"The calico cat?" Evelyn replied brightly.

"Yes, yes." Molly put a hand to her cheek.

"She's fine, was really hungry though." Gavin half-smiled.

A look of relief came to the woman. "Ms. Penelope was everything to Rhonda."

"I took her home with me," Evelyn said. "She's a lovely little kitty. Affectionate."

"I know," Molly began as a well of tears came to her eyes. "Please, I would like to take her. If that is all I have left of Rhonda, I will welcome her to my family. I'll give her to my sister, who adores animals."

"Sure, no problem. We will make it happen," Evelyn commented, smiling. "I'll bring her over this weekend."

Molly leaned over and hugged Evelyn tightly. "Thank you," she said.

"There is one more thing," Molly interjected. "I mean, it might be minor."

"Anything is helpful," Gavin said.

"Rhonda had this thing all the time. Maybe it was part of her issue, I don't know. As long as I knew her, I just accepted it. More or less dismissed it." Molly fidgeted with the cross again. "She always thought someone was watching her. Eventually, for the longest time, she stopped telling me about it. But in the last three months, she said that she felt someone watching her."

"Do you know who?" Evelyn inquired, shooting Gavin a

quick glance.

"Seriously, no. I loved Rhonda, but I couldn't buy into her crazy all the time." She added, "She said something odd about a month ago. On the phone. She was hysterical. She said, 'I saw him again today.' I asked her who it was, but she just replied with, 'I was looking at him and don't think he saw me.' She wouldn't explain anything more. Strange, huh?"

"Yes, indeed," Evelyn said.

"Well, thank you," Gavin began as he stood up. Gavin handed her a card and told her to give him a ring if she thought of anything. When he turned his back and closed the door, he heard Molly begin to sob again. Sills had a true friend, probably the only one in her life.

As they descended the narrow stairs, Gavin thought he was sure Sills knew who was coming for her.

TWENTY

Already running about a half an hour behind, Gavin swung his car into the parking lot, parked, and raced into the building. The sensations of Chad's warm embrace, his musky delicious scent, and the feel of his cock inside him created a lingering, sassy grin on his face. After meeting with Baker last night, he decided to surprise Chad at his apartment. When Chad greeted him, he wore only a towel. His lover enjoyed being nude in his house. Honestly, Gavin could not resist the swaying manhood between those gorgeous toned legs. That morning, Chad had joined him in the tiny shower, where their bodies hung halfway out. Chad's tongue had pleasured him sweetly and kindly.

Walking down the busy corridor, Gavin continued to ignore the texts from both Evelyn and Derrick. Late last night, Mylo had left him a message that he had some information to share. Making a quick dash for his desk, he dodged other officers, detectives, and staff along the way. In the far corner near the interrogation rooms, Evelyn poked her head around the corner and flagged him over to a meeting room.

Must be that important. He dropped his coat and bag over his chair.

Casually, he glanced over at Creighton's dark office. While a couple of days had passed since he last saw Quinn, the captain was still answering emails and distributing important new polices as needed. Probably better that he was not here.

As he approached Evelyn, she said excitedly, "Hey, I want to show you something."

"Sure," Gavin returned.

In the room, Derrick sat at the table with his jacket off. The crisp, pressed white shirt sculpted his muscular torso as he nodded, speaking to someone on the phone. "Yeah, can you send the report over?" he said loudly. "Yep, yep."

"Here, Gavin." Evelyn pointed at the table, where several files were opened. "We have a couple of minutes. Mylo is waiting for his sister out front."

"What do you have?"

On the table were military pictures of Gable, Carlton, and Sills. Each of them wore serious, dark expressions in their photos.

"Got the vics' military files late last night," Evelyn said. "Don't get mad, but I took the liberty of adding Sills' name to the list. Somehow I knew that they *all* would be in the military."

"Continue." Gavin glanced over at Derrick, who seemed lost in his conversation. Or *purposely* lost in it.

"First," she explained, "I thought their military past wouldn't reveal anything. Sills and Carlton were in the army, and Gable in the marines. No connection. But then I looked at this." She flipped each one to the next section and pointed to a highlighted piece. "Each of them were stationed at the same place. Afghanistan."

Derrick turned slightly in the chair, facing away from them.

Gavin replied, "That can't be a coincidence."

"No, not at all," she said. "It gets better. Here." She flipped over the next page. "Gable left voluntarily, as did Carlton. But Sills was discharged for mental instability. And here, look, all of their files have this notation."

Gavin looked to the lower right corner. It read: *Pending prosecuting case: unresolved.*

"What the hell is that?" Gavin blurted out.

"Exactly," Evelyn stated.

At that moment, Derrick got off the phone. He appeared more serious than usual.

"Hey, D," Gavin began.

"Before you ask," he replied with his hands up, "like I told Evelyn, I did not know these women."

That's not the question I was going to ask. "No, I was wondering if you knew what that notation meant," Gavin returned, standing straight.

Sighing heavily, Derrick responded, "Not really."

Before Gavin could ask another question, Mylo rounded the corner. His face looked grim as he pushed up his thick glasses. A second later, a thin young Asian woman slid into the room. She took a seat next to Derrick, her long black hair with streaks of red and bright purple framing her narrow face.

"Everyone, my sister, Lily," Mylo announced and anchored himself near the laptop. On the wall, the screen came to life as he pressed some buttons.

Both Derrick and Evelyn nodded and greeted her, introducing themselves. When it came to Gavin's turn, he reached out a hand to take her cold small hand and briefly shook it.

"Glad you could help us on this," he said to her.

"Yeah," she replied grimly, putting her small purse on the table. "Wish I didn't get involved in this shit. Don't know how my brother can deal with it."

Mylo shifted in his stance and stated, "Ready?"

"Last victim's apartment view," Mylo said and pressed a button on his laptop. Instantly, the far gray wall displayed a dark, grainy image of Sills' apartment.

"That's near the back entrance," Derrick pointed out lowly.

"The action happens about thirty seconds into the video." Mylo took a sip of his coke.

The scratchy image of the building displayed the rain falling. In the lower corner, shadows crossed the building. Within seconds, a sizeable man in black clothing carried an unusually long duffle bag over his shoulder. His back was to the camera as he headed west down the leaf-strewn pavement. The man seemed not to slow down his quick pace. He disappeared out of range, causing elongated shadows to follow.

"Best you have?" Gavin questioned.

"The suspect didn't turn around," Evelyn commented. "Don't even have a profile."

Derrick remained quiet, tapping his fingers.

"Sorry, this was the best I could find, given the area," Mylo returned. "Without decent camera feeds on any of the nearby buildings, I was lucky to get this one." He closed the file, and soon another file was loaded. "Are you to the next clip?"

Gavin only nodded, giving a side glance toward Derrick, whose fingers tapped nervously against the table. A troubled expression covered his partner's face.

On the screen, a slightly clearer image of Sills' front

apartment building was to the far left, about a hundred yards away. The camera angle was turned down toward the traffic light, surveying the non-existent traffic on the desolate street. A moment later, the same man in dark clothes appeared from the side street with the large duffle bag over his square shoulders. Walking steadily, he headed toward the back of a black truck. From the angle, Gavin couldn't make out the license plate. The figure climbed into the vehicle and drove off.

A black truck—just like Eric Holtz and the dishwasher mentioned.

"Still nothing," Derrick spoke up.

"Best footage I could pull," Mylo sounded disappointed. "I may go back to the toll booth cameras at the time of the alleged abduction and—"

"You can if you want, not pushing you into doing it though," Derrick interrupted.

"I agree," Gavin stated. "We may need you for more pressing matters."

"Still, he knows how to creep in and out of a camera view," Derrick returned grimly. He added, "Mylo, you could have just sent us the images."

"Brought you here for the recovered CD," Mylo said. "We pulled together some footage."

"Footage?" Evelyn sat up, looking curious.

"Lily?" Mylo gave a small nod toward his sister.

Rising slowly from her chair, she stepped near her brother. Oddly enough, they did not appear to resemble reach other at all.

"I assumed the disk contained data," Derrick stated, giving Gavin a serious look.

"No." Mylo adjusted the laptop for his sister. "Initially, I thought it would have contained data as well. But it was an early formatted digital CD."

"CD?" Evelyn questioned before sipping her coffee.

"That's what we both discovered," Mylo stated. "Not my area of expertise, the reason why I brought in Lily."

"I actually work for an insurance adjuster," Lily announced, "who takes video surveillance files of probable fraudulent claims. I go through them to reveal the actual moments before the incident."

She clicked on the laptop, opening the file below.

"Because the disk was physically complete, pulling data

strings was easier," she said. "When data is damaged due to fire, water, or otherwise, everybody assumes the data cannot be retrieved. Much like deleting emails, files, pictures, and whatnot, the information is still sourced. Relatively speaking, the damaged data can be re-coded. It takes time. In the case of this particular data stream, the data can be enhanced and strung together. Mind you, Detectives, sometimes the data information can be broken. For audio, film, and picture data, you can capture the data bits, or at least what remains significantly, repair the data streams, and find the information.

"In this case, the film was created by an older format, which can be a bit trickier than it entailed. In essence, the data images we pulled together are only a snippet of the entirely broken data stream. The damage to the surface of the disk did keep some missing data from being retrieved." Turning toward Gavin, she added, "I worked endlessly for the past several days to show this snippet. Again, the fire did significant damage to the disk, yet I was able to pull off a good two-minute, thirty-two second snippet."

"The quality of the picture," Mylo interjected, "must be how it was filmed. Or whoever held the camera."

"Also, because of some of the broken data stream," Lily said, "the color of the picture is distorted and will show a prism of colors. Not necessarily of the intended piece. However, I could not attach the sound to the scene."

"Are you ready?" Mylo asked.

"Let's see what you have," Derrick replied, his tone oddly quiet.

"On a personal note," Lily commented and then looked at Evelyn, "this is some fucked up shit."

At that same moment, she pressed a button, and the wall came to life.

A shadowy canvas backdrop opened up, and the jiggling of the images indicated whoever was filming was not steady. In seconds, the image stopped shaking and began to pan from the canvas to the dirt floor, then up to a dark green cot, where Rhonda Sills was tied up. As the picture tightened, the camera scanned her body, which was covered in cuts and bruises. From how her head was rolling around, she appeared to have been drugged. Her swollen eyes couldn't focus, bloody drool seeped from the corner of her puffy lips, and her hair was matted against her head. The camera sharpened on the woman's naked body, panning over her small breasts down to her cleft. It was difficult to tell through the grainy color, but it appeared she was bleeding slowly from her vagina.

Suddenly, the camera turned on its side, the image falling quickly away from the woman. They got a brief glance of another cot and a pair of legs covered in dark camouflage pants. The man was barefoot.

The camera was set upright again, revealing the man's naked lower back, glistening in sweat. The pants were loosened, exposing some of the man's buttocks. Casually, the man ambled toward the woman, showing more of his cut, muscular frame. The grainy distorted images began to blink and shake. As he approached the woman, he held a long wiry strap.

Suddenly the film stopped.

Everyone was silent for a long moment. Only the hum of the overhead lights invaded the space.

"That's what we have now," Mylo said with a shaky voice, looking over at his sister.

"Should have more soon," Lily simply stated. Pulling out her phone, she said to Mylo, "Have to go. Another errand."

"Fine. Thanks," Gavin said.

"We sent you these pieces already," Mylo stated as he packed up his computer. "I'll call you as soon as I have more information."

Soon, they departed the room. The awkward silence remained.

******

"Who made the home movie?" Evelyn was the first to break the unusual quietness.

"Better yet," Gavin added, "it looked like Sills was drugged, then beaten, and then what?" He looked at Derrick, who stared back at him. "Sexually assaulted?"

"If this is the case," Evelyn said, "then we can assume that Carlton and Gable were filmed. Could that have been those pieces of plastic in the other bodies?"

"Let's assume so," Gavin stated. Then he said to Derrick, "You've been unusually quiet. Your thoughts?"

Sighing heavily, Derrick rolled his eyes away from Gavin. His fingers still drummed the table.

"Not sure, man," Derrick finally commented.

"Not sure?" Evelyn returned heatedly. "That's all you got?"

"Whoever is doing this," Derrick replied calmly, "my gut says it's our guy raping Sills. But we have no clue who the sick son of a bitch is. The camera doesn't show him."

"The film says it all," Gavin jumped in. "The tent, the camouflage, and the cot. It was some army scene."

"Exactly." Derrick seemed more annoyed than concerned. "It looks like it. Could be some stage setting."

"Bullshit," Evelyn exclaimed and pushed the military files toward Derrick. "What about the fact that they were stationed in Afghanistan, these pending cases, and…"

"What?" Derrick exclaimed. "Think I'm the one who's fucking killing these women, Evelyn?"

"No, nothing like that, D," Gavin said, attempting to defuse the ignited dynamite. He took a moment to wonder why his partner had jumped to that conclusion, then added, "What about these women? Did you know them? The fact that they were stationed the same place you had toured…"

Derrick shot an evil glare at Gavin. "Fuck you," he growled. "I had nothing to do with this."

"Well, you ain't helping us," Evelyn joined in, collapsing her arms across her chest.

Standing up, Derrick pushed back his chair into the wall. He shook his head at both of them and walked around the table.

"Where are you going?" Gavin asked.

"To get some fucking fresh air," he stated.

"Are you going to tell us what you know?" Evelyn declared.

"Evelyn, you are treading on goddamn thin water," he said, his voice a low rumble as he reached for the door handle. Then to Gavin, he said, "Think you better have a chat with this one. I'm taking the rest of the day off."

"Derrick," Gavin attempted as he stood up.

Soon his partner disappeared around the corner and headed toward the back of the station. Gavin looked at Evelyn.

"Are you going to scold me now?" she remarked as she gathered her files.

"You shouldn't have talked to him like that," Gavin said,

shutting the door.

"You mean like a cop? Not a friend?" She stood straight up.

"That's not what I meant," Gavin began.

"Whatever," she said. "I'm the new kid. You two are partners. I come in, start asking the right questions, and your partner loses it. Am I the bad one here?"

"No, Evelyn," Gavin interrupted her. "You need to think before you speak. Gather your evidence and work the case—"

"Think I've been sitting on my ass this whole time?" Her face reddened. "I regret calling you in. Sorry I fucking inconvenienced you guys." She shook her head and said, "Another goddamn boys' club."

Evelyn grabbed her pile of papers and marched up to him. He moved aside as she reached for the door.

"Guess I'm still working this one alone."

On that note, she threw the door open and it slammed against the wall, making a couple of nearby uniformed cops look over at him.

******

When Gavin made his way back to his desk, Evelyn was nowhere to be found. Although he wanted to text her, he decided to give her some space. Perhaps she'd pushed Derrick more than he had realized when he arrived before the meeting. Derrick's hot head attitude was truly out of character. Needless to say, he had to push onwards and figure out how to get the two together again.

Arriving at his desk, he noticed his phone was blinking with a voicemail. Most people would know to call his cell phone to reach him. Even his outgoing message told the caller to reach him by his cell phone.

Hopping on, he pressed in the code and listened.

"Hello, Gavin. Not sure if you remember me. This is John Clariden. Aidan's old partner. Your father's old partner." The man's voice was husky and dark. "Just want to catch up with you. Talk about a couple of things. My number is…"

At the same time, Gavin dialed John. Someone answered on the second ring.

"John?" Gavin said. "You just called me. It's Gavin. Gavin Nolan."

"Yes." The man coughed. "Sorry. Gavin, good to hear from you."

"I haven't seen you in a long time," Gavin stated. The last time was at his wedding—his mother had wanted John there.

"I know, that's my fault. How's your mother?" He paused. "Is she still in that home in Hinsdale?"

How did he know about her? "No, LaGrange," he corrected. "Why are you calling, John?"

"Can we meet tomorrow?"

"Sure."

"There's a bar called Rusty's Nail off of Cumberland and about two blocks west on Foster. Meet me there."

"Okay, what time? I have something in the morning."

"Don't worry about time. I'll be there waiting for you," he replied.

"Can you tell me what this is about?" Gavin asked, hearing the trepidation in his voice.

For a moment, John did not say anything and breathed heavily into the phone.

"Not over the phone," John said. "It's better to tell you in person. See you tomorrow." The man hung up.

Staring at his phone, Gavin shivered slightly and realized that it was no ordinary call. Why did John suddenly want to speak to him? After all this time? Sitting down at his desk, he retrieved his father's case file from the lower drawer. It was mind-numbing, the amount of times he'd read the report. Still, looking down at the photograph of his father's body, covered in black plastic, he wondered if he had missed anything. Once again, he read the words he had memorized. The report stated that his father had been shot three times squarely in the chest by a suspect who was breaking into a warehouse.

In the grainy picture, a young, mournful John Clariden stood in the background, speaking to someone whose back was to him. Even through his expression of anguish, John Clariden seemed genuinely surprised.

But why?

At the end of the report, the various investigators listed their names, which totaled eleven officers and detectives following up on non-existent leads. The suspect seemed to have clearly *vanished*, as one person noted. Finally, right at the bottom, next to then Captain

Ronin's signature, there was a simple notation: *Presently unsolved case.*

Setting the file down, Gavin looked up to see that Evelyn had returned to her desk and was on the phone. Her slender back was to him, indicating that she wanted to be left alone. Perhaps she needed her space. Between Derrick abruptly leaving, the video, and John's call, his head was pounding. He'd left a couple of strong pills in his car, thankfully.

Glancing over at Creighton's darkened office, he ambled toward the back of the station. He was glad that Quinn was not present today. Another mess that he could not deal with.

Begrudgingly, the day pressed on.

TWENTY-ONE

Situated near Oak Park's bustling center, Dr. Simmons's cream-colored office building was reminiscent of 1950s postmodern architecture. As with the town, the combination of Victorian, Craftsman, and postmodernism blended within the neighborhoods and the facades of the downtown area. It was perhaps why Gavin enjoyed coming to Oak Park. As he crossed the street, the nearby Metra's whine screeched to a stop. Upon entering the building and stepping into the elevator, the stillness of the office complex was deafening.

Gavin glanced down at his phone; neither Derrick nor Evelyn had texted him.

A ding signified the floor, and the doors opened to a white industrialized corridor. Several offices down, the stately Simmons and Associates nameplate hung on the door. Inside the small lobby area sat five tattered taupe pleather chairs, two blond side tables, and three inexpensive silver floor lamps. A large glass window to the right allowed the natural light to stream in. A heavyset receptionist, who wore unflattering dark-rimmed glasses, spoke on the phone as she sat at a neatly organized desk. Behind her, two more desks—which were covered with the clutter of paperwork, files, and older desktop computers—were smashed against the far wall of the tight space. Once she hung up, the woman acknowledged him and told him to wait. He took a seat and noticed the plethora of older tattered magazines on one of the tables. Moments later, the door to the left opened.

"Detective Nolan?" Dr. Simmons poked her head out. Unexpectedly, she was stunningly attractive. Her deep chocolate brown hair loosely fell across her shoulders, a pair of simple wire rim glasses clung to her petit nose, and a cordial smile caressed her burgundy-colored lips. Yet, a hint of despair showed in her dark eyes.

"Yes." Gavin stood up and shook her cold delicate hand. "Pleasure."

"I apologize for the wait," she said quickly, pivoting on her heel. A faint flowery perfume emanated from the doctor. "Let's go back to my office."

"You own this practice? Who are the associates?" He ambled casually behind her.

"Struggling part-time therapists." Her husky voice sounded like that of a classic jazz singer. "I charge them very little rent for their space."

"Very kind on your part."

"Detective," she replied, "my father built this practice when the concept of psychiatry was a folklore. He had a solid reputation within the community. After his death, I still maintain his tradition."

She stopped at the last office and directed Gavin into an understated, plain space. He found himself taking the chair near the desk. Dr. Simmons did not sit behind her glass desk but in the nearby chair, showing a passive responsiveness to his authority.

Doctor, what are you not going to tell me?

"Beautiful space," Gavin commented instead and shrugged off his jacket, placing it over the couch.

"It makes my clients feel welcome in their sessions. I try to take the stress out of their days." She smiled and leaned back in the chair. The tight jersey caramel dress highlighted her ample bosom.

"Did you find Rhonda Sills to be stressed during her sessions?" Gavin inquired.

"Detective Nolan," she replied, "understand that I can give very little information about her."

"You mean the patient-slash-client privilege?" Gavin said softly. "Your client was murdered."

"What Rhonda and I shared in this office was between ourselves." Simmons straightened her back.

"Dr. Simmons—"

"Please, call me Beth," she interrupted.

"Dr. Simmons," he continued, ignoring her, "withholding important information from a case can put you in contempt of court."

The smile increased on her thick lips. "Attempting to defuse me with alleged court procedures will not get any more information out of me. I don't apologize for it."

Guess I have to be blunter. He then queried, "So, how long had you and Rhonda been together?"

"I don't understand your question." A poker face remained.

"Rhonda liked women, and her friend said that she was seeing someone, but never knew who." Gavin leaned closer toward her.

"Just because Rhonda was a lesbian doesn't mean that I am." She shifted slightly in her chair. "Obviously, your own homosexual issues or phobias distort your perception of the people around you. Your tone suggests some hidden fears and doubts. Was there some past guilt?"

"Is that the same type of therapy you used on Sills, Doctor?" he replied. "Tackling her self-doubts and twisting them around for your own pleasure?"

A stern face stared back at him. "I don't have to say anything—"

"When was the last time you saw Rhonda?" Gavin interrupted.

"I checked the books. Five weeks ago."

"How did Sills behave at the time of the visit?"

"Listen, Detective Nolan," she said carefully. "Rhonda had some serious issues. We were working through some anger management problems."

"Is that why you prescribed several psychotropic medications? Was that part of the therapy?"

"Rhonda," Simmons said, "required some balance to her daily routine. Her, um, outbreaks needed some restraint."

"Overmedicating her was the best solution?"

"Detective, medication effects each individual. I prescribed Rhonda various combined strengths in hope they would quell her anxiety." Simmons shifted slightly in her chair. Her eyes pierced Gavin's. "Needless to say, her symptoms were quickly devolving over the last couple of months."

"Is that when you stopped seeing her?" Gavin asked. He added, "Privately speaking."

Simmons said nothing and clasped her hands on her thin legs.

"Doctor," he returned. "We are trying to establish a timeline of Sills' whereabouts prior to her abduction."

"Abduction?" A genuine look of concern washed over the woman's face.

"Yes. We believe she was taken, murdered, and then preserved," Gavin stated.

"What do you mean, preserved?"

"The suspect had other intentions for her corpse," Gavin said, trying to get a better read on the doctor.

Still reserved, Simmons tugged her skirt down. Her dark eyes seemed to water, and she looked away from Gavin toward the long, slender window.

"I think Rhonda knew who it was. Perhaps she told you. Either professionally—" He paused, and then said softly, "or otherwise."

The room was unusually quiet. Gavin imagined the unnerving silence as part of the therapy to draw Simmons's patients to speak.

"Detective, this practice is the threshold of my very existence," she began. "What I tell you must be kept quiet."

"To be honest, I cannot guarantee it entirely," Gavin said. "But I will make sure that information will be kept only within the investigating officers. Is that fair?"

Nodding, the woman kept her posture rigid. "Very well," she said.

Gavin pulled himself up straighter in the uncomfortable chair. "Can you let me know when you began seeing Rhonda?"

"Professionally," she stated, as her eyes drifted away from him. "Rhonda came to me about three years ago. She was referred to me by a fellow colleague who spoke about her resisting to open up. My first sessions, I attempt to have the person open up about their troubles. Typically, the types of people I treat respond in the first ten or fifteen minutes. Rhonda was different. Reserved. I asked her many questions, but she barely uttered a word. At the very end, I explained the concept of therapy and how it worked. Instead of reacting negatively, Rhonda nodded and told me she liked me and wanted to return."

"How many times did she see you?"

"Once a week. The first couple of months were a challenging period. I began to detect she had a delusional paranoia syndrome, almost bordering schizophrenia. She discussed her nightmares. They consisted of her running down a long alley or hallway while many arms grabbed at her. At the end of the dream, she woke up in a panic and felt as if someone was in the room with her."

"Did that sound out of the ordinary to you?" Gavin questioned.

"Yes and no," Dr. Simmons replied. "Dreams are just a reflection of the subconscious trying to cope with a real issue. Figuring out the symbolism was challenging, as Rhonda held back information."

"Would she ever discuss her work?"

"Sometimes." Simmons seemed to reflect and gather her words. "Her work environment gave her solace. Caring for sick people gave her a sense of accomplishment. The moments of interacting with her colleagues gave her anxiety. Rhonda's emotional state was unpredictable at best. I never knew what kind of Rhonda would walk into my office. If she had to wait for me while I finished up with another client, she would be agitated. Several times, I'd have to calm her down. At that point, I suggested prescribing her medication."

"Why so many different kinds?"

"As In stated before, I had to prescribe the right amount and correct dosage in order for Rhonda to maintain stability."

"Did it work?"

"For the most part," she answered unconvincingly.

"When did your relationship turn from professional to private?" Gavin asserted.

A gloomy smile caressed the doctor's lips.

"About a year and a half ago, in therapy," she stated distantly. "I never expected it. It just happened. She always had the last session of the evening. It was late, she was in a dark mood, and I was trying to relax her. One thing led to another. Please understand, I never had the intention of being with Rhonda. As I knew her privately, she opened up more to me. Her trust in me as a romantic partner solidified it.

"Rhonda had a dark, lonely childhood. Her mother had a major mental illness, which she could not describe. She locked it away in her mind. She had no clue who her father was. Her grandparents raised her until she was five, then they died suddenly.

Without anyone, she was forced into foster care and bounced around from home to home. Professionally speaking, some of her symptoms derived from her childhood. The constant sense of loneliness truly substituted her acceptance of belonging to a group at any level. Because of her irrationality of not belonging, she lashed out more against society and removed herself as much as possible.

"Personally, I felt sorry for her." Simmons glanced over at Gavin. "Her disturbing upbringing affected me the most, I would say. Rhonda spoke of no other friends. I felt as if I was her only world. I hadn't been with another woman for years, before my first husband. The time I spent with Rhonda beyond these office walls was special."

"How so?"

"Despite her erratic behaviors against social norms, she was completely different with me. Affectionate, caring, and doting."

"Did she ever talk about her military experience?" Gavin shifted slightly.

Simmons's eyes went down to the floor, and she kicked the air slowly with her slender leg. "Yes and no."

"Can you elaborate?"

"She would briefly describe her days as a nurse in Afghanistan. She talked about some conflicts, how long she was stationed."

"Did she ever say why she left?"

Shaking her head, the doctor seemed more upset. "No, but I sensed it was bad."

"How so?" Grainy imagines of the video of Sills bleeding and tied up circulated in Gavin's mind.

"When I pushed for more details, Rhonda withdrew from herself, and well, us. I should have pushed her more on it. But…" Simmons's chocolate eyes watered. "I lost myself and forgot how desperately Rhonda needed help. She grew even more hostile and volatile toward other people and me. I could no longer tolerate her outbursts in the office. Beyond these walls, it was absolutely unacceptable, especially toward me. She became possessive. She showed up at my apartment at different times. Then she came here every other day. I couldn't handle it. So I ended it around four, five, months ago. August, I think."

"How did she take it?"

"She walked away," Simmons stated simply. "Said nothing."

Probably the reason why she disappeared. "Did you see Sills after that?"

"Yes," she confirmed. "Professionally."

"I'm sure that was awkward."

"No, Rhonda knew I was her therapist first and foremost. Our sessions reverted back to before our involvement. I quickly lost ground with her. About six weeks ago, I gave her a list of new therapists, explaining to her that another person would be best for her."

"How did she respond to that?"

"Not well," Dr. Simmons stated. "She yelled at me, and then cried. I wanted to comfort her, but I dared not return to that place in our lives again. Then, she said something odd to me. She said, 'Beth, I need you now. I can't be alone.' Her voice was full of fear. Just as quickly, she shoved me away, yelled at me, and told me to go fuck myself. I did try to contact her, call her, text her, email her—just tried to get ahold of her. I should have done more. It feels as if I am to blame for her... her death."

Simmons stopped for a second. Gavin could see a single tear slide slowly down her face.

"It wasn't your fault," Gavin said softly. He leaned forward, almost wanting to take the doctor's hand.

She sat up in her chair even more rigidly and stoically, and replied, "You are right, what you said."

"What do you mean?"

"I think she did know who was after her." Her eyes fixated on Gavin evenly. "When she missed the session before her last one, I grew even more concerned. I called her at work, but they wouldn't allow me to speak with her. Of course, she did not return my calls. I went by her apartment the week before—I'd been there once—but she wasn't there. Then, suddenly, she showed up for her... her last session."

Taking a deep breath, she explained, "She was about fifteen minutes late. I was wrapping up and ready to leave. Rhonda was frightened. I asked her about her medications. She stopped taking them for some weeks, said she needed to be clear headed. I tried to calm her down by having her sit. I then asked her what provoked her. Almost as if she wanted to kill me, she said, 'I have to be alert. I keep seeing his truck.' She sprung up from the chair, the same one you are sitting in, and went toward the window. She kept looking down at the street. I went over to the window and couldn't see anything. I asked her who she was seeing. She didn't say much. Only shook her head—almost angrily. I realized that her psychosis was teetering on the edge of something terrible. As I reached for the phone, she said to me, "*Aleadui*'. Before I could ask her more, Rhonda said, 'He's following me. I have to go.' She just took off. I went after her, but she was already way ahead of me and had disappeared."

"That's the last time I saw her." Dr. Simmons's voice cracked slightly.

Gavin imagined Sills' frantic state as she looked out the window. "What did she mean by *aleadui*?"

"It bothered me," Dr. Simmons said softly. "I have some Middle Eastern friends who were able to translate. It roughly means 'enemy.'"

*****

The cold air wrapped around Gavin while the sun's rays hit the nearby snowbanks, making them sparkle. Simmons' conversation rattled him. Sills knew she was being followed. Much like Gable and Carlton. *He* was after them. These were not random women being picked off. After waiting for a bus to pass, Gavin darted across the street toward his car.

He had purposely held back with Simmons about the video. The footage was about Sills. But were the other fragments from the other bodies also CDs? And were they tied to the other women?

His phone rang.

Without looking at it, he answered and spoke automatically, "Nolan."

"Hey, G." Derrick's voice was low, almost hushed.

"Derrick," he replied, somewhat surprised.

"Yeah. Did you already talk with the doctor?"

"Just finished up."

"Shit," he stated. "Was about to text you that I'd meet you."

"No problem. I took care of it."

"I should've been there," he responded.

"Well, Simmons was insightful." Gavin then relayed the conversation.

After a full minute of silence on his end, Derrick finally said, "Sills definitely knew the suspect."

"Seems that way," he said, noticing Simmons leaving the building. A pair of round, thick-rimmed sunglasses covered her eyes. "Sills did say something to the doctor that was interesting. She said 'aleadui'.'"

"Enemy," Derrick said immediately. "First word you're taught when you're over there. We were usually them."

Got it. "Do you think that means anything in particular?"

"No, frankly," he said. He paused and then added, "Sorry, G, for yesterday. I shouldn't have left like that. Before you got there, Evelyn kept pushing me. And G, you know I don't like that shit."

"We've worked long enough together to know what pushes our buttons. Give her time." Gavin admitted.

"She just kept probing me," he said matter-of-factly. "She's new at this bullshit. But she needs to step down when she's fucking wrong."

"I'll talk to her," he began.

"No, I will," Derrick interrupted. "My fight. I'll make peace."

"No referee?" Gavin mused.

"Naw, man, we're fucking grown-ups here," he retorted. "At least I am."

"Fine."

"One more thing," Derrick said. "I requested files on those questionable military cases."

"Do you have some contact there?"

"Yes, but I can't use him for that one." His voice lowered. "I have no contacts other than my former recruits who escaped that shit-show. I just sent an email to Creighton."

"It may take longer than we need."

"Yeah," Derrick answered quickly. "But it's through the proper channels."

"I'll drop Creighton a note to speed it up," Gavin returned.

"Not sure if he'll help."

"Worth a shot."

"Hold on." There was a muffling sound from Derrick's end and some low talking. He came back on the line. "Alright. Want me to come in today?"

"Naw, we're off today." Gavin started up his car, hearing the soft purr of the engine. "Plus, I have my own plans."

"Understand that," Derrick said. "Listen, G, I'm sorry again."

"Don't be."

Derrick hung up.

The warm air from the vents finally began to fight off the cold. On his phone, Gavin mapped the route to the bar.

Yeah, I'm done for the day, D, he thought. *I've got a different meeting.*

He maneuvered the car into the traffic and snaked his way down toward O'Hare.

TWENTY-TWO

The bar, Rusty's Nail, was situated at the end of a nearly vacated strip mall close to a vast industrial park in Rosemont. Being so close to O'Hare, the rumbling of an overhead Boeing airliner rattled the car windows when Gavin parked. The landing gear was already down as it quickly descended to the earth. As he got out of the car, he could see the passengers in the windows, probably staring back at him. Stepping toward the bar, the sounds of I-290 and the Kennedy traffic echoed off the darkened windows and cement facades. Even if the strip mall was empty, the parking lot sure wasn't. More cars came in and parked, and people in purple and orange jerseys ran into the bar entrance.

Inside, the crackling noise of the college game on TV and loud conversation reverberated around him from the packed narrow space. On the flat screens, Northwestern was playing Notre Dame. Ironically, the small dive bar was a college bar more fitting in Evanston neighborhood than near a bustling airport. Shifting his way through the crowd, a few young women eyed him hungrily while their college men were too busy tuning into their game, beer, and friends to care.

Inching his way through the packed bar, he imagined what John Clariden looked like now. It had been over fifteen years since he had last seen him. On the end, John perched on a stool. His bulky body leaned on the bar surface as he spoke to another person near him. Nodding his head, he flagged for Gavin to come over and said something to the other man who then stood up, finished off his dark drink, and walked away.

"What'll you have?" John said loudly as he pointed to the nearby stool for Gavin.

Sitting down, Gavin noticed a tall Pabst can and several shot glasses in front of the man. A short, husky woman behind the bar came by, and Gavin ordered a beer on tap.

Putting out a hand, John said, "It's been too long. How's Emily?"

"We got divorced a few months ago," Gavin returned as he shook the clammy fat hand.

"Goddammit. Sorry, Gavin," he returned. Shaking his round thick head, the man's jowls jiggled slightly.

"Didn't work out, that's all," he replied. "You look good," he added, lying.

"Bullshit," John quipped back, rubbing his white, wiry whiskers. "The wife says I should start losing some weight. Hell, I like to eat."

"Come here often?" Gavin asked. A few young college kids pushed their way up to the bar, appearing tipsy already as they talked noisily.

"Grew up around here about a mile or so over on Foster in Norridge," he returned. "Just like the feeling. Get here less and less."

"Unless you have something to do in the city," Gavin shouted over the cheers that marked a Northwest touchdown.

The bartender came back with the beers and a fresh shot glass of whiskey for John. Then she paid quick attention to the young group and asked for ID.

"Yeah, suppose." John grinned at him. "This place used to be a small little place. Some of my friends hung out here." His eyes scanned the chaotic scene. "Now, new fucking owners. Young kids moving in around here. Revamping the old into new goddamn hipster spots."

"Seems the trend lately." Gavin sipped the cold lager.

"Barbara," he said, nodding at the bartender, "has been here since I can remember. Reason why I come back, mainly on Saturdays."

His stubby fingers reached for the whiskey and he downed it quickly. For a couple of lingering minutes, the game on the flat screen occupied their silence.

"Why the call, John?" Gavin stated matter-of-factly.

"Took me," he said, barely audible, "a long goddamn time to call you. I should've talked to you earlier."

"About Dad?" Gavin glanced over at the elderly man.

"Aidan," Doug said, his voice low. "Your father was the finest, best goddamn officer. A great partner. Honest, by the book, and so bullheaded. Told you straight to your face what he felt. His Irish temper pissed people off." The man wore a lopsided grin.

Is this a walk down memory lane? "So, what did you want to tell me, John?"

"Your frankness reminds me of him," he commented as his light blue eyes looked upon Gavin. "Have no other way to say this, but Aidan's death wasn't an accidental shooting."

The bar stool seemed to pivot underneath him. "Why do you say that?" Gavin's voice sounded a whole lot calmer than he felt.

"The year before your father's death," John explained, "the neighborhood went downhill. Fast. *Unusually* fast. The number of muggings, assaults, property damage, robberies, and B and E's went up overnight. It didn't make any sense to any of us on patrol. The assholes were working goddamn overtime."

"I remember my dad working a lot," Gavin admitted.

"Yeah, we couldn't keep up," John said, downing the rest of his beer. He signaled Barbara for another round. "We all thought it would die down. No, it just kept getting worse."

"Was it a gang hitting the neighborhood?"

Smiling, John said, "Your father thought the same. Because he was sergeant, Aidan instructed the other officers to locate gang signs or any unusual people hanging out. Nothing out of the ordinary. Plus, no one came forward. People weren't talking. And it got fucking worse."

"Did you talk with gang unit?" Gavin turned to him.

"No. The gang unit was more interested in Cabrini Green and South Side," John grumbled. "They didn't care about the constant issues at hand."

"What about Ronin? Wasn't he the captain?"

"Ronin? Fucking shithead," John replied bitterly. "That asshole only ever cared about kissing the next alderman's ass. Like that fat fucker does now. He didn't care about the people. Just his position. Told us to do our jobs. Goddamn serve and protect. Fuckin' fucker."

Two of the college students looked over at that.

"Did Dad approach Ronin?"

"Not at all," John said adamantly. "Aidan hated that fucker the most. Ronin told us to focus our attention on drug dealers and prostitution. Which there was none of, Gavin. After that, your father never trusted him. Not as bad as that little son of a bitch Creighton."

"Captain Quinn Creighton?" Gavin delicately touched the frosty

Pilsner in front of him.

"Captain Creighton," John spat, "was a complete asshole. Never liked him either."

Another person who doesn't like Quinn. "But I know this isn't about Creighton," Gavin replied, attempting to quell the old man's anger.

"Yeah, yeah. Where was I?" John huffed, lost in thought or too drunk to think. Over the cheers of the patrons, John said, "Around March, before he was killed, Aidan came up to me and told me that a couple of people came forward about the break-ins, robberies, and the other shit. They were too scared about any consequences." He drank a good portion of his beer and continued. "The same time that Matterson threw his hat in the ring to be alderman."

"Matterson?" Gavin looked at John, surprised.

"Yeah, same one you busted a couple of years ago. Before you say anything, I saw you on the news," John confirmed. "Anyway, he came rallying at the precinct to get our support; said he wanted to help control the violence and promised us more pay. All goddamn bullshit. Of course, Ronin was his right-hand man and followed him like a dog. Maybe it could be the other way around. Not sure. Can't be sure these days. Still, your father was adamant about stopping the increasing crime. Despite Ronin's orders, he continued investigating." John swung his head over to Gavin and said, "Thinking back, I was a fool not seeing it now. But, no one was listening to him. Most of the other guys were buying into Matterson's promises. With the help of Ronin. And of course, goddamn Creighton.

"I'll never forget that night. Aidan and I were on our usual route. Rundown area between Cicero and Pulaski. We were called on a B and E in the abandoned warehouses about two miles south. Strangely, Labanowski and Griffin were closer, yet Aidan obediently responded, and we went instead. Pulling up to the warehouses, we heard glass breaking, some voices, and a car starting up. Before I could park, Aidan already had the door open and was running down the north side of the building. I drove the car around the south side."

John took in a heavy breath and drank a deep gulp of his lager. His eyes watered as he gathered his thoughts.

"When I rounded the building again," he said, "Aidan was in pursuit on foot after a suspect. He was tall and slender. But I couldn't tell if he was white, black, green, or whatever. The suspect was a good few feet ahead of Aidan. Quickly, I pulled off to the side to get out. As I got out, three shots were fired from the side of the building. They hit Aidan directly in the chest. Dead center." His voice was shaky. "I ran to my partner. Your father… your father died in my arms."

Gavin stared at the man, who wiped his eyes. Despite the crowd, he felt as if he and John were the only ones there.

"I've read the report numerous times," Gavin stated, his voice low.

"Yeah, I bet you did." John attempted to regain his composure. He leaned closer to Gavin and said, "The warehouse had been long closed. Whoever was there was waiting for us. For your father. Maybe I thought about it too many times, but I swear on your father's grave, those goddamn perps were waiting for us. For your father."

"John, I don't—"

"One more thing," John interrupted. "That very day, Aidan was nervous. Almost antsy. Not like him. Your father was always calm and cool. When I asked him why, he shook his head and just said, 'I have to do the right thing.'"

"Do you know what it was about?"

After another long gulp of beer, he said, "After Aidan's death, asshole Ronin transferred me out of the district and landed me a job up in Libertyville. While I hated him, I was glad to be away. And I raised my kids and learned the peaceful life of the suburbs. Recently, I went to a friend's retirement party. Your father's name came up."

"Why are you telling me this?" Gavin straightened his back.

"Gavin." John leaned closer to him, smelling of whiskey. "My friend told me that Aidan was going to be interviewed by internal affairs the following day."

"For what?" Gavin returned, staring deep into the man's leathery face.

"Never knew." Doug emptied the beer even quicker and threw three twenties on the counter.

"Who told you?" Gavin asked.

As his eyes darted around the bar, a complacent smile appeared on his lips. He simply stated, "I've already said too much."

"Where are you going?" Gavin began to stand.

"I like you and your family," he said, standing and putting on his coat. "I just want to give you a, uh, heads-up. Just watch yourself,

Gavin."

"What do you mean by that, John?" Gavin queried anxiously.

"Doesn't matter," he said halfheartedly. "I promise to see your mother soon. Have a good holiday."

Waddling through the building crowd, John headed toward the double doors and disappeared into the blinding light.

******

In the early hours of the next day, Gavin rose out of bed silently, trying not to disturb Chad. He ambled toward the dimly lit kitchen, where the remains of Chinese takeout were still evident along with two empty bottles of wine at the end of the counter. While Chad had described his new training sessions and debated competing in an IBPP competition that following May, Gavin tried to encourage him, but it had been halfhearted. The thoughts of his father's death, his shooting, and John's words madly buzzed in the back of Gavin's mind.

He pulled out his laptop and set it on the counter. The screen's light pushed away the early morning shadows.

Quickly, he googled his father's old district and scrolled through numerous archived news reports. After a few minutes, several dozen articles captured his attention. Skimming each one and saving the pertinent ones, he read that the area had indeed been inundated with crimes: break-ins, robbery, vandalism, property damage, and the like. Seemingly small items, yet enough to cause stress on the community.

A half an hour later, Gavin googled "Matterson running for office in '92-'93." A series of articles appeared that described Matterson's campaign throughout the area at schools, churches, Senior homes, and libraries. Pictures showed an overly exaggerated smile on that familiar gaunt face as he shook hands, gave hugs, and accepted support. No matter, Gavin could see the cold eyes staring back at him.

Scrolling down, he noticed an article from April of 1992 and clicked it. The article was titled: *Matterson and Local District Enforcement Working Together*. In the photo, Matterson and Ronin were side by side, both half-smiling. Behind them, a group of officers were the backdrop. There on the second row near the left side, his father stood. *Looks pissed off*, he thought as he blew up the picture. Next to him, a much younger and thinner John Clariden stood, equally pissed off.

Was John telling the truth?

In the article, the reporter asked Matterson what he was going to do about the rising crime in the area. Matterson responded, "After speaking with Captain Ronin, and if I win the coming election, I will solicit more funding for the district for our law enforcement in order to stop future criminals."

Leaning back in his chair, the cool metal touched the middle of Gavin's naked back.

Somehow, the picture looked so staged.

Hitting the web again, he searched for the November '92 elections. Moments later, he found an article that showed a picture of Matterson at his campaign office, surrounded by supporters cheering and celebrating. He noticed Ronin leaning against a wall in the far right corner. Zooming in, he saw that two officers stood near him, speaking to him. A look of mild disgust washed over his face. How well did Ronin know Matterson?

Closing his laptop, Gavin looked out into the darkened city. Why did John really meet with him today? He could have spoken to him at any point. But why now? Why bring up his father's shooting? John looked nervous, but he'd also been drinking. Why was John warning him? Craning his neck to the side, Gavin had one final thought, which kept his mind racing even after returning to his bedroom and lying next to his lover.

Why would Dad be interviewed by Internal Affairs?

TWENTY-THREE

Gavin exited the cramped elevator onto the thirty-third floor of the CNA building. The hallway leading toward Sanford and Pierce Realty was a luxuriously inviting space. The caramel-colored walls displayed various houses and buildings throughout the Chicago metro area. The modern art sculptures flanked the portraits, and the sleek blond wood floors were pristine. Next to Gavin, Evelyn's heels tinged lightly off the surface as Derrick's heavy shoes pounded just behind him. Ahead of them, a large embossed logo of the realty company was etched into the frosted glass doors.

"Smells too sterile in here," Derrick commented.

"Almost too clean," Evelyn replied. The scent of her flowery perfume wafted into his nose.

They'd met in the grand lobby below. When he arrived, Derrick and Evelyn were talking jovially with each other. He figured that they'd reconciled from the argument days ago. Yet, they caught a sense of his sour mood. Evelyn brought him up to speed on Mary's findings. Yesterday, Gavin hadn't been in the mood for the case; he'd seen the emails but didn't open them. In fact, Chad quickly pointed out his sour mood and suggested going for a walk on Michigan Avenue. While Chad gleefully chattered on about the decorations in the various stores, the upcoming holidays, and buying presents for his family, Gavin's mind wrestled with his father's death and John's words.

Gavin opened the door, allowing Evelyn to go through first. Derrick entered next, and Gavin followed behind. A woman with large brunette curls in a loose red sweater noticed them and pasted a fake smile on her round face. Evelyn approached and informed her of their meeting with Mr. Pierce and Mr. Sanford. In his peripheral vision, Gavin saw Derrick shrug off his long coat and place it over his thick forearm. The stone features of his face probably made the receptionist nervous as his eyes scanned the place. Within moments, Evelyn produced a set of manila folder files Mary had created. While they did not hold concrete evidence, the lease agreements, sale notifications, and other tax-related items of each property would be enough to trigger the conversation.

"Detectives," the woman said, placing the phone back on its cradle. "I'll show you to the conference room. Please follow me."

Taking the lead, Gavin followed the woman through a tight hallway to the left. There were doors and long narrow windows on each side, and Gavin noticed that each room was being used to store files. Silently, he let out a heavy breath, and his brain began to wrap itself around the case at hand.

Evelyn looked straight ahead. The soft hue of red gloss caressed her lips, which made them appear more delicate against the hard-lined edges of her midnight hair. Perhaps she could sense Gavin's mood and wanted to stay quiet. Near him, Derrick's heavy breaths echoed dully in the noiseless hallway as the overly cushioned carpeting muted their footsteps.

The wall of doors opened up to a bland gray cubicle center. The desks were clear and void of any human contact. Against the far walls to the right, several empty grand offices were half opened to reveal empty desks. Soon, they arrived upon open space where several long couches and chairs were placed. Ahead of them, the wall of floor-to-ceiling windows revealed the Chicago cityscape. As they continued on, the clicks of their shoes clattered over the wood floor of the hollow vestibule.

The receptionist told them to wait for a moment and headed to the right of them, toward a window-encased room. The window was blocked by a curtain, but they could see the movement of shadows inside the room.

Taking a couple of steps forward, Gavin ambled toward the dark leather couches and took in the beautiful city. The towering steel and glass buildings poked out of the dense concrete jungle and seemed to go on forever. To the right, the dark cobalt lake churned violently and splashed savagely against the shoreline.

"I count five people," Derrick said behind him.

"Wonder who they brought?" Evelyn returned softly.

Turning toward the glass-encased room, Gavin replied, "Doesn't matter. We'll see what kind of answers we get."

Gavin felt his partner's frustration as Derrick shifted in his stance and sighed heavily. Gavin's mind was back in the game.

*****

Shortly, the receptionist invited them in. Evelyn stepped forward this time, followed by Derrick, and Gavin last. The floor-to-ceiling windows in the narrow space overlooked the shoreline. Whispery snowflakes danced off the pane and floated away into the air.

Four men and one woman sat on the opposite end of the long rectangular pine table. He recognized Sanford immediately due to his thin features and short white hair. His serious light eyes still pierced Gavin as he shook his hand. Next to him, the vice president, Barry Schumacher, a portly man in his late forties with ginger hair, seemed to be unnerved by their presence. Next to him, the vice-president of acquisitions, Paula Bolder, a tall, slender woman with a firm handshake, greeted him formally. Larry Hewittson shook his hand quickly and almost nervously. Finally, Pierce remained seated and only nodded pretentiously at Gavin.

"Detective Nolan," Hewittson grandly announced, "I am present for legal representation for the S and P Realty Group. Questions and/or inquiries should be explicitly regarding the properties in question. Having consulted with my clients, if I should feel the questions do not pertain to the business, we'll end our conversation."

"Both Mitchell and I," Sanford added quickly, "would like to share as much information about these sites and help you in your investigation."

"Perfect," Gavin replied, faintly smiling.

Next to Gavin, Derrick leaned on his elbows and slid over some documents that Evelyn had placed on the table. Catching a glimpse of Pierce, Gavin took in his stone face.

"In our research," Derrick began, commanding their attention, "your company has leased three of the properties in question for an outside vendor."

Casually, Evelyn picked up a piece of paper and slid it toward Sanford. "What do you know about Zanders Holdings?"

Bolder scooped up the paper before Hewittson could take it, and then handed it to Schumacher, who then gave it to Sanford.

"Can you please be more specific, Detective Nolan?" Sanford questioned as his eyes scanned the document.

"Who is the key contact you are subleasing and purchasing properties for?" Derrick answered instead. "For example, who purchased the Henderson house on Ashland?"

On cue, Evelyn slipped a copy of the faxed house sale over to Sanford. He, Bolder, and Schumacher peered at the document for a moment. Pierce seemed the least interested in the paper, while the lawyer jotted notes down.

Before Sanford could speak, Pierce stated, "We have many properties within the Chicago metropolitan area. We would have to look into who in our company controls and maintains these properties on a consistent basis."

"In fact, it would take time to round up the employees—" Mr. Sanford interjected.

"No," Gavin cut him off quickly. "Not necessary. We do have a list of six employees who have been connected with these properties." He handed over the list Mary had created for him yesterday.

"Where did you get this?" Hewittson inquired.

"All public records, sir," Derrick said and sat straighter.

"As you well know, since you have a realty business," Gavin stated, staring at Pierce the entire time, "all property must be properly acquired and sold with proper permits from the city. A simple standard procedure, gentlemen and Ms. Bolder."

For each of the properties, Mary had been able to uncover the names of the said listing agents. Gavin had a newfound appreciation for the Land and Title Division of Chicago Public Administration. While it may seem a pain in the ass for most businesses, one could not execute land deeds without getting the proper paperwork in order. Sanford cleared his throat loudly and glanced at Pierce, who seemed oblivious to the paperwork.

"Our business relies on the employees," Sanford said quickly, "of the company to run the daily operations as seen fit. We, myself and Mitchell, run a clean, honest business, which we have worked over the last thirty-some years to build. I have no clue as to what these properties in question have to do with our business."

Pierce remained quiet and leaned further back into his chair. His short salt-and-pepper hair was cropped to a fine military perfection, making his face appear much rounder. Unequivocally and confidently, his dark brown eyes did not turn away from Gavin's stare.

"Well, we do have a list of potential employees we would like to question about the properties," Gavin said. Flipping over a stack of papers, he produced a simple document with the names of the employees and handed it to the bulky lawyer.

Immediately, the lawyer snatched the piece of paper and placed it in front of his clients. While Mr. Sanford did look it over, Mr. Pierce only intensified his glare.

"Of the said employees on this list, I can assure you that they no longer work for the company," Sanford answered.

"It doesn't matter. Your company still has third-party rights to the possession of these properties." Gavin leaned onto the desk, positioning himself to face Mr. Pierce. "I ask again, please provide me with the key name and contact information for Zanders Holdings."

"My clients will give you the numbers of these former employees," Mr. Hewittson answered back as his thick fingers fumbled the piece of paper.

"That may be," Derrick stated, "but the fact remains that Pierce's signature is on the deed of the property."

At that point, Derrick pulled out copies of the final page of each agreement, which provided the signatures of the seller. Then he slid them over the table. Along with Bolder and Schumacher, Sanford studied the documents. They looked at each other, shrugging shoulders and softly whispering to themselves.

"Mr. Sanford," Gavin spoke up, looking directly at the man, who seemed surprised. "I do believe that you run an honest business. I am sure that you conduct your affairs ethically. Yet," he turned his attention to Pierce, "we believe your partner does not hold the same standards."

"Detective, that course of discussion is on the lines of slander," Mr. Hewittson rebutted.

"What are you trying to say?" Sanford's voice was scratchy as he finger-combed his salty-colored hair back. "Mitchell, explain to these officers that we have nothing to do with these properties."

Pierce remained firmly silent.

"Mr. Pierce, can you verify this is indeed your signature on these documents?" Evelyn inquired.

"Honestly, this is the most absurd thing I have ever heard," Sanford said, slumping back into his chair. "Mitchell, just tell them that we are not involved. Just tell them—"

"Shut up, Donald," Pierce commanded. His dark eyes did not shift away from Gavin.

Sanford's hands flew up. He stood and exclaimed, "Enough! This is enough!"

In unison, Bolder and Schumacher stood up and left the room without issuing a goodbye to Gavin, Derrick, or Evelyn. They were scattering like cockroaches under a bright light.

"Shut up and sit down, Donald," Pierce commanded, his voice deep and authoritative. "You are making a fool of yourself. Detectives, we need to consult our lawyer at this time. Please excuse us."

"I expect an answer when we return," Gavin replied.

******

"Got their cages rattling," Evelyn softly spoke as they gathered near the couches.

"Sanford's pissed." Derrick nodded toward the now closed door.

Hushed, inaudible words could be heard from the aquarium-like room. Gavin particularly noted how Sanford's angular shadow was distanced from the still-sitting Pierce shape.

"Their partnership must be at a crossroads," Gavin surmised, keeping his voice low.

"Keeping secrets in any relationship is a death kill," Evelyn stated.

Abruptly, Sanford pulled open the door, which slammed against the wall, and marched toward them. His gaunt face appeared to be reddened from either anger or embarrassment—Gavin could not decide. A few paces behind him, the portly lawyer followed.

"Detectives, I did not know about Pierce's involvements,"

Sanford huffed slightly.

"Please, Donald, let me take care of this," Hewittson finally said as he caught up.

Without turning around and still staring at Gavin, Sanford replied angrily, "Larry, you have enough to handle now." Then he said to Gavin directly, "I am no longer in this portion of the conversation."

"Your involvement is key to our—" Derrick began.

"Larry," Sanford said as he turned to look at the lawyer. "You no longer represent me. I will freely speak to the detectives on my own accord."

"You are making a huge mistake," the lawyer warned with a furrowed brow.

"Get the hell away from us," Sanford demanded.

The lawyer scuffled off, looking bruised, and escaped back into the room.

Folding his arms across his chest, Sanford's eyes darted from the conference room and back onto Gavin. "This is such a mess," he said gravely.

"How long was Pierce lying to you about business dealings?" Derrick inquired.

"It's recent," the elderly man returned.

"You must have known longer, Mr. Sanford," Evelyn commented. "This place is almost completely deserted."

"Mitchell was always an aggressive business person," the man said softly. Sanford's light eyes drifted from them to the window. "He really created and developed our business. His steadfast stubbornness and willpower challenged my own practices as we joined together years ago. Outside of work, we shared most of our lives together—family gatherings, our children growing up together and becoming friends. Now, it's all for naught."

"Did you know about his purchases and leases?" Gavin asked.

"Yes, I did," Mr. Sanford stated simply. "After some time. I did not question the acquisitions. I should have followed up. When a couple of risky pieces fell through early this year, I hired Paula for that reason."

"Like a watch dog?" Derrick added.

"Yes," he admitted. "Typically, on larger pieces, we would

both give approval." Slowly shaking his head, the man sighed heavily. "I knew about the warehouse and the theatre. Mitchell assured me that he was handling the buyer. I had my own accounts and businesses to woe and keep happy. It was… is, all a game. And I was a fool."

"Did you know about Zanders Holdings?" Gavin inquired, looking at the man.

"No, not until last Friday." He put a hand to his chest feebly. "I swear on my grandchildren."

"But that doesn't mean you aren't part of this," Evelyn stated.

"Detectives, I am confiding in you," Sanford seemed to plead, "because when I saw the reports on the news about the fires, they were our properties. I asked Schumacher to quietly dig into them. Mitchell's hands were all over them."

"Why didn't you come to us?" Derrick said.

Sanford's lips pursed. "I couldn't." Then he added quickly, "Last week, when I heard through the receptionist that you called, I approached him about the sites. In typical Mitchell fashion, he told me not to worry. His usual bullshit. It was the final straw, among many, with him."

"Is that the reason why the floor is empty?" Derrick said.

"Since *his* business dealings have been jeopardizing *my* livelihood," Sanford replied carefully, "in the recent month, I officially dissolved our business partnership and opened my new office out in Oakbrook. Most of the realtors and staff are out there now."

"So they jumped ship too, to join you," Derrick said. "Must have pissed off Pierce."

"He dug his own grave, Detectives," the man replied simply. "I still run a clean, ethical business. I assure you I had nothing to do with these lease agreements with that company. Next time you would like me to discuss S and P business dealings, my own lawyer will be present. Have a good day."

Sanford turned and walked down the same long hallway where Schumacher and Bolder were waiting for him.

Obviously, they were not staying for the rest of the show.

TWENTY-FOUR

Settling back into the same chair, Gavin purposely sat directly in front of Pierce as both Derrick and Evelyn flanked his sides. The elderly bulbous man, who wore thick-rimmed rectangular glasses, contemptuously grinned, much like a malicious clown baiting young children to the back of a tent. The sternness of his round face created deeper creases around the edges of his lips and eyes. In front of him sat several files, neatly stacked.

At the same time, Evelyn spread out the property leases and purchases of each building. Out of the corner of his eye, he could see the parts Mary had highlighted in various columns. Next to him, Derrick subtly cleared his throat, leaned further back in the chair, and gave Gavin a quick nod. His partner was ready to fight.

Clearing his throat, Hewittson stated, "I am here as legal representation only on behalf of Mr. Mitchell Pierce. As discussed out in the foyer, Mr. Sanford did not retain any legal representation, and therefore, any words you and Mr. Sanford exchanged can be considered inadmissible in court."

"Mr. Pierce, can you please explain your involvement with the Zanders Holdings Group?" Gavin questioned, staring straight at him.

"I represent their interests." His scratchy voice indicated years of smoking.

"Then, please, can you explain their interests?" Derrick asked lowly.

"Gentlemen, and lady," Pierce replied sardonically, nodding toward Evelyn, "I am not a judge for what other businesses do. I only provide them given locations with the best potential to make their models come to life."

"From the lease agreements of the theater and warehouse,

which date back to oh-one and ninety-nine," Gavin said as he slid two documents in front of him, "it looks like you've had business dealings with them for a while. May we ask how you began your relationship with Zanders Holdings?"

Grinning more, he said simply, "A friend with mutual interests."

"Who's the friend? Can you give us a name?" Derrick questioned.

"What does that have to do with your murder investigation?" Hewittson interjected.

"We need to know all parties involved," Derrick stated.

"Mitchell, you do not have to give that information," the lawyer said to his client. "It does not pertain to properties in question."

Pierce remained quiet.

"Mr. Pierce," Gavin casually reiterated, "why do you represent this company for these lease agreements? What do you have to gain from it?"

"Profit," he said. "Plain and simple."

Shifting through the paperwork, Derrick pushed over a lease document with a red circle around a name and queried, "Who is Fernando Guerillo?"

Pierce said nothing for a moment. The grin slipped slightly.

Derrick's contact in public works had given him that name on three of the four locations from various utility statements.

"A person," Pierce replied.

Next to him, Evelyn shifted slightly in her chair and gave Gavin a side glance as she took copious notes.

"We need to speak with Guerillo," Derrick stated. "His involvement could be key in our case."

"I don't see how he—" the lawyer began.

"Mr. Pierce," Gavin deflected Hewittson. "Several young women have been abducted and murdered, with close to two dozen other casualties—all killed in your locations. All of which are specifically linked to Zanders Holdings properties. We believe that the person is purposely using them to carry out a message."

"Still don't see how speaking with Guerillo could possibly benefit you, Detectives," the lawyer responded indignantly. "Seems awfully circumstantial at best."

"We can subpoena all necessary documents pertaining to a possible suspect," Derrick counter-attacked. "And even possibly personal accounts."

"That's enough, Mitchell," the lawyer announced as he started to stand. "You don't need to take this abuse. I believe that this meeting is adjourned."

"We know that you can assist us, Mr. Pierce," Gavin returned, looking straight at the man. "We are here to find a serial murderer."

"While crucifying my client?" Hewittson stood up, seemingly aghast. "That hardly seems..."

"You made a lot of profit with Zanders Holdings, did you not?" Gavin interrupted.

"You don't need to treat my—"

"All that profit was shared equally between you and Mr. Sanford, correct?" Gavin pressed on.

"Mitchell, let's go—"

"Imagine if we subpoena your accounting reports and discover that Mr. Sanford was indeed benefiting from your questionable business practices. Imagine that we have to get the district attorney to investigate Mr. Sanford. After many costly court proceedings, he will eventually have to pay for restitution for illegally avoiding taxes."

"That's impossible," the lawyer huffed out.

Gavin put his elbows on the table and stared at the elderly man. "Mr. Pierce, your relationship with that company also affected Mr. Sanford. If you are willing to see your old business partner go to a federal prison for your misdoings, you have a far stronger conscience than I."

"Outrageous!" the lawyer exclaimed as he pushed back the chair.

Gavin noticed that a small smirk came and went from Evelyn's lips. Next to him, Derrick leaned back in the chair, watching them like a bulldog.

Subtly, Pierce put his hand on Hewittson's forearm and said softly, "Sit down, Larry."

"What?" The lawyer was amazed.

"I will answer your questions," Pierce stated, "under one condition."

"What would that be?" Derrick stated.

Pierce's eyes shifted from Derrick to Gavin. "Sanford is not to be investigated in any manner."

"What are you saying, Mitchell?" The lawyer was in disbelief.

Without turning, he said, "Larry, you are my counsel. But you need to learn to shut the fuck up. And just listen."

Slowly, the lawyer sank to his chair and leaned back, shaking his head.

"We can arrange that," Gavin said. "Sanford will be free from any charges for dealings involving the Zanders Holdings Group."

Nodding, Pierce said, "Very well. Let's proceed." He glared at Gavin bitterly for a few moments before reaching for the glass next to him and drinking the rest of his water. A few drops fell from his chin onto the table. Gavin could tell that Pierce was carefully forming what he was about to say.

"I met a representative of Zanders Holdings in the mid-nineties," Pierce finally said.

"Can you give us a name?" Evelyn asked quickly, her pen tapping the paper.

A smug smile settled onto his thick face.

Without answering her, he continued. "The same time, Sanford and I expanded our burgeoning realty company. With my few connections and courting many Chicago officials for government business, our firm had many possible opportunities. For the most part, Donald catered to mainly residential and small business clientele. A section of business that was, and still is, less than forty percent of the profit. Even now, Donald believes his new company will grow and become successful. Did he not learn his lesson from the last economic downturn? Only time will tell.

"I, on the other hand, was more aggressive. I sought large corporations, both national and international. In fact, many of the new businesses that are resurging in the large towers downtown are some of my work. To drive more profits, I aggressively went after new businesses. Any business that needed space. Since the Chicago area had an ample supply, I was willing to drive it."

Gavin noticed Evelyn had stopped taking notes and sat back straighter in her chair. Derrick leaned forward and rested his elbows on the dark table.

"In ninety-eight or ninety-nine," Pierce continued, "I

convinced Donald it would be necessary to purchase some buildings and lease out offices. Various buildings, sections in high-rises and such, were easily available. Donald understood how much profit was to be made. After some financial maneuvering, I began to purchase spaces, rehab them slightly to suit any business needs, and then began our leasing program."

"Including residential homes on the South Side," Derrick commented.

Pierce's eyes scanned Derrick briefly, and then Evelyn. Soon they settled back on Gavin. Clearing his throat, he stated, "When my *mutual* friend introduced the Zanders contact to me, their interest in obtaining several unique properties throughout the city was astounding. With their contracts, I was able to increase yearly fees, add extra fees for increasing space, and tack on maintenance fees. Truly, out of all my leasers, they were the best clients and most…"

"Profitable," Gavin finished.

"Exactly." Pierce sat straighter. "Again, their requirement for many types of venues and locations varied throughout the city, but one in particular had been the theater on the South Side. I didn't care. We were making money. They approached me about the warehouse, explaining that the company needed space for distribution of goods."

"Did you ever ask what the nature of their business was?" Derrick questioned. "I mean, to see what your company was representing, that is."

"Detective," Pierce returned sarcastically, "does a realtor ask what kinds of belongings you possess when you move into your new house? No. Yes, I know I've assisted technological companies, phone companies, oil and gas businesses, steel businesses, and some retail clothing distributors. Because those clients divulged their needs to me directly. Some clients don't explain their exact needs and just request space and size requirements."

"You never directly asked what Zanders Holdings Group was based on?" Evelyn then asked.

"No," he said softly. "I obtain properties for businesses to meet their needs and, if applicable, that of their customers."

Enough of his slippery responses. "When did you become involved with Guerillo?" Gavin asked.

"About three years ago or so," he replied. "He was one of many main contacts I dealt with for that company. Upon our agreement, any Zanders Holdings representative would directly contact me, and I would assist in their needs. Thus, the buildings in your investigation are only a small group within the city."

"We will need a listing of their locations," Evelyn quickly stated.

His smug smile widened. Without turning toward his lawyer, he said, "Larry, can you give them that folder now?"

Instantly, the lawyer slid a dark blue folder over to Evelyn. She opened it and then passed it over to Gavin. Briefly, he looked down and saw three pages of locations. Many, many locations. Derrick leaned over and pointed at the house on Ashland Avenue and the Opus Theater on the first page.

"As far as I know," Pierce added, "about two-thirds of those locations are empty. They continued to change locations."

"Did they ever explain the reasoning?" Gavin stated.

"Never," he said. "They paid their contract fees from old locations in order to set up a new location."

"Extra profit?"

"Yes." Pierce folded his arms onto the table. "Recently, Guerillo's interest was in some townhomes and smaller local front businesses throughout the north part of the city."

"How recent was that?"

"About six months ago."

"Do you have a number we can reach him at?"

"Certainly." Pierce straightened his back. "The condition is that I can be pardoned from any possible criminal actions on their part."

"Protecting your profits, Mr. Pierce?" Derrick asked.

"No, Detective, reputation."

"Mr. Pierce," Gavin returned sardonically, "you are going to be charged for aiding a fraudulent company, which is a federal crime. You do realize that the IRS will be sifting through your business and personnel bank accounts for not reporting your actual income over the last decade. Also, the DA will charge you for impeding and obstructing a murder investigation. If you would like to keep your charges simplified, please provide Guerillo's contact information."

After a few long moments, the soft hiss of the heater filled the quiet room.

Pierce finally said, "From what I understood, while working

with Zanders Holdings Group, the representative was in charge of wholesale and distribution of their products."

"What kind of products?" Derrick inquired.

"Mitchell, you don't have to answer," the lawyer returned.

"As part of our lease agreements," Pierce said, ignoring Hewittson, "we make several surprise inspections once a year. For maintenance purposes only. Check the structure and condition of the property. While I did not personally inspect any location, the reports indicated that, um, adult-related merchandising was obvious throughout their company. Like the warehouse on Damian."

"The porn industry is a billion-dollar industry," Derrick commented.

Briefly looking at Evelyn, Pierce seemed almost embarrassed. "Yet it was one report that disturbed me." He paused for a moment and then continued. "Several months ago, I went to the Merchant Mart, where the last fire had been, to see for myself. Knowing that Guerillo was not there, a colleague and I observed the rows and rows of, um, adult toys, items, clothes, and movies."

"So they were selling adult materials—what's the crime in that?" Gavin asked.

"We did not go there to look at that, but to confirm something else," Pierce returned. "In the back, there were two rooms with cameras and lights. A king-size bed with white silk sheets was in the center. On a nearby table, several sex toys, oils, and boxes of condoms were laid out. In the next section, there was a makeshift film editing bay, which was in complete disarray."

"They were making their adult videos?" Derrick inquired.

"Yes," the elderly man replied angrily. "Not part of the lease agreement. We don't have liability for that. Two days later, Guerillo finally replied to my calls. He told me to, um, go fuck myself. Within the next six weeks, the last of the nineteen locations closed up simultaneously. The company broke the agreements and did not pay out the rest of their contracts. I lost a lot of money, which affected *our* business."

"That made Sanford dissolve your partnership, correct?" Evelyn said.

Nodding his head, he said, "Yes. I lost nearly half of my wealth in less than a year."

You are going to be losing more than that, Gavin thought. "May we have your information on Guerillo?"

Pierce opened a nearby folder and slid a paper over to Gavin.

"As part of our current procedures," he stated, "we require all leasers or managers of the property to have a picture ID submitted. You know, in case of situations similar to this."

The photo of the California driver's license showed a man who appeared to be Mediterranean. He had a strong build, a rather round face full of thick facial hair, and menacing dark eyes.

*****

Back at the station, Gavin was typing up the report from their Sanford and Pierce meeting. As he recounted Pierce's opinion about the Zanders Holdings Group, he thought the possibility of the Sills video being connected to Zanders Holdings seemed highly likely.

Could the suspect have known about this all along?

"Have a question for you," Evelyn said, scooting over on her chair.

Continuing to type and not looking at her, he said, "Go ahead."

"Just scanned over the documents," she stated. "How did you know that Pierce was on the take?"

Stopping, he glanced over at her with a coy smile.

"Evelyn, sometimes you have to look at the whole picture," he replied, leaning back in his chair. "Remember Pierce? The Armani gray suit, the large gold Rolex, the diamond pinky rings and manicured hands? Sanford wore a dark blue suit, worn sleeves, a faded dress shirt, and worn brown leather shoes."

"Got that just from clothing?"

"No, the response to the murders," he reaffirmed. "Sanford was surprised and even concerned. Whereas..."

"Pierce had a grudge the minute we walked into the conference room," she finished.

"Exactly. You get it."

"Are we going to investigate Pierce's financial records any further?" she inquired.

"No." He shook his head. "We are homicide. But when I'm done with the report, I'll tell Creighton he should hand over a copy to the DA. Probing fraudulent businesses is their specialty."

"What about Sanford?"

Shrugging his shoulders, Gavin returned, "I made a special note about it, but not my call."

Before Evelyn could say anything, Derrick dropped his phone down and said loudly, "Seems as if this Guerillo is a ghost."

"What do you mean?" Gavin sat straighter, seeing the frustration wash over Derrick's face.

"For the past two months," he explained, "no activity on his bank accounts and credit cards. Rent was paid in advance, in cash mind you, for the last six months."

"No one disappears," Evelyn stated as she stood up.

"They do if they don't want to be discovered," Gavin said simply.

"G, I'll dig deeper into his life and see what I can find," Derrick said. He looked up at Evelyn. "Want to help?"

Evelyn nodded and joined him in the search.

As he was about to return to his work, Gavin's phone rang. A seven-zero-eight area code.

"This is Detective Nolan," he answered.

"Yes, Detective. This is Dr. Kimberly Saunders from the University of Chicago," a strong, soft feminine voice breathed into his ear. "You made an inquiry about the manager of the Opus Theater. I'm not sure what information I can provide. I was just recently made in charge of the property in the last two years."

The theater. Almost forgot. Grabbing his notes on the theater, Gavin said, "I understand completely. Does the realty firm, Sanford and Pierce, mean anything?"

"No, not at all."

"What about Zanders Holdings Group?"

"Zanders what?" She paused. "No, does not ring a bell. Sorry."

"Then who was in charge of the theater from the university?"

The sound of papers flipping rustled in the background. "Ted McFarland."

Writing the name down, he said, "Do you have any current number for McFarland?"

"Sorry, no. That would be in Human Resources," she said abruptly.

"Very well," he said, knowing this was a dead end.

"But I can tell you why he was let go," she replied in a hushed tone. "When I became part of the department several years ago, I heard a rumor through the faculty grapevine that the theater was being investigated by the police."

Not exactly. "Well, that was true," he lied.

"Yes," she said. "I heard from the student body that they would go to the midnight showings. I wondered what they were talking about. One of my PhD students informed me the theater was playing pornographic movies."

"Obviously scandalous for the university," Gavin returned.

"My gosh, yes!" She bit off some laughter. "When the school did an internal investigation, they found out Ted McFarland was behind the whole thing, charging tickets on the side and keeping the money." She paused. "McFarland was fired immediately and supposedly forced to pay back the stolen money to the university. That never happened."

"So will HR give me his current number or address?"

"Actually, Detective," she said, "no."

"Why?"

"Because he died last year. A car accident. He was drinking, I guess."

With that, he ended the conversation.

On the surface, the business was legitimate in selling and distributing adult merchandise, and operated perfectly in several locations. However, Zanders Holdings Group also was involved in some non-legitimate dealings: pornographic films at the Opus Theater, making adult videos at the Merchant Mart, and strange noises at the Ashland house. While the list contained proper warehouse locations like the one on Damian, the other properties— single family homes, apartments, condominiums, and townhomes— seemed rather questionable.

Was the suspect leading us to these spots? Why kill these women in these locations?

Then there were the fragments of CDs that were found on Gable and Carlton, and the entire disc found on Sills. Remembering the video, Gavin knew Sills had been filmed, tied up, beaten, and even raped. How was Zanders Holdings connected to the fires and the bodies? Suddenly, he stopped typing and looked over at the whiteboard. The suspect had created these explosions and purposely targeted these women. Gavin glanced over the destruction of the locations. *The suspect knew about all of this. But how?* Standing up, he stared at the three victims' faces and then back at their charred remains. They never knew they were being filmed.

Yet, thinking about the film, the cameraman was always there.

The suspect is telling us about the other guy. Putting a hand to his chin, he glanced over at Derrick and Evelyn, who were absorbed in their own work and did not notice him.

The son of a bitch had a partner.

PART IV

COLLEEN

"He had been defeated by that which he had sought to destroy."
—*Richard Wright*

"Why can't I get you off my mind
Clips of your body on rewind
If I come over would it be right…"
—*Tank*

TWENTY-FIVE

"Your hand's clammy," Chad commented softly to Gavin.

The elevator doors before them opened to his mother's floor. The all-too familiar nursing station was straight ahead. Behind the orderly desk, handwritten patient names were displayed on a large wall, indicating daily statuses on medicines, check-ups, and the like. His mother's name, *Josephine N*, was near the middle. On the corners of the counter, papier-mâché turkeys guarded some decorative gourds and corn. On either side of the desk, the signs of the holiday season were fast approaching: a small, sparsely decorated Christmas tree to the left and a menorah to the right.

"This way," Gavin replied nervously, letting go of Chad's warm hand.

A bemused smile caressed Chad's thick lips as he clutched a small bouquet of daisies. He insisted on bringing Gavin's mother something as a gesture. Gavin had suggested those because his mother loved daisies, having grown them in their backyard for years and letting them spread throughout the garden like a rustic open field.

Sounds of laughter and conversation drifted down the hallway from the activity room. Reaching room seven fifty-six, Gavin guided Chad inside.

"Mom," he said quietly, taking a couple of steps inside. Clearing his throat, he said louder, "Josephine."

Her bed was empty and neatly made.

"Not here?" Chad asked behind him. "Her room is nice."

Chad went past him and surveyed the younger pictures of himself, Evan, and their father on the wall. His fingers touched the photographs, and his smile increased.

"Probably down the hall," Gavin said, pivoting on his heel.

Chad turned to him and said, "You were a cutie as a kid."

Feeling a knot in his stomach, Gavin began to walk back to the hallway when he nearly bumped into Mavis. She was one of the regular nurses he saw on his Sunday visits.

"Oh, Jesus, sorry, Mr. Nolan," she said. Her crisp uniform fit her stocky frame snuggly.

"Mavis, it's Gavin," he said with a half-smile.

"Yeah, yeah," she answered quickly as her black eyes darted down the hallway. "Part of new policy is to address family by last name." Suddenly, she noticed Chad standing behind him and gave him a syrupy smile.

"What're you doing working a holiday?" Gavin stepped aside to let Chad out of the room.

"Well, I can either work Christmas or Thanksgiving." Her eyes remained on Chad. "I'd rather work today. 'Cause my daughter is forced to make me a turkey feast."

"Is she a good cook?" Chad asked.

"No, honey," she cooed slightly, smiling wider and showing her teeth. "Not like me, sugar." She then asked, "Mmm, what's your name?"

"Chad," he replied, taking her petite hand. "Gavin's best friend."

"Such a tall, fine man, aren't you?" Mavis pressed back her hair, licking her lips and touching her chocolate-toned face subtly.

"Did anyone get my message?" Gavin asked before Chad could reply.

"Yes, I just brought her down there," Mavis stated, glancing over at him. "I wish you'd bring Mr. Chad here more often, Gavin."

"I think he might," Chad answered for Gavin.

"Would love to get to know more of you, sugar," she said, her voice extra husky. A room buzzer suddenly sounded beyond the elevators. Sighing heavily, she stated, "Never stops." She glanced over at Gavin, smiling. "Your momma is in the usual place. She's been real talkative the last couple of days. More alert too. I told her you were coming to see her today, and she seemed happy about it."

Another buzz echoed down the hall.

"Yeah, yeah. Have to go, sugar," the nurse moaned to Chad, gripping his arm softly and letting go. A savvy smile was plastered on her face. "Maybe we all should go for some drinks sometime." She winked, turned, and walked away.

"Thanks, Mavis," Gavin replied, taking a glance over at Chad, who seemed to be holding back a laugh.

"Guess she likes you," Gavin mused.

"Cougars usually do," Chad replied.

*****

The clicks from their shoes off the hard laminate flooring hushed as they stepped onto the carpeted floor of the activity room.

Because of the holiday, more families than usual had gathered and sat in tight clumps throughout the place. Gavin noticed the same three elderly men sitting in their usual spots near a TV that played the Macy's parade, their somber faces staring blankly at the other new people. Over these years visiting the Alzheimer's floor, Gavin would often catch distant expressions on the men's faces as they took in the strangers around them. Perhaps they were recalling their own memories of familiar faces from long ago. However, as Mavis explained to him one time, those men no longer had family visiting them. A part of him ached for them, realizing they had become invisible to the kept surroundings.

Chad's hand clamped onto his shoulder and he asked, "Is that your mom over there?"

Across the vast space in the bright sunlight, his mother sat with her slender back facing them near the corner window. Her favorite spot.

"Yes," Gavin replied softly.

As if feeling his hesitation, Chad whispered softly, "Come on. It'll be okay. I'm excited to meet her."

As they approached her, his mother sat quietly in her wheelchair, and she stared out into the sunny sky. Her long, gaunt face had a touch of makeup, which was rare for her, so a glimpse of life seemed to capture her emaciated features. With a long dark brown skirt and hazel-colored top, his mother appeared more put together than the rest of the patients, most of whom wore lounging outfits. Unaware of their presence, her lips moved as if she were speaking to someone.

Thanks, Mavis.

"Mom," Gavin said uneasily. "Happy Thanksgiving."

Chad moved around to the other side of her, hunkering into

an overstuffed chair.

"Josephine," Gavin said louder as he crouched down, taking her cool, fragile hand.

At that moment, she saw him, and her face lit up. Her thin, pale pink lips smiled.

"Bogie," she said softly.

"Bogie," he said to Chad, "was actually William, my mother's brother. My uncle. Not sure why the family called him that."

Chad said nothing and stared at his mother with an endless smile.

"No, Mom, it's Gavin."

Slowly, her head craned over to Chad. A more perplexed, almost curious expression overtook her face.

"Hello, Josephine. I mean, Mom," he said quickly. "I'm Chad." Chad's dark eyes fluttered between his mother and Gavin.

"This is, um," Gavin started. His hands were sweaty and his heart raced slightly. "This is my friend…my…"

"I'm Gavin's friend," Chad interjected, eyeing Gavin.

Her head rotated back and forth slowly between Chad and Gavin. Then she gave a small grin of acknowledgement—something he had not seen in a while.

"Donnie?" his mother asked Chad. "How can you be here?"

Chad looked at Gavin, who shrugged his shoulders.

"Who's Donnie, mom?" Gavin asked.

"Bogie, you know," she said simply and pointed at Chad.

"No, that's Chad," Gavin said louder.

"Silly, Bogie, always silly," she teased back. She put her hand on Chad's arm, patting it gently. "Donnie, you were always so strong. What are you doing here today?"

"It's Thanksgiving," Chad replied warmly.

"My goodness, Thanksgiving already." She seemed more excited. "Such a nice holiday to be together. Is that why you are here, Donnie? Taking a break from school out east?"

"Yes, I am." Chad put his large hand tenderly over hers.

"Bogie, why don't you invite him for dinner?" Then she looked back at Gavin and pointed toward the window. "Mother made enough."

"I think I will," Gavin stated, and then he looked at Chad. "Mom, I have to tell you something."

"What is it?"

"Chad is more than my friend. He's... my... um... my..." His voice was quivering slightly, and he stopped. His eyes began to well up as he looked at Chad holding his mother's hand, realizing she would never really know the truth about him and his new life.

"What's wrong, hon?" his mother asked sincerely.

Gavin turned away slightly and felt the sting of tears come to his eyes.

"Josephine, what Bogie's saying," Chad answered. "Bogie and I have feelings for each other. And we are more than friends."

For a few lingering moments, the murmurs of talking, music piped in over the speakers, and the faint sounds of the television seemed to take over their small space. With a sense of guilt, he wiped the tears from the corners of his eyes and then looked over at Chad, seeing the compassion in his lover's equally teary eyes. Chad extended his hand, and Gavin held it in front of his mother, who watched carefully.

"Good," his mother finally said. "Bogie, I was waiting for you to tell me. I've known for some time."

"You did?" Chad inquired softly before Gavin could speak.

Placing her hand back on her leg, she leaned into Chad slightly. "Yes. I saw you and my brother kissing the other night. When you got home."

Gavin looked up at his mother. "You saw that?"

"Yes, and more." She smiled. "Please don't be angry. I didn't want to talk to you until you were ready."

"I suppose," Gavin began, feeling a sense of relief release from him.

"You know," she whispered, "be careful of Father though. He doesn't like to hear about that sort of thing. Especially in our house."

Uncle William was gay... That was news to Gavin. "Right," he agreed. "We won't tell Father."

"If you don't mind, Donnie," she inquired softly, "please tell me what you like about Bogie so much?" Then she turned slightly to Gavin and said, "A sister has to know these things about her baby brother."

"You are right, Josephine," he replied, holding back his tears.

For the next hour or so, Gavin listened to and observed the

conversation between Chad and his mother. As Chad described their first few dates in detail, his mother lapped up the stories, nodding her head and intermittently asking questions. She seemed so enthralled and in the moment. His mother was actually engaged, lively, and almost herself in those moments. Perhaps it was Chad's charm working a certain magic on her. Sliding closer to Chad, Gavin placed his hand onto his leg and squeezed it.

Noticing the gesture, his mother leaned into Gavin and commented, "You make such a lovely couple."

"Thank you, Mom," Gavin replied and felt Chad kiss him quickly on the cheek.

"Bogie, Donnie," she carefully said, "don't worry. I won't tell anyone. It'll always be our secret."

"Sure, Josephine," he replied.

They stayed for another half an hour, until his mother began to grow tied. As Chad wheeled his sleepy mother back to her room, Gavin placed a hand on his lover's back and kissed him on the shoulder.

Gavin's feelings for Chad had solidified.

TWENTY-SIX

Derrick took the seat at the head of the dark oak rectangular table, with Maria to his left. Throughout dinner, the conversations did not cease when the turkey and all its prepared fixings arrived; instead, the chattering noise of talk and laughter filled the handsomely decorated dining room with life. The packed table held most of Maria's relatives, including her mother, who sat next to her. Gavin sat just to the right of Derrick, and next to him sat Chad. At the moment, Derrick and Chad were engaged in a conversation about the football stats, playfully arguing about recent plays and even predicting the Super Bowl.

After they'd arrived at Derrick's beautiful home in Riverside, a proud Maria whisked both Gavin and Chad on a tour of their three-story Craftsman style house. Each room reflected the old architecture with the dark wooden beams and thick baseboards, while a flair of Spanish influence modernized and echoed Maria's passion for interior design. While not going down to the basement where the kids and other family were hanging out, she informed them that they had just finished it off with a bar, play area, and large screen television. She termed it Derrick's Den. Briefly, she even showed off her mother's suite, which was a converted maid's quarters and looked spacious and comfortable. Throughout the tour, Chad continually complimented Maria about her taste in décor, pointing out things like the magenta color in the new baby's room and the Frida-inspired wall hangings. She was just excited to have Gavin over for the first time.

The holiday meal laid out before them had been mostly devoured, yet some lingering tidbits of food remained on each of the platters. The smells of roasted turkey, corn bread, spicy chilies, and even a hint of cumin continued wafting into his nose. Shifting slightly in his chair, he took a sip of the remaining wine in his glass. Maria reached for a bottle near her and filled it. Saying something to Lucinda, she looked over at him.

"Come on, Gavin, you have to eat some more." Her smile was wide. Then she added, "You're looking too skinny."

"That's what I keep telling him," Chad added in, stopping his conversation with Derrick, who was distracted by a young nephew.

"I'm good, really," Gavin replied with a smile back.

"*Dios mio*," Lucinda said with a grin, holding up the empty wine bottle. Her tightly woven bun showed off gray vines carefully intermixing with her rich black hair.

"Mama, I can do that," Maria snipped. At that point, she took her plate.

"Let me help you." Chad rose. "The least I can do."

"You're my guest," Maria replied. She then turned to her brother's wife, Angela, and said something in Spanish, gesturing toward Lucinda, who marched off into the kitchen. Angela complied and left the room, taking several dishes with her.

"You have a lot of dishes here," Chad began.

"Fine," Maria agreed. "But you have to open another bottle of wine."

"Great, cleaning up will go faster." Chad moved his chair back. A long groan of other chairs moving across the wood floor filled the space. As he moved away from the table, he said, "Maria, you have to explain to me how you made the chorizo corn stuffing. Fantastic!"

Several of her cousins at the end of the table chattered in Spanish to each other as they took plates into the kitchen as well. The male cousins, on the other hand, patted their stomachs, saying something to Maria before ambling to the basement. From the kitchen, the sounds of the clanking of dishes, murmurs of conversations, and running water began to fill the quiet space.

Ramone, Maria's brother and Angela's husband, stood. His large stomach stretched tightly against his royal-blue button-down shirt, made his loose tie appear smaller. He announced, "I'm sneaking downstairs to watch the beginning of the game. Got a hundred on this one." A loose grin stole his dark lips. "Want to come down with me, *papasito?*"

Derrick held up a hand and said, "Not yet."

Ramone nodded and slipped down the narrow corridor, keeping an eye on the kitchen. He looked like a school boy avoiding the mean teacher on the playground.

Leaning over, Susan whispered softly in Gavin's ear, "I just never knew you were, uh, batting for the same side. Especially for one of my soul brothas."

Earlier, when Susan arrived alone, bearing gifts of wine and chocolates, she hadn't said much to Gavin as she hungrily eyed Chad. As she stuck out her chest in her deep plunging red dress, ready to make her move, Gavin said softly to her, "Lay off my boyfriend." Before she could say anything, Maria had whisked her away to give her a private tour of the house.

"It doesn't just happen overnight," Gavin returned.

"Apparently not." Her husky voice oozed with sarcasm.

Casually, he glanced over at Derrick, who was already leaning back in his chair.

"What happened to your date?" Derrick questioned, resting his arms on the table.

"That ass-fuck," she groaned, rolling her eyes.

At that very same moment, a niece appeared around the corner, who looked to be about twelve, and came over to Derrick. Derrick shot Susan an evil glare, then spoke with the timid girl.

"Sorry." She pretended to zip her lips with her fingers. Subtly, she slid into Chad's empty chair and said to Gavin, "Stood me up this morning. I shouldn't date another paramedic."

"Sorry," Gavin said.

"No biggie." She leaned closer to him. "I'm happy for you."

Redness flushed his cheeks. "Thanks."

With a caring squeeze of his forearm, she replied, "I knew for a while that you weren't interested in women anymore."

That so? Gavin said nothing, letting his fingertips caress the rim of the wine glass.

"I like him already." A smile transformed her dark lips.

"Good. He's a good guy."

"You need that, especially after Emily," she commented. Drinking the last of her chardonnay, she whispered, "Plus, that boy's just fucking fine."

A grin hit his lips. "Yes, he is."

Then into his ear, she commented, "Bet the boy's packing a huge one. A stallion body like that."

Gavin leaned over and looked into the kitchen. Wearing a small apron over his dark sweater, Chad was hunched over the sink, washing some pans and talking with Angela and Maria. They laughed and jeered with him, along with the other cousins. All females in the room were either longingly scanning Chad up and down with their eyes, or finding some excuse to touch his back or arm or shoulder. Gavin turned away from the kitchen, knowing Chad was enjoying all the extra attention.

"The ladies are loving him." She stood, grabbed her glass of cabernet, and reached for a platter that had once contained roasted asparagus, portabella mushrooms, and squash. "You don't mind if I cop a feel of his tight ass?"

"Depends on him." Gavin gave her a wink.

Susan leaned over and kissed him on the cheek.

"You're a great friend." Her feline qualities showed themselves as she lazily ambled into the kitchen and pretended to be part of the conversation.

"What was that about?" Derrick leaned over. The niece looked down at her phone with a small smile and headed off.

"Acceptance," he replied back.

As promised, Lucinda returned with a gracious smile and a fresh bottle of wine. She poured a generous amount of wine into the glass.

"Gracias, *senora*," Gavin stated.

"*Tu amigo est...que hermoso*," she said softly with a grin. She grabbed a heavy platter containing the turkey meat with both hands and hobbled off.

"I think Lucy's got da hots for your new bitch," Derrick chided.

"She's not the only one," he stated. Then he asked, "What do you think of him?"

"He seems genuinely nice. Smart. A football fanatic too," he said simply. "As long as you're happy, I'm happy."

"So far," he admitted.

"You two went to see your mom before here?" Derrick queried and drank the rest of his wine.

Explaining the visit, Gavin finished with, "At least she was coherent today."

"All that matters is he got to see your family," he stated. "What about Evan?"

Shrugging his shoulders, Gavin returned, "Haven't told him yet."

"Understand." Derrick's eyes looked into the kitchen and went back to Gavin. He cleared his throat slightly and stated, "If he dumps you, I'll be the first one to kick his motherfuckin' black ass. Don't care how big he may be, I can take that fucker down."

Choking on a sip of wine, Gavin gave a quick laugh. Near them, the tan Pack 'n Play rustled with movement. Derrick's son, Ernesto, poked his head over the side. His dark complexion and radiant hazel eyes melted Gavin instantly.

"Good evening, little man," Derrick cooed, scooting his chair back and reaching over to the toddler. He scooped up the child with his large arms and placed him on his lap. "Have a good nap?"

Ernesto blinked over and over again while he sucked on his pacifier. His tiny fingers stretched out as Derrick's large hand covered his entire torso. The child's eyes stared relentlessly at Gavin in wonder.

"Is this his normal nap time?" Gavin drank some more of the delicious dry wine.

"No, but it was a big day." Derrick was looking down at his son, smiling. He prattled, "That's right? Huh? Bunch of people now? Right?"

At that moment, Maria came back into the dining area.

"*Ah baba, que vas? Bien? Bien?*" Her voice took on a high-pitched level of happiness. She went around the table to Derrick. Her dress billowed behind her, showing off the delicate curves of her small frame. No one could tell that she had given birth only a few weeks ago.

Ernesto jumped on Derrick's lap in response and clucked out monosyllabic tones and chants.

"Baby, why don't you sit and let them take care of the kitchen," Derrick said to her.

Tickling their son, she replied, "No, they already have it done anyway. Plus, I have to get this little *bambino* fed." She reached for Derrick's wine and took a generous sip. "That's better."

"Everything was exquisite, Maria," Gavin said.

"Thanks, anytime. You guys should come over more often." Scooping up Ernesto, Maria placed him on her hip. She then added, "Chad's funny, intelligent... and shit, hot as hell. That kitchen was getting too warm for me."

Gavin began to laugh.

"Shit, baby, what am I?" Derrick wrapped an arm around her waist.

"Potent baby maker." Maria hit his shoulder with a coy smile. At that moment, the baby monitor lit up and emitted sounds of screaming. "With that, I think I'll have you feed him while—"

Lucinda came around the corner then and turned off the monitor, saying something in Spanish quickly to Maria. Maria responded just as quick. Then in English, she said, "I can take care of her too."

"*No, tengo mi nieta, relajarse con sus amigos,*" the older woman said and went up the stairs.

Maria sighed heavily and looked at Gavin.

"Love her to death, but she's such a martyr." With that, she took another sip of wine and finished off Derrick's glass. "Getting ready for some tequila," she said to Derrick, who smiled. Then she looked down at Ernesto and said joyfully, "But you need something to eat. *Si. Vamonos. Comminda.*"

Soon, Maria left with the toddler.

Leaning on the table, Gavin listened as the sounds of the conversation took on a lighter, brisker tone. Perhaps Chad would have some stiff competition with the one-year-old. No matter. Gavin picked up the wine bottle and leaned over to fill Derrick's glass.

"No more wine." He placed his hand over his glass. "Too much wine, and I'll be shit tomorrow. Have to switch to Scotch."

"Never knew you liked Scotch." Gavin placed the bottle back on the table.

"Well, not since the kids came. I need to knock out at night." He shrugged his shoulders. "Work and shit."

"Yeah," he said. "Do you ever regret having kids?"

"No, couldn't imagine life without them." He slid back in his chair and slowly got up. "Not planning space between both of them has been tough. But Maria wanted them fast and out."

"Does she ever want to get back to work?"

He stifled a laugh. "She's ready to go tomorrow and escape the house. She has something lined up in January at Northwestern Hospital. Since Lucinda is here, daycare is covered."

"Smart."

"Yeah, but it has its consequences." Derrick looked over at

the empty stairs. "Lucinda is good with Ernesto and loves Gina, but Maria's right though. She fuckin' becomes pious and judges us on our parenting skills. Seriously old-school."

"Sorry, man."

"What about you?" he inquired.

"What?" Gavin was surprised.

"Kids? You know, having them."

"I don't know, never really thought of it," Gavin lied.

"Well, I know you and Emily were trying at one point."

"That was a different time, different place."

"So?"

"So I'm with someone new, a different lifestyle and—"

"And you have to consider expanding your family, right?" he pressed on. "Many gay couples have children."

"D, I just started introducing Chad as my boyfriend," he stated.

"Well, baby steps. I get it." Derrick held up a hand. "Just keep it in the back of your mind, Gavin. You would be a great father. So would he."

"You're buttering me up." Gavin's cheeks reddened again.

"No, it's the fucking wine." Derrick rose up from his chair. "Time to switch my flavor. Come on."

Glancing into the kitchen, Gavin saw Chad holding Ernesto in his strong arms as the child touched his dark chin in fascination. Maria was tickling his feet and cooing at him while Susan seemed to be enjoying the moment. Angela scrubbed dishes but took side glances at Chad, smiling. In that moment, somehow, children seemed like a plausible idea for his future.

Chad caught his glance and gave him a small but sexy grin, as if he enjoyed holding the child.

Lucinda came down the steps slowly with a pink bundle and went toward the kitchen. Gavin turned to hear the soft sounds of laughter and happiness.

TWENTY-SEVEN

They sauntered over to Derrick's living room on the north side of the house. Against the opposite wall, dark-stained built-in shelving bookended a huge fireplace with speckled olive granite surrounding it. The wood crackled in the hearth and radiated a pleasant warmth and richness to the space. Above the mantle, an elegant abstract picture of floral shapes popped against the rich indigo wall. Opposite the fireplace sat a nice dark leather sectional, where Gavin settled. The softness of the couch was undeniably comfortable and extremely inviting.

Derrick ambled toward the fire, opened the screen, and threw a couple of logs on the dying embers. Soon, the licks of orange flame slowly engulfed them. Over the crackles, the subtle sounds of Mary J. Blige could be heard.

Setting his glass on a nearby table, Gavin commented graciously, "You have a magnificent house."

"Thanks, man," Derrick replied with his back to him. "Not all my doing. Maria should be an interior designer."

"That she should be." He looked at several beautiful Talavera vases near the bookcases in the corner, close to the long window. "Can I ask a blunt question?"

"Never stopped you before," Derrick stated and looked at him.

"How did you get a house like this on a cop's salary?"

Smiling, he replied, "Not a cop's salary. A marine's." He ambled toward a small but beautiful liquor cart covered in silver etchings.

"Forgot."

"Never lived off the base. Rent was cheaper," he said matter-of-factly. "I just sacked my checks away for a rainy day."

"It's a beautiful payoff." Gavin glanced over at Derrick pouring himself a generous amount of Scotch in a crystal glass.

"Hell yeah." With his drink in one hand, he went over to a nearby recliner in the corner opposite Gavin and plopped down. "Only goddamn advantage I had when I left. Now, can *I* be goddamn blunt?" He shifted in his chair and then queried, "What's been on your mind? You were thinking a lot at the table."

"What do you mean?"

"I know you. You wanted to tell me something about the case."

Got me. True. "It's the holiday. Can't talk about work all the time," he began. Derrick had taken off Tuesday and Wednesday for the holidays—something Quinn had granted months ago.

"Bullshit," he interrupted. "What's up?"

Glancing over at Derrick, he said, "Before I tell you mine, tell me yours. What's up with Guerillo?"

Derrick's eyes rolled away. "He's a sticky little asshole. So many aliases. Hard to pin him down here in Illinois," he said. "I may have a lead. I'll check into it tomorrow."

"Thought you were taking Maria and the kids shopping?"

"It's going to be a motherfuckin' nightmare on Black Friday," he spit out and drank some Scotch. "Lucy's going to watch the kids. And, uh, we are going out. Santa has to come, you know."

A smile caressed Gavin's lips. "Yes, Santa. Forgot."

"Santa's the man, G," he retorted. "Besides, I can run in tomorrow real quick and check some emails. Look like I was in, you know."

"Got that right." Gavin raised his glass and took a sip of wine.

"And you?" His partner's tone reassured Gavin.

"I was getting nowhere in the past few days with this company." Gavin could hear the exasperation in his voice. "Zanders Holdings is a huge, huge, huge company. More or less an oligopoly. If a corporation can be considered a psychopath, then Zanders is the serial killer."

"All monies earned off of selling adult toys? I'm in the wrong fucking business," he replied.

"No shit," Gavin answered. "Started in the late eighties and only sold sex toys. Within two years, the company did so well that it bought several other adult business franchises. And grew and grew. In the early nineties, the company took a new shape and involved itself with media print. Ever hear of Big Ass Hooters and Asian Clickables?"

"Do I look like that type of person?" Derrick replied sardonically.

"The company grew exponentially," Gavin continued, "swallowing up smaller businesses. Its earnings hit half a billion dollars in sales by 1997. That year, the company ventured into the film business. It gobbled up small film franchises then rebranded them with a clear single name: Wet Valley Studios. Their biggest movie hits were based on typical girl-on-girl action. Around the turn of the new millennium, Zanders decided to purchase some smaller gay adult production companies, renamed Spurting Films. With both studios, Zanders reached two billion in sales by 2002. Even with 9/11, their company didn't hit rock bottom. It actually boomed."

"I'm following your lead here," Derrick stated. "But what does this have to do with real estate?"

"Good question—you did pay attention in school."

"Fuck off, asshole," Derrick chided and sipped more of his Scotch.

Remembering what he read, Gavin continued, "Zanders bought land and property for their warehouse distribution centers and whatnot. Like the theater on the South Side, it provided a platform for movies to be seen. Because the films were horribly produced, the sales fell in the theater and, evidently, they sold it to the university. As far as the warehouse, they moved their distribution site across the borders, just like any good American industry. Cheap labor and high profit.

"This is where it gets interesting." Gavin leaned forward, resting his elbows on his knees. "Around 2004, a particular church group, the name I've forgotten right now—some holy roller Baptist bullshit group—began protesting their Southern stores with large picket signs, rallies, and radio campaigns. In return, Zanders actually closed down the store fronts from the media pressure. Yet, they reopened similar stores with different names in the town over. In the same spots where the old stores had been, new Christian bookstores were placed under Brother's Keepers, a subsidiary of Zanders Holdings."

Derrick wore a suspicious expression on his face.

"Mary found a couple of case files about film studios in California and Hawaii being raided a year later. Turned out to be the very same Wet Valley Studios where underaged girls were being filmed. Some arrests were made, but the charges were dropped for lack of evidence."

"Sleazy fuckers," Derrick grunted. "Someone was bought off, I bet."

"Guess what Zanders Holdings did about it?" Without giving time for Derrick to answer, he answered himself, "The studio doors closed and are now located in Central America."

"Off the radar."

"Exactly." Gavin finished his wine. "In the last couple of years, Zanders profits have been falling significantly. The company lost close to half a billion dollars in revenue. From the information, I've read that smaller companies were sold off, but the film industry still remained. Now this leads us back to Chicago and the conundrum of the day. What does the savage murders of these women, the real estate company, and Zanders Holdings have in common?"

From the kitchen, dishes clanked slightly, and oohs and ahs over the children could be heard. Soft laughter from below the floorboards seeped through the air. The smell of cinnamon and fragrant spices drifted into the living room.

"Shit!" Derrick stood up. His eyes widened and he replied, "We're looking for two people."

Exactly. Gavin stated, "We have one person, the killer, who wanted us to find this out."

"We've been so focused on the brutal murders," he said excitedly, "we weren't seeing the other person. But..." His voice trailed off as he went toward the liquor cart.

"But what?"

"But," Derrick said with his back to Gavin, "is the suspect just playing name blame? Like he's using Zanders Holdings as a symptom of the problem?"

"No, the video says it all," Gavin responded back. "Our suspect—"

"Is the cameraman," Derrick replied, turning around. "Goddamn it."

"If we are on the same wave length," Gavin stated, "we have

to bring Evelyn in the loop. Perhaps that's why none of us were seeing the second person. He's the one really pulling the strings."

"What about Guerillo?"

"The key to finding our second guy," Gavin stated.

"I just don't get how we missed it." Derrick's voice was slightly angered and frustrated.

"Missed what?" Maria came into the living room. In her hand she held a glass of clear liquid with a couple chunks of ice and a lemon slice.

As if he'd been caught snooping in *Playboy Magazine*, Derrick changed his tone and a large smile came over his face. "Nothing at all. We were just talking about—"

"The Bears," Gavin piped in.

"Hell no," Maria replied with a slightly scowling look. "You guys were talking shop."

"Yes, we were. Sorry," Gavin added unconvincingly.

Maria's eyes darted at Derrick. "You have to change little Ernesto. You're turn today."

"Fine." Derrick shrugged his shoulders at Gavin. "I clean up the shit around here."

"You think you do," Maria retorted.

Walking over to her, he leaned over and kissed her on the forehead. "Mmm, I like this feistiness. Maybe later on, you and me—"

"Get the hell off of me." She smiled and hit his back. "*Va. Va.* He stinks bad. Chad's holding him."

Derrick smiled back at Gavin. Soon, his large frame turned the corner and was out of sight.

*****

With a smile, Maria stepped around the glass and metal coffee table and sat on the other end of the couch. Her light frame hardly shifted Gavin as she sat. Sighing, she sipped on her drink and glanced over at him with an exhausted face.

"You outdid yourself today," Gavin remarked. "Everything was exceptional."

"I enjoy entertaining," she said. "You should see when the entire family comes over. Drives Derrick absolutely insane."

Stifling a laugh, he returned, "I'm sure." Then he quickly added, "Look, Maria, I apologize for talking about work."

Holding a hand up, she responded, "Both of you are cops. I get that. Always on call."

"Yeah, but—"

"Derrick has been getting a lot better about bringing that shit home," she interrupted. Her eyes floated away from him toward the fire. "Having a family made him more, ah, centered."

Centered? I'll try that one next time.

Before he could speak, she continued, "Listen, I don't ask about his work, the cases you guys are on. Sometimes, I would like to know. And sometimes, I don't want to know. Like your last case, when you were in the hospital." She paused. "That could be Derrick one day. I get it."

"I'm sensing a 'but' here," Gavin commented softly.

"Since he has been partners with you, he seems more relaxed and at ease." Her subtle Spanish accent was fluttery and intoxicating, even though she had a serious tone. "He admires you, Gavin. He has a lot of respect for you and the work you put into each case. When you were in the hospital, he was upset. He probably never told you, so I'm telling you."

Never knew. Sipping his wine, he too stared at the orange flames.

"Gavin, what I'm saying," she said softly, "Derrick is a beast. Either he likes you or he doesn't. It's his nature. And when he does, he'll always have your back."

"Unless I piss him off."

"Easy to piss him off," she agreed. "He's such a military man, makes me sick really. So regimented. When I left the military, I turned it all off."

"What was he like in the military?" He glanced at her. Maria seemed lost in her thoughts as the glow of the fire accentuated her fine features.

"Never told you how we met, huh?" Maria took another generous sip of her drink. "Figures. When we met, he was broken. I'd heard stories about how great he had been, about his fine reputation. He could've been in the military still."

"What happened?"

"I'll let him tell you when he's ready. It angers me 'cause it was all just bullshit." Her back straightened on the couch. "When I met him, I was a nurse and he was injured. I knew the moment I saw him. He was the one."

Gavin was more intrigued. "Is that the reason why he retired from the marines?"

"Retired?" she returned. "No, Gavin. Not exactly retired. Discharged."

Discharged? What is Derrick not telling me? Gavin's eyes went toward the door. Soft voices and laughter could be heard over the ubiquitous rhythmic music. Maria craned her neck slightly and her eyes darted toward the dining room. Her motherly instincts seemed to take over and then relaxed at the sounds of the baby squealing in content.

"I have to ask," Maria finally said. "You two were investigating a death involving a person named Rhonda Sills, right?"

Should I answer her? "Yes." Then Gavin inquired, "Why?"

Her lips pinched together and her finger tapped on the glass. "Don't know if I should say anything."

"How about this," he said. "Tell me, and it goes no further than us."

"Promise?" Maria asked. "Derrick hates when I keep shit from him."

"Seriously," Gavin replied. "I'll check into it personally. He won't know."

A dubious look came over Maria's face. "If he trusts you, I trust you." She stared at him benignly. "If this is the same person, then I may have known her—well—helped her. Back in Afghanistan, I was a nurse. I'm sure he told you. That's how most of my education was paid through the military. Being deployed there... it was awful. Gritty and just goddamn nasty. Sand everywhere, roaches, huge-ass spiders... I hated it.

"It was about the middle of my tour when a Hispanic woman was brought in. She was discovered on the side of the road near the base just outside the village. She was semiconscious, delirious, stuttering, obviously on drugs. Her clothes were ripped and dirty. She had circular abrasions on her back and arms with teeth marks—like bite marks around her breasts and vagina—and narrow superficial cuts. When she came to, she panicked, hit one of the helpers, and wanted to escape. We had to restrain her and give her something just to calm her down. When she was calm, I asked her name. She said Rhonda Sills, an army private from a division in East Afghanistan."

"Did she explain what happened to her? Or even how she ended up with you?"

"She said that she couldn't remember. By her stats, she was severely dehydrated and malnourished. There was no determination on how long she was in the desert or how she got there." Maria looked straight at Gavin. "I felt bad for her."

"Was she sexually assaulted?"

Maria cocked her head to the side. "Yes, the doctor found evidence of vaginal bruising and scarring, along with anal bleeding. Clear signs of being sexually traumatized. No semen was discovered. Why?"

"Just curious."

"You wouldn't ask unless you knew something." A wave of clarification came over her face. "Was she the victim in the Merchant Mart last week?"

"Maybe," Gavin implied.

"I can help you," she replied excitedly. "I'll reach out…"

Suddenly, they heard the sounds of laughter and loud voices coming closer. Maria eyed the doorway and stopped talking.

Derrick turned the corner with Ernesto on his shoulders, who was giggling contentedly. Derrick's powerful hands engulfed his son delicately as he held on to him firmly. Behind him, Ramone was saying, "Then right at the quarter, they missed the fucking ball to score a touchdown. Those idiots are going to fucking lose, man!"

"Watch the mouth," Maria snapped instantly. Her mind was no longer on their conversation. "Be careful, baby."

"Always am," Derrick said.

Ramone went past him and came toward Gavin. "Missing a great game."

"Yeah, sorry," Gavin said.

"Not as sorry as I'll be when I tell Angela what I lost."

More voices could be heard then as the rest of the guests began to mingle in the dining room. Chad was carefully placing a chocolate torte in the center of the table, talking to Susan. She held a platter of sugar crescent cookies, and the smells of sweetness filtered into Gavin's nose. His stomach actually growled.

He returned to the dining table along with everyone else. Chad sat next to him with an arm around his shoulders.

Even as everyone was laughing and conversing about the horrible weather, the holidays, shopping, and everything else, Gavin's mind kept envisioning Rhonda Sills wandering through the Afghanistan countryside.

Unaware her rape had been filmed.

TWENTY-EIGHT

They encountered a horrendously packed freeway on the Kennedy. The first holiday weekend always brought people to the city for some shopping on Michigan, to relish in the holiday window displays, skate under the bean in Grant Park, see the latest play or musical, or even just walk around and take in the splendor of the city. Needless to say, the drive from O'Hare was longer than it should have been. Because of that, Gavin's mind lingered over Chad's goodbye. That morning, Chad had insisted on cooking an extravagant breakfast and serving Gavin in bed—wearing nothing but a tight apron around his strong hips.

A smile creeped across Gavin's lips.

Never had he felt this strongly for someone. Something about Chad electrified him and intoxicated his senses. With Emily, the sense of commitment and undying love had never truly surfaced, and he blamed himself for those years of not trying harder to salvage their crumbling relationship by seeing a marriage counselor.

He lifted the flap of his coat and sniffed Chad's rich woody scent. Chad's strong embrace at the drop-off clung to him, making him feel protected. Up ahead, the Division Street exit finally appeared and Gavin snaked his way over. Behind him, a car laid on its horn in reaction to a small delivery truck cutting in. Shaking his head, He navigated the car into the turn-off lane.

Near him, his phone flashed on, indicating a text from Derrick: *Only fifteen minutes away from the station.*

Quinn had texted him as he was driving Chad to the airport. A simple message: *Got your files as promised. You owe me.* Once he saw it, he called Evelyn and Derrick, leaving them messages.

Oddly, the focus on the case would be a good distraction.

However, his thoughts still slipped back to Chad and his lover's thick manhood pleasuring him.

*****

Gavin slipped out of his coat. The warmth of the station seemed stifling as moisture was building at the base of his back. Nearby, Evelyn sat at her desk, hunched over the screen. She seemed oblivious to Gavin's presence.

A large courier box sat in the middle of his desk. The address was directed to Quinn, and the return address was from Virginia. While Derrick suggested that normal protocol in civilian matters typically took several weeks, the fact remained that Quinn had the right connection to retrieve these files. But Gavin could not linger over the how—Quinn had produced them, as he stated he would.

Who would Quinn know in the military to be able to get these results so fast?

"Have you opened them?" Derrick queried behind him.

Turning slightly, Gavin noticed the dark bags under Derrick's eyes. Lumbering awkwardly forward, his partner shrugged off his khaki overcoat and set it over his chair. As if on cue, Evelyn stood up, straightening her shirt before snatching a piece of paper from the printer.

"Some good news, guys," she said matter-of-factly. "Thomas emailed me last night." She handed the paper to Gavin. "The explosives were tracked to an address in South Carolina. Their grade and the plastic equal the same potential amount in each explosion since the warehouse."

As Gavin glanced over the email, Derrick craned his neck to see over his shoulder. Thomas had written that they did not have sufficient conclusive evidence the explosives could be linked to the cases, further explaining that, *"It is highly probable the components and compounds are linked to the distributer given the quality and grade of the explosives."*

"Doesn't prove our killer had the means to obtain the explosives," Derrick stated.

"Yeah, but I can call and get records from any shipments to the Midwest," Evelyn replied.

"Do you realize how many addresses that could be, Evelyn?" Gavin returned.

"I'll go through it." Her voice sounded agitated.

"Fine," he concluded. "If you need Mylo to help you, and probably another officer, do it."

With a smile, she said, "Good."

All their attention went to the brown case. With a quick reach, Derrick opened the package and slid out the contents. He handed both Gavin and Evelyn one and kept one for himself. The insignias of the Marines and US Pentagon were stamped over the top of the folder. Gavin noticed the large stamp on the corner of the first page: *CLASSIFIED*.

"Fuck, I knew it," Derrick grumbled. "Goddamn military assholes. They redacted everything."

Gavin flipped through the document. All statements, witnesses, and locations were inked out by a black maker. No photographs were included, and signatures were clearly blacked out. The other files were the exact same way.

"Means we have shit, right?" Evelyn sounded equally as pissed as Derrick.

"Can anyone just redact a document?" Gavin asked naively.

Throwing the file on the desk, Derrick stated exasperatedly, "If any case involved a secret operation where American Intelligence could possibly be compromised, then the document can be redacted to protect potential secret missions and such. Standard fucking military procedure."

"Isn't there a copy?" Evelyn asked, paging through the file.

Shaking his head, Derrick stated, "No, this is it. Goddammit!"

About three desks over, a couple of other detectives glanced over at them.

"Then that proves it," Gavin replied.

"Proves what?" Evelyn crossed her arms over her chest, still clinging to the file.

Nodding his head, Derrick said, "You're right. Not dealing with just one."

"One what?"

"Evelyn, we have a theory," Gavin said.

He then explained their theory about the current killer and the person who was assisting him. For a moment, Evelyn did not say a word.

"The video backs up the claim," Evelyn finally said. "With this, how can we prove anything?"

"We can't. Not yet." Derrick spoke up. "My friend at the CIA sent over some last known addresses on Guerillo."

Friend at the CIA? Gavin said, "Do you think they'll be dead ends?"

"Not sure," he said. "Anyone want to go on a ride-along? It's a long shot, but someone must have seen him."

"I'll go," Evelyn offered. "While you're driving, I can contact the explosives company. Rattle their cage to get some addresses."

"Good work, D. Better than what we had before," Gavin stated. To Evelyn, he said, "Don't rattle too hard. So far it's all circumstantial. No hard proof. And copy me in any email. I can help."

"Got it." She stepped over to her desk and grabbed her wool coat.

"I'm going to keep digging into Zanders Holdings," Gavin told them. "What our suspect wants to know."

"If you two are right, and I believe you are," Evelyn said, placing a furry hat on, "that means the other guy is much more dangerous than our killer."

"Why do you say that?" Gavin asked, setting down the document.

"He was the one calling the shots," she said. "If he was the cameraman in the videos, he was directing our killer all this time. Perhaps the director and the actor had a problem. An argument."

Derrick stopped buttoning his coat and had a pensive look on his face. "Like creative differences?"

"Control," Gavin added in. They both looked at him with an astonished face. "Both of these guys had been partners, and then a shift between them occurred. Something our killer didn't like one bit." Gavin nodded at the victims. "They were an unfortunate consequence to his anger."

"If that's the case, G," Derrick simply said, putting on his jacket. "Our asshole is going to create a larger spectacle soon."

I couldn't agree with you more.

With that, Derrick and Evelyn left the station for the remainder of the day. Gavin stayed behind and clicked at the computer. Diving deeper into Zanders Holdings businesses, he searched the company's vast array of subsidiary companies. Many of which were located in Eastern Europe and the Middle East. A nagging thought began to form in the back of his mind: how did they meet? Evelyn was correct though—the two men had an argument. But over what? What made the killer start his rampage?

After a couple of hours, he sat back in his chair, his head throbbing. He dry-swallowed a prescribed blue tablet and rotated his head back and forth. His eyes landed on the darkened captain's office; Quinn had not come into the station at all today. That was absolutely fine with him.

Texts from Derrick and Evelyn broke up his afternoon. One from Derrick told him that the dead ends were too many. Another one from Evelyn explained an email from the explosives company would be sending a list of addresses in the next forty-eight hours. Both decided to call it a day around one o'clock, since it was still a holiday weekend. About that same time, he decided to leave as well. Later that evening, Chad called him from Brazil, and his voice was refreshing to hear.

Even though his final thoughts before sleep were of Chad, the victims from the fires haunted his dreams

*****

Instead of lying in bed on a Sunday morning, Gavin forced himself up around seven. With such a restless sleep, he had a nervous energy. In about two and a half hours, he had to meet Derrick and Evelyn at an address on the near South Side. According to Derrick's voicemail, someone had recognized Guerillo's face and given him an ex-girlfriend's number.

Gavin threw on some warm running gear and headed out the door into the brisk air on a cloudy day. The cold forced his eyes open, filled his lungs, and woke up his brain even more. Although his legs slipped to and fro on several patches of black ice, he managed to stay upright during the entirety run as his feet pounded the street. For the next hour or so, his mind seemed more refreshed and alert than earlier.

After an incredibly hot shower, which thawed his body, he dressed into his custom suit for work. As he walked toward the kitchen counter, he opened the cupboard, gathered some ingredients, and began to make a protein shake. Another one of Chad's subtle influences on him. Glancing over at his phone, he noticed it was lighting up.

Grabbing the phone, he saw it was Evan, and that he'd already missed several calls from his brother. He accepted the call and said, "Hey there—"

"Where the hell have you been?" Evan's voice cracked.

"What's wrong, Evan?"

Evan said nothing. Quietly, he choked back a sob.

"Are you okay?" Gavin was grabbing his keys and making a quick stride for the door. "Want me to come over?"

"No, no, we're not there." He paused.

"Is Sharon with you? Where are you—"

"It's Mom," he said at last.

Gavin stopped right next to the door. "What happened?"

"Don't know. The home called me an hour ago..." He trailed off. Another sob. "Thought you were first on the emergency call list."

I am. Taking a deep breath, he asked, "Where are you? Where's Mom?"

"Hinsdale Hospital," he replied. "Doesn't look good."

"I'll be right there." His eyes watered. He knew that this day would come. *But not yet. Not so soon. Chad just met Mom—*

Gavin felt a heaviness in his chest. Throwing on his jacket, he called Chad, not sure if he would answer.

"It's me," he said as he raced down the stairs. "Call me. It's my mother, she's in the hospital..."

Gavin stopped when he heard the crack of his own voice.

*****

Early in the afternoon, the sparsely filled waiting room seemed utterly too silent. Every so often, a doctor and nurse would stride up to one of the few small groups of people waiting for news. Their conversations were quiet, yet their expressions of relief—or anguish—filled their faces.

Gavin settled back on the couch near his brother. Evan put his arm around Sharon, who looked off in a different direction. Swallowing the last sip of his cold vending machine coffee, Gavin set the cup aside. While they'd had very little conversation, Gavin just liked being near his brother. The redness in Evan's eyes slowly dissipated. When he'd first arrived, no one had given them much information. About eleven o'clock, Dr. Adhul appeared and explained their mother had suffered another severe stroke. When they rushed her into the hospital, the initial scan discovered that blood was forming at the base of her brain. He was moving her into surgery to help relieve some of it.

It just became a waiting game.

Occasionally, Gavin glanced down at his phone. There was still no word from Chad, even though he'd texted him several times. Perhaps his phone was out of service at his current location. But Gavin knew Chad's company was expensing all international calls because he still had to work and be connected.

On his way to the hospital, he called Derrick to give him the news. Derrick was concerned for his mother and simply said, "You take care of your family."

Already hitting the two-thirty mark, Gavin was becoming slightly restless and even hungry. He shot a glance at Evan, whose eyelids appeared to be getting heavy. Gavin fished out his wallet and took out some twenties.

"Here," Gavin said to Evan, folding the cash and handing it to him. "Take this. You guys go. Get some lunch. Take a break."

Shaking his head, Evan returned, "No, we can stay."

"Really." He leaned over and opened Evan's hand to place the folded money in it. "Lunch, on me."

"Gavin." Sharon straightened up with a meager smile. "You don't have to. We can take care of ourselves."

"I know. But you were here longer than I was."

"By an hour," Evan stated. Acquiescing to the temptation, he grabbed the cash and shoved it into the front pocket of his jeans. By the scruff on his face, Gavin guessed he probably had not showered since yesterday. Sharon wore some thin sweatpants and a big sweatshirt, her glasses sitting slightly crooked against her round face.

"Go, seriously," Gavin insisted.

Evan looked at Sharon, who shrugged with an equally exhausted smile. Then he said to him, "Thanks. I owe you."

Trying to smile, Gavin replied, "Maybe you can make me dinner some night soon."

"Yeah, sure," Sharon attempted to sound more upbeat, allowing her South Side accent to come through. "You can invite your new friend along."

What? "Don't know what you mean," Gavin lied.

"You've been busier than normal." Evan stood up and stretched slightly. He forced down the tattered baseball cap over his thick dark curly hair. "It ain't work this time."

"Work's been busy, actually," he said, feeling his cheeks blush.

"Stop lyin', Gavin," he remarked. "The nurse, Mavis, told me that you brought someone to meet Mom. I don't know who she is, but she must mean something." He pointed to his phone. "'Cause you keep looking at that too."

It's not a she, Evan. "Work."

"Bullshit." Evan took a step toward him. Sharon stood as well. "Why didn't you let her come?"

Suddenly but softly, Sharon hit Evan's arm. "Dumbass, you don't invite your new SO to a family emergency."

"Out of town," Gavin admitted.

"Business trips? Hmm, after Thanksgiving weekend. Must be important." His brother eyed him up cockily.

"Whatever, Gavin," Sharon piped in. "I'd be happy to cook something for you and your new girlfriend. I make a mean lasagna."

Boyfriend. "Sure." Then with his hands, he shooed them along and said, "Now go. Go. Won't tell you twice."

Unexpectedly, and even surprisingly, Evan leaned over and hugged Gavin firmly. Then he whispered, "Call me, and I'll come running back. Love you."

"Me too." Gavin let him go.

Watching them walk down the corridor, hand in hand, it was a pleasure to see Evan come alive once again after a short few months. After Vincent kidnapped him, Evan had been a wreck for a good few weeks. He felt so guilty and helpless, then Sharon walked back into his life to nurture him back to health. Occasionally, she called Gavin once in a while about Evan's nightmares and him waking up screaming. In the recent months, Evan had found a decent psychiatrist, which meant he was willing to deal with the darkness Vincent had inflicted. Evan was still working through some minor physical therapy as well. Vincent had wanted to take him away from Gavin. Instead, Gavin made sure that Vincent was no longer a threat.

For either of them.

TWENTY-NINE

About a half hour later, Derrick called. Gavin picked up and walked near a window, wishing it were Chad instead.

"How's your mom?" Derrick inquired.

"Same. Still in surgery."

"Sorry." His deep voice was low and quiet. "Your mom is in our prayers. Maria and Lucy said a prayer at church for her."

"Thanks."

Briefly, the doors to surgery opened. Only a nurse came through the door. She approached a nearby family and then ushered them through the doors.

A brief moment of silence fell between them.

"Not a social call, is it?"

"No." A sound of shifting paperwork could be heard.

"At the station?"

"Yeah." He paused. "Bad time to talk?"

No, absolutely not. "Go ahead."

"Alright," Derrick began. "After a couple of addresses that led nowhere, I knocked on Guerillo's ex-girlfriend's door. A Ms. Anita Dias. Lucky for me, Evelyn was there because Dias spoke only Spanish. Anyway, she said that she hadn't seen him for couple of months. I made Evelyn push harder. It turns out that she broke up with him about a month and a half ago. She claimed that Guerillo had some deal that was going bad and he had to leave."

"What deal?" Gavin asked softly.

"Exactly," Derrick responded. "She started spilling more about him. She knew that she was not the only girlfriend."

"Only?"

"Motherfucker had six or seven at the same time."

"Jesus." Gavin scanned the snowy train tracks below.

Derrick continued excitedly. "About four weeks ago, Guerillo came knocking on her door and wanted to stay at her place for a couple of days. She said that he looked scared. But she was still pissed off and told him to go away."

"Last time she saw him?"

"Yeah. She found out that he might be hanging out at another place, on the South Side. Turned out to be his kid's house."

"Guerillo's kid?"

"Yeah," Derrick breathed out. "Has a daughter about six years old. Diaz knew about her and met her a couple of times. The daughter lives with Guerillo's aunt or something. I already have a patrol sitting on the house right now."

"Good work."

"She also mentioned another house Guerillo used to live in, when they first met," he said. "She knew he brought his other girlfriends there. So when I got back here, I just happened to cross reference the address to S and P Realty…"

"A Zanders Holdings property," Gavin interrupted. *A connection. Finally.*

"Yes," he said. "If you're up to it, tomorrow we'll go swing by the place. If not, Evelyn and I can handle it."

"Did you contact Creighton about a search warrant?"

"Done. In the works. Think we are getting closer, G."

"You're right," he replied. "Keep me in the loop. Call or text me the address."

Derrick told him that his mother was in his thoughts, and they disconnected.

The grim reality came into focus as he looked down at the phone.

*****

Around four thirty, Dr. Adhul ambled through the double doors, spotted Gavin, and sat near him. The scent of surgical antiseptic lingered on him like an invisible jacket. Delicately, he explained how his mother sustained a major stroke that most likely caused extensive paralysis on the left side of her body. Currently, she was still unconscious. Although he was able to stop the internal bleeding, his mother would remain in ICU for the next several days so they could monitor the bleeding and determine the extent of the damage the stroke placed to her already weak body. Even as he spoke, Dr. Adhul's compassion drifted through his words, which helped Gavin suppress his building despair.

Before he left, the doctor said softly, "Only time will tell what the stroke did to her body. Have some faith that your mother is strong enough to fight it."

As the doctor left, Gavin felt worse than before.

Once his mother was settled in ICU, he called Evan to come back to the hospital. Over the phone, he began explaining her condition, but soon his brother's muffled sobs stopped the conversation. Within a half hour, Sharon and Evan returned, appearing slightly more refreshed. Throughout the evening, a parade of nurses came back and forth to her room while Evan, Sharon, and Gavin skirted around them.

His mother lay perfectly still in the center of the bed with her eyes closed. The low light above the bed illuminated deeper, harsher lines on her alabaster skin. The netting of tubes jetting out of her body seemed to float around her, as if she were some cyborg creature, while the constant sound of the respirator forced air into her thin body. Images of his mother rushed to him: he thought of her digging in the garden, cooking dinner at the stove, wiping his face from a cut, kissing him on the cheek, and mouthing the words *I love you*. He forced the tears to remain inside—he had to be strong for Evan.

His brother was taking the situation even harder, breaking down every so often. Gavin stroked his long back while Sharon held his head on her shoulder. Perhaps the years of him being alone with her while Gavin was attending school had developed their bond. Perhaps the years after their father passed away had truly created their relationship. Either way, Gavin did not want to see his brother suffer through another tragedy.

Though they spoke very little, just being together was enough for him. Feeling his stomach rumble at one point, Gavin asked them if they were hungry. They humbly declined.

"Why don't you take a break?" Sharon queried, glancing up at him.

"No, I'm fine."

"Gavin, you've been here all day," Evan spoke louder and stood up. "We can't do anything more. We'll be leaving shortly. Don't worry, I'll be back tomorrow. After work."

"Really," Sharon stated. "You kicked us out. It's our turn."

Nodding, Gavin knew his brother was right. Tiredness overwhelmed his mind. "Think I will go."

In that moment, Evan hugged him tightly and briefly, and then patted his shoulders. "Rest. I'll call you if there's any change." He paused and said softly, "Love you, big brother."

"Love you too," Gavin returned. He hugged Evan once more, and then Sharon.

Waves of guilt washed over him as he rode down the elevator, walked through the deserted lobby, and made his way to the parking lot. Part of him wanted to remain, but he knew he had to go home. Evan was correct—there was nothing else they could do. The fresh chilly air welcomed him once again.

Once inside his car, the phone vibrated. A text from Chad.

Finally.

Quickly, he read the message: *G man! U should B here! Holy Shit! Watch this!*

Gavin glanced up ahead of him with a sigh. He knew this message was meant for Gordon, not him. Did he dare to open the video clip Chad had sent by accident?

Gavin hit the play button.

The screen erupted with a blaring rhythmic Latino beat as strobe lights flashed all around in the background into a grainy darkness. By the swirling motion of the camera, the video was shot above Chad. Many half-naked men were dancing in an open club on the beach front. As Chad panned around, the city of Rio was off in the distance, and the ocean waves crashed against the shores. Men were splashing and playing in the thunderous waves, naked, kissing and touching each other. Suddenly, hands were in the air with glow sticks bopping to the quick beat.

"Look at this!" Chad boomed over the noise. The screen changed suddenly to the selfie lens. With a long extended view, Gavin saw that Chad was shirtless, glistening with sweat and wearing only a pair of white briefs. He was packed against a sea of nearly naked men, all dancing.

Suddenly, two thin caramel-colored men—one with a thick

mustache and the other draped in colorful tattoos—were grinding on Chad's body. Their hands were feeling and exploring his muscles, while their hips rubbed against him. Soon, the tattooed man kissed and licked Chad's back while the other one slowly got down on his knees, licking his well-formed abs on the way down. Not stopping them, Chad danced to the music even as the mustache man slid off his briefs. Then two more men noticed what was going on and began rubbing Chad's body. A couple of hands were on Chad's thick manhood. In the last shot, the camera went straight down, revealing the mustache man as he engulfed Chad's hardened manhood in one gulp.

"Yeahh—" Chad shouted.

Gavin stopped the video.

Anger tore into him. He threw the phone into the empty seat next to him and banged his fists against the steering wheel. While Chad was partying and having a great time, he ignored Gavin's messages. Tears stung his eyes, and suddenly he wanted a drink. A lot of drinks. Gavin knew if Chad wanted to play that way—

"Fuck, fuck, fuck you," he grunted. He threw the Mustang into drive and squealed out of the parking garage.

Once he was on the Stevenson, Gavin made a different call.

******

"Don't understand why you didn't use your own goddamn key," Quinn said behind him. "The one I gave you."

Gavin stood at the windowpane of Quinn's apartment, which was located in the narrow buildings across from the Museum Campus. When he'd walked in, Gavin was in awe at how spectacular it was.

The apartment was situated on the corner edge of the building, overlooking both the city and the campus. A semi open-concept space was laid out before him, with rich wooden floors contrasting the sleek slate-colored walls. The dark navy-blue furniture looked bold atop the wool geometric rugs, and the pops of stainless steel fixtures and appliances added a sense of ultramodern along with the seemingly endless wall covered in abstract paintings, which stood opposite of the floor-to-ceiling windows.

Gavin stared down at the churning mysterious dark lake

before him. In the dim light, he could see Quinn's bare back in the near corner by the exquisitely clean white kitchen. Quinn's rigid posture was accentuated by the leather strap around his shoulders and mid-deltoids, while his tight-fitting leather chaps hugged his bare, round ass.

I shouldn't be here. Quinn came toward him; the black jockstrap he wore surrounded his manhood, making it bulge with each step.

Gavin could not bring himself to move.

Concentrating on the darkness, he felt a cold glass touch his hand. He sipped the rich whiskey without a word while Quinn gulped down half his glass in seconds.

"Did I interrupt anything?" His eyes went to Quinn.

"My day off"—Quinn scratched his hairy chest and grinned—"my rules."

I can tell. "My mom was a little much today," he began, already regretting what he'd said.

"Where's your chocolate lover?" Quinn questioned sarcastically.

Gavin said nothing and took a sip of his drink.

"A lover's quarrel?"

"Away," he replied softly. "On business."

"Must be a big shit to be out on a holiday weekend." Quinn sidestepped toward Gavin. A hint of musky cologne and sweat danced off his body.

"You weren't in for a few days," Gavin commented, looking down onto the seemingly desolate campus.

"Signed my fucking divorce," Quinn stated. "The cunt's heading back to California. She can fuckin' stay there too."

"Take it the settlement was hell?"

"No, her," he retorted dryly.

Quinn's hand touched Gavin's lower's back as he looked him up and down. The captain's fingers slowly came to rest on the crook of his belt loop. His touch did not make Gavin uncomfortable, but unusually at ease.

"Did you go in today?" he asked. "Because your standard cop look—I could do without it today."

In the reflection, Gavin saw how the black suit jacket clung to his frame. The white shirt was untucked and his pants were rumpled: the clothes were wearing him, not the other way around. The thought of heading home to change had never occurred to him.

"Nice place here," he said, craning his neck away from Quinn. "A captain's salary must be pretty good."

"Shit, it sucks," he remarked. "Just lots of good investments."

I wonder. Gavin drained the rest of the drink.

On cue, Quinn said, "I'll get you another drink."

He walked away from Gavin, and after a moment, the sounds of ice clinked in a glass. At that point, the subtle sound of music came from nearby. Facing the window, Gavin noticed the bedroom door was cracked open.

"I love this view. Especially at night." Quinn handed him the drink and stood within inches of him. "The water always relaxes me. Such a beautiful and destructive force that no one can fuckin' control."

In one subtle motion, Quinn swept his arm around Gavin's waist and slipped a hand into the front of his pants pocket. Taking a slow, deep breath, Gavin did not move away.

"When I was young, my mother took me to the beach often." Quinn sipped on his drink and seemed pensive. "Those were the best and only fond memories I have of her."

Hmm, first time I heard about your family.

"What was your mother like?"

A small smile caressed his lips. "Beautiful, strong willed, very delicate looks that showed off her French heritage. She was my life."

"What happened to her?"

"Died of cancer." He then added, "But she taught me the most important life lesson."

"What's that?"

Quinn shifted closer to Gavin, allowing his hand to slip down deeper into Gavin's pocket. A familiar sensation began to fill within Gavin, and his desire began to grow. At the same time, the drink warmed him up, and he felt a little lightheaded. Perhaps the small bags of chips he'd downed did not suffice.

"Always get what you want," he whispered in Gavin's ear.

Through the fabric, Quinn's fingers touched the tip of his cock, rolling it around gently as he leaned in closer. "Tell me, Gavin." His thick voice was hot near his skin. "Why the fuck did you come here tonight?"

Attempting some composure, he looked over at Quinn, whose

devious smile seemed too intoxicating. He could feel the warmth of his bare skin. Slowly, he lifted his hand and placed it on Quinn's chest, feeling the leather strap. Quinn's hand went deeper into his pocket, stroking his manhood. Gavin let out a soft breath.

"Is this why you came here tonight?" Quinn's lips were so close.

Not saying a word, Gavin leaned in and kissed Quinn savagely. Quinn's scratchy beard sent a shockwave of familiarity through his body. Gavin's other hand moved up toward the back of his head, and his fingers tussled through his short bristly cut. The taste of whiskey on Quinn's tongue was delicious.

Quinn took Gavin's glass and set it next to his own on a nearby table. Then their hands were exploring each other aggressively. Quinn ripped open his shirt suddenly and began kissing his neck.

Gavin caught a glimpse of their reflection in the window. Then he noticed another man emerge from the bedroom. Stopping, he pushed Quinn back slightly.

"Thought you were alone," Gavin huffed.

Glancing over, Quinn smirked. "You never asked." Then, nodding at the younger man, he said, "This is my other friend. Scott, come here."

Scott was as tall as Gavin and had long, wispy sandy-blond hair that spread down to his shoulders. As he sauntered toward them, Gavin's gaze followed the constellation of nautical stars tattooed crossed the right side of his sculpted chest. The tattoo continued a narrow path over the man's abs and down to his naked groin. They also extended down his right arm and disappeared over his shoulder. His body art flinched exquisitely with every movement of his muscles.

Quinn left his hand inside Gavin's pants and continued to massage his awakening manhood.

"Scott," Quinn said softly, staring at Gavin. "Say hi to Gavin."

"Hi." His deep voice was luxurious as he wrapped an arm around Quinn's hip. Scott's dark eyes stayed on Gavin while his other hand reached up and played with Quinn's nipple.

"I should leave," Gavin said softly. "I interrupted your evening."

"No, no, Gavin," Quinn whispered, leaning closer. "Stay. I think you'll like Scott. He's fantastic."

"Best mouth in the city," Scott stated with a surly grin. The man's long cock dangled against Quinn's leather pants.

"Amazing, really," Quinn reaffirmed, turning to him and kissing him on the mouth ferociously.

"Thanks, babe," Scott finally said.

"I really should leave," Gavin stated softly. Yet, Quinn's grip on his cock was harder, exciting him all the more.

Suddenly, Scott's grin widened. "I know that name. Is this the Gavin you talk about, baby?"

"Yes, the one." Quinn's sultry smile widened.

"You talk about me?" Gavin asked. The room seemed to be spinning under him.

In that moment, he felt warmer and could feel his heartbeat soundly in his chest. His erection wanted to bust out of his pants. *Did I drink that much?* He needed to leave. As he attempted to move, his body swayed slightly.

"Whoa, whoa, there." Quinn propped him up. "Let me get you to the couch."

As if moving through the air, Gavin fell onto the couch.

"You look warm," Quinn said seductively, and he took off Gavin's jacket and shirt. Already, Scott was undoing his pants and peeling them off.

Oddly, Gavin no longer felt like resisting. Scott's touch was brilliantly dazzling on his flesh, while Quinn's kisses on his chest made him tingle. Then Scott began to kiss the inside of his thighs, his tongue sliding out of his mouth as he did so. Quinn unsnapped his jock then and let his dick flop onto Gavin's stomach.

It isn't right. I need to go.

"You're so goddamn big," Scott said softly behind Quinn. Then Scott's wet lips surrounded the tip of his penis.

"Time to play by my new rules," Quinn whispered softly.

Quinn began to kiss Gavin deeply, letting his tongue roll around his mouth. Scott's wet tongue left Gavin's thigh, and the young man placed his hands on Quinn. Gavin felt Quinn's body shudder as he they continued to kiss, and he realized Scott's tongue was exploring Quinn's crevice. Moments later, Quinn slid himself onto Gavin's thick shaft slowly. At the same time, Scott's tongue and mouth engulfed Gavin's scrotum before traveling downward to his crevice. The pleasure from the multiple sensations was undeniably incredible. As Quinn rode him, Scott's hot tongue made him quiver with delight.

Closing his eyes, Gavin slipped into a cloudy, delicious, tantalizing haze.

THIRTY

Everything was so goddamn disorientating.

Closing the car door, the refreshing cold air did not alleviate the floaty, foggy haze that engulfed him much like another layer of heavy skin. Gavin headed straight toward the townhouse protected by a single uniformed officer. Since his eyes had opened that morning, a gripping headache had latched on to the back of his skull.

Earlier, he found himself askew on Quinn's bed with Scott lying near him on his stomach, naked. Rising out of the obscenely large bed, Gavin could not remember much of the night. When he'd looked at himself in the bathroom mirror, he found handprints on his hips and ass, bite marks around his groin and chest, and some scratches across his tight stomach; it must have been a rough night.

Gavin was furious with Quinn. Had he really been bold enough to take advantage of Gavin like that, when he'd come to him feeling so vulnerable? Much less introduce another person to their scenario…

Gavin counted only two drinks. He could not have gotten that drunk that quickly. And he was even angrier at himself for not controlling the situation. For not leaving. What enraged Gavin the most had been Quinn's note that he left on Scott's bare ass. It simply said: *Fuck of the decade. Q.*

Discovering his clothes in a neat pile in the bright dining room, he'd quickly dressed and left.

Looking down at his phone, he saw that he was an hour late. Several texts from Derrick and Evelyn indicated they'd already entered Guerillo's townhouse. Derrick's texts carried an angry tone: *Where the fuck are you? Everything alright with your mother? Why aren't you fucking picking up?*

In his car, just before he'd left Quinn's place, Gavin had texted Derrick back: *On my way.*

Too late. Already in. Get your ass here now.

Gavin quickly walked toward the brief flashing of lights and heard muttered conversations. Rounding the corner, he found that the narrow townhouse. From wall to wall the corridor was less than five feet wide, making it nearly impossible for people to walk through with their equipment. The long living space held no furniture and shot out toward a small, bare porch. To the right, the somewhat updated galley kitchen seemed devoid of any belongings, just blank stone countertops. Several CSI members emerged from a side passage, and one pointed him down the other hallway.

He found Derrick speaking with a different CSI member, his bulky frame filling the small space. As Derrick muttered something to her, he noticed Gavin, and a sour expression spread over his face.

Behind Derrick, a small six-foot table held headphones, a stationary computer, a film editing unit, and numerous small empty boxes. On the floor, several knocked over boxes spewed out their paper contents. As Gavin approached, he saw that the contents on the floor were blank order forms, shipping labels, and blank item tags.

"'Bout time you got here," Derrick grumbled.

"What's all this?" Gavin ignored his dig.

"If you were here when we entered the location an hour ago," he replied quickly, "you'd be a little more informed."

"Sorry," Gavin began.

"Bullshit," he said and let out a sigh. The harsh single light in the room deepened the dark circles under Derrick's eyes. "Looks like a makeshift editing studio. CSI's going to take samples off the equipment to get any fingerprints."

"Think this is like what Sanford discovered?" Gavin craned his neck to look over the table's contents.

"Not sure," he replied. "Looks like it hasn't been used in a while. The hardware was taken."

"Empty house." Gavin pointed at the impressions in the rug. "But it had been furnished at one point."

"Let's go to the master," Derrick commanded and then walked out of the room.

Taking one final look, Gavin followed Derrick through the living room, toward a small staircase at the end of the short hallway, which banked right and up. Ascending to the top stair, he noticed one more empty dark room, a tiny bathroom, and a couple of double doors. More flashes of a camera went off as he entered the room.

Inside, the large narrow room had a wall of windows at the end and a balcony. Yet, it was a three-foot-long table on the right side that grabbed Gavin's attention.

On the table, various colored wires were scattered on the surface, along with nuts and bolts of different sizes and a small torch. A simple chair sat behind it. Nothing else was in the room.

"That seems a little out of the ordinary," Gavin stated as he walked toward it.

"And convenient," Derrick added, flanking his right side.

"Detective," Greg, Thomas's assistant, said to Gavin. "Good to meet you again." Then to Derrick, "As far as I can detect, no explosive materials are in the house. The dog would have sensed it. I made two thorough sweeps."

"Thanks," Derrick replied. "You can start bagging it up. Tell me if you get anything."

Greg indicated that he would as he put on latex gloves. He then pointed at another fire marshal, whose gloved fingers danced over the objects. Derrick took a couple steps to a nearby corner to get out of the way.

"Bomb assembly in here?" Derrick asked, putting his hands on his hips.

"Doesn't feel right," Gavin said, darting his eyes around the vacant place. "So planned."

"Yes. Convenient. Same feeling Evelyn and I had," Derrick stated. He turned and walked toward the bathroom. "I noticed something before I got pulled."

The modern opulence of the tight master bedroom seemed a stark contrast to the rest of the plain home. Quickly, Derrick hopped on the edge of the soaking tub and pointed toward the ceiling in the corner.

"Notice something?" Derrick's baritone questioned with a raised eyebrow.

At first he didn't, but then he noticed the slight shift in the vent register. A small dark smudge against the pristine white, as if someone had moved it back and forth. Derrick extended his arm and pushed it up. Fishing out his flashlight, he pointed it up and aimed it into the dark space. He then reached in with his long fingers.

"Feel something," he said, looking over at Gavin. "Just about got it. There."

Quickly, his fingers emerged with a flash drive. He threw it over to Gavin, who caught it. Looking down at it, he noticed the slim object was scratched on the side.

"Wonder what's on it?" Derrick asked as his foot stepped hard onto the marble floor.

"Guess Mylo will have to find out for us," Gavin stated.

"Detectives?" A stocky man from CSI approached them. "We have something for you."

Pocketing the flash drive, Gavin followed Derrick once again, still trying to shake off the dizziness.

*****

The CSI member took them back to the vacant living room, which was now dim. Even the overhead lights in the open kitchen were switched off. Nearby, Evelyn leaned against the wall near the kitchen, talking on the phone. As soon as she saw them, she ended the conversation.

"Glad you could make it to the party," she said to Gavin. A brief scent of light flowery perfume washed over him. "How's your mother?"

Don't know. Scott's naked back, his hands on his cock, Quinn's tongue on his chest all flashed in his mind. A quivering shudder erupted over him.

"You okay?" She looked concerned.

"She's stable," he replied.

"Good," she said.

"Alright," the CSI guy said loudly, holding a long purple fluorescent flashlight in his right hand. "I was doing a usual sweep with the UV light. As you asked for, Detective Williamson." He nodded at the young woman near the blinds. "Alright, Peggy."

Quickly, the woman twirled the cord, and darkness invaded the space.

"Look what I found." The purple light switched on, and the man kneeled down. He waved it slowly back and forth to illuminate an oval spot about two feet to three feet in diameter.

"That's a lot of blood," Derrick said.

"This has to be at least four pints of blood," he replied and then looked up at Gavin. "More than a papercut, I'd say." Then his eyes went over to the young woman. "Okay, Peggy."

Instantly, the muted sunlight flooded in as he turned the purple light off.

Stepping over to the man, Derrick began to give him instructions about the carpet. At the same time, Evelyn said to Gavin, "I may have something."

"Listening," he replied.

"A tenant above in 2D recognized Guerillo coming in and out. Said there was unusual sounds coming from the house. He knocked on the door several times, but no one answered. Even called the super.

"About five weeks ago," she continued in a more hushed tone as two bulky CSI members passed by them, "a large moving truck came and cleared out the house. The movers blocked the main entrance for a time, which made everyone in the building pissed off."

"Did he catch the name of the moving company?" Derrick queried.

"No," she said. "But I bet someone else may remember."

"Alright, keep at it." Gavin pulled the flash drive out of his pocket. Evelyn looked curious. Before she said anything, he said, "Derrick found it."

"I think that whoever removed Guerillo from the equation," Derrick stated, stepping over, "was looking for that."

"Any idea what could be on it?" Evelyn folded her arms against her chest.

"Nope, but Mylo can figure it out." Gavin looked at Derrick and then Evelyn. "So, we have an editing production station in one room, a makeshift bomb-making work station in the master, no furniture—"

"No belongings, just useless paperwork," Derrick added.

"And a quick move out," Evelyn finished.

"What does it sound like to you?" Gavin asked Evelyn.

Her dark eyes darted to the CSI team carefully pulling up the rug. She bit her lower lip. "If we weren't working the case before, and this was just an average call, Guerillo would have been our bomber. But it all doesn't seem to add up."

"Do you think it's our killer?" Gavin asked her matter-of-factly.

"No," she said.

"Good," Derrick replied. "Who then?"

"The second guy," she stated firmly. Then she asked, "Why go through all this trouble to set up Guerillo, then kill him? And how did Guerillo contact our killer?"

"Maybe the other guy figured that *our suspect* must know, and he's covering his tracks," Derrick commented.

"How?" Gavin questioned. Then he said to Evelyn, "Mind staying here, rapping this up? Keep knocking on doors. See if anyone remembers the name of the moving company."

"Fine." Evelyn nodded and headed out of the apartment.

"Gavin," Derrick said. "Just a word."

"Yeah," he replied casually.

"I don't know what happened this morning, or why you were late." He stepped closer to him. "I understand that your mom's stroke was bad."

"What are you getting at?" Gavin straightened up and stared back at Derrick.

Pulling his phone out of his pocket, he handed it over to him, and said, "Read that—from Creighton."

On Derrick's phone, a message read: *Expect Nolan late. Rough night.* Gavin felt a sudden anger flow through him. His cheeks reddened.

"I know you guys have a history as partners," Derrick began.

"Fucking asshole," Gavin muttered under his breath.

Before he could say anything, Derrick got a call and turned his back.

How dare Quinn send Derrick anything! What the fuck was he thinking?

"Hey, it was Mylo," Derrick began. "He finished the next part of the CD. Said we need to see it."

At the same moment, Greg found Derrick and began asking him some questions. Without so much as a word, Gavin left.

He needed to see Quinn.

THIRTY-ONE

Arriving at the precinct first, Gavin walked quickly inside. All he needed was a few minutes with Creighton. The bull pen was unusually chaotic, which was not a concern for him. As he headed for Creighton's office, he discovered it empty. Nearby, a uniformed officer said she saw Creighton head into the bathroom. Without appearing to be anxious, he picked up his pace and dodged people along the way.

When his phone vibrated, he glanced down to read a text from Chad: *Gavin, sorry I missed your calls. How's Mom? Call me pls.*

Shaking his head, he pocketed his phone. *Not now. I have other matters to take care of.*

Gavin opened the door to find a quiet restroom. Taking a couple of steps inside, he heard the sound of sniffing, a couple of subtle grunts, and then a stall door unlatching. Quinn came out of the far stall, adjusting his tie and peering over at Gavin.

"Nolan," he stated with a coy grin. "Fuckin' scared the shit out of me."

Pinching his nose, Quinn sniffled more and walked toward the mirror.

"What the hell were you doing?" Gavin demanded angrily. He suddenly recalled the rolled-up bills, razor, and white residue still on the glass coffee table that morning.

"Taking a shit," he said, leaning closer to the mirror. "Goddamn crime in that?"

"I think you were doing more than that." Gavin stepped toward him and met Quinn's eyes in the mirror.

"Wondered *if* I could take a shit after last night." He ignored Gavin's accusation, grinning maliciously. Quinn flipped his tie over his shirt and began washing his hands.

Abruptly, Gavin grabbed Quinn by the shoulder and hissed,

"What the fuck happened last night?"

"Told you." Quinn's smile widened. "Fuck of the decade."

Trembling, Gavin shoved Quinn backwards into the nearby radiator.

"I don't fucking remember," he grunted, stepping toward Quinn, who regained his balance, still smiling. "What did you put in my drink?"

"Come on, Nolan," he remarked matter-of-factly. "You came on to me last night. I was just making you more at ease." He patted down his pants and adjusted his crotch. "Did you like it?"

"You put something in my drink," he said, a statement this time rather than a question. He took another step toward Quinn.

"Didn't you like having two men fuck you, Gavin?" His deep voice echoed against the tiles. "You liked it when Scott was fucking you while you fucked me. Don't you remember?"

A flash came back to him. In the large shower, Quinn was pressed against the wall as Gavin was slipping his cock inside of him, and then, behind Gavin, Scott entered him. The rhythmic grinding was incredible as the hot water poured over his body—

"Son of a bitch," Gavin grunted and tightly grasped Quinn by the shirt collar with both hands. "You had no right to—"

"To take advantage of my innocent little Gavin?" Quinn finished for him. "You fuckin' liked it, over and over. On my face, in my mouth…"

Gavin's hand wrung Quinn's shirt, tearing it. The wide smile remained planted on his captain's face.

"You even swallowed Scottie's big dick," he continued, his hot breath cascading over Gavin's lips. Then Gavin felt Quinn's hand on his crotch, squeezing it. "Guess your new black fuck's got a big-ass dick too—"

"Shut up, I'm warning you," Gavin uttered throatily.

"What are you going to fuckin' do, Nolan?" He leaned closer to Gavin and pressed his lips against his ear. "All you are doing is making me fucking harder."

With a quick snap, Gavin released Quinn backwards and threw a punch at him. Quinn blocked it, but a second jab toward the captain's face clocked him in the jaw. Instantly, Quinn returned with several quick undercuts that caught Gavin off guard and forced him back. When Gavin attempted another swing, Quinn landed a couple more hits to his abdomen. The strength of the blows knocked Gavin back into the sink with the faucet still running. Hanging onto the side of the sink, Gavin looked to Quinn, whose fists were raised in the air, poised to attack. There was a wickedly wild smile plastered on his face.

"If you wanted to get spanked, Gavin," he returned loudly, breathing heavy, "all you had to do was fucking ask!"

Grunting, Gavin lunged toward him. "Goddamn bastard!" he yelled.

Gavin's arms went around Quinn's waist, forcing Quinn back into the wall. At the same time, Quinn punched the narrow of his back, swiftly and directly.

"Like it rough, bitch?" Quinn grunted back. "Next time we fuck, I'll show you what I really like!"

Hearing the pleasure ooze through Quinn's words, Gavin saw red and threw some blind punches back at him, missing him and striking the wall. Under his breath, he returned, "Fucking asshole!"

"Hey! Knock that shit off!" Derrick cried out behind them. "Help! Guys! Get in here!"

In the fury of the moment, Derrick savagely pulled Gavin off Quinn and threw him against the nearby wall. Derrick pressed his forearm and chest against his body, pinning him tightly. The adrenalin pumped in his body as he watched Quinn being helped by other uniformed officers. Derrick forced Gavin to the other side as more cops and detectives began to enter the tight space.

"You're going to fucking regret that, Nolan!" Creighton snapped at him loudly. A trickle of blood dripped from his swollen lip.

"Go!" Derrick commanded and pushed Gavin out of the bathroom into the bull pen. All eyes were on Gavin. He could see the surprised looks on their faces and sensed the eerie silence.

"I said you'll fucking regret it, Nolan!" Creighton repeated from the open door.

"What the fuck, G?" Derrick stated, eyeing Gavin up and down with a sour expression. Then he stated, "Go clean yourself up. Meet me in room three."

Straightening up his posture, Gavin felt the warm heat of Quinn's sharp blows on the narrow of his back. Ambling toward the locker room, he glanced back at Quinn emerging from the bathroom while a cop tended to him. Their eyes locked. Even then, Quinn's snarky grin remained on his face. Gavin turned away from him, tucking his shirt back into his pants and avoiding the continuous stares.

Not done with you yet, Quinn.

*****

About fifteen minutes later, Gavin emerged from the locker room and bumped into several detectives along the way. The scuffle between himself and Quinn had already made the rounds, and he received some unusual responses: "Never knew you had it in you," "Wish I was there," "He can't do that shit to you," and such. Glancing over at Creighton's office, he saw that all the blinds were down and the door was shut.

Fuck you, Quinn.

Shaking his head, he headed for the interrogation room.

As he rounded the corner and entered the room, Derrick was standing near the laptop.

"Mylo on his way?" Gavin questioned in a heavy breath.

"No," Derrick replied, frowning. "Sent him off to go work on the flash drive."

"Good," Gavin replied and closed the door. The dull hum of the fluorescent light above filled the space. Then, he said, "Derrick, I apologize for—"

"Right now, not my concern," he interrupted. His eyes looked away from Gavin to the laptop. "You ready?"

"Did you already watch this?"

Without saying a word, Derrick clicked a key, and the video on the wall came to life.

The first shot was a close-up of Sills' arms tied above her head. As the camera panned down, Gavin noted that Sills had new cuts and bruises added to her once beautiful face. Her body was slightly suspended in the air. A soft, low moan came from her lips, making bloody bubbles on the corner of her mouth. Suddenly, a hand appeared and grabbed her shoulder, and her body began to jerk around.

The cameraman pulled back the shot, turning the camera toward the ground, and then panned up. There, the same man from the first video appeared. With his back to the camera, the screen displayed his entire muscular naked backside. With a quick grip, the man opened Sills' legs and assaulted her once more.

"Come on, bitch," the man groaned. "Take my big cock! Yeah, fuck yeah!"

Looking up, Gavin glanced at Derrick, who turned away from him slightly. His hand gripped the wall for support as he hung his head low. His eyes were shut, and he was almost wincing at the brutal sexual noises.

The camera tightened on the man, who leaned back and pulled out his swollen cock. It quivered and then ejaculated onto his hairy navel. While his tight stomach concaved rapidly from the vigorous fucking, the man smeared the creamy mixture into the splatters of blood around his pubic area. He turned back to Sills, whose faint groans subsided as her head lay to the side like a ragdoll.

"That's the money shot," the cameraman's thick Southern voice returned.

Slowly, the camera panned over the man's body, showing his chiseled hairy chest and part of his face. As the man turned away, Gavin caught a flash of red beard and sculpted bicep. The angle of the shot displayed a tattoo of an eagle with a number on it. As the camera jerked slightly, a faint image of the man's face appeared, looking straight at the lens. His piercing green eyes and red hair made him menacing. The image went blurry, and the screen froze.

"That's it?" Gavin said, standing up straight.

Derrick said nothing.

"Now we know for sure that Sills was viciously raped," Gavin stated, moving around the table. "Plus, we have a possible ID on our guy. But that tattoo. I swear I've seen it before."

"I lied to you, Gavin," Derrick stated, still keeping his head low.

"What do you mean?" Gavin replied.

Derrick turned to face him as water filled his large dark eyes. His fists balled up.

"What's wrong, Derrick?"

"I just never thought," he said quietly, "that part of my life would affect this life. Goddamn ashamed of it!"

He hit the table with his fist furiously, rocking the laptop.

"D, explain." Gavin stared at him, declining the urge to step near him.

"The poles, the victims' hanging, and even the goddamn

wires," Derrick stated, shaking his head. "All in my fucking face. The son of a bitch was right there!"

"Who?" Gavin was perplexed.

"I lied to you and Evelyn." At that moment, Derrick loosened his tie, unbuttoned his navy-blue shirt, and slipped it off. In the tight white tank top, his muscles twitched in rage. "A part of me knew who it could be. But I was trying not to admit it."

"Derrick," Gavin began.

"See, when I went into special ops," Derrick ignored him and turned to the right side, pointing at his thick upper bicep, "our troop all got the same goddamn ink job. *He* said it was for ID if something happened to any of us."

"When you were in the military?" Gavin stepped closer to him, examining his arm. Derrick had the same eagle tattoo as the red-haired man in the film.

"Squad twenty-one." Derrick leaned back against the wall. "Shit, he was here all along."

Sucking in a deep breath, Derrick shook his head. Then his eyes went back to the computer screen.

"Derrick, do you know who the killer is?" Gavin asked him.

Shamefully, Derrick nodded as a single tear dropped from the corner of his eye. "Yeah, yeah I do."

For a long, lingering moment, silence enveloped the room.

"That motherfucker was my commander," Derrick finally spat out in disgust, pointing at the image on the screen.

*****

About a half an hour later, Derrick plopped onto the dark chocolate leather couch. His eyes still seemed lost in thought as they scanned Gavin's apartment. Gavin had realized the station was not conducive to his partner feeling comfortable enough to explain himself. When he had suggested his place, Derrick jumped at the option.

"Not a bad place here, G," he finally said.

"Thanks," he replied, handing Derrick a beer.

"I can see why you like it here," he commented. He pointed at the construction across the street. "The view of the city is breathtaking, but that's an eyesore."

"It calms me most days," Gavin replied, sitting in the nearby chair. He casually sipped his beer, trying to suppress his headache.

"I've been to a lot of places." Derrick eased further into the couch, leaning his head back and looking up. "I was stationed in Italy, Germany, Thailand, and Japan. I always thought about Chicago though. Nothing could fucking compare to it." Within seconds, Derrick had drained the bottle and wiped his mouth. "Anything stronger?"

"Scotch? Neat?" Gavin queried as he stood up. A tinge of pain hit his lower back.

"Whatever the hell you want to give me," he replied with a brief, forced smile.

Gavin ambled over to the kitchen and reached up into the cabinet for the un-cracked Johnnie Walker bottle. He pulled out a tumbler and poured his partner a generous amount. While the silence was uncomfortable, Gavin did not want to push Derrick. The angry, or, rather, disappointed expression on his face lingered. At that point, Evelyn texted, asking where they were. He shot back that they were running on a hunch, and then asked her to follow up with both Mylo and Mary.

"When I was in the service," Derrick said behind him, "I only came back three times to Chicago. Two times to visit Momma. Those times, I took her out. To museums, other places we'd never been, nice restaurants. Just let her feel like a queen. She deserved it."

"You were a good son," Gavin replied as he took down another glass. He reached for the Grey Goose and some seltzer. He too needed something stronger.

"Naw, man." His voice was entrenched with sadness. "I was an asshole son. I left Momma when I entered the marines. Left her with my bitch sister. Every month, from when I got my first check from the government, I sent Momma money. Turned out she never used it for herself, but on my sister's kids. My goddamn nephews and nieces. Shit, G, I was so fuckin' pissed when I found out. But that's not it though. I just wanted Momma to get out of the hood. To get a good place. Not to hear gunfire in the middle of the night. Not to be harassed by the fucking gang bangers on the block."

"You can't control everything," Gavin returned, heading back and handing Derrick his drink. He set his own on the coffee table near him.

"In hindsight, no," he replied. "But goddammit, I should have. I was too… too getting lost in the Corps to pay attention to what the fuck was happening to Momma. The letters she sent me. Her not feeling well. Her having harder days, a harder time getting up in the morning. Her dealing with her grandkids. Her dealing with my sister's bullshit."

He took a drink.

"The third time I came back to Chicago," he said, "was to bury Momma. And after that, I left the city. I still have some things in my house that I stored away, of Momma's. I feel like I never really buried her. She's still with me. When she died, man, I wasn't in a good place. Perhaps that's why I ended up where I did in the marines."

"Can't blame yourself," Gavin began.

"Can't I?" Derrick returned loudly. "I wound up with that squad, under *his* fucking command, because I was broken. And I thought being more willing to be in the thick of fighting would make up for neglecting my life here. I didn't care if I fucking died on a mission, man. Sometimes I ran to death."

Derrick stopped for a moment as his eyes remained on his drink. Slowly and not quite willingly, they fell on Gavin and filled with water. Derrick shook his head slightly, turned his attention to the view ahead of him, and took a generous gulp of Scotch.

Taking a sip of his own drink, Gavin could see Derrick was lost in another time, in another place. The silence of his apartment engulfed them until Derrick began to speak.

THIRTY-TWO

"I was just a kid when I joined the military.

"Don't get me wrong, I'm proud that I served. The comradery, the unconditional respect, the brutal training, the mundane daily tasks, the smell of sweat, gas, and smoke all day long, the sounds of yelling commands, and even the goddamn rigorous schedule. Military blood still flows in my veins. If you asked me early on, I'd say I was a fucking marine for life. My career was to be entirely in the military, serving my country. I was their fucking puppet, and I conformed to their commands. Eat, sleep, and shit green.

"I *thought* I needed that life. People entered the Corps for many different reasons.

"I joined to escape. Escape the fucking hood life. Escape my family. Escape everything. There were other people like me. We all wanted to shake our old lives and become something different. The military was the perfect choice. Like Sills and Carlton, I used the military advantage and earned my bachelor's degree in history.

"I was committed solidly to the marines. After being abroad for nearly a decade, I wound up stationed in Texas and became staff sergeant. I trained new recruits on firing weapons both close and far range. Could I have been a sniper on the field? Yes. I was passed over several times for missions for different reasons that I won't get into. It was a fantastic job where I could mentor the recruits who wanted to learn, much like training Evelyn. However, I somehow notoriously became the asshole to recruits, especially those who disrespected a black man in charge.

"Anyway, Colonel Coniston was my commander at the base. An incredible man who served all his life. He may have looked menacing, but he was the best. We got along very well. During my tenure, he promoted me because the colonel appreciated my honest opinion and demanding training exercises for the recruits. Remember I told you that I went fishing in the Keys from time to time? That was the guy.

"When Momma died, I was a mess and my attitude changed. The years of forgetting my past seemed to smack me in my goddamn face. In the months after her death, I had to reassess who I was, where I wanted to go, and what I wanted out of the military. Colonel Coniston took me off training exercises for a while, telling me I could get it back. Honestly, I was fine with that; sitting behind a desk and pushing endless amounts of bureaucratic paperwork probably helped me with being a detective now.

"But I was not distracted enough.

"When the Twin Towers fell, I needed more purpose. I just had this restless unexpected adrenaline rush. I wanted to run into that danger. Even against the wishes of Colonel Coniston, who spoke to me more as a friend than just another soldier. He explained how risky the assignments could be, that the deployments would be extraordinarily long, and that I would be on enemy grounds nearly all the time.

"I didn't want to hear him. I didn't fucking want to. I was just a stubborn son of a bitch.

"In the end, he honored my request."

*****

"In late fall of the same year, the colonel informed me that I'd been selected as a possible candidate for an elite team. In a week, I was to participate in a tactical exercise under the supervision of the commander in charge. Of course, with my obedience to the Corps, I accepted the challenge.

"On test day, Colonel Coniston explained the nature of the exercises: combat skills, weapons cleaning and firing, shit like that. What struck me as fucking odd was how the colonel was telling me what to do. Immediately, I noticed a major I had never seen before standing near the colonel as I performed the exercises. He was about my height, wore mirrored sunglasses, chewed on tobacco, and had the most coppery red handlebar mustache. After completing the exercises, I really wanted to approach the colonel and the mysterious major. But my military discipline instinct kicked in, and I waited for permission. For some time—which seemed like goddamn forever—

the colonel and the new major talked to each other. Oddly, the colonel kept his back to me as he spoke. The major nodded, not looking at me, and then stepped into an accompanying jeep with a private at the wheel and drove off.

"I walked over to the colonel and asked him what happened

"'Tests are done,' he said to me. He had a stern look on his face. 'Williamson, you did a fine job in my eyes. Better than any soldier I've seen in a long time. But it's not up to me, son.' Taking off his sunglasses, he looked directly at me. I could see sadness in his dark eyes like a parent letting go of their child. 'Always remember you can say no. You don't have to go. You don't have to at all. Yeah, we are marines. We do what we are told. But Williamson, sometimes it's okay to say no. If it doesn't feel right in your gut, then you don't have to do it. It's not insubordination. You always have a choice.'

"'Sir, I understand what you are telling me,' I said. 'But it's my choice. I want to do this. It feels right to me.'

"I had a heavy heart when I climbed into the back of the jeep behind the colonel in the passenger seat. As the private threw the vehicle into gear, the colonel didn't say anything more to me as we headed back to the base. He seemed more or less disappointed in me.

"A few hours later, I was requested to meet with him in his office. Sitting behind his desk, he barely looked up at me while he scribbled items into a folder. Once the colonel finished up, he told me how impressed Major Stanton had been. So much so, that I was ordered to head out to a San Antonio base, where I would be flown out. He did not give a location, nor did I dare ask. Before I could get a word in, he informed me that my personal belongings would be packed up and stored until my return.

"He stopped for a moment and leaned forward slightly as though he wanted to confide in me. 'Williamson,' he said. His eyes were so sad. 'Derrick, I've known you well enough these past couple years. I know what kind of man you are. A good person. Don't let that ever change you, even when you are in the field. Even if you feel that this is the right thing for you.' He paused for a second. 'My gut says it's wrong. And if you ever need anything, anything at all, reach out. I can try to help you. Understood?'

"With that, he rose and walked around his desk. I stood at attention out of respect. He clasped his hand on my shoulder and said softly, 'Derrick, I tell you this as a friend. Not as your *commander*.

I will miss you, son.'

"Once he dismissed me, I could see him wiping his eyes discreetly. At that same time, my gut told me my decision was not right. But I was too stubborn to let that control me.

"I said fuck it and tried to move on. It'd be the last time I'd see Colonel Coniston for quite a while.

"That night, I boarded a plane full of inexperienced privates. These young cadets were fresh, barely legal, and ready to fight when the opportunity presented itself. The scared looks on their faces, I can't forget. They didn't know if they were returning or not. While they could not control their fate, I was running straight into that danger.

"After a short bumpy flight, we landed in Florida. I was singled out by a lance corporal, who instructed me I had an overnight stay ready on their base. Could I fucking sleep? Hell no. My mind churned like an angry wasp's nest. I was awoken by a different corporal, who ushered me onto another plane. I didn't ask where I was heading. No. Me, the stubborn asshole? I just did as I was fucking told.

"A large freight airliner was commissioned with supplies, heading for the Middle East. Unlike the other one, where the seats somewhat resembled an ordinary commercial airliner, this one was full of crates secured to the walls and strapped down by reinforced nylon netting. As I boarded, I inventoried the amount of mortar shells on board. Shit, if the plane crashed or was gunned down, we'd all die instantly in a huge-ass fireball.

"As the corporal pointed out the seating area, a dozen other people were taking their seats. I quickly strapped myself down and got ready for the flight. Next to me, a nervous-looking white guy was adjusting his belt over and over. Thick black-framed glasses were pushed against his round face, and his fatigues hugged his portly body.

'First flight, Bauerman?' I asked him, reading his name badge.

'No, just hate freight flights,' he yelled back with a crooked smile.

'Don't fucking vomit on me,' I returned, extending a hand out. 'Williamson. Where are you heading?'

"The plane revved up and shook madly as it began to move. The color disappeared from Bauerman's face.

'Not sure,' he replied. 'Just following orders.'

"Leaning closer to him, I said, 'Major Stanton?'

"His eyes widened under his lenses. 'Yeah. You in too?'

"Almost too cheerfully, I said, 'Fuck yeah. Good to meet you.'

"A slim, tall woman sat a seat over.

'You said Stanton?' she said. Her nametag read Sheridan.

'Yeah,' I said.

'Going to Turkey,' she stated simply.

'How did you know?' Bauerman asked over the roaring engines.

'Have to ask.' A faint syrupy smile caressed her thick lips.

"Suddenly, the plane jerked around more as the speed increased. Next to me, Bauerman was wiping his hands on his pants over and over, closing his eyes, muttering a prayer. Sheridan was too calm when the plane began to prepare for ascent. As if she'd done this before. Once the engines were at full blast, the noise was piercing and the plane's frame rumbled under my body.

"For the remainder of the flight, we didn't speak. Sheridan went to sleep. Bauerman spent most of the time in the latrine. I gazed into the cockpit watching the blue horizon.

"Once we landed in Istanbul, Turkey, we were met by some more privates who took our belongings and escorted us into some vehicles. Winding through the streets of the ancient yet modern-looking city, I couldn't help but to think of the history: the old stone facades, the temples, the iconic squares, the people, and the market were right at my fingertips. I wanted to stop the car to get out and explore. Instead, we headed out of the city and drove for another several hours toward the Syrian border.

"Sheridan and I took one car, and Bauerman took the other car. I was exhausted but kept my eyes on the road ahead, admiring the rugged landscape and passing small, scattered villages.

"Outside a small town, the convoy stopped where a muscular white guy was waiting near a military jeep. The detailed tattoos popped on his forearms, and his angry, no-bullshit glare meant business. Getting out of the truck, the smell of fresh air and warmth of the sun felt refreshing.

'Bauerman, Sheridan, and Williamson,' the man announced.

'Yes, present,' I answered for all of us.

'I'm taking you to our camp,' he said. 'Grab your shit and let's go.'

'And who are you?' Bauerman questioned.

'Taylor,' he stated. Even then, I knew that he was just an asshole.

'First Sergeant Taylor. Get your asses in gear! Major Stanton is waiting. And you don't want to piss him off.'

"Dutifully and reluctantly, I threw my gear in the back. I slid into the passenger seat since Bauerman and Sheridan had already taken the back-seat. Not saying anything more, Taylor cranked the jeep into gear and sped off. We journeyed through the backside of Turkey, taking rocky roads that jostled all of us around. I thought that Bauerman was going to lose it halfway through. Sheridan was still so quiet. Taylor didn't look at me nor attempt any conversation. The muscles just twitched on his biceps with each hit. An hour later, he lifted up his radio and spoke clearly, saying that we were only five clicks away. There was no response from the other end. Rounding a deep bend in a shallow valley, the vehicle pulled up to several tents. Taylor slowed down to the center tent.

"We were in fucking nowhere Turkey!

"As I climbed out of the jeep, Major Stanton came out of his tent. He was chewing tobacco, like he had the day I was testing. He glared at all of us and ordered us to fall in. Taylor just leaned against the engine hood watching us.

'I selected each of you for a specific reason,' he stated. His harsh, guttural voice was demanding. Worse than Creighton's on a bad day. 'You're the best. But here on the field, that means shit. Right, Taylor?'

'Yes, sir.' He yawned like he was bored with the whole thing.

'You fuckers are mine,' he stated. 'What I say goes. No fucking double talk. There's no bullshit when we get out there. We're a fucking team and that's it. Any questions?'

"We said nothing.

'Good.' He looked each one of us in the eye. 'I got you space in the tents. Get some rest because we pack up at oh-six hundred tomorrow morning. For our first mission.' He then stepped toward Sheridan. 'Just because you have tits, doesn't mean that you don't sleep with the rest of the men. Got it?'

'Yes, sir,' Sheridan returned.

"Then he looked right at me. 'Forgot how big you are, Williamson. Taylor here thinks he can take your ass out. Right?' He says.

'Yes, sir,' Taylor grinned as he stepped away from the truck and came toward me.

'What do you think, Williamson?' Stanton asked me.

"I snapped off, 'Tell Taylor not to fuck with me, and we'll get along just fine. Sir.'

"Stanton smiled. He was pleased I stood up for myself. 'Like that spirit, boy. Gonna need that out in the field,' he says to me.

"Taylor gave me the finger and walked off.

*****

"At oh-three in the morning, the other members of the squad wrestled around and broke down the camp- site. All the while, Stanton barked out orders and commands to get the shit done quickly. His goddamn pious attitude was relentless and overbearing toward Sheridan, Bauerman, and me. However, he was even-toned with the others. I wasn't sure what I was getting myself into. I felt like I was starting boot camp all over again. Instead, there were no drills, no practices, nothing like that.

"Two hours later, while the sun rose in the sky, we drove past the Syrian border and toward the fighting. In the distance, I heard the echoes of a couple of mortar shells exploding in the far distance off the canyon walls. Faintly, the sounds of screaming, car alarms, and the rat-tat-tat of responding gunfire followed.

'Music to my goddamn ears,' Stanton said out loud, maybe to Taylor, who was driving. 'Nothing like a shit-ton of explosions ahead of me.' He looked at me with a devilish smile. 'Today would be a great day to fucking die. Don't you think, assholes?'

"Taylor snickered like he was in on a private joke. Sheridan just gave me a stern look. I kept my mouth shut, hunkered down into the seat and watched the plumes of white smoke in the far distance. Stanton turned his attention back to the road, humming something inaudible.

"That's how I met Major Zachary Stanton."

THIRTY-THREE

"For the following months, our missions were solidly based on the Syrian-Iraqi border, and then deep within Iraq. Technically, I can't disclose the true nature of the missions. I can say that we were typically extracting high-level personnel who were trapped behind the border. The fighting and retrieving of said personnel was, at times, seriously fucking risky. Sometimes we had to go after insurgent militants to take down their camps, or to claim as much intel on them as possible. In the marines, you relied on each other and protected one another. Quickly, you learn to trust each other, especially behind enemy lines.

"Stanton always took the lead, and we followed.

"The squad was full of people like me, people who were escaping their past lives to do something new. Torres, a small Puerto Rican guy highly trained in martial arts, was communications. He could drink like a real motherfucker. Zeller, a thin guy who smoked like a chimney, was explosives. He taught Stanton the braided wire trick, by the way. But Zeller never really talked much about his family. Not sure if he ever had one. Then came Pope. He was an odd one. Not exactly the fucking smartest, but he was brute force. A big-ass fucker too. Yet, he could sneak up on anyone so quietly that you'd never see him coming. Typically, Stanton sent him out first with Zeller. Finally, there was Parker. He was as tall as I am, fairly built frame, lighter skin than I have, and unusually smart. Not school smart, street smart. If he wasn't in the military, I think he would have been a leader in a major gang. And he was just a mean motherfucker. Always sharpening his long blade against a stone whenever we traveled.

"Bauerman settled in as well. Probably too well in my opinion, always trying to come across as too likeable. He did whatever Stanton or Taylor told him like a fucking dog. He did all the miscellaneous bullshit things around the camp. In the field, he usually went in with Taylor, Torres, and Parker. I was assigned to ammunition and weapons because Stanton was so impressed with my test. Sheridan was actually a doctor. Still, she and I seemed to always be teamed up together. Even though she was a medic, in the field she handled the gear and vehicles, usually finding our escape in any situation. Like me, she and I would be the ones laying down cover for the others. I considered her to be a much better sniper than me, and I asked her how she became so good. In confidence, she told me that her father taught her to aim a gun and respect a weapon's power.

"By that point, we all trusted each other.

"About four months in, after getting back from a mission, we were hanging around our camp, sharing a couple bottles of whiskey. Bauerman asked Stanton why he needed three more people in his unit.

'Simple.' His voice was always guttural like he'd just choked on something and was clearing it. 'Because they died.'

"Later on, I did uncover information that Stanton was telling the truth. The squad was in a classified mission near the Iranian border when one of their vehicles hit a land mine. The soldiers—Wong, Ross, and Hankel—died instantly. We drank a lot that night.

"A couple of days later, me, Sheridan, and Bauerman were rounded up. They found a nasty tattoo parlor in a little town nearby. Stanton came along with us.

'To be in combat against motherfuckers like these, we need to be one team.' He was an arrogant son of a bitch. He rolled up his sleeve, and on his bicep was the very tattoo you saw in the film. Each of us got one.

"I'm ashamed to say I actually felt like part of the group—like I had a fucking purpose. Stanton had a way of making a solider feel indestructible. The missions flew at us, and I no longer cared about whatever else was going on in the world. We never really had downtime, no real time off.

"Yet, being around each other so much, it didn't take me long to figure out how Stanton operated."

******

"The missions blended into one long epic bullshit day: wandering the desert, the valleys, through the high heat, the chill night air, setting up camp, tearing it down, and lugging shit from place to place. Of course, we'd have to watch our backs being in hostile environs, only clicks away from enemy camps and sometimes abandoning our vehicles and huffing it on foot. The excitement lost its appeal real fucking quick. When traveling to key locations, I witnessed Stanton's cruelty. He wasn't just a son of a bitch to us, he passed it on to the non-hostiles, the innocent ones who didn't even want the war.

"Like one time, I remember distinctly, we entered a village just on the western Iraqi border, about a good forty or fifty clicks from the actual fighting. We had a long day of travel to get where we needed to go, and we needed to get some rest. Instead of setting up camp on the outskirts, Stanton commanded Taylor and Zeller to scout out a village. A half an hour later, we rode through the small streets. The impact of the war could be seen in the villagers' eyes, their sadness and hidden rage. About three or four streets in, amongst the shanty buildings, Taylor popped out of a house and flagged us over. Stanton got out of the car and entered the house. Along the way he blocked off the herds of small kids begging for food with his arm, as if they were pesky mosquitos.

"Over the crowd, he gave an all-clear and yelled out, 'Come on you, pussies! Unpack, let's go! Sheridan, first watch!'

"Helping Torres with some bags, I went through the crowd and noticed shadows floating in the back of the houses. When I turned back, Sheridan stood on top of the jeep with her rifle pointing at the growing crowd. As I entered the building, an older woman spat near my boot and yelled at me with disdain.

"Inside, the tight space was claustrophobic to say the least. In the far corner I caught sight of, a man in his mid-thirties with fresh bruises on his face protecting the young girl just behind him. In the opposite corner, Taylor had stripped off his shirt, and his tank was speckled with blood. Stanton emerged from the side kitchenette with a bottle of booze in his hand and cursed at the man in the corner. Taylor and Parker snickered as they also sipped from the bottle. I didn't want to touch it, but Stanton called me a pussy for not drinking any.

"I felt like the invading force we were, and I was on high alert. Stanton didn't see it as he plopped on the sofa and stretched out his long body. His eyes remained on the girl for some time, until she eventually snuck out. For the rest of the night, while Torres, myself, and Sheridan took watches, the others partied, wrecking the place.

"Was this the first time I saw this? Fuck no. Every town was different. Every place showed gutted shells of people. Stanton took and stole from the desperately hungry, impoverished, and sickened families, leaving destruction and fear as a result. Eventually, I became so used to Stanton's actions that they became just a common thing. A pretty fucked up situation.

"Then the missions, man.

"What can I say about them? I was never exactly privy to the actual communications with base. Stanton kept the details between him and Taylor. The major never gave us exact locations or let us know ahead of time who we needed to grab and what we needed to infiltrate. All of it was done through cryptic commands and snap decisions. We were puppets in his fucking malicious hands. As the months wore on, we captured possible hostiles for intel on enemy bases. We did what was necessary to complete each mission. Some were easy in-and-out pulls. Others were rather bloody. Too much blood on my hands, I admit.

"The extractions and rendezvous points were always on a need-to-know basis. Simple. Later, I would learn that our successes on missions were actually pinned on Stanton. He absorbed the accolades and reviews from the generals above. The Corps is built like that. The upper commanders receive the credit, and the underlings get shit. Our missions decorated his jacket.

"Then I woke up one day to what was really happening. It took one supposed extraction to get me thinking what the real purpose had been.

"Probably around ten months in, late summer, we brought in a possible suspect. A young kid, maybe no more than eighteen or nineteen. We killed several of his buddies in a fast assault. I found him trying to escape through the back door. When I pursued him, Parker appeared around the corner and stabbed the kid in the leg. We were on orders not to kill the subject.

"Setting camp out of the village, Stanton ordered me to set up a spare tent for the prisoner. Lying in my cot later, I was exhausted from watch duty. As I was closing my eyes, I heard this muffled shouting. I snuck out into the shadows and, easing my way closer to the prisoner tent. I spotted some movement just outside of it. In the bright moonlight, Stanton was shirtless and his pale skin glowed like a ghost. He was wiping his hands on a bloodied towel and chewing on a lit cigar, an obvious look of frustration on his face.

"Taylor, who looked sweaty, came out of the tent and said something inaudible to Stanton. Not turning to look at him I heard him reply, 'Get Bauerman and bury it near the valley.'

"Of course, his pet, Taylor, nodded and ran off. As he walked toward his tent, I noticed splatters of blood all over his chest, like he'd been butchering an animal. Bauerman, Parker, and Taylor came around the tent and entered. I saw them carry a bundle in a wrapped tarp to the jeep and take off southwest in the dark. Once they left, I snuck into the tent.

"Inside, a folding chair was knocked over and spattered with blood. On a nearby desk, I curiously sifted through some papers, which were signed by General Norquist. I then noticed a photo of some other man, slightly older and chunkier, who didn't look at all like who we had taken. I crept behind the flap of the tent when I heard a noise.

"Cautiously, Sheridan crept inside and went to the table. Her long thin fingers danced over the same papers I had just touched. It surprised me when she asked softly, 'What are you doing in here, Williamson?'

'I should ask you that.' I stepped out, keeping my eye on Stanton's dark tent.

'On patrol, asshole. Saw movement in here.' She seemed distracted, as if I weren't really the issue.

"Out of nowhere, Pope entered the tent and gave us a suspicious look. 'What the hell are you doing here?'

"I tried to cover my presence there. 'Going to take a piss, got mixed up,' I said.

'All you need is a bush, idiot,' Sheridan stated behind me.

"Pope just eyed me and I took off toward the nearby rocks. Glancing back, I saw Sheridan speak to Pope and then head in the opposite direction. Early in the morning, Stanton announced that the prisoner had died overnight. Sheridan dared not make any eye contact with me. At the same time, Bauerman, Taylor, and Zeller conveniently and uncharacteristically tore down our camp.

"As we walked on that day, my mind kept picturing the young man. Our missions were never to torture hostiles, just extract and let the others get information. *Who the hell was that kid? What did*

Stanton want with him? I kept wondering. Keeping my mouth shut, I realized then that I couldn't trust anyone on the squad.

"Especially Stanton."

*****

"A month later, we finally got a break and Stanton gave us some much needed R and R.

"I was thrilled because the missions could not distract me enough from what I had witnessed. And my eyes had opened to the true reality of how divided the squad was. You see, Taylor, Parker, Pope, and Bauerman hung around Stanton, eating up his stories, kissing his ass, and doing much less work around the camp. Then there was us: Torres, Sheridan, and me. We worked harder, had to take the night watches, and lugged most of the shit. Even if I was one of them, I couldn't stand how they looked, how they sounded, even how they smelt. Fuck, man, I wanted to be away from them!

"I went to London to decompress. Guess being submerged in the squad for so long, I lost track of the rest of the world—the protests about the war, Islamophobia, extraordinarily heightened security, the tension in Europe, and the existing financial crisis. Shit man, I felt lost in the real world. Before I knew it, time had slipped away and I reluctantly returned to the Middle East. When I reached Turkey, a lance corporal greeted me and informed me that Stanton had rerouted us to East Afghanistan. I found Sheridan, Torres, and Pope on board the plane. They were all talking about their time off. I remained quiet.

"The cordial flight attendant asked Sheridan and me for anything to drink. She ordered some Scotch and I asked for a couple of beers. Sheridan stared out the window. She was anxiously tapping the armrest. A faint, sad expression covered her beautiful face. I leaned near her so Torres or Pope couldn't hear us.

'Did you and your husband have a fight?'

'No, not really.' She didn't look at me.

'Sheridan, he didn't want you to come back,' I suggested.

'After what we've been through, you can call me Colleen.' She acknowledged my good guess with a faint smile.

'Fine.' I extended my hand. 'I'm Derrick.'

"Her smile increased as she blushed and shook my hand.

'Good to meet you.' Then she added, 'Yes, you're right. He didn't want me to return.'

'Did he give the 'me Tarzan, you Jane' guilt trip?' I quipped.

'No, not at all,' she said. 'He's really understanding. He knows my job is hard.' She stopped and looked away, sipping on her Scotch. Maybe wondering how much more information she could trust me with.

'Well, what we do is fucking nuts.' I glanced over at the guys to double-check that they were asleep. 'Working for an asshole boss in a shitty place.'

"Nodding her head in agreement 'You don't know the half of it.'

"A small, quiet moment passed between us.

'I have a question to ask you,' I said.

'How did my tits get so big?' she quipped. 'It's called genetics.'

'No, but thanks.' I know I blushed slightly. Even after all I'd been through there was still a part of me that was innocent. Leaning into her more, I got all serious. 'That night, the one when the prisoner died.'

"She said nothing.

'Did you see anything?'

"She didn't focus on me. She was watching the other guys. 'What do you mean? I was on patrol that night.'

'I mean, I saw a picture of the man we were supposed to capture. Why did Stanton order us to grab that other guy?'

'Orders are orders.'

"I leaned even closer to her. I wanted an answer from her. A confirmation that I was on the right track. 'Something's wrong with our squad. I think it has to do with Taylor, Parker, and even Stanton.'

"Sheridan still had trouble looking at me. Finally, she looked up from her drink.

'Listen, Derrick, I'll tell you this. Taylor requested me to do a full sweep of the perimeter of the base camp. He claimed he heard some noises a quarter-click away. I cut it short because I heard some screaming. When I returned, I found you in the tent. No prisoner.'

"I wanted to ask her why she covered for me. Instead I asked, 'Did you see Bauerman or Taylor while on post?'

She shook her head. 'No. About an hour later. Parker said

he'd take over my shift. Told me I should get some rest.'

"I let it digest for a minute.

"She leaned over and whispered, 'Derrick, just be careful.'

"I asked her if that was a warning?

'No,' she whispered. 'Because I think something's wrong too.'

"Before I could say another word, I felt Torres hit my shoulder, then ask me why Sheridan and I were so close to each other. Abruptly, Sheridan dismissed him with a cocky remark, which made him laugh. For the rest of the long flight, I drank more beer and couldn't sleep at all. Sheridan curled up next to me and slept soundly. As the plane entered Afghan air space, a sense of dread overwhelmed me. Not because of the pending missions, but because of Stanton and the others in the squad."

THIRTY-FOUR

"When we arrived on location at a base just north of Kabul, near the capital of Afghanistan, Stanton gave us the customary ass-chewing speech about being late. Apparently, the others received the message earlier than we had. Stanton gathered us near a large hangar. I remember the major's words: 'Hope you ladies enjoyed your leave. It'll be the last one for a fucking long time. Because of you, and your hard fucking work on capturing all goddamn insurgents, General Norquist assigned us here. Our missions are going to be run out of here. This is our permanent residence.'

"Naturally, the squad was fucking thrilled by the news. I instantly felt restricted. I looked at Sheridan for a response, but she was quiet. For the following weeks, our squad helped with construction, organization, and setting up tents for incoming troops. Much to the displeasure of the locals, our base infringed on a small town nearby. Even though a handful of locals were pleased about the American base, the rest took to the streets in protest.

"In a matter of days, I found myself in newly constructed barracks, where I bunked with Torres. The other guys took nearby rooms, while Taylor remained on his own at the end of the hallway. Sheridan took a room by herself in another barracks just opposite of ours. As soon as we got settled, the missions came at us again. I suppose the luxury of having an actual bed to return to was better than nothing. Like before, behind enemy lines, we gathered intel on possible terrorist groups, captured possible suspects, and rescued important American delegates. Honestly, man, some of those missions come into my dreams and I wake up in a cold sweat. Scotch isn't enough to chase them away.

"While we were in the non-hostile villages, Stanton's aggressive and vicious reign was fucking relentless. He gave orders to pilfer houses, kill their animals, and take what we needed. At times, I felt like he was one of those Caribbean pirates on the seas, ruthlessly raiding small vessels. While Bauerman, Parker, Pope, Taylor, and even Torres played along with his cruelty, I began to stop catering to his demands. It just wasn't right. This one time, he commanded me to empty out a woman's pantry. She barely had enough to survive much less feed her kids. So, I didn't do it. Outside the village, Stanton unexpectedly sucker-punched me in the ribs, spat a huge wad of chew into my face, and yelled, 'Sergeant, when I tell you to do something, just fucking do it. Otherwise, next time, I'll leave your goddamn black ass out here to die.'

"That fuckin' motherfucker!"

*****

"Days later, we were back at the base for some down time. I seemed to separate myself from the squad even more. Soon, I made some local friends who spoke broken English; in turn they taught me simple phrases. I even struck up some friendships in other divisions. I didn't care. I couldn't deal with Stanton's bullshit.

"Stanton requested me to do an inventory and resupply of all weapons. As I was conducting inventory, a local guy, Aymaan, asked if I needed any help. Technically, he was not supposed to, because locals were strictly assigned to construction detail. Having met him before and learned about his huge family, I trusted him more than the others. Plus, the extra hand was helpful. As he was pulling down some equipment, Aymaan told me that he'd never met a black man before. Of course, I just laughed it off with him. He followed it up with the statement, 'No, you are much nicer than that other one.'

"I didn't know who he meant. 'There's a lot of black people on the base.'

'The other one in your group,' he said.

'You mean Parker?' Parker was practicing at the range that day.

'My people don't like him.' He shook his head in disgust. 'He just bad.'

"For some reason I felt a desire to cover for him even though I knew he was a little shit. 'Why? He's not that bad,'

"Aymaan came closer to me. 'Your boss go to a place where

he should not be,' he said. His dark eyes looked past me.

'Major Stanton?'

'Yes.' He stopped counting and looked directly at me. 'West of here. Not far.'

'What's there?'

"Before he could say another word, some air force and army groups entered the area, and we went about our business. I sent Aymaan on an errand, I purposely searched the base for Stanton, pretending I needed him to check the inventory. A half an hour later, I found Taylor with Bauerman and Pope in the maintenance shop. I asked Taylor if he had seen Stanton.

'What the hell do you want him for?' Taylor was shirtless. He loved showing off that ugly-ass eagle tattoo on his chest every chance he could.

'Need him to check my inventory and supply list.'

'Never needed goddamn permission before. Why now?'

"I shrugged and tried to act cool. 'New base. New rules, I guess. Where is he?'

"Taylor dropped the wrench in his hand and came up to me angrily. 'Do I look like his goddamn babysitter?'

"I decided to push it. 'You are second in command. You should know where the major is.'

'I'm getting fucking sick of your know-it-all attitude, Williamson.' He was within inches of my face. 'Parading around here like your fucking shit don't stink.'

"That pissed me off. I got braver, or stupider. I got into his face. 'Well, you're just a goddamn white asshole who uses large muscles and tattoos to compensate for a small dick size.'

"Taylor threw the first punch, and I returned with several direct hits to his pretty-boy face. I'd been waiting for an opportunity to hit that asshole. Several others in the garage egged us on, along with Bauerman and Pope. Before I realized it, he'd knocked me on the ground face first, trying to pin my arm. Instinctively, I wrapped my other arm around his neck and strained to flip him over my body.

"Suddenly I heard Sheridan. 'Goddammit! Stop it! Enough!' Then a pair of arms pulled Taylor off me. He was breathing heavily, wiping blood off his nose and mouth. Looking over, I saw Sheridan stepped in and separated us.

'What the hell is going on?!'

"Taylor snapped at her. 'Ain't none of your goddamn business, *Doctor.*'

"I confirmed his statement as I walked away. 'Like the asshole said, ain't nothing.'

"Later that evening, I purposely waited for Stanton, who came back to base just after midnight. His diligent little pet, Parker, was in the driver seat."

******

"The very next morning we were awakened by the sounds of artillery exploded all around us. A large insurgent faction was attempting a coup over the government. As a result, we were engaged in major fighting and resistance for the following months. Many Afghan people died, and nearly a third of the outlying areas were destroyed. Many of the injured were brought to the makeshift hospitals, and the infrastructure was ripped apart. I came to learn that the   fighting   was   always   a   constant.

"Stanton led our squad into the thick of it. Naturally, we worked as a unit and took out the leaders of the insurgent group. We weakened their stronghold, and they retreated back to the west. Even though Taylor and I had our fight, we were neutral on the field. No one ever mentioned our scuffle to Stanton. I didn't give a fuck either way.

"The devastation of the fighting affected me, man. Each day, funeral processions went down the broken, rubble-ridden streets of the nearby village. It seemed like the smell of continuous burning buildings and even dead bodies worsened by the hour. The American presence was being met with resistance as thousands and thousands of protestors surrounded the base and shouted in their native tongues, 'Go home, Americans!' I understood their anger. They didn't want us in their problems. However, the Afghan, U.S., and other Aliant governments did not agree. While I helped, I was spit at, shoved, yelled at, and hit.

"Never felt so unappreciated.

"Three weeks later, we got a new mission. On my way to gather materials, I found Aymaan in a nearby medical tent. As I approached him, I saw the distress in his face. He was kneeling next to a cot where a young, severely burnt boy was covered in bandages across most of his torso. Aymaan muttered prayers and held the boy's hand. When he looked up tears flowed down his face. He told me his family had perished in a fatal attack, and his son was the only survivor. I didn't know what to say and felt tears come to my eyes. Without a single word, he dug into his pocket and reached over to my hand.

'Here,' he said.

"I palmed the items in my hand. They were gun shells.

"I pocketed them as I asked him what he wanted me to do with them.

'You a good man, my black friend," he said in his broken English as more tears coursed down his cheeks. 'Took those out of my daughter. The Qahhar killed her with those.'

'Qahhar?' I couldn't believe it.

'Yes, from the west.'

'I don't know——'

"He whispered, 'your boss go to west. Ask him why he do this,' 'Leave me.' Aymaan said no more. His eyes went down to his dying son.

"I snuck around a building and pulled out the shells, which were standard issue M4 carbine casings. Part of me did not want to believe Stanton was dirty. Yeah, he was an asshole. Not dirty though. Of the hundreds and hundreds of troops in Afghanistan, how could it be Stanton? Why would he do it? I couldn't believe it.

"Oddly, my gut told me otherwise."

******

"Knowing about the shells ate away at me. I was in my own head, just thinking about Stanton, watching his every movement, hearing his voice. I was angry, concerned, and even felt helpless. As a result, it almost cost me my life.

"On the Russian-Pakistan border, we were heading down an embankment when rapid firing occurred. I laid out a suppressive fire to hold off any intruders while the others ran for safety. I nearly got hit by the gunfire, tumbled down the ravine, and was stabbed in the arm by a thick branch. When Stanton caught up to me, he unleashed his fury and told me I was a fucking idiot. Behind him, Taylor ate it all up. Sheridan came to my side and checked out the injury. Stanton's face was in mine, and I could see the red lines around his piercing green eyes. He yelled savagely, 'Better get your fucking head on straight, Sergeant! Don't know what the hell's going on with you, but we're a goddamn team. Taylor, Torres, and Pope almost got taken out due to your fucking lack of attention!'

"I looked directly at Taylor and grunted back, 'Maybe they should have been.'

"Taylor tried to jump me, but Stanton's thick arm held him back.

'Fuckers think I don't know what happened between you two?' Stanton glanced back at Taylor. 'Think I'm a fucking idiot?'

'Naw, Sir,' Taylor barked back. One of the few times Taylor's Southern drawl came out.

'*William-son.*' Stanton over-exaggerated my name all the time. I hated it. 'Whatever's distracting you, better get it the fuck out! Need a soldier, not a goddamn menstruating pussy!'

"Then he and Taylor huffed away.

"Sheridan wrapped up my forearm. 'Though I hate to agree with Major, that was a dumbass move.'

"I was in no mood to take any correction. 'Fuck him.'

"Sheridan questioned my actions and what had gotten into me.

"I wasn't sure who I could trust anymore and I told her so.

"She leaned closer and whispered, 'Think we have something in common. When we get back, we should talk.'

*****

"When we returned to the base, I inquired about Aymaan's son, and, to my relief, the son was being flown out to a major hospital in India. Instead of finding Sheridan, who was already busy with patients, I decided to perform my standard post-operative inventory on supplies. Walking toward the hangar, I noticed a double shipment of the last order, sitting in the way of everything. Another guy, a Sergeant Foreman, army guy, also worked in the hangar and happened to be there that day. He declined that shipment was his stuff and told me it was what *I* ordered. Thinking back, I tried to look for the shipment or even purchase order, but I never found it. Maybe it was a simple mistake, not like the Pentagon didn't ever fuck up here or there. I simply called it into requisitions to put the shipment on return notice.

"About two days later, I headed for the showers after a hard workout and overheard a couple of other guys talking. With the noise outside, I couldn't really hear who it was. One thing about the military, there ain't no such thing as true privacy. Anyway, I jumped into a nearby stall and turned on the water. After the passing trucks went by, I heard Bauerman's squeaky-ass voice say, 'What're you going to do with your cut?'

"I heard Taylor reply, 'What the fuck you talking 'bout?'

'From the shit, you know.'

"Slowly, I turned off the shower so I could eavesdrop easier. More rumbling jeeps passed by and blocked out the rest of the conversation.

"I heard Taylor's angry hiss once the vehicles had passed, 'Never say a fucking thing again!'

"Bauerman sounded panicked when he answered. 'Alright, man!'

"Taylor lowered his voice further. 'Not alright, asshole.' Say one more thing outside of the circle, I'll personally make sure you go back in a body bag. Got it!'

"I could hardly hear Bauerman's frightened reply of, 'yeah'.

"I watched Taylor's inked legs leave the stall. He threw on a pair of pants and headed out the door. About a minute later, Bauerman left too. Without thinking much, I threw on my pants and followed Taylor into the busy base.

"Soon as I got out the door and turned the corner, I ran directly into Taylor, who was on the phone. Before he could say anything, Sheridan shouted behind me, 'There you are!'

"I turned to see Sheridan running toward us with a large smile. In the corner of my eye, Taylor seemed to be equally surprised, lowering his phone. With a sudden burst, she sprinted over to me. Several other officers and soldiers noticed it as well.

"She clasped her arms around my bare shoulders and grinned up at me. 'I so missed you. You smell fantastic.'

"Taylor shook his head and stepped back. Sheridan had him going. 'Are you guys a couple now?'

"Sheridan had him hooked like a big mouthed bass. 'Of course," she says, and looks me straight in the eyes. 'Isn't that right, baby?'

"On cue, I wrapped my arm around her waist. In my lowest voice, I said to Taylor, 'Got a problem with that?'

"A huge grin formed on his nasty lips. 'God, can't wait to tell the major this. You guys're fucked!'

"Sheridan kept up the act. 'Whatever.' She spit out and coyly giggled, slapped her hand on my chest. 'Derrick can fuck the shit out of a nun. His mammoth black cock fills me up for days!'

"At the same time, a couple of lovely young new female recruits eyed me.

"I grinned and lowered my face close to hers. 'Girl, don't be telling that stupid redneck motherfucka my secret.'

"Taylor shifted gears and asked her, 'Aren't you married?'

"She rubbed her fingers along my stomach tenderly. She would have made a great actress. 'Hey, don't Vegas rules apply in Afghanistan?'

"I stood up straighter. 'That's right, sugar.'

"Taylor started off. 'Stanton's going to shit.'

'Hmm, I don't give a flying fuck,' Sheridan hollered after him. 'Do you, honey?'

'Naw,' I said. Before I knew it, she kissed me, passionately and aggressively. There were a few shouts from soldiers, and Taylor was gone.

"Sheridan let go of me and grinned as she scanned the area. 'I just bought our cover.' She pulled me close for one last kiss on the cheek and whispered in my ear, 'We need to talk. As soon as possible. I have a perfect place in mind. Meet me at the gate at eighteen hundred hours, tonight.'

"I agreed and Sheridan began to walk away and then turned back to look at me with a naughty smile. 'Derrick, you should be shirtless more often. Me like-y.'

"She disappeared behind a nearby building. I was beginning to realize even then that she wasn't telling me everything."

THIRTY-FIVE

"Once I met Sheridan at the gate, she whisked me away into the depths of the village, hardly speaking along the way. She wore a loose beige dress and matching hijab. I dressed the part and wore some khakis and a light colored button-down.

"Several blocks in, she took me to a small restaurant, which reminded me of a diner where Momma took us for breakfast after church. The clunky tables had mismatched chairs, the cigarette smoke hung in the air, and the smell of grease hit you immediately. A small chubby man walked over to Sheridan and gave her a hug, speaking something quickly in his native tongue. The other people stared briefly at me, then went back to their own worlds.

"Hurriedly, the man showed us to a table in the back, far from the window. He left and quickly returned with some room temperature sweet white wine, some naan, and garlic-eggplant spread.

"Sheridan immediately got down to business. She asked me what I knew about Stanton.

"I was cryptic. I didn't know who to trust. 'He's the boss,' I said.

"She wasn't falling for that line. 'Don't bullshit me,' she said. 'You haven't been yourself lately.'

"I tried to pass her off. 'Some shit's been on my mind,' I said.

"She seemed to relax and smiled at me. 'Enlighten me.' she said.

"I asked her how I knew I could trust her and she pointed out I wouldn't have been with her otherwise.

"I held my tongue.

"She leaned in and put her hand on my arm. 'You wouldn't have played along with me today. Unless...'

'Unless what?' I prompted. I wanted some reassurance.

"She smiled. 'Unless you didn't want Taylor to know that you were following him. Rather poorly, I might add.'

"I tried to sound convincing when I denied it.

'Then what were you doing? Stalking him? Got a man crush on him?' She was playing with me.

'Fuck no,' I said louder than I meant to. A couple at a table near us turned and looked at me.

"She leaned forward on the table. 'Tell me what you know. In return, I will show you the reason we came here.'

"I joked with her. 'You mean you didn't bring me here for the fucking ambiance?'

"She gave a brief laugh. At that point, our main course came. Sheridan warned me to use the naan instead of the silverware because the utensils were never washed. Between bites and sips of wine, I shared what Aymaan told me about Stanton. Then I explained about the double shipment, the conversation I'd heard between Bauerman and Taylor in the showers, and the bullet casings.

"She finished off her wine and stood up. 'Come on, my turn,' she said and off we went.

"Sheridan and I stepped through the ragged curtain into the narrow kitchen. My stomach churned after seeing the filth in the corners, the raw meat covered with flies, and one of the cooks scratching hard at his spotty scalp. Through the narrow doorway to the alley, Sheridan ascended a nearby wooden staircase. As I followed her, I caught a glance of a young man with a rifle in a doorway, smoking a cigarette. The man was a lookout, not a threat.

"Reaching the top floor, Sheridan ducked beneath some linens hanging from a clothes line and walked into a shabby doorframe. Inside, a dim light above exposed a small room, where three people sat on a broken couch. A television displayed a translated American cartoon while two young children in long dirty clothes sat on the floor and stared at the screen. We shuffled over to a small alcove, where a petite, thin elderly woman with a long dark brown burqa smiled sadly at Sheridan. The woman grabbed her hand and nodded, and Sheridan said something kind back to her. I didn't realize how quickly Sheridan had picked up the language. A taller anemic-looking man stepped in the doorway across from us. His bloodshot eyes were swollen with grief, and he signaled for us to enter the next room.

"My heart squeezed tightly from what I saw.

In the corner of the very small bedroom, a bed was on the bare floor with a light netting over the top. While the open window gave minimal fresh air, the smell of blood and sickness hung in the room.

Under the netting, a young woman lay resting. She seemed to barely cling to life by the sound of her raspy breaths. In the dim light, her face and arms showed signs of multiple lacerations, and thick bandages stained with dried blood covered half of her body. Near her, the mother was holding her hand, muttering some prayer under her breath.

"Sheridan knelt down near the young woman and examined the bandages diligently. Underneath her long dress, she pulled out some clean bandages that had been secured against her legs. For the next few minutes, she changed the dressing on the woman's wounds. It was then that I saw the deep, badly infected knife cuts in her stomach and upper thighs. The young woman did not moan nor stir as Sheridan touched her body.

"After a few minutes, Sheridan spoke softly. 'Amalia, here, found her daughter at the edge of town like this, discarded into one of the fields.'

"Innocently I asked, 'why can't you take her to the base?'

"Sheridan looked up. 'They don't want to step near it at all. They say we brought them here.'

"I still hadn't caught on. 'Who?[22] I asked.

"She continued to clean the wounds. 'The Qahhar.'

"I could not help but stare; the gurgling sound of the woman's breath meant death was close. That was the second time I'd heard of the Qahhar."

******

"Back outside, the crisp air was refreshing as I scanned the dark streets around us. I knew that what Sheridan had shown me was kept hidden for a reason.

"I finally asked, 'What does the Qahhar have to do with Stanton?'

"She replied in a heated breath. 'The locals tell me that for nearly a decade, the Qahhar was no longer a threat in this region. Back in the late seventies and early eighties, they attempted an assault on the capital, and failed miserably.'

"I still didn't get it. 'Is the Qahhar a new faction that was to take over the government?'

"She continued to explain. 'Not exactly. The fighting that occurred for the last couple of months was unexpected. In the late eighties, the government began to round up Qahhar leaders, imprison them, and dismantle their organization. In ninety-seven, the highest leader broke out of the prison and headed west to the mountains. In a short time, he was able to reorganize and reestablish the Qahhar quickly."

"She made them sound like a gang, and I told her so.

'Actually, close,' she said. 'They are the largest drug cartel in Afghanistan.'

"My mind was trying to wrap around the idea of drugs. A couple of kids poked their heads out of the window and stared at us. The little girl whispered to a younger boy and giggled. Sheridan told me the girl thought I was handsome. Then an angry voice scolded them, and they moved away from the window.

"She continued to weave her story. 'Being near the capital the villages were fairly safe from possible attacks. They are not a normal cartel.' Her fingers adjusted her hijab for a second, revealing more of her concerned face. 'They are highly weaponized and resourceful. Since ninety-nine, they were buying weapons from ex-Soviet war criminals. In Russia, you can buy anything if you really want it.'

"Up ahead, the light pollution of the base could be seen over the housetops, and the noise was increasing. As we turned a corner, I noticed a couple air force soldiers heading our way. Quickly, Sheridan wrapped an arm around my waist and came in close to me. As they passed, she kissed my cheek, pretended to whisper something to me, and I smiled back at her. The soldiers went on their way. Since we were only a couple of streets away, she insisted that I hold her hand tightly.

"She continued to tell me the Qahhar wanted one thing. More drugs to buy more weapons. What they needed was more land to grow their product. They were growing *Papaver somniferum.* she said. Poppies. For heroin, the drug of choice in that part of the world.

"I still hadn't made the connection. 'What does this have to do with Stanton?' I asked.

"She slowed down her pace as we came to the crowded streets. 'Remember that night before I found you in the prisoner's tent?' She paused. 'You were right. That young man was not the intended target. He was captured for a different reason.'

"I finally had it. 'To learn more about the Qahhar?' I guessed.

'You're smarter than you look,' she joked. 'Yes, he was one of the higher members of the organization. How Stanton knew to grab him, I'm not sure. One more thing. Since our arrival on the base, drug use has gone up. That's not a coincidence.'

"I said nothing for an entire block. When we entered the noisy bright strip leading to the base, the sounds of the soldiers in bars shouting, the loud music blaring in the street, the rush of sellers going from person to person, and the cars honking at people crossing the street created a scene of chaos. I never let go of Sheridan's hand the entire time.

"Once we were on base, Sheridan leaned closer to me, and I automatically wrapped my arm around her.

"I asked what we should do next?

"She needed me to find copies of the squad's weapons inventory and shipments.

"I didn't think Stanton would be that dumb.

"She agreed but wanted me to start there. 'You'll know it when you see it. That's your thing.' She assured me

'I'll do my thing,' she added. She stopped and scooped her arms around my waist. A look of concern fell over her face. Then she said, 'I *knew* I could trust you.'

"Slowly moving her hajib back, I touched her hair. Several soldiers from the mess hall were coming toward us. I asked her how were we going to share information?'

"Sheridan leaned in close and whispered, 'When we sneak out and fuck, baby.'

"With a half-smile, I softly replied, 'Fine with me.'

"On that note, we kissed. As the soldiers passed, she stepped away and smiled. She walked toward the door. I went to my own room. All I could think was: *What kind of shit was I getting myself into?*

"If anyone found out, or if Stanton found out, I was fucked."

*****

"For a whole week at the base, no missions were assigned to us, and Stanton actually took a short leave. It made it easier for Sheridan and me to begin our work.

"The illusion of Sheridan and me as a couple hit our squad over the next couple of days. Pope, Zeller, and Bauerman thought I hit the sweet spot. Torres, who was not as convinced, scolded me for sleeping around with a married woman. Naturally, Parker and Taylor were complete assholes. For all the eyes on base, we walked hand and hand in the open with fake smiles, pretending to be in love. In the mess hall, we purposely sat next to each other, picking at each other's food, laughing, and talking with large smiles. Maybe we were overdoing it. But it worked. Other staff members, recruits, and officers asked us questions about our relationship, like how we met and when we had time to be alone. Most of the time, Sheridan took over the details. We were convincing.

"All the while, we dug into Stanton's connection to the Qahhar. I should say, *supposed connection*, but my gut was right about Sheridan's hunch.

"On my end, I could not find any proof or correlation between shipments. I received copies from the requisitions office, which was standard. One thing about the military, paperwork is a bitch. There's a copy, form, or document about anything you could ever want. Probably a week later, Parker slithered into my work space, noticed all the old purchase forms in front of me, and questioned it. Thinking quickly, I explained that I was just double-checking quantities from past missions and wanted to lighten up the load on future missions. He bought my bullshit enough to get off my back. Truly, I was comparing quantities of supplies.

"Later that week, I had just come back from getting some coffee when another shipment was dropped. Looking around, I cautiously went up to the wrapped crates. I heard a truck approaching and noticed Taylor and Parker in the front seats. Diving behind some crates, I saw them pull in front of the hangar.

"Taylor shouted for me. I heard a couple feet land on the ground. 'Hey asshole, are you here?' he bellowed.

"I heard Parker say, 'Probably fucking Sheridan.'

"Both Taylor and Parker headed toward the shipment. Their voices lowered slightly as a couple of convoy trucks passed by. The noise vibrated the ground and shook loose a desert spider from the top of a nearby bench. It landed on its feet and crawled quickly near me. Goddamn, I hated those things. They were so big, and all their eyes stared back at you. In a quick move, I grabbed a loose rod, hit it, and sent it a few feet away, stunned and crumpled. The slight clack of the metal scraping the floor made Taylor and Parker stop talking. Their feet came closer to me. Slowly I crawled under the bench, where the spider's web still clung. Looking over, I saw their shadows along the crate above me.

"Taylor shouted, 'Fucking bugs!' I strained to see the spider, and a boot went down on it and splattered its guts all over. Right behind him, Parker insisted that they leave so I wouldn't see them. Still seeing the bug twitch, I heard Taylor tell Parker to meet him back at the hangar later that night. Soon they were gone.

"I crawled out of my space and ran out to the hangar's edge. When I walked back to the shipment, part of me wanted to crack it open and see what was in the crates, but I couldn't risk tampering with it.

"That night I went back to the hangar at twenty-two hundred hours and waited. As expected, a half an hour later, Taylor and Parker returned along with Pope. The truck pulled up without lights and silently coasted in. Of course they all worked diligently to load the crates in the truck, shooting half-assed remarks at each other.

"I heard Taylor say, 'We only have less than an hour to meet at the rendezvous point.'

"Within minutes, the truck fired up and slowly took off. As I made my way through the hangar door, I could barely see the truck in the distance. Its headlights were off in the far west part of the base.

"The next morning, I needed a new approach. Call it thinking outside the goddamn box. Or I was thinking like a fucking cop, you could say.

I headed over to requisitions with a dozen donuts. Oddly enough, the clerk behind the desk had a thing for me. When she saw me come in, she stopped what she was doing and wet her lips in anticipation. Handing her the donuts, I made some remarks about how beautiful she looked that day, which made her smile more. Finally, I sat on the edge of her desk and said something like… 'wondering if you can help me. Assistant Major Taylor is going on leave and I need to take over his orders for a couple of weeks. Just wondering if you can give me copies of his past purchase orders.'

"She placed her hand on my leg. 'Wish that asshole would leave for good. I hate him. Tells me that I'm fucking up his orders. Got me into trouble twice.'

"I looked sympathetic. 'I'm sorry. the prick didn't give me any instructions other than 'go figure it out your fucking self.' Here I am.'

"She was getting worked up on my behalf. 'Stupid-ass white

mothafucka.' She frowned and looked me up and down. 'You know, I'd really like to. I have to get proper release documents.'

"I touched her hand and smiled. 'Please, it'd help me a lot. Otherwise, my ass is going to get chewed out by my major. And he's an even worse prick.'

"A small smile came to her lips. She whispered, leaning near me, 'For you. Anything.'

"I've always had a way with the ladies. The clerk told me that it would take a couple of days to gather the information. Of course, in return, I promised to go out with her for a drink. After I left and was heading back to the hangar, I noticed Bauerman coming toward me in jeep. Once he pulled up, he told me that Stanton wanted to see me.

"I didn't know he'd returned."

THIRTY-SIX

"I entered Stanton's office. Sheridan and the major stopped talking when I opened the door. A flushed look flashed over her face. She planted her eyes somewhere on the ceiling while she stood with her hands behind her back. Stanton stood up from his chair an evil smirk gracing his lips, and then it quickly vanished once he looked at me.

'Williamson, glad you could fucking make it.' His deep voice echoed off the thin walls.

"I solidly planted myself next to Sheridan, not looking at her. 'What's this about, Sir?'

"Slowly, Stanton stood from behind his desk, his uniform hanging loose on his fit frame. His piercing green eyes scanned both Sheridan and me for a long moment as he let out a sigh.

'I hear you two are fucking,' he stated angrily.

'Yes, Commander,' Sheridan spoke up before I could.

"He was exasperated. 'Never in my days have I had to deal with this goddamn problem.'

"He was going to kick our butts no matter what we said, so I blurted out, 'You mean Taylor and Parker aren't fucking, Sir?'

"He pointed his finger at me and shouted, 'Cut that shit out, Williamson!'

"I piped up, 'Our sexual relationship will not affect any missions, Sir.'

"Sheridan added, 'Nor has it before, Sir.'

"He was bewildered. We probably surprised him being so up front about our relationship. 'How long have you two been fucking?' He asked. 'It's against military code. Stop it or you will be discharged.'

"Sheridan started to spout off... 'Pardon me, Sir, that's completely false. As soldiers, Williamson and I can have a consensual relationship within any military branch. Many men and women in the military—'

"Stanton hit the roof. 'Stop!' He barked back. 'Yes, I know the fucking rule! I'm fucking ordering you to stop fucking each other now!'

"Sheridan stood up straighter. Looked him in the eye and said, 'No!'

"I seconded her statement.

'Do you agree with her?' he asked.

'Yes, we're not going to stop fucking, Sir.'

You should have seen him… The redness on his cheeks equaled the color of his hair and thick mustache. For what felt like forever, he didn't speak in order to calm himself down.

"Finally, Stanton declared, 'From now on, you two will not be in the same tent. Other members of the squad will be present around each of you at every part of the day. You're not gonna be spending any time alone, around each other, or speak privately with each other. By fucking God, if I catch you even looking at each other, you better goddamn hold me back. Got it, you assholes?!'

"Sheridan and I both confirmed we heard, but neither of us looked happy with the prospect.

"Stanton went on. 'Fine. We leave at fourteen hundred hours. Meet me back in the hangar in fifteen minutes with the rest of the squad for debriefing." He rattled off some bullshit orders before the leave.

"Looking at his new gold Rolex, he grinned and said, 'If you need time to get a quickie in, you've got exactly two minutes.' He eyed me up and down. 'Don't think of you as a minute man, Williamson.'

"I grinned back. 'No, I ain't, Sir." I replied.

"He ordered us out.

"At fourteen hundred hours, as we headed off base, I truly believed we'd caught him off guard. Or at least I fucking thought so."

*****

"Stanton kept his word the moment we hit the caravan on the mission.

"On one truck, I rode with Parker, Bauerman, and Zeller, while Sheridan rode with Stanton, Torres, and Taylor in the other. While we may have fooled everyone, our deception unexpectedly took a toll on Sheridan and me. The others were always around us, like they were babysitting us. Our duties were divided so that Sheridan and I couldn't interact with each other.

"Despite Stanton's petty vengeance, we were all marines, and we did the job.

"Knowing something was wrong with the team, remembering my conversations with Sheridan, and being constantly watched weighed on me each day, man. I drifted back to my dark place, remained silent, and adapted as a functional soldier. What was Sheridan thinking? Who the fuck knew? All I know was her stone face meant business. We dared not exchange glances. We avoided each other and barely spoke more than three or four words in front of the others.

"Nevertheless, something occurred before we were scheduled to head back.

"One day, Torres, Pope, Bauerman, and I were tasked with taking the north end of the village, where the insurgents held a major encampment. We were teamed with some British Royal Air Force who'd joined forces with us to take down the targets. As we were scouting the area, when the gunfire temporarily ceased, I crawled around the rocks and met up with the English guys. They scored a better advantage to take out potential targets. A half a click behind, Pope, Bauerman, and Torres planted themselves in several spots and had their weapons on the targets. We were the countermeasure for the approaching troops, who were about fifteen clicks out.

"Near me, the young Brit pulled out a pack of cigarettes and offered me one. I declined.

"Eyeing the fence, he said, 'Got some time to wag off for a bit.'

"I asked him if he had any dice?

"Coughing out a laugh, he puffed out a tall pillar of smoke. He leaned closer to me and almost whispered, 'Got any more charlie?'

"I didn't understand what he was talking about and said so.

'That bindle went quick.' He pretended to snort some coke.

"The other Brit called over in an irritated voice, 'Stupid arsehole, not the right American.'

"The young guy eyed me and shrugged his shoulders. 'Bollocks, my fault.'

"I decided to take the opportunity to dig. 'Talking about my friend, Parker?' I asked. 'The other black guy?'

"He turned back to me with a look of suspicion on his face. 'Aye,' he says

"I told him he was on the other side.'

"Not saying anything else, the Brit soldier scooted to his other teammate. Eventually, they moved on, leaving me there. As I stared down at the simple dwellings, I realized that Parker, Taylor, Bauerman, and Zeller were connected. All to Stanton. And the Qahhar? I wasn't convinced on that yet.

"I really wanted to talk to Sheridan."

*****

"After the grueling, unnecessarily long mission, Stanton informed us that he had to leave for a week, and in return, he gave us all R and R. Honestly, I fucking needed it. After you spill so much blood, it starts to get to you. When I returned, the major still had not come back. Seriously, I could give a shit if he ever returned.

"Sheridan came back the day before I did from her brief leave and left me a message to meet in my hangar the next day. The paperwork was piled up on my desk. Like being a cop, it was a necessary evil. Because Sheridan was running behind, I filtered through my mess. Off to the side, I saw a simple envelope from requisitions with a handwritten note: *Heard that you were just sent out. Here are those docs. Drinks on me, baby.*

"Pulling out the order forms, I paged through the staggering amount of invoices. Simply put, Taylor had been. requesting small orders of supplies. Not enough to cause a stir, but over a period of time, it was substantial. With that amount of items, Stanton would have to store it some place off base. Then again, remembering the over-ordered shipments, I realized they would have to be stored in a huge facility. Shifting through the documents for the next half an hour, two things struck me: the large shipment invoices were not included, and only Taylor was ordering the items. Had I realized then what I had in my hands, perhaps the outcome would have been different.

"Nonetheless, I needed to get them back to the reqs clerk, because internal audits were notoriously common hell in the military. With a quick stride over to a nearby building, which housed office supplies, a couple of hardwired computers, and copy machines, I made two sets of copies. Once done, I marched back, stashed them for the time being, and then ran over to the reqs department. Finding my special clerk, I quietly asked for more documents. I explained to her what I would need.

"Running a quick half mile back, I found Sheridan waiting for me, staring at the planes and the nearby mechanics doing maintenance. She asked where I had been, but I dismissed her and wiped the sweat off my face. Turning around, she asked me to follow her. She walked to the rear of the hangar into the dim light. Behind some large cases, she began to remove her fatigues.

'Take off your clothes,' she says big as brass with an idiot's grin.

"I slipped off my shirt, but asked her what she was up to.

"She reminded me to call her Colleen as she slipped off her pants. Even in the shadowy light, I could tell her figure was taut and lean. She said simply, 'We have to fuck, Derrick.'

"Not like I was reluctant, Sheridan was a hot woman, but I wasn't sure about the move and said so.

"She laughed. 'Really? Like I'd fuck you? I mean, if I were single, I think I'd try you out.' She stared at my crotch, and then added, 'For size.'

"She was a real prick teaser. My cheeks flushed. It was the first time I couldn't fucking say anything! Sheridan was the first woman to leave me tongue-tied.

"She was already standing in her panties and bra. Smiling, she performed some basic calisthenics in place, and I soon I joined her. Without much air circulation, the heat of the desert baked us, making the sweat come easily. As we did our routine, she talked about her trip home to see her husband and her visits with her parents and friends. One thing about Sheridan was her love for her husband. After fifteen minutes, she stopped and wiped sweat off her chest and stomach. I pulled on my pants and retrieved some water from the front.

"She smiled and teased me some more. 'Was it as good for you as it was for me?' she asked, breathing hard. She took a drink of her water.

"I told her it was and then asked her if she knew where Stanton went. He took a two-week leave.

"She was casual about her answer. 'Went back to the States. Back to his wife and kids.'

"I was surprised he was married. I never saw a ring on his finger.

"Sheridan said his wife's name was Jacquelyn and they had four or five kids."

"I stood there with sweat rolling off my forehead and dripping in my eyes. I couldn't figure out how she knew that information when Stanton was so close-mouthed.

'I'm the doctor, you know." She smiled. She had the nicest smile. Almost contagious. 'Have to know the next of kin. You know, if something happens.' She paused and then looked at me. 'You should have one, Derrick.'

"True, I didn't. But it stung me that she had access to my jacket.

'Is that what you were talking about before I came into the office?' I questioned her.

'No.' Her eyes turned away and her lips pursed. 'Different thing. I hate that asshole. He tried to make a move on me.'

"I lost it. I couldn't believe he would do that after the lecture he gave us. I wanted to pound him. More importantly, I wanted to know when and how?

"She put up a hand on my arm to cool me down and returned, 'It was a while ago. When we first got on the base, I was stupid and decided to go for a couple of drinks with them. You know, Bauerman, Parker, asshole Taylor, Zeller, and Stanton. Torres was with us, so I felt some safety. Don't know what I was thinking.

'It was late, and I'd had too many. At the end of the night, it was Torres, Parker, Stanton, and me. Of course, Torres was too drunk to stand, so Parker took him back to the barracks. After the last one, I said that I was done. He told me that he'd walk me back. We were about thirty meters from the barracks, where it's not well lit. He grabbed my hand and pulled me hard against his body. He leaned into me and tried to kiss me. I resisted, but his mouth was on me. He forced my arm so hard behind my back, I thought I heard a crack in my shoulder. His other hand went to unbuckle my pants. I couldn't scream. I was just so shocked.

'Suddenly, I freed one of my arms and gave him a severe undercut and cross hook. That made him growl like an animal. He said to me, 'Come on, bitch, you wanted me the moment you laid eyes on me.' Behind us, I heard someone ask if I needed any help. He let go then and spit some blood onto my shirt. We both looked over at the military patrol. He stormed off, and I walked away. When he asked about our relationship, he brought it up again that day in the office. Fucking asshole. He's just pissed because he thinks I'm fucking you and not him.'

"I told her she could've reported him.

"She shook her head. 'No, no, Derrick. Not so easy. He's a major. I'm a staff sergeant. His word against mine. He has more seniority. I would look like the weak soldier while he twists it around. Too many white men control the Corps.'

"I asked if that was the reason she wanted to start our relationship?

'Partly,' she admitted. After a moment, she asked me if I had anything since was had seen each other last.

"Again, I peeked around the crates and looked for any signs of people. I was sweating and the crate I leaned against was almost hot enough to blister your skin. I told her about the shipment, Taylor and Parker finding it, how I watched them load it, and the two Brits. Like the bullets, I gave her a brief idea about the invoices I'd looked over, not giving her too much detail. Sometimes less is more, you know. When I finished, she remained still and absorbed the information. Outside, the roar of the plane engines squealed noisily, and the rumble of the engine shook the boxes.

"As soon as the plane was far enough away I asked her if she had anything new.

"She spoke with some MPs about the drug issue. Being a doctor, she got a few extra perks. They claimed that they couldn't figure out how it was coming into the base. They had a lead that it might be coming from the locals. But she knew that wasn't true.

"I asked her if her assumption was based on those locals we met a couple of months ago.

"She confirmed that, and added with a hint of sadness in her eyes, that the daughter died two weeks ago."

"I said nothing, visualizing the girl's horrible state in my mind.

"She surprised me by saying that she was working on something and that we might have to take a small road trip soon. I wondered how we were going to pull that off, but she said she would take care of the details.

"By time time, we had both lost our sweat camouflage. I removed my pants and asked her if we should go for another quickie? She was shameless. She said, 'You're going to make some lady very happy.'

"After another vigorous round of calisthenics, we were grossly hot. Without putting my shirt back on, we left the hangar, and I held her hand. She of course pretended to whisper things to me, letting her hands touch my skin affectionately. And yes, the other soldiers saw us come out of the hangar. I felt like I needed to protect Sheridan more.

"In the following weeks, after he returned, I watched Stanton."

*****

"As time progressed, Sheridan purposely found places to meet that were highly visible around other soldiers and officers. Typically, I greeted her in a tank top, or shirtless, and paraded around with her. While we didn't talk in the open about Stanton, we talked more about ourselves. Eventually, I discussed my mother and family back here. She seemed to empathize with my story. All the while, I discovered how much Sheridan was a unique woman—so confident, brilliant, and actually attractive. Seriously, she became more of a sister than anything else.

"I also trailed Taylor, Parker, Bauerman, and Zeller. Because we were trained to be unseen, I fucking reversed it. I sought them out: the repair shop, the bar, the gym, or wherever. I played dumb most of the time and talked about stupid shit. Stanton was more difficult. Sometimes, I would casually bump into him here and there on the base. Make sure he had seen me. However, I noticed how often he and Taylor met. Not in his office, but near the officer's barracks, eating together in the mess hall, or going for runs.

"About a week later, Stanton, Taylor, and Parker went off base. For what, I can't say. Finally, I got the nerve up to search his office without telling Sheridan.

"No one questioned me entering his office. It was immaculate—organized. Stanton was good, real fucking good. It was pissing me off.

"Sheridan knew it too.

"A couple of days later, Stanton and Taylor had to meet General Norquist off base, meaning they'd be gone for a good two to three days. I knew I wanted to get into Stanton's apartment. I told Sheridan of my plans. She traded her shift so she could come along with me. Later the same evening, Sheridan picked the lock and we entered his small officer's apartment. Much like his office, everything was clean and clutter free. What surprised me was there were no pictures of family: no wife, no kids, no parents, nothing. As if that part of his life did not exist.

"After, I informed Sheridan that I was going to search Taylor's room. Because of her rotation, she couldn't join.

"Around two o'clock in the morning, knowing Torres was already passed out from whiskey, I quietly entered. The idiot never kept his door locked. I could see why Taylor wanted to be alone. He was a filthy pig! Leftover food was piled in the corners, dirty clothes were stacked on the floor, and books and CDs were thrown all about. Worst yet, roaches, beetles, and other things crawled in and out of the stuff. God, I felt itchy just being in there. When I searched the closet, I noticed the back wall was a different color than the rest. It was non-regulation to paint your own room. The wall moved slightly under my touch. Leaning over, I discovered he had a stash of bondage porn magazines. The dog-eared pages were bent and crumpled. Just below it, a map of Afghanistan poked subtly out. Pulling it out, I saw that five red circles dotted the map—they were locations northwest of the base. Quickly, I wrote down the coordinates on the inside of my forearm. I put everything back and slid out of the room effortlessly.

"The next day, I found Sheridan in the medical building, speaking with a nurse. Smiling, she nodded her head for me to follow her. She escorted me to an unoccupied room and closed the door behind her. The noise of the hospital faintly echoed through the paper-thin walls.

"She figured it must be important if I came to the hospital. I confirmed her thoughts by producing the map I just bought at the Base Exchange with the locations circled like I saw in Taylor's room.

"She wanted to know what they were. I admitted I didn't know, but had found them in Taylor's room under a stack of porn mags.

"She pointed to one of the circles located about forty miles from the base. She thought she might know what they signified. She slapped the map back into my chest. 'Hold on to this,' she said, 'and meet me at my barracks, fifteen hundred hours. We're going on that road trip I talked about.'"

THIRTY-SEVEN

"We didn't speak as we traveled to the middle-of-fucking-nowhere Afghanistan. I kept my eyes out for any potential threats—the paved road was riddled with potholes that were once land mines. The barren land gave way to the effects of the war: burnt down houses, crumbling buildings, families with their only belongings walking east, and then the vast nothingness. Sheridan clutched the automatic tightly against her hip while my gun rested on my leg as I drove. The restaurant owner had given us an old Datsun as well as clothes to wear. He insisted we needed to blend in better. I wore a dark turban and loose dark clothes. Sheridan had a longer hijab and a loose cream-colored robe.

"Approaching an even smaller village that appeared around the bend of the mountain, the coordinates indicated that we were only seven clicks from the spot. The shabby housing flanked the sides of the road as children happily ran about. Suspicious glances from elderly men glazed over us while the women, dressed in burqas, turned away. The town felt like any small town—close-knit, generations of several families, pretty quiet. To me, the twenty-first century had yet to arrive.

"Pointing ahead toward a steep hill, Sheridan told me to take the next right. The old car almost crawled at the incline. Its engine whined under the hood. I hoped like hell it didn't stall. As we headed further up, the town disappeared and the slender road became dirt.

'There,' she pointed.

"Ahead, a small mosque with huge cracks on the sides of the building that indicated mortar fire sat on a ridge. Outside, several women in dark burqas descended the steep stairs, weeping and bowing their heads. Some children in thin long clothes followed suit, their eyes stained with tears. Parking the car on the edge of the road, I could see a straight drop into a deep valley was within ten feet.

Carefully, I got out of the car, slipping my gun behind me in my waist and under my robe. Sheridan got out as well, slung a backpack over her shoulder, and ascended the stairs. As I climbed the stairs, whiffs of heavy incense floated around me.

"At that moment, a tall slender man opened the door and stepped into the waning sunlight. His long dark beard masked the dark acne scars on his face. Sheridan greeted him, and he nodded at me. She introduced me as her friend. The man, Khari, welcomed me. I gave him my name and complimented him on his English. He informed me that the former Indian British rule allowed higher ranked families, like his to learn the language. Sheridan asked if we could visit the patients. He said yes and led the way.

"In the mosque, the walls were simply decorated in gold and silver, and the scuffed white tile floors were rather plain. Several woven rugs were scattered about, and candles lit much of the room.

'How many patients are there?' Sheridan asked.

'Right now, seven remain,' Khari replied. 'I lost one this morning. You may have seen the family who left.'

"Sheridan asked if the patients' conditions were the same? Khari confirmed they were. We came to a long wooden door that had to be at least three hundred years old, and the man opened it with ease. He described their injuries as we entered. 'The deep internal wounds pierced most of the major organs. Each patient lost a significant amount of blood. Infection exacerbated the conditions.'

Gavin tilted his head and studied Derrick as he paused for the first time in his recitation. He started to speak, but Derrick waved his question away.

"Let me finish," he said quietly.

Gavin nodded and poured himself another drink. He had a feeling he was going to need it.

"We entered a small hallway and descended a spiral staircase. It felt like we were in the mountain. The air was chilly. Yet, like in that young woman's room, I smelled the blood, urine, and unearthly sickness and faintly heard the soft groans below us. Glancing up, I saw that the stairway was almost dark; we saw no one else in the long shadows.

"As I hit the bottom stair, Sheridan followed Khari through the narrow doorway. Ducking slightly, I entered as well. Two dozen beds were housed in the long narrow windowless room. Only seven were occupied. The male patients were of different ages, half naked and wrapped in bandages that covered their waists and upper chests. Dark yellow-reddish stains were on the wrappings that covered their wounds. Two young women with dark headwraps attended the patients. If I hadn't seen any of the men's chests move, I would have thought they were dead. Even worse, the soft buzzing sounds of flies echoed in the room as the insects flew and landed on them. Of all the things I've seen, those men always appear in my worst nightmares.

"Sheridan and Khari went up to the nearest patient. I stepped up to the end of the bed.

"Sheridan slipped on some gloves and asked permission to examine the patients. Khari granted it. Diligently, she removed the upper bandage. A foul stench filled my mouth. The round wound in the patient's upper chest was clearly infected. The hole was distinctive, like someone had shoved a rod into him. The patient himself was unaware, barely breathing. His closed eyes did not flinch as flies freely walked across the lids.

'Where is the exit wound?' Sheridan asked, leaning closer to examine the flesh.

'They found the stake protruding out of his anal cavity.' The man took off his glasses and wiped off the lenses.

"I asked how long they had been there? Khari replied they were only the most recent to be brought in. About a week or so ago.

"Where were they discovered? I asked and he said they were all found near their land on the side of the road.

"Sheridan put in words what we men could not. 'They were impaled,' she said without looking up.

"Sheridan lowered her bag and opened it. She took out a new bandage and some antiseptic. After she applied the solution to the man's flesh, one of the helpers came over to continue cleaning the wound. Sheridan backed off and removed her gloves, glancing over at me with a somber look.

"For the next half hour, Sheridan examined the other men who were equally as bad off, if not worse, than the first patient. I needed some air. I just could not handle seeing any more of that shit. Remaining quiet, I gulped back my own rising vomit. Once she was done and satisfied, Khari escorted us back outside. The hot air seemed unusually refreshing.

"Sheridan said the bag had enough supplies to last Khari for two weeks. Morphine, solution, etc. She wished she had brought more, but she didn't realize the need was so great.

"Khari said unfortunately, he didn't think they'd last long. We asked if there had been more men like this.

'Not that I'm aware of,' he replied. His eyes scanned the dusk. He warned us to be careful on the way back. Too many eyes watched the road from there to Kabul.

"I shook his warm hand. I turned and headed back to the car. Sheridan remained with the man for a few minutes. As I started up the car, she opened her side and hopped in. For the first time, throughout all of our missions together, a frightened look was on her face.

*****

"As we headed back to the base, her endless quietness frustrated me. I asked her why she took me there? They weren't the coordinates on Taylor's map. I told her if I was just driving Miss Daisy, I hated to tell her, but I didn't do that shit."

"When she finally started talking I began to get the picture.

'The last few days,' her voice was calm as her eyes focused on the dark road ahead of us, 'I heard rumors from the locals. They claimed the Qahhar was tired of waiting for their *owed* land. They started to take it. The Qahhar went into those land owners' houses, raped the women, brutally beat the kids, and killed the livestock. As a final warning, they staked the owners onto poles in the hot sun. The Qahhar want to take what they believe is deserved. Plain and simple. It doesn't matter about the American presence."

"I asked what Stanton had to do with it?

"She looked over at me with a steely stare. 'We both know that drugs have entered the base. And it's steadily on the rise. Already, over two dozen men and women have been discharged just in the last month. It all happened the moment our squad began living there. Plus, you met up with those British soldiers.'

"I was still being thickheaded I suggested it was maybe just Parker and Taylor running drugs.

"Her eyes turned back onto the road. 'The coordinates on Taylor's map is a key Qahhar location, only fifteen clicks away from that mosque. That cannot be a mere coincidence. I think you and I know that Taylor doesn't have the brains to coordinate such an operation.'

"I asked her if she was thinking it was Stanton?

"She put it as simply as she could. 'Some of the villagers approached me about Stanton's trips out west. Those men you saw are on strategic land for the Qahhar to use for planting. They would have enough land to control a major portion of drugs in Central Asia and become a major threat to the already weak Afghan government. Stanton is part of it.'

"For a few moments, she didn't speak. The town was just behind us. The road seemed more dangerous in the black nothingness.

"I thought we should tell someone, but she pointed out that it wasn't just Stanton. Someone else was assisting the major. An operation like that was too vast. It took years of planning to make this happen.

"I asked her if she had any ideas of who would be helping him?

'Khari told me that he dug out the bullets from the patients. American bullets.' She spoke as if I weren't there. 'Someone above Stanton must have clearance to approve vast weapons shipments.'

"Her hand slid through the break in her cover-up, and she pulled out a plastic bag. She took one object out in the dim light and held it close to the dashboard light.

"I recognized it as the same shell that Aymaan had given me. My head was spinning. Standard M4 rounds. American issue.

In the rearview, faint headlights appeared in the distance. Sweat was running down my back.

"I was putting two and two together. The shipments that randomly appeared were actually going to the Qahhar. Taylor, Parker, Bauerman—all of them were part of it. Maybe Torres. Stanton was coordinating the drops. I voiced that to her and she nodded her head.

'We need proof,' I said. The distant headlights became two different sets. I stepped harder on the accelerator, hearing the engine race.

'What about the young girl who was assaulted?' I asked her.

"Shaking her head, she replied simply, 'Don't know. Not sure how she fits in yet.'

"We both agreed that when we got back to base, we needed to formulate a new game plan.

"For the rest of the trip, I kept my eyes on the growing amount of headlights behind us. My paranoia was just fucking going crazy.

Sheridan kept to herself. In the dim light, the concerned look washed over her face while her grip on the semi-automatic remained constant.

"I knew someone was following. My gut told me so that night, and I should have listened to it. Maybe I should have went to someone—a general, military police, not sure—and told them about our suspicions. Instead, I trusted Sheridan too much and thought that we needed to dig further.

"When we finally got back to the base, Sheridan went to her room in the barracks. I needed a drink and wanted to wash what I had seen out of my mind.

"I fucking regretted being in the squad."

*****

"Early in the morning, Torres shook me awake.

'Come on, Williamson!' he yelled. 'Got another assignment. Now! Major Stanton wants us lined up in an hour. Gear and all!'

"I woke up groggy; the bourbon from the night before kicked my ass. Automatically, my body responded—I was showered, dressed in fatigues, and prepped for battle in twenty minutes. I found Torres waiting with Bauerman and Pope in a jeep just outside the barracks. Their grim looks equaled my hangover. The sun was just peeking over the dawn, and the chill of the desert hit me hard. On the way there, another jeep with Taylor, Parker, Zeller, and Sheridan sped along the side. Naturally, Sheridan ignored me. At the hangar, Stanton stood. His form was rigid in his battle gear as the wad of chew in his mouth made his cheek appear deformed.

"He greeted us with his usual slander, saying 'Took you pussies long enough!'

"We fell in line. Of course, he took his customary inspection of us, eyeing us slowly. 'Insurgents have penetrated the line of defense sixty kilometers out.' Stanton's voice was loud and echoed in the hangar. 'British defense was weakened by several surprise attacks over the night. We must infiltrate a key base only forty kilometers out. How the fuck the insurgents obtained a defense base, I don't fucking know. Our job is to take down their base camp. The orders are to kill on sight. Got it?'

"We all chimed the affirmative in unison.

"His green eyes dug into me; I would never forget how much rage simmered in them. In the corner of my eye, I saw Parker and Taylor smirk. 'Maybe you'll kill them with whiskey breath, Williamson,' he stated angrily.

"Walking away from me, he shouted, 'What are we!'

'Marines!'

'What do we do?'

'Act as one!'

'What do we do?'

'Fucking kill or be killed!'

'That's right! Are we going to be killed?'

'Fuck no!'

'Alright assholes,' he shouted. 'You have fifteen minutes for detail! We ride out in twenty-five! Move, you sons of a bitches!'

"Scrambling around, weapons detail and loading gear took us less than twenty minutes. Surprised, Stanton ordered us out through the back of the base. Toward the open desert. Sheridan was in the convoy jeep ahead of me. Torres was behind the wheel of our truck, keeping up with Taylor's crazy speeding. Whizzing through the west gates of the base, the stark terrain was fucking endless.

"While the jeep bounced around, my head imploded. The booze was trying to get back up through the back of my throat, but I was swallowing it back down. Since I was behind Torres, the fresh air at least was on my face so I could breathe. Glancing over, I saw that we were parallel to the very road Sheridan and I had traveled the night before.

"Parker's voice crackled over the radio. 'Target location is twenty minutes away.'

"Something was not right in the mission. I sensed it. We never had to quickly gear up and run into a mission before. This was different.

"Taylor headed northwest toward the same village. Ahead of us, billows of black smoke drifted into the morning-blue sky. As we came closer, I saw that the town was leveled. Many of the houses and buildings were rubble. The sounds of emergency vehicles could be heard, and many American military trucks were just arriving. Troops geared with guns were hopping out and running into the burning streets. Although we were passing the village, the sound of gunfire was faint. My eyes drifted up to the mosque. I almost choked—a roaring fire was in its place. The entire structure was gone. I eased back in my seat and looked the other way. A sense of panic overwhelmed me.

"Unexpectedly, I heard a familiar whistle coming toward us.

"I yelled at Torres.

"Ahead of us, Stanton's convoy narrowly missed incoming mortar fire, which exploded just behind them. Torres made a sharp turn to miss the new crater. Another whistle was louder. In a flash of light, the explosion hit on my side of the truck. The truck toppled over several times, and we all rolled over each other. The sound of screeching metal and Bauerman shouting flooded the space. My body slammed into the front seat, into Bauerman, and then I felt myself being ejected out the window.

"Once my body landed on the ground, I heard a snap and felt intense pain on my side. I didn't hear the other whistle come in, but I felt another explosion near me. The rock debris rained down over me, and the dust made it impossible for me to see anything. I choked on the thick air and began to stand. Looking down, I felt something in my side. A small piece of metal stuck out of my midsection. Without thinking, I pulled it out and put pressure on the wound.

"Near me, Torres's body was twisted backwards and crumpled like a piece of paper. Half of his head was missing. I walked toward the truck, holding my gun with my weak, shaking hand. No sign of Bauerman or Pope.

"As the ringing died in my ears, I heard some shouts and gunfire. I tried to run toward it. Through the blowing smoke, I saw the other convoy truck on its side. Parker was behind it and firing toward the west in the dust cloud. The pain intensified in my stomach, and I knew I was losing blood.

"I heard Zeller in the distance cussing.

"A series of gunfire exchange took place. I couldn't tell which way. Then I felt an arm grab me. It was Taylor.

'They fucking took Sheridan!' he shouted in my ear. Without a word, he scooped his arm around my waist. 'Fuck, Williamson! Lie down! Parker!'

"Who took Sheridan?" I asked.

'Couple of terrorists,' Taylor stated. He was already ripping open my jacket. 'Major went after him with Zeller.'

"Parker took one look at my wound and started cussing. 'Fuck!

Fuck! Fuck!' He kept repeating.

"I remember Taylor ordering Parker to put pressure on my stomach. Before I blacked out, all I could think of was Momma. And how disappointed she would be in me.

"Then I fucking felt nothing."

*****

"When I opened my eyes, I was in the med center. The noise of the hospital startled me, and I tried to sit forward. As I did, a pain ripped right through me and made me fall back onto the bed. I ⌐ noticed a large wrapping around my stomach. Near me, Pope was unconscious, lying on a bed. His head was wrapped tight, and an IV drip was connected to him along with a heart monitor. His slumber was not comforting.

"I twisted my head when I heard a soft woman's voice call my name. I looked up to find a Hispanic woman touching my chest softly and taking my pulse. She touched my scalp, where I felt another bandage. Soon, her light fingers grazed the bandage on my stomach.

"I was disoriented and asked who she was.

'I'm your nurse. My name is Corporal Maria Dominquez,' she said. Her sincere smile was comforting. 'You had a bad injury. When you arrived, you had lost a lot of blood.'

"I tried to move, but the intense pain was unbelievable.

"She tried to calm me. 'If you move any more, you'll rip your wound open again,' she said.

"I asked about my squad.

"A sadness glimmered in her sincere face as she said, 'Some didn't make it.'

"I was worried about Sheridan. 'Who?' I demanded.

'Two of your men,' she stated simply. 'Sorry.'

'What about Sheridan?' I asked, looking over at Pope.

"Maria licked her lips and whispered in my ear, 'Dr. Sheridan is stable at the moment.'

'What happened to her?' I asked

'I'll let your commander tell you,' she replied. I could see how nervous Maria was.

"Stepping aside slightly, I saw the MP standing outside the door, guarding entry. As I tried to move my right hand, I discovered it was cuffed to the rail.

'What the hell,' I demanded, but before I knew it a dreary darkness overcame me."

*****

"For the next couple of days, I remained in the hospital, isolated in that fucking room. No one came and saw me. No one from the squad. Not even fucking Stanton. Even at that time, Maria could tell something was wrong about my situation, but she never asked. She kept me monitored on Sheridan's status because I wasn't permitted to see her. I remained strapped to the bed and guarded.

"When I was able to move more, I was sent over to the officer's barracks in the large conference room. Wheeled in by a different nurse, I found the major of MP, General Norquist, Stanton, and Taylor sitting behind a long foldout table. No one else. Stanton spoke up. God, I remember every fucking word to this day too.

'It came to my attention, Sergeant Williamson,' he stated firmly, 'that you have been the one supplying and distributing illegal substances on the base.'

What the fuck? I thought. Looking him straight in the eye, I said, 'I think you have it reversed, Sir.'

"The major of MP turned slightly to Norquist, who looked absolutely bored. My career hung on a false allegation. How I wanted to punch Taylor in his big-ass smile.

'We found said drugs stashed not only in your hangar behind your desk,' Stanton added, so confidently, 'but in your personal room. It seems like you and Torres were running a little operation, considering the amount of cash hidden.'

"I went ballistic, which did not help. I screamed. 'Fuck you! What the fuck are you talking about?! Sir, General Norquist, these are all lies!'

"Norquist ignored my rant and said, 'Staff Sergeant Derrick Williamson, you are now discharged for the illegal selling and distributing of drugs on a US-based military ground. Thereby, you will be immediately extradited to the US for further prosecution.'

"Without much delay, I was escorted out in my wheelchair. At the hangar, I sat there with a bag of my stuff, the exact items I'd left with from Texas. As though I had no one else in the world, Maria found me and gave me a hug. She said that they were wrong. The entire base was already talking about me. Before I knew it, she kissed me and told me that I wasn't that kind of man."

*****

Derrick stopped and stared outside. The soft drifting snow bounced off the dark windows.

"Is that how you ended up in the CPD?" Gavin inquired. He looked at his phone; it read twelve thirty-three.

"No, man," he said. "When I got back, I didn't know what to do. I went to my only friend, who did not believe the trumped up charges. Whatever he did, the military did not pursue it any further. I had a clean slate. It took another few years before the military changed my status to honorable discharge. He's the one who pulled the strings to get me in the CPD."

"You could have gone anywhere," Gavin commented.

With a tired grin, he looked at Gavin and said, "Maria wasn't just anywhere."

"I get it," Gavin stated.

Derrick grabbed his phone for the first time all night.

"Shit, it's late," he said. "Maria's going to kill me."

Instantly he rose off the couch, wobbling slightly.

"Need an Uber?" Gavin asked.

"Naw, G," he said as he slid on his jacket. "I'm fine. Actually, too sober now."

"One question," Gavin said, slowly standing up. "Whatever happened to Colleen?"

Derrick stopped buttoning up his jacket and glanced over at Gavin with a bleak expression. His eyes again lost in another world, he said, "Sheridan actually was sent back to the United States due to her injuries. I did locate her when I got back. Somehow, I just couldn't make myself call her until two or so years later. When I called her house, her husband, Mark, answered the phone and informed me that she had committed suicide. A rifle to her head."

Gavin said nothing.

"An honorable way to die as a marine," Derrick said finally.

Ambling toward the door, Gavin stated, "We are going to get

Stanton, Derrick."

Before he reached the door, he replied, "You see, an army patrol found Sheridan on the side of the road. Nearly naked. She'd been beaten severely." He paused as his eyes watered up. "Sheridan was sexually assaulted, much like Sills had been in that video."

Derrick opened the door and left.

Even though Gavin was tired, he cracked open his computer. He logged into the CPD locator and noticed the moving red ping leaving his house. When Derrick had used the bathroom earlier, Gavin had placed a tracker on his phone. He needed to keep an eye on his partner, whether he liked it or not.

Because in the pit of his gut, Gavin also realized that Stanton's dirty work was far from over.

PART V

JACQUELYN

"No hour is ever eternity, but it has its right to weep."
—*Zora Neale Hurston*

"I can't get over you
You left your mark on me
I want your hot love and emotion, endlessly..."
—*Drake*

THIRTY-EIGHT

Sitting at a small family diner, Gavin fretfully glanced at his phone. While it was already a quarter to eleven, Derrick had not called or texted. That was unusual. Opposite of him, Evelyn poured a couple packets of sugar into her fresh coffee and stirred it briskly. While Derrick was talking last night, Gavin had texted Evelyn info on Stanton's name and a possible wife. Turned out that Stanton and his family resided in the Chicago area. Somehow Gavin was not surprised about it. That morning, Evelyn informed him that she'd set up this meeting with his wife in Schaumburg. Mrs. Stanton was willing to give over the keys.

Already she was twenty minutes late.

"Did you find out anything else on Stanton? Or Mrs. Stanton?" Gavin sat straighter, glancing out onto the nearly empty parking lot.

"Yeah. Several domestic dispute calls between the late 90s and mid twenty-tens," she replied. "Neighbors called in. Claimed loud shouting, breaking objects, and crying kids. When officers arrived, they discovered no issues."

"Huh," he said.

"Can I ask you how Derrick knows Stanton?" Evelyn queried innocently.

Wondering if she was going to ask or not, he remained silent. Last night, Derrick's military life rumbled chaotically through Gavin's dreams. He'd dreamt he was part of the squad and under Stanton's command. When his alarm went off, he could have sworn it was the mortar shells descending on him.

Before he could say the right word, she said, "I understand. You boys have your secrets."

"It's not that," Gavin began.

"No, don't explain anything," she retorted quickly and looked directly at him. "I'm the third wheel. When we capture Stanton, I'll have my own partner. I'll be out of your hair."

"Are you done being whiny?" Gavin returned impatiently.

Evelyn avoided eye contact and sipped her coffee.

"Evelyn, you're a great detective," he stated softly. "Don't ever forget that. I enjoy having you around, and I think even Derrick is smitten with you."

"Not exactly sure about that." Her eyes went down to her phone nearby.

"When this is over," Gavin said sincerely, "I'll talk to Creighton. Keep you in our fold. Work cases together."

Her posture shifted slightly. She ignored him and said firmly, "I think Mrs. Stanton is here."

A white BMW had pulled up to the window and the doors opened. A portly man in his fifties with salty wispy hair walked around to the passenger side. A shorter woman in a drab gray coat stepped out of the car and took the man's hand carefully. Her thick, oversized sunglasses engulfed her thin face. Soon, they made their way to the entrance.

Sliding out of the booth, Gavin stood and straightened his suit coat. Evelyn followed suit, pressing down her dark skirt.

"Jacquelyn Stanton?" Evelyn prompted as the woman approached them, still not taking off her sunglasses.

"Detective Lopez?" Her shaky voice was somber.

"Yes," Evelyn said. "This is my partner, Detective Nolan."

"Nice to meet you." Gavin put out his hand to shake, but she hesitated and recoiled her own hand deeper into her pocket. Not saying a word, the man instead shook Gavin's hand and only nodded.

Jacquelyn turned toward the man and said softly, "Steve, I'm fine. Go to work. I'll call later."

The man kissed her cheeks softly, nodded to both Gavin and Evelyn, and walked out of the restaurant. Evelyn and Gavin slid into one side of the booth while Jacquelyn Stanton leisurely slid into the other. The bored waitress came over immediately and asked if they needed anything. Jacquelyn ordered a hot tea with lemon. As Evelyn took out her notepad and readied herself, Jacquelyn finally took off her sunglasses.

"Mrs. Stanton," Gavin stated quietly, after the waitress had placed the tea in front of her. "I'm glad you could meet us on such short notice."

The woman straightened her back against the booth as her long fingers gathered themselves around the hot white cup.

"Before we start," Jacquelyn stated simply, "don't call me Mrs. Stanton."

"What should we call you?" Evelyn asked.

"Jackie, Jacquelyn, or by my maiden name, Mrs. Lenard." She stared at Gavin with dark eyes and a sour expression. "But don't call me *Mrs. Stanton*."

*****

Glancing over in the same direction as Jacquelyn, Gavin noticed the white import car remained in its spot and idled. With a subtle and effective nod, Jacquelyn turned her attention back to the cup of tea in front of her. Soon, the car pulled out of the slip and headed away.

"May we ask who that was?" Evelyn inquired.

"My boyfriend, Steve," Jacquelyn answered. "Does he have to get involved in this?"

"Not unless you want him to," Gavin returned.

"No, no, he already knows too much about Zach."

Digging into her handbag, she placed a key on the table. "There you go. For the house."

"Don't you want to come and be there while we search the house?" Gavin reached for the key. "It's your legal right."

"No, I have nothing there." Her light, buttery voice hinted at sadness and even bitterness. "I live with Steve. Kids and all. Have for quite a while now."

"May we ask why you left your husband?" Gavin questioned.

Apprehensively, her thin fingers tugged at the dark scarf around her neck. For a moment, she collected her thoughts, seemingly forced a smile, and simply said, "Detective Nolan, Zachary was a highly decorated commander in the marines. I believe his years away in the Middle East took a toll on him. While he was away fighting for our country, I raised the children and ran the house. I'm greatly appreciative that Zachary was able to serve and protect our country. He had an honorable record."

"If he was such a loving husband," Evelyn stated, "then why have there been more than a dozen police reports from your house?"

The smile disappeared. "The war was hard on him." She tapped her well-manicured nails on the table. "When a soldier comes back from such a traumatic experience and readjusts to civil life, there's a time of, um, adjustment. The neighbors did not understand him as I did."

"You never explained why you left, Mrs. Lenard," Gavin said.

"We were growing apart," Jacquelyn said unconvincingly.

"Typically," Evelyn remarked nonchalantly, "women who have been physically abused change their names and revert back to their maiden names."

Turning his head, Gavin noticed the conviction in Evelyn's face. Still, Jacquelyn remained poised and proper.

"I don't know what you are talking about." She raised her voice as she spoke, as if she'd been insulted. "Zachary was a loving husband. And a fantastic father figure for the children."

"Interestingly enough," Evelyn continued, "it's common for battered women to only discuss the ideal happiness of their partner. She puts him on a pedestal and speaks about that person with confidence."

Jacquelyn's face was unwavering. "Detective Lopez, I believe you're mistaken—"

"Also, battered women always blame themselves and their actions—every single time."

"I gave you the key. It's *yours*." She let go of the cup, grabbing her bag.

"Jacquelyn," Evelyn said louder. "Are you frightened of Mr. Stanton? Are you scared that he may come and do something harmful to you? I see a small scar just below your chin."

"Are we done, Detectives?" Jacquelyn was sliding out of the booth. "I gave you what you needed."

"Should we talk about the emergency room visits?" Evelyn pressed on. "Or are you scared he might do something to the kids?"

"Okay, I am done now." Jacquelyn stood up and shoved her hands deep in her pockets.

Quickly, Gavin rose and said softly to her, "Don't you want to know why we want to question your husband?"

"No, not really." She remained planted.

"We believe he has done some horrible things to other women." He paused and stared into her watery eyes. "A dozen people are dead because of him. Can you live with that?"

Saying nothing for a moment, her body shook slightly, and a couple of tears crested her lids and fell down her cheeks. Nervously, she glanced over at the new customers at a nearby table.

"Can you give me a moment?" she said quietly. "I need to use the bathroom."

"Of course," Evelyn said.

She walked with an uncertain gate toward the rear of the restaurant, pulling out a tissue and dabbing it against her eyes.

"Should I go with her?" Evelyn asked.

"No," he stated. "You pushed her hard."

"I know. I had to," Evelyn returned, sliding back into her spot. "Abused women are a soft spot for me. My aunt was horribly abused by my uncle for years. I had seen the scars, heard the screams, and had my cousin stay with us, crying about her mom. Aunt Tia was a beautiful woman."

"Was?" Gavin remained standing and looked down at her.

"On New Year's Eve," she said matter-of-factly, "Tia and Javier went to a big family party. A lot of people. A lot of family. Javier thought that Tia was hitting on someone at the party. Once they got home, Javier grabbed her by the back of the hair and dragged her up to their apartment. Once inside, he beat her with their metal kitchen chair. When Tia cried for help, he took a kitchen knife and stabbed her thirty-nine times. Thank God my cousin happened to be staying with us that night."

Stunned, Gavin could not say a word.

"I was just a kid at the time," she said. "I didn't know. Until I read the official police report."

"Where is he now?"

"Downstate," she replied crisply. "No one ever visits him. Except for my cousin, who's now my age. She said that he found God."

Gavin spotted Jacquelyn heading back to them. Before he could comment, Evelyn straightened her back and nodded in the woman's direction. Silently, she slid back in her place. She fixed her scarf and clasped her hands in her lap.

"Jacquelyn," Evelyn uttered calmly, "Detective Nolan and I have your safety and your children's safety as priority. When we finish talking, we will have patrol cars sit at your house until Mr. Stanton is apprehended."

A grim smile came to Jacquelyn's face, almost as if she had heard that line before.

"Are you willing to help us, Jacquelyn?" Gavin inquired.

"Yes, Detectives," she spoke softly.

"So, I am going to ask again," he replied. "Why did you leave Zachary Stanton?"

"I…he, uh," she began.

"Take it easy," Evelyn said, reaching over and scooping the woman's hand into her own.

Sitting straighter, she looked dead on at Gavin and remarked, "Zachary physically and mentally abused me for most of our marriage," Jacquelyn said. Her striking gold-colored hair seemed to float around her delicate face, much like a Greek goddess. "When we first met, his military charm worked on me, even against my parents' wishes. I was young, I had hardly dated anyone else. We happened to meet at a friend's party. At first, he was such a gentlemen, opening doors, holding my hand, pulling out my chair at the dinner table, things like that. While we dated, he never encouraged any sexual activity. And I was fine with that. I had never been with anyone else.

"It wasn't until our wedding night that we consummated our marriage. He was a devoted Christian, as I had been. I understood Zachary's life in the military was important. I understood that we would move a lot, and I wanted to see other parts of the country. In the mid-nineties, we lived on the base in South Carolina, where he was stationed. There, I gave birth to our first child, a son. When he was not working on the base, he doted over our son. He didn't want me to work. He just wanted me to be home, to raise our son. And I accepted that role. But I was so far away from my family in Wisconsin. I felt alone, not knowing what I was doing.

"As my therapist said, the little things, things I began to make excuses for, were the first signs of abuse. When I did not have his uniform pressed for the next day, he yelled. When I did not have dinner ready exactly at eighteen hundred hours, six that is, he yelled louder. If I did not get up with our first son when he was crying in the middle of the night, he would shout and push me from the bed. Then I would get these remarks like, 'What good are you if I don't have my whiskey waiting for me'; 'Lay off the makeup, you look like a whore, not a mother.' Or my personal favorite: 'Latrines are meant to be scrubbed with a toothbrush—get on your effing knees and scrub.' I never told my parents these things because I was too embarrassed.

"A couple of years later, we moved to Florida, and I was pregnant again. At the same time, he was assigned to serve in the Gulf War. Of course I was scared for him. Zachary was, how shall I say, exhilarated by the opportunity. Being pregnant did not stop Zachary's excessive ridicule. He'd say, 'Just 'cause I knocked you up, doesn't mean you have to go any slower.' My second child was harder on me, having another son to care for already. I pleaded with him to have my mother come down. I hadn't seen her for a while. Zachary hated that. I knew it. I could see that look in his eyes, just of pure anger. When she was there, instead of yelling at me, he went out drinking with his friends. My mother didn't like his behavior at all."

Jacquelyn took a deep breath while her fingertips played around with the empty sugar packet. She looked out the window, seemingly staring off into space.

"We had a beautiful little girl," she continued sadly. "How I wanted a girl. I was unbelievably happy. My mother was thrilled as well. Zachary was not as pleased. He would not hold his daughter. He spent more time with our son, pretending to shoot our daughter with his fingers. I saw such a dark anger in his eyes when I held her. After my mother left, he was at the kitchen table, most of a bottle of whiskey gone. The baby was screaming, and when I asked him why he didn't get her, he just glared at me. Even before I could get my coat off, he struck me so hard that I hit the wall. That was the first time I tasted my own blood. He came straight into my face and said, 'How dare you give me an effing girl. They're weak, they're nothing. Next time I expect a g-d boy.'"

"Did he apologize?" Evelyn asked.

"No... yes... I don't know," she responded weakly. "Five days later, he was shipped out. I was alone with a newborn and a young child. I never felt so alone. He called me every so often, but his conversations were puzzling at best. I hated living on the base, not having anyone around me. I wanted to be near my family. He then suggested that I go visit them for a while.

"I stayed with my family for six months. I didn't care about the belongings at the house on the base. In a way, I really had nothing there. I did fly back once to pack up some suitcases of stuff and returned with them. The next time I spoke to him, I told him that I was done in Florida. He said that as long as I was happy where I was, I should be there. Then he said something unsettling, 'I will always find you, Jackie.' When he returned from the Gulf, a good year and a half later, I'd made my life in Wisconsin again. I even got an apartment near my parents' house in Oak Creek, just south of Milwaukee. It was where I grew up. My friends were there, and I was home. I was happy.

"For the first couple of weeks, we were where we had once been. He was a loving, caring, doting father to both children. Then it started over again. Zachary's expectations of my *wifely* duties never changed, only worsened. He was crueler in his words and drank a lot more. He was even more aggressive in, um, bed. I felt like he forced himself on me. I hated it, actually. About two months later, he said we should not live in a 'backward state' and wanted to live in the Chicago area. Within a month, he found a house. The same house you will go to. He made an offer and bought it. Not asking me if I would like it, not letting me see it. Of course we all left together. After we moved, several months later, I was pregnant again.

"The house was not bad, nice and spacious. But I hated it and hated the neighborhood. I couldn't show it though. He was so accustomed to being in the military and insisted I was one of his soldiers. He ordered me around like a fool. I just fell back into that lifestyle again. In the course of a year, I severed my relationship with my family, making excuses not to see them. Zach's torment was excruciating. One time, our little girl happened to be sick and I was taking care of her all night long. I needed some sleep. That morning, he dragged me by my hair, while the kids were screaming, into the kitchen to make him breakfast. Because I loved her more than him, he slammed my face in the fridge, laughing about it. Another time, I forgot to wash his clothes and left them in the basket, because I'd decided to take the kids to the park instead. When I put them down for a nap, he struck me across my back with his belt a dozen times, calling me a selfish b. On and on it went."

"Why didn't you call the cops?" Evelyn asked.

"I thought it was me," she returned simply. "We had been apart for so long. He needed to adjust to real life. You know. I made many excuses, let's put it that way. Anyways, the weeks he was home were hell on Earth. Out in public, in restaurants, he looked like the loving and concerned husband and father. No one would have believed me, especially since he was a Gulf veteran. No one would question him. Plus, the kids were too small to notice. And then his demand for intercourse was just painful and rough. Much different."

"How so?" Gavin asked.

"What does that have to do with anything?"

"I understand it's personal," he stated as he propped his arms on the table and leaned toward her. "But it's crucial."

"I don't know. Just rough. He liked to take me from, you know," she answered sheepishly.

"Anal sex?" Evelyn finished, making a note.

Jacquelyn nodded slowly and her eyes teared.

"When was the next time Mr. Stanton left for duty?" Gavin asked, remembering Derrick's story.

"His next tour happened when I gave birth to our third child," she stated simply. She paused for a moment to take a sip of her tea. "He called a month later to ask me how I was doing. Never asked about his new son. He seemed so preoccupied, like I was an inconvenience to him. The following years were especially hard. I raised the three kids by myself. Zachary's tours kept him out of our lives the majority of the time. Sometimes six months, seven months. Each time he returned, a very short time—a week, five days sometimes—he pretended to be in love with me and the kids for one day and then became a tyrant the rest of the time. He'd be rougher, even meaner. Of course, each time he came back, he wanted to sleep with me. If I faked a headache, or something like that, he would beat me and then have his way with me. I was afraid of him while he was home. Soon, I was pregnant with our fourth child when he went away. It was 2001. Same year as 9/11."

"How had he been then?" Gavin asked, leaning back so the waitress could pour him some fresh coffee.

Jacquelyn retorted, "Zachary was different. It was July when he returned home. He was upset. Angry. Not at us. Something else. Never really spoke much about it. He was horrible though. One time, I asked him why he came back so early. He claimed that some of his soldiers perished in a horrible accident. I actually pitied him. Then 9/11 happened. I know watching the towers fall affected us all that day. He was different. He changed. He was rather quiet."

"Was that unusual?" Evelyn stated, looking up from her notepad.

"Yes," she whispered. "It was the rage in his eyes. Shortly after, he received a phone call from a general."

"General Norquist?" Gavin added. Next to him, Evelyn looked over at him, but he dismissed her.

"Think so," she replied. "Soon after, he was gone again. For a much longer time."

"Is this what made you finally leave him?" Evelyn then inquired.

"No," she replied simply. "I stayed in that awful relationship for the kids. I had four children to take care of. Plus, my oldest two were going into school, and I had to take care of a baby. It was a lot of work. I then decided to go on the pill. I couldn't be pregnant again. And Zach never found out. I hardly saw him, which was great for all of us. But when he returned, he was just as brutal. When my youngest was around two or so, he finally showed his true colors in front of the older kids. He began to snap at them and treat them like his little soldiers. That's when he would strike me in front of them. My oldest tried to protect me, but Zachary backhanded him out of the way. He wound up getting stitches. As far as Zachary was concerned, he thought the kid deserved it."

"Did you file a report?" Gavin asked.

"No," she said. "I was stupid then. I felt as if no one would understand. I was too afraid to ask for any help. When my mother died, l thought I had nowhere to turn. At her funeral, I don't know who I cried for more, my mother or myself. I was glad he wasn't there though; even my family saw how much I'd changed, and I didn't want to answer their questions. He never called back about my mother's death. I left him some messages on his voicemail, but nothing.

"Finally, one day, I decided to go back to school," she said. "The youngest was three. The others were in school and I knew I had to get a job soon. I realized I had to get away from Zachary. I received a two-year degree in accounting through an online program. Zachary never saw the tuition bill because I paid for it entirely in cash. I even used my maiden name. In between, he came back only once. And he was an absolute bear. Luckily, it was a short time, and soon he left again. I began to work. For the first time in my life, I felt some freedom."

"Did he ever discover that you were working?" Gavin asked.

"It was only a part-time job," she stated. "My hours were flexible. Usually, he called before coming home. They never knew my situation. The money I was making, I was sacking it away. I was cashing my checks and hiding it in a place he'd never find. That was my first plan to leave. I thought I had it all worked out.

"When he came home," she said, "he was more distant. He decided to start sleeping on the couch in the den. But his beatings worsened. That week, I wound up staying overnight in the hospital. Zachary told the doctors I fell on some ice and hit my head, but they didn't believe them. I couldn't tell them that he'd smashed a whiskey bottle on my lower back and kicked me several times. When I got back home, he gave me a bouquet of red roses and said he was sorry. Of course I didn't believe him. Oddly, before the taxi came to pick him up, he said that he was working on something. He was going to get a pay raise."

"Is this when Mr. Stanton went to Afghanistan?" Gavin interrupted.

"Yes, actually," she said. "About a month later, I noticed that a huge sum of money began hitting the bank account. I emailed him about it. If I remember right, his response was: 'Only the tip of the iceberg.'"

"Did you ever look into where the money came from?" Gavin asked.

Softly, she finally responded, "No, I didn't care. With my own money and this new money, I began to stash away more cash."

Evelyn glanced over at Gavin and sat straighter in the booth. "You had money," Evelyn stated. "Why didn't you leave?"

"It had to be about a year or so later," Jacquelyn explained, "when I had enough money stashed away to leave. I had a realtor ready in Wisconsin, and I was planning on living with my father for the time being. I had boxes in the basement ready to go. I was set. Or at least I hoped. Then Zachary came home out of the blue, unannounced. I was absolutely shocked."

"Why did he come back?" Gavin asked.

"Zackary told me that he had to meet an investor or something in the city," she said confidently.

"Do you know who it was?"

Shaking her head, she said, "Not really. Maybe from the same place where I was getting the extra money. Think it was called Enders, something or other—"

"Zanders Holdings Group?" Gavin completed for her.

"Yes, that was it." She looked at him. "I remember that I do have some old bank receipts from them. Would you like them?"

"If you could, please," he requested.

"Getting back to moving, did Mr. Stanton discover your plans?" Evelyn jumped in.

"Yes." Jacquelyn's shaky voice matched the slight tremor in her hands. "My youngest told him that we were moving. He was innocent, only four or so, and wanted to know if Zach was excited too. A look of silent rage came over him. He was completely different. When he struck me, I told the kids to run over to our neighbor's house. The older ones were at practice, or meeting with friends, not sure which. It was only the two youngest at the house." Tears began to form in her eyes, and a single one escaped to roll down her cheek.

"What happened, Jackie?" Evelyn asked.

"By the time the police came, or at least what I was told by them later, he'd already beat me unconscious. They had to force him off of me because he was already slicing at my throat." She lowered her scarf to reveal a scar right next to her artery. "If they had not come, I would have been dead."

"Did you press charges? Make a statement?" Gavin inquired.

"Because we didn't find a report like that," Evelyn admitted.

"I thought I did. I know I did. I remember talking to an officer about it. Can't remember the name." Jacquelyn looked surprised.

"That's okay, we will look into it." Gavin touched Evelyn's arm, and she wrote a note. "Continue, please."

"I was in the hospital for almost a month. He had broken my left collarbone and several ribs. My father came down to watch the kids. I was too embarrassed to talk to my him about it. Before I knew it, Zachary was out of the country. He never was arrested, nothing. I was so angry. It was then I told my father about Zachary. He cried and told me I needed to leave. But I couldn't. Zachary had discovered the cash in the house and had taken it all. I lost my job because I was out so long. I was again back to nothing."

"How were you able to leave Mr. Stanton?" Gavin asked.

"Being in the hospital was my tipping point," she said. "I found a full-time job shortly after. That's when I met Steve. He became a good friend, and then eventually my companion. Within a couple of years, I moved out and into Steve's house. He loves the kids and they love him. Since that time, Zachary has not come back. I have had little if any contact with him. It was Steve who pressed separation papers, which I filed."

"Did you file for divorce?" Evelyn questioned softly. "We haven't found any documentation."

"Yes, I did," she said matter-of-factly. "Under my maiden name. I have legally changed my name back to it. About four and a half years later, I emailed him that I was divorcing him. It was then he told me that he was coming back home.

"I planned to meet him at the house again. Steve wanted to come along, but I said no." Jacquelyn was confident. "When he arrived in the taxi, I was waiting in the empty house. Never touched his stuff in the basement. Never went near it. He came in, and I did not see any anger. Zachary broke down and pleaded for me to stay with him. He confessed that he was not the best husband, and everything under the sun. I told him that I could not live with him anymore and he had no rights to the kids. When I turned to leave, he grabbed my arm. I thought that was it, I was going to die. Zachary said calmly, 'This is not over. I will find you and the kids.'"

"Did he sign the papers?" Evelyn asked.

"No, still to this day. We are legally separated," she stated. "Even after he was discharged."

"Discharged?"

"Yeah, he called me a year and a half ago that he was back in the States." Jacquelyn's eyes darted out toward the parking lot. "He wanted to reconcile. I had already started my life with Steve, and the kids were finally happy and settled."

"How many times did he contact you?"

"I changed my phone number so many times, I can't tell you. Somehow he found it." She then added, looking at Evelyn: "I filed restraining orders on him. Steve knew someone in the court system who could protect me and the kids."

"Did he ever say why he was discharged?"

"No, Detective Nolan," she replied. "I no longer cared."

"Do you know if he will be there?"

She shrugged. "Not sure. But you'll know because he owns a stupid ugly black truck."

"Really?"

"Yeah, keeps government plates on them too," she said. "Thinks he's still in the military." She looked at her phone. "Will this take any longer? I have to get to work; I promised them I would be in by noon."

"No problem. You gave us enough information," Evelyn stated.

Jacquelyn stood up and grabbed her clutch.

"Detectives, please be careful of Zachary," she warned. "He's unpredictable."

"We are trained professionals," Evelyn replied as she shook the woman's hand.

"Not military," she rebutted.

"Thank you for your time," Gavin stated.

"One more thing. This may sound trivial. But..." She looked at her phone and then into Gavin's eyes. "Last year, he contacted me for something. He was in Colorado at the time. I tried to give him condolences about his mother."

"His mother?"

"Yeah, the reason why we lived there, his mother lived over in Hanover Park," she replied. "I never really got along with her. She was a rather nasty, bitter woman. Last year, I think it was, his mother died in a house fire. When I spoke to him about it, he seemed even less... emotional about it."

"Well, thank you, Jacquelyn."

Quickly, she walked out of the restaurant. Within seconds, the white BMW appeared and she slipped inside. It pulled out onto the road and disappeared.

Evelyn said that she was going to the restroom as Gavin grabbed his coat. Looking out on the gray day, he thought of Jacquelyn, feeling her pain under a savage tyrant. Now, she was in survival mode, protecting herself and the kids.

The house key seemed to burn in his pants pocket.

THIRTY-NINE

The established neighborhood reflected a late-seventies to mid-eighties façade. The two-story houses were reminiscent of split-level dwellings with typical red brick on the first floor and a variation of white siding on the second level. The square lot gave way to a variety of fences, natural shrubbery lines, or cleared space. As the vehicle slowed down, the presence of children could be seen in the small snowmen, snow forts, and snowy footprints. Very little movement could be seen in the dimly lit houses. Most likely, many of the people were at work.

"Should be the fifth houses on the left," Evelyn said softly, slowing the car down even more.

Pulling out his phone, Gavin saw that he still had not received any text messages from Derrick.

Something's wrong.

He glanced up to see the Stanton home, which seemed especially dark. The long white curtains covered the front window, the paint on the garage was peeling, and the pathway to the front door was covered in snow. The place appeared to be vacant.

"No black truck." Evelyn eased the car into park across the street from the home.

Without a word, Gavin nodded and opened the car door. The quietness of the street enveloped him, as did the chilly air. As they crossed the street, soft snowflakes gently drifted down. Evelyn flanked his right side, already gripping her gun in her left hand. She stopped at the mailbox at the end of the driveway.

"Doesn't look like he's been here," she said behind him. "Lots of mail not picked up."

"Maybe that's the point," he stated.

Gavin stepped in the undisturbed snow bank and stomped his way to the front door. The icy snow fell into his shoe, causing an instant chill to run right through him. His eyes remained on the windows, and he hoped no one was returning his gaze. Once he reached the small snow-covered porch, he signaled Evelyn to stop walking, and the crunches ceased.

Unsnapping his gun holder and placing his hand on the cold piece, Gavin rang the bell. No sound. No chime. Nothing.

Stanton might have disconnected it, but why?

The screen door squealed open like a screaming child, and he pounded the door with his fist several times.

"Mr. Zachary Stanton?" Gavin raised his voice. "It's the CPD. We'd like a word with you."

No response. Looking back, he caught Evelyn's eyes darting back and forth between the window and the door.

Sliding out the key, he opened the door and announced loudly, "Mr. Stanton, we are coming in!"

Even then, his words echoed.

Inside the house, the room's dim light caused lingering shadows to become elongated dark specters on the bare walls. As Gavin stepped further into the bare front room, Evelyn snuck in with her hands firmly grasping her gun, pointing it down at an angle. The dated carpet, which was in need of replacing, absorbed any sounds. The long olive curtains on the bay window were dusty, and tendrils of cobwebs hung from the ceiling lights to the curtain rod. Various marks in the carpet indicated where the furniture had once been placed.

Evelyn nodded toward the staircase near the long hallway. She crept silently and ascended the stairs.

Cautiously, Gavin walked further into the darkened house. Reaching into his side pocket, he retrieved his flashlight and flicked it on. He noticed the house was unusually cool as the carpet gave way to large square industrial white tiles. The clicks of his heels bounced faintly into the empty, dated moss-colored kitchen.

On the floor above him, the soft creaks of Evelyn's footsteps seemed unusually distant.

In the kitchen, he searched through a couple dark brown lacquered cabinets, finding nothing but dust, more cobwebs, and mice droppings. Opening the fridge, he discovered that only a limited number of contents remained: three bottles of Pabst, a half-jar of mayonnaise, and a package of mold-covered Oscar Mayer bologna.

In the freezer, the frost and ice took over much of the space, though three frozen Hungry Man dinners lay in the middle. The blinds were drawn on the huge window above the sink. Casually, he flicked the blinds open and peered through the slats. It was the neighbor's garage side; they wouldn't have witnessed Stanton's movements.

Gavin followed the flow of the kitchen into the family room. Near the kitchen, a stone fireplace anchored the wall. Ahead of him, a bank of windows covered one side as well as two patio doors. The long blinds were tightly closed. Making a slight turn, he saw that the tile gave way to carpet once again. The obvious signs of stains and marks were engraved in the dark beige carpet. To the left was a single door, followed by another one in the far corner. He opened the door cautiously. Flicking on the light, he found the garage to be empty and cold. The entire space was void of any maintenance items; no shovel, snow blower, tools, or car necessities. As if Stanton didn't live there.

As he turned back, Evelyn rounded the corner.

"Nothing," she reported. "Huge cobwebs, a dead rodent in one closet, and big water stains in the ceiling in the master bedroom."

"Seems like Stanton doesn't live here," he said softly. His light flashed over the ceiling near them to reveal another water stain dripping down the wall. "He's letting the place go."

"Do you think Jacquelyn was lying to us?" Evelyn inquired as she stepped toward the patio doors. She cranked one side of the long metal blinds, and the shards of light cascaded over the space.

Gavin looked down and noticed a clear traffic pattern in the carpet from the garage door to the door in the corner.

"Someone's been here," Gavin stated and followed it.

Opening the far door, he flicked on the switch, and a high fluorescent light pushed back the inky blackness. A set of gray stairs descended into the basement. Gavin took the first step clutching his gun in his hand. He took each step carefully as he lowered his head, ready to catch a glimpse of any pending trouble. Right on his heels, Evelyn crouched, aimed her gun in the opposite direction, and matched each step.

Gavin took a couple of strides into the large basement. The intense light lit up every corner. Lowering his gun, he noticed Evelyn sidestep to a narrow area behind the stairs, still pointing her gun forward.

Ahead of him, a single cot was in the very center of the room, a simple gray blanket and pillow resting on top of it. Approaching the cot, he noticed a six-foot metal table placed a couple feet away with some files stacked on it. The basement windows were boarded up and painted black. No light entered the space. Or rather, no one could see in. But what struck him the most was a chalkboard on an angle near the table. Behind him, Evelyn's soft steps echoed.

"A large freezer was behind the stairs," she said. "Large enough to store a body."

"Perhaps," Gavin replied.

"Is this a DIY bunker?" she questioned, lowering her gun.

Walking toward the table, he took out his phone and began to snap some pictures. *Bauerman* was written on the side of the first one. Gavin's heart raced slightly. He fished out a pen and used it to open the folder. A photo of a middle-aged white man appeared. The angle of the shot meant that Bauerman was unaware that his picture was being taken. The man was walking out of an office building, tie undone and suit coat over his arm, a look of anger on his face.

Derrick's marine past is coming to life.

The next file was labelled with Parker's name, and inside, Gavin found a picture of a thin black man in tattered clothes. Gavin snapped a picture on his phone. Before he could get to the one that read *Taylor*, Evelyn said softly, "Gavin, you need to look at this."

Looking over at the angled board, he saw Evelyn on the other side. Stepping around the corner, he found military headshots of Bauerman, Zeller, Parker, Pope, and Taylor. Each photo had a black X over the face. There was also a shot of Derrick's military picture. Near it, a picture of him leaving his house was pasted in the far corner. A series of Derrick pictures were below it: Derrick entering a grocery store, coming out of a Macy's store, walking down the street with a stroller, and even one of him getting out of the unmarked car in the police lot. Stanton was following him. But for how long?

In his peripheral vision, he saw Evelyn walk over to a metal trunk near a post a few feet away.

Getting on his phone, he texted Derrick: *Call me now. Stanton has been tracking you.* He took a quick picture of the board.

"Holy fuck!" Evelyn cried out. Turning in her direction, he watched her backing up.

Stepping toward the case, Gavin saw the self-made bomb, counting down. The red digital numbers read: *:23, :22, :21…*

"Run!" he shouted and sprinted to the stairs.

Just ahead of him, Evelyn had already hit the staircase. Taking the stairs two at a time and rounding the corner, Evelyn was just a quick pace ahead of him. Their pounding footsteps echoed in the kitchen as they raced to the front door. Quickly, Evelyn grabbed the doorknob and opened it, slamming it against the wall. The moment she was out of the house, the vibration of the explosion shuddered the foundation, and the sound of a train barreling at him overtook Gavin's ears. A surge of force combined with an intense heat lifted him up slightly just as his foot touched the doorframe. He could see Evelyn becoming airborne as he heard her scream. Around him, Gavin felt objects being hurdled past.

Suddenly, he descended and landed in the packed icy snow mound near the street. Glancing back, he saw the entire house disintegrate before his eyes in an immense orange ball. Near him, Evelyn was face down and not moving.

"Evelyn!" He crawled over to her and turned her over. A large gash had ripped her skin from the base of her jaw down the side of her neck. Blood dripped down and splattered the white snow. He placed pressure on the wound and saw the scarlet viscous liquid ooze between his fingers.

In the far distance, faint screaming sirens were heading toward them.

*****

About thirty minutes later, the tight street was filled with emergency crew vehicles. A couple of fire trucks took up most of the space, police cars blocked the intersections, and an ambulance was parked near their unmarked car. Finally, turning off their hoses, the firefighters were wrapping up their work and talking amongst each other. Near one side of the block, various news vans were already up and reporting the explosion. The uniformed policemen ushered them along with the growing bystanders.

Leaning against the ambulance, a dull pain ached in Gavin's right shoulder—the very spot of impact when he hit the ground. He said nothing though; his concern was for Evelyn, who appeared to be more disgruntled than hurt.

"Pissed off?" Gavin asked, watching the EMT bandage up her

neck.

"It was set for anyone," she replied back, wincing slightly. "What if Jacquelyn happened to nose around in there? That's an asshole move." She pointed at the rubble.

"Couldn't agree more, ma'am," Gavin replied.

Suddenly, his phone rang.

"Detective Nolan," he said without looking down, hoping it was Derrick.

"So formal, aren't ya?" Mary quipped back.

"Little pissed off," he admitted.

"Remind me not to piss you off." He heard a series of soft clicks in the background. "Bad time?"

Glancing over at Evelyn, who was rising off the cot, he stated, "No. Perfect."

"Okay then," she said. "After I got your text, I did a quick dig on Jacquelyn Lenard. She did put a restraining order out on a Zachary Stanton three years ago. A strict one too. Mr. Stanton cannot come within a thousand yards of the house, two thousand yards of four named children, and two thousand yards of her in any public space. Judge Matthews from Circuit Court twenty-one approved the order, stating clearly that Ms. Lenard's husband must be arrested on site for a violation, etc., etc." She stopped. "Really, Nolan, I haven't seen an order this severe in a while. I think she has some powerful friends."

"Seems that way." Gavin recalled that Jacquelyn never gave Steve's last name.

"Next, I found the divorce petition and proceedings." Another series of clicks. "All legit. Okay, now, a little funky here because Mr. Stanton has pleaded no contest on the case. His lawyer—"

"Does it say what firm?"

"Hold on." A couple of seconds later she said, "A Larry Hewittson."

"Really?" Surprised, Gavin looked over at Evelyn, who gave him a suspicious look. "Go on."

"Looks like they are holding up the divorce proceedings. The lawyer has been filing extensions, injunctions, and other petty legalities in order for the proceeding not to occur. From her filing and her witness testimony that I quickly skimmed through, her husband was a real SOB. Sorry for the language, but this guy's bad."

"Did you find out any information involving a situation at their home address about a potential stabbing?"

"No," she said. "Nothing so far. I did find several hospital emergency records on Jacquelyn Stanton."

"Huh," he said softly.

"Let me keep digging though," Mary responded quickly.

"Alright."

The EMT helped Evelyn down off the cab end. She adjusted her coat, almost hiding her bandage.

"Talk soon," Gavin said. "I may need your magic fingers soon."

"You betcha," she replied cheerfully and hung up.

Stepping toward Evelyn, he was about to recap Mary's findings when his phone rang again. His eyes read the screen: *Quinn*. Not Derrick. He was about to let it go to voicemail, but that would be worse.

"Yeah," he stated begrudgingly.

"Nolan," Creighton replied back. His deep voice was unusually soft. "I know about the explosion. It's all over the news."

Fuck. "Yeah, about that," he began.

"Never mind that," he interrupted. "You and Lopez need to come back ASAP."

"I can explain," Gavin raised his voice, which alerted Evelyn.

"It's Williamson," he stated matter-of-factly.

Feeling like he couldn't breathe, Gavin returned, "What about Derrick?"

"He's fine," Creighton said calmly. "He's here. In my office."

"Okay." Gavin stared at the smoldering ambers. "What is it?"

"Gavin," Creighton said softly, "it's Derrick's wife, Maria."

"What happened to her?" Gavin pivoted on his heel and headed toward the car before he even head the answer.

"Maria Williamson was taken," the captain answered solemnly.

FORTY

Well into the late afternoon, the precinct was actively involved in the case against Stanton. Yet, conversations amongst the other detectives and officers were muted, as if they were tiptoeing around Derrick, attempting not to disturb him. The combined effort seemed to dissipate some of Gavin's trepidation while Evelyn physically moved many of the conversations away from their area. Even more, the rally to find Maria was compassionately heartfelt—not just rudimentary business at hand.

When Gavin and Evelyn had arrived at the station, Derrick was sitting in Creighton's office, his hands covering his face, his large frame unusually slouched in a stiff chair. Saying nothing, a thick, heavy sigh escaped from his mouth.

"Derrick," Gavin said delicately, squatting near him. "Are you sure it was Stanton?"

"Only blame myself," he conceded. His voice was barely audible through his fingers. "My fault."

"Don't blame yourself," Evelyn returned compassionately, placing a hand on his shoulder.

"Gavin... Evelyn," Creighton said.

He looked up at Quinn, who closed the door slightly, even while the other detectives' curiosity showed in their prying eyes. Handing him a cell phone, Creighton whispered, "Look."

Taking it, Gavin pressed the button, and the messenger instantly opened up. There was a dark, angled picture of Maria, bound, blindfolded, and gagged in the back of a dark truck bed. The text read: *Find me and maybe she'll live. Or maybe not. Depends on you, Sergeant.* The time stamp was the same moment he and Evelyn had entered the Stanton home.

In an unprecedented move, even before Gavin could say a word, Creighton stepped out of his office and summoned everyone in the precinct for a meeting. A stern look of concern covered the captain's face. As other detectives and uniformed personnel gathered, Gavin ambled out of the office and turned at an angle so that he could keep an eye on his partner. Evelyn lingered in the doorframe and folded her arms over her chest, seemingly to shield Derrick.

"As of right now," Creighton bellowed before the crowd, "each and every one of you is working Nolan and Lopez's case. Their case involves the several explosions killing a number of people. We are now concerned about the three specific women the killer has targeted. As you may be aware, this killer was after a certain type of person. He, a Mr. Zachary Stanton, has taken someone I believe to be part of our lives, too. Mrs. Maria Williamson, Detective Derrick Williamson's wife, has been abducted by Stanton."

A mumbling of conversation occurred amongst the officers.

"Time is of the essence." Creighton's voice grew louder. "All other cases are on the back burner. He will not get one of our fucking own! Got it?!"

All of their eyes briefly locked on Gavin and then slid past him into the office. In the next few minutes, Creighton gave out specific orders to set up a task force in the hunt for Zachary Stanton. As he emerged from the office, Derrick did not utter too many words, receiving some sympathy from fellow workers, hugs, and brief positive remarks about Maria. As if he were a zombie, he ambled slowly through the bull pen and plopped down at his desk. A sense of hushed conversations buzzed around the station as the others worked madly to dig into Stanton's life.

Gavin proceeded to summarize the case thus far, including the recent conversation with Jacquelyn Stanton. Then both he and Evelyn were bombarded with questions and endless emails. During this time, Creighton blanketed other detectives with details by sending reports of the case through email. Despite the distraction, he would not allow himself to take his eyes off his partner. Even Evelyn, who answered the majority of inquiries, watched Derrick. Within forty-five minutes of the announcement, Detective Rodriguez had pinned Maria's picture on the whiteboard amongst the other victims.

A certain sense of dread came over Gavin, who attempted not to look at it.

In between this, Derrick received calls from Maria's family. Gavin could only imagine the panic in their voices, the grief from Maria's mother, and the rage from her brothers and sisters. Quietly, Derrick spoke to them in monosyllabic responses, avoiding any eye contact with the staff around him, and tapping his fingers on the desk. Each time Derrick stopped talking, an expression of fury washed over his face. When he went back to the case, Derrick forced himself to look over evidence. Was he actually reading it? Or was he in another world? Gavin could not tell.

The last piece of visual evidence of Maria's vehicle was seen on Bode Road in Schaumburg. On the very street he and Evelyn had turned off after they'd left the little diner on Roselle. The time registered at four twenty-three, yesterday afternoon. At the same time yesterday, Derrick was at Gavin's apartment, explaining how he was picked for Stanton's team. The car disappeared off the city cameras when she entered the subdivision's labyrinth of streets. He could see Derrick stare at the picture of the car, probably looking at the pixelated image of his wife in the driver's seat. Even with the grainy image, you could see Maria was talking on the phone. Derrick said that her mother had spoken to her for the last time in mid-afternoon.

Around four or so in the afternoon, Mary approached Gavin and Derrick. Distress caressed her face. Softly, she touched Derrick's shoulder and looked down with a grim smile. Derrick did not say a word and stared at the screen. Or probably pretended to.

"I did some digging into those pictures you sent me." Her voice was nervous.

"Pictures?" Derrick said. Nearby, Evelyn hung up her phone and stepped over to them.

"The one I took before the house went up," Gavin replied. "I showed you earlier."

Nodding, his eyes went back to the computer screen.

"Alright, all of these men have indeed died over the past year or so." Opening a manila file in her hand, she handed Gavin a couple of accident reports. Gavin took and placed the sheets next to him, making the pile of papers taller.

"Steven Bauerman." Mary looked down at her notes. "Lived in Denver. He died in a car accident by driving off a cliff. After an inspection of the car, no tampering of the motor, brakes, or gear shifted were detected. His blood alcohol level was well over three points of the legal limit."

"That's nearly lethal," Evelyn pointed out.

"I dug further into Bauerman," she replied. "He was a recovering alcoholic. The death was ruled as a suicide. That was in September of last year."

Derrick said nothing.

"Moving on, Joseph Pope was killed in a farming accident." Mary puckered her lips faintly. "His father discovered that his son had fallen into a corn forager. There was no autopsy because the body was shredded. The father said that his son was always careful, and it seemed unlike him to do such a thing. Pope died in November last year. According to the police report, ruled as an accident. Now, Dwayne Parker. His body was discovered in the Hudson River on the Queens shoreline in late February this year. According to the autopsy, he died from hyperthermia. His ex-wife reported him missing the week before."

"No one just jumps into a frozen river during winter," Gavin said as he sifted through the papers near him.

"Detective Nolan," Mary said. "Parker had an issue returning back to the States from his tour. Numerous reports on his house about domestic violence, shouting, and whatnot. Parker had been going to the VA hospital nearby. He was prescribed some heavy meds by his doctor."

"Why try alternative therapies when you can just drug the mentally ill," Evelyn commented.

"Also noted in the autopsy," Mary continued, "a large dose of his three prescriptions were in his system. The report cannot conclusively state whether it was a suicide or not."

"Why?" Gavin asked.

"The coroner reported subtle abrasions under his arms, meaning someone dragged him," Mary said. "Since Parker was in the water for so long all the evidence could be questioned."

"Maybe I'll send that one over to Dr. Hobart," Evelyn stated and fished it out of the pile.

"Finally," Mary said. "Cody Taylor died in a house fire in South Carolina."

Derrick looked up from the computer screen to Gavin.

Promptly, Mary cleared her throat. "He was found on the upper level of his two-story home, while his wife and three children were located in the den. Their bodies were all burned beyond recognition. This is where it gets weird. Taylor's neck was clearly broken. He and his family died in early August."

"So what was Stanton doing for those months in between?" Evelyn asked, looking at Gavin.

"Studying his targets," Derrick croaked. "On the field, he loved the sense of the hunt. He'd watch the target's base for some time—learning what they did and the change of guard routine—waiting for the right time to strike. The perfect time to strike."

For a brief moment, the soft sounds of the station filled their space. Mary finally asked, "Is there anything else?"

"Yes," Gavin stated. "Can you look into Stanton's credit card? Bank account? I want to know how he's paying for his plane trips. If you are stuck, ask Mylo to show you. And tell him I told you to ask him."

Mary nodded and put a hand back on Derrick's shoulder for a second. "We are going to get Maria back, okay?" she said. Then she straightened up and walked away.

Before she could respond, Evelyn's phone rang again. As she answered it, Gavin leaned closer to Derrick, staring at his dark red eyes.

"Are you sure this was Stanton's work?"

A brief snarl pierced his lips. "Yes, Gavin," he growled. "I know how he works. He didn't give up. Especially on the target."

"I'm going to ask you something you may not like," Gavin prefaced hesitantly.

Derrick remained still.

"Why do you think he didn't just take you out first?"

"Hmm." His partner's eyes turned away to look at Maria's picture on the board. After a few seconds, he finally replied, "The motherfucker wants me to suffer."

Instantly, a text message came from Mylo that read: *Nolan, come to my office now! URGENT!*

Standing up, Gavin casually glanced over at Creighton's office. The door was closed and the blinds were down. Nearby, Evelyn sat with her back to them, still talking on the phone.

"Hey," he said to Derrick. "I'll be right back. Going to be okay here?"

"Don't need a goddamn babysitter," he answered bitterly. His attention went back to the computer screen.

*****

Upon entering Mylo's tight office, a faint whiff of body odor drifted into Gavin's nose. Behind his desk, Mylo looked up at him, pushing his thick-framed glasses up the bridge of his nose. Mylo's dark thick hair seemed pasted on his skull, as if he'd been wearing a wool hat.

"What do you have?" Gavin stated.

"Close the door," Mylo requested.

Gavin didn't want to because of the stale air, but he obeyed. He sidestepped several stacks of files and boxes in the cramped office. Mylo insisted on keeping the overhead light off and instead had only task lighting, which cast barely enough light to see what was stuffed in the corners. Knocking over the pile of Coke cans, takeout boxes, and crumpled papers, Gavin hoped no little creatures would pop out. As he reached the desk, he noticed the same boxes Creighton had been digging through weeks ago, stacked near the desk.

"May I ask why these are here?" Gavin queried, opening a box top.

"My next pet project." Mylo sounded agitated. "Captain Asshole's orders."

"What are you supposed to do with them?" He pulled a file and looked at a random case number. *Don't recognize this number. Definitely not our precinct.*

"Scanning all this bullshit, like I'm his personal secretary," Mylo grumbled and then added, "Didn't ask you to come and search my office, Nolan."

"Sorry," he replied and slipped the case file back into its slot.

"Alright," Mylo stated simply and twisted his screen monitor so Gavin could see. "Those serial numbers on the flash drive took more digging than I thought. I assumed they were barcodes. That was the most logical guess, because they typically run from twelve to fifteen number increments. Since you gave me that video to restore, the only logical assumption was film or video sequences, correct?"

"Yes," Gavin confirmed. The screen flashed on, and endless digits appeared hypnotically on pages and pages of spreadsheets.

"Numbing, right?" Mylo glanced over at him. "Allowing my computer to run the numbers against possible produced films in the last, oh, I'd say, fifty years. A high projected number of probability."

"Your point," Gavin said impatiently.

"On this file, these barcodes are associated with some sort of porn film," he retorted. "I'm talking thousands and thousands and thousands of them. I randomly took several barcodes to see what film producer created them. I only came up with one brand. Wet Valley Studios."

Zanders Holdings. "I'm interested now," Gavin replied. "What significance is this…?"

"I was getting to it," Mylo interrupted. "The partial random code that I discovered off the burnt CD from the victim matched to one of the films. It came from a subsidiary distribution brand, called Sweet Treasure Studios that specialized in brutal sex, BDSM, young children, and teenage girls. Real amateur. All handheld devices."

"Like snuff films?" Gavin leaned back slightly.

"Yes," Mylo said, lowering his voice. "I mean, I like my share of porn. But this shit is sick. Nasty. But the victim's film was part of a series titled *Desert Blossoms, The Ultimate Military Reality.* She was part nine."

Before Gavin could speak, Mylo hit a key, and a small box popped up in the corner—a movie cover. The canvas of a military tent flapped in the wind with the desert in the background. A man whose face was hidden by a green cap was looking down, showing off his sweaty, bare muscular chest with its eagle tattoo. On the opposite corner of the screen was Sills, tied to the tent pole.

"How many parts are in the series?" Gavin kept staring at Sills' sleeping face.

"Not sure yet." Mylo typed on the keyboard frantically. "But that's not why I brought you here."

The screen flickered, and the same image of Sills appeared.

"After discovering the barcodes, I went back to the original film. And I was bothered by how it abruptly ended," Mylo stated solemnly, leaning back in his chair. "I misspoke, Nolan. I realized the video was the original content. Unedited, raw footage. I scrubbed the background noise and reran it through my sound mixer at home. I came across a piece that probably was not in the released film. It would require a comparison of the two."

"Run it." Gavin leaned in closer to Mylo's monitor.

The video flickered to life.

The angle of the shot changed on Sills' limp and bleeding body. The subtle noises of a busy base echoed in the background.

"Zach," a man off-screen said. "Hold the camera up at a forty-five-degree angle. Yeah."

Quickly, the camera shifted slightly, aiming downward at Stanton's naked body, and then at the dirt on the ground, before finally resting on Sills. The shot tightened to show the wounds and bruises across the light skin of her entire body. A moment later, a shadow appeared in the corner of the screen, and an older man's hairy back blocked the camera view for a few seconds. Then the man stepped toward Sills and bent over. Without a word, he firmly struck her across the face several times and grunted, "Whore, take that!"

With his back to the screen he called out, "Cory, get your ass over here."

Within a second, the man who was on the cover appeared and stumbled slightly forward with a whiskey bottle in hand. The older man then said, "Alright, you take her from behind. I'll take her from the front."

The eagle-tattooed man pulled up Sills slightly and went under her, slipping his manhood deep into her bleeding anal cavity. As the camera tightened, the older man guided his cock inside of her vagina. Sills let out a horrific cry of pain. The older man mounted Sills and thrusted himself over and over into the woman's body as the younger man penetrated her. Slowly, the angle of the camera shifted toward a mirror in the background. The film suddenly froze on that image. There was a naked Stanton in the background with the camera, part of Taylor's body under Sills' limp legs, and the older man on top of her.

Staring at the corner of the screen, Gavin could see a faint image of yet another face in the mirror.

"Are you saying you have a picture of the director?" Gavin inquired.

"I just finished this section this morning. With some editing, I can make that image better," Mylo said. He looked up at Gavin. "I don't think I ever told you this, but I have this thing about faces. Once I see it, I'll just automatically remember it. Probably my photogenic problem. Anyways, I just saw that face the other day." He pointed at the screen. "It bothered me so much that I went digging. Then it was right here."

Mylo handed him *The Tribune*. In the Local Section, a brief article discussed an award ceremony being held that night. Six pictures of the recipients were posted. The last picture resembled the image on the screen.

"Holy shit, right?" Mylo stated with a big smile.

"Keep this between us," Gavin said in a hushed voice. "Clean up that image. We're going to need it."

Quickly, Gavin left Mylo's office and reluctantly headed toward the only person who could help him.

*****

Determined, he knocked on Creighton's door, seeing that another uniformed officer was inside. Their conversation immediately halted, and their eyes locked on him.

"Can we talk?" Gavin said. He could hear the anxiousness in his own voice.

"Sure," Creighton replied. Then he said to the young cadet, "We'll rap this up later."

Nodding, ever obedient, the officer gave Creighton a coy smile and headed out the door.

"What's on your mind, Nolan?" Creighton's tone changed slightly from overly commanding to concerning in an instant. "How's Williamson?"

"As well as expected," he lied, closing the door behind him and staring at Creighton. "Need to speak to you about the case."

Oddly, a brief silence fell between them. Creighton leaned back slightly in his chair and patted down his tie.

"Can't read your goddamn mind," he retorted.

"With Mylo's help," Gavin said quickly as he approached his desk, "I uncovered a piece of evidence that will possibly apprehend the second suspect, the man who assisted Stanton."

"What the fuck are you talking about?" Creighton's eyebrows furrowed.

Briefly, he summarized the possibility of a second suspect, involving Zanders Holdings, Guerillo, and Stanton. He intentionally left out Derrick's time in the military. Then he asked Creighton for two things to happen next. For a lingering moment, a brief silence fell in the tight space.

"Okay." Creighton studied him. "Do you have any irrevocable proof? And what about Williamson's wife?"

Believe so. "Yes," Gavin replied. He added, "Working on Maria now."

"Okay fine. Let's deal with one thing at a time though. Find Maria, and let's bring this Stanton into custody," Creighton returned.

Gavin felt as if he'd been punched in the face. "Didn't you hear what I just explained?"

"No offense, Gavin," Quinn returned. "I believe your story. You're emotional. We all are—"

"Fuck you, Quinn!" he yelled back and pounded his fist on the desk.

Not stirring, the captain replied harshly, "Better watch yourself."

"This time," Gavin stated sardonically, standing rigidly, "this isn't about you or me. It's about Maria. We need to find this demented asshole. He's going to lead us to the other guy, his partner."

"I still don't—"

"Just fucking do this for Derrick, goddamn it!"

Quinn leaned further back in his chair and stroked his stubble. A flash of anger reddened his cheeks, and Gavin waited for a backlash. Letting out a heavy sigh, his eyes bore into Gavin, and finally he said, "All you had to say was fucking please."

"Asshole," Gavin grumbled, stepping away from the desk and walking away.

"I'll make it happen, Gavin," Quinn stated behind him.

Putting his hand on the doorknob, Gavin said, "All of it?"

"You want to play this fucking dance, Gavin?" He seemed not to question, but to hiss. "Because you and I are far from done. I'm not doing this for Williamson. I'm doing it only for you. And there's going to be fucking repercussions."

Not saying a word, Gavin opened the door quickly and escaped into the station. He dared not look back. His gut was right about this. Immediately, he texted Mary some information to search for, and shortly after, he texted Mylo some items to explore. Almost bumping into someone, Gavin finally looked up. Only then did he notice that Derrick was not at his desk.

Gavin picked up his stride, circumvented several desks, and scanned the area for him. A few desks over, he spotted Evelyn speaking with a couple of people and made a beeline toward her.

"Evelyn," he said to her, interrupting their conversation.

"I'll talk later with you two about those things, okay?" she said to the other detectives. Then she spoke softly. "What's wrong?"

"Nothing. Everything." He was scanning the room. "Seen Derrick?"

"No," she replied. "Said he had to use the bathroom."

"Shit," he muttered.

"What's going on?" Her voice was becoming tense.

"Just listen," he said softly. "I'm going to go check the bathroom. If I'm right, Derrick's not here."

Already walking over to their desks, she stated, "Where would he go?"

"Grab our stuff," he replied as he fished out his keys. He palmed them into her hand. "Meet me out back. I may know."

Breaking away from her, he walked quickly to the bathroom. As expected, Derrick was not there. He pulled out his phone as he headed toward the locker rooms. He immediately pressed a button on his phone and saw a red dot on the city map.

Got you, D. You're not doing this one alone.

FORTY-ONE

"Ay, *chingados!*" Evelyn grunted as she braced her hand against the dashboard.

Saying nothing, Gavin hit the accelerator and swerved around the slow-moving cars. Ahead of them, the Lake Shore lanes on the right side were bumper to bumper and nearly stalled. Rush hour seemed even more packed than usual. Derrick's phone had stopped moving at Navy Pier. The exact spot where the gala was to be held that evening.

Not a coincidence. Stanton wants to make headlines.

Glancing over, he saw on Evelyn's phone that Creighton was calling her. He'd already ignored the plethora of text messages from him.

"Seventh time he called," she remarked.

Fuck him. Gavin said nothing.

"Why are we avoiding the captain?" Evelyn questioned, wide-eyed. "We need help. Backup…"

"Because this sick asshole…" Gavin finally growled, running a red light and dodging three cars to the right. Honks and screeching tires blasted outside. "Will kill Maria and Derrick before Creighton can assemble anything."

"But—"

"I need you to work on that," he glanced over at her. "I need to try and stop Stanton right the fuck now!"

Under the viaduct, the amount of traffic increased. Slamming on the brakes, he maneuvered around the merging traffic, heading east. Quickly, he switched into the next lane and pressed down the pedal. He could feel the sweat on his hands. Blasting his horn so some pedestrians could back up, he sailed through the next red light easily. Before them sat Navy Pier.

The large Ferris wheel was lit up for the holidays. The fresh snow on the ground and buildings made the holiday decorations appear quintessentially festive. However, a line of cars, limos, and taxis were forming a massive jam near the circle. On the sidewalks, people were bundled up and heading toward the entertainment spots.

"So many people," Evelyn stated as she put on her gloves.

Turning left, he went to the other side of the street and into oncoming traffic, heading out of the place. Several squads were haphazardly parked at the north side of the pier. While the south side contained the shops and restaurants, the north side was really for parking and deliveries.

Stopping within inches of the squad, Gavin got out of the car. The icy wind hit him instantly.

"What the hell are you doing?!" one of the young officers stated, putting his hand on his gun.

"We're detectives!" Evelyn shouted out and held up her badge.

"Did you see another detective come through here?" Gavin stated. "Big. Black. Like a football player?"

"Yeah," the other young officer answered. He pointed down the side. "Went almost to the end. Looked real pissed off. Figured he was part of security for the thing tonight."

"Thanks." Gavin turned to Evelyn and said anxiously, "Call Creighton now. Get as many people as possible out of the end of the pier."

"What are you two talking about?" asked the squattier officer.

Before he could hear Evelyn's response, he shut the door. He slipped into reverse, backed up slightly, and then put the car in drive. Stepping on the gas, he went around the squad by going on the sidewalk, honking at people to move out of the way. With one last glance in the rearview, he saw Evelyn on the phone and speaking to the police officers. Her red jacket blew in the harsh wind.

Speeding up, Gavin haphazardly veered around a couple of parked cars, delivery trucks, and people. Near to the end, he noticed the unmarked car to the side of the building. Derrick had parked it on an angle. Following his lead, Gavin parked the Mustang near it. He got out of the car and pulled out his gun.

Gavin tightly gripped the weapon and entered the nearby cracked exit door.

It was almost as if he too were being lured in by Stanton.

*****

The slender service hallway was brightly lit. From a distance, the sounds of clanking dishes and glasses chimed quietly while the smells of garlic and seared steak perfumed the air. At that very moment, the noises stopped; murmured conversations erupted and the shuffling of footsteps echoed further away.

Thanks, Evelyn. The catering group had received word to evacuate.

Nearby, the exit door cracked open wider by the force of the strong wind, letting the bitter temperatures cascade inside. He stepped carefully, and noticed another door was ajar about twenty feet ahead of him. No matter, the thick stuffy atmosphere still hugged him. As he constantly looked back and forth, a small droplet of sweat fell from his forehead. Without lowering his weapon, Gavin undid his heavy coat and dropped it onto the floor. As he approached the open door, something felt odd about it. *Why was Stanton purposely leading Derrick to this location, of all places?*

Pushing the door open slowly with his shoulder and steadying his weapon in front of him, Gavin slipped into the darkened event hall. Faintly, he heard muffled conversations nearby.

Gavin had to get to Derrick.

The empty hall engulfed him. The extraordinarily high ceiling made the space unusually hollow, and his footsteps seemed loud, even against the carpet. On the opposite side, the massive floor-to-ceiling windows allowed the dim city light to invade the shadowy space. Glancing outside, he saw the museum campus lights in the far distance, glowing against the black lake water.

The conversation was getting louder.

Heading toward the next set of double doors, Gavin looked back into the vast emptiness. Only the creeping shadows stared back at him. Putting a hand on the knob, he cracked the door open.

"She had nothing to do with it," Derrick growled savagely.

"Bullshit, Sergeant," another man replied matter-of-factly. "Maria had fucking everything to do with it."

Easing into the next room, the inky darkness lingered as he crept behind a row of steel-blue fabric dividers. The six-foot-wide dividers extended along the perimeter of the wall and stood nearly ten feet high. He stepped quietly and saw a hideous orange glow breaking through in several places. He inched closer to one of the seams.

Perhaps he could use it to his advantage.

"Let her go!" Derrick demanded.

"And they thought I didn't know," Stanton returned.

Derrick repeated, "Maria had nothing—"

"Shut the fuck up!" Stanton roared back, his scream echoing throughout the empty space.

In that instant, Gavin heard the slap of a hand hitting a hard surface, and Derrick let out a brief grunt. Reaching the nearest crack, Gavin peeked into the room.

Derrick was on his knees, slumped over slightly with his hands behind his head. A trickle of blood mixed with drool oozed out of his mouth. His partner shook his head slightly, lifted his eyes, and said, "That all you got, asshole?"

Stanton walked around him, his bulky muscular frame snuggly filling his black tactical outfit. His ginger hair glowed in the iridescent light as he held a long hunting knife in one hand and clutched something else in the other.

"You stupid son of a bitch," he retorted. "You just don't fucking get it. Never fucking respected authority!"

"No, Major," Derrick returned, staring up at him. As he lifted his head up slightly, Gavin noticed the splatters of blood dotting his shirt and the deep cut in his right cheek. "I don't respect the authority of those who abuse it."

Stanton let out a maddening laugh. He commented, "Sergeant, you're still a goddamn idiot."

At that moment, Stanton turned away from Derrick and faced Gavin. Quickly, Gavin stepped back slightly into the darkness. Above the man's rugged coppery-colored beard and strong cheekbones, a hidden wrath swam around in his light green eyes. It was similar to the rage Gavin had seen in Vincent's eyes not so long ago. Subtly, he stepped over to the next slit in the fabric, which was a couple of feet down. He needed to locate Maria.

"Don't you think people are looking for me?" Derrick questioned.

"That's what I'm fucking banking on," he replied.

Keep him talking, D.

"You wanted me," Derrick continued, "you got me. Do what you want. Torture me. Kill me. Whatever the fuck you want. Like Bauerman, Pope, Parker, Taylor…"

"Ain't that goddamn simple," Stanton stated calmly. "They

needed to be taken care of. No loose ends. My orders were clear. You're different, Sergeant."

Gavin moved closer to them, managing to stay hidden. To the right, he noticed a large circular barrel. Then he noticed a length of rope leading up to the ceiling. The end was tied to an anchor in the floor, just to the right of Derrick.

"What the hell are you talking about?" Derrick appeared to be perplexed.

On the move again, Gavin crept closer to a crack in the fabric where the light was brighter.

"Maria knew exactly what was happening," Stanton rattled on, pointing the knife up in the air. "She couldn't mind her business. Fucking spic cunt. Should of done her, too! I bet your sweet little Maria has got a nice, sweet pussy. Maybe my thick cock in her mouth would have shut her up."

"Fuck you!" Derrick shouted.

"Huh-uh," Stanton returned right away. "Don't fucking move, Sergeant."

Gavin peered through the seam. Stanton's back was facing him, blocking Derrick entirely. He was holding the knife over the extended rope.

"One more inch," Stanton declared maliciously, "she fucking dies."

Gavin's eyes followed the rope, tracing its long line up to the nearby balcony and then down.

Before him, Maria Williamson's naked body was lit up by a portable fluorescent light. She was suspended from her hands above a long, thick metal shaft. Her long, curly hair covered her face, and her head barely moved, but her bare chest heaved slightly, signaling life. As his eyes drifted down, Gavin noticed the tip of the pole already inside her, causing two small streams of blood to flow down her legs.

"Good." Stanton stood straighter. "I finally got your goddamn attention."

"Son of a bitch," Derrick retorted, his voice thick with rage. "I'm going to fucking kill you!"

"Think I've got the upper hand." Stanton turned slightly. "Either way, we all die."

Craning his head, Gavin saw the entire explosive device. It was only a couple of yards away from him, near the curtain line. Five yellow barrels of explosives were intertwined in a spider web of wires. On the top, a simple red digital counter was set for three minutes. How soon before it would start counting down? A sick knot fell into his stomach.

Reaching for his phone, he texted Evelyn: *Found Derrick & Maria. Get bomb squad ready to go.*

Instantly she responded: *Done. 40% cleared. Creighton's ETA is 10 min.*

He then replied: *Work faster.*

Pocketing his phone, he squatted down slightly and began to contemplate his next move. With a slight shift of her head, Maria's puffy face seemed to aim down toward him. The slight movement caused the curtain of her hair to part, and her lackadaisical dark eyes rolled around in their sockets, as if attempting to focus on him. Taking a deep breath, he shed his suit jacket and gripped his gun tightly.

Time was running out. He had to act quickly.

******

Stanton steadily held the knife over the taut rope and shifted slightly.

Derrick's rage was pasted all over his face and showed in the stance of his rigid body, as if her were readying to pounce on a big savage lion.

"You didn't know what you were doing though, Sergeant," he said. "And you thought I didn't notice either. I know you and that whore doctor were trying to find shit on me. On shit I was doing. No, I had the upper hand. Money buys respect. I had a lot of respect on that base."

Stanton scratched at his beard. "Everyone fucking loved me. I was the fucking star. But you and Sheridan insisted on playing games behind my back. You think you knew what I was doing? You barely hit the fucking tip, Sergeant. After your sorry black pathetic ass got kicked out, I was revered. I was a hero there. A fucking god to the people."

"Depends on who you ask," Derrick returned.

Spontaneously, Stanton lashed out at Derrick and kicked him

squarely in the gut several times. Derrick bent over and clutched his stomach, gasping for air and spitting up more blood. Grinning, Stanton stepped aside just out of view. Gavin could only see his arm.

Even though he wanted to jump in, Gavin held himself back, gripping the gun tighter and waiting for the right moment.

"As I was saying, Sergeant." Stanton's voice sounded louder. "We had a plan from the get-go. All was fine and dandy. I did my thing. And *he* did *his* thing. Then we celebrated our victories from time to time."

"Who…" Derrick gasped as he straightened himself up.

"Was really Maria who fucked it up," he stated. With a slight movement, Stanton appeared just to the right. "Since our relationship was going so well with the faction…"

"Faction?" Derrick questioned, staring at him.

Stanton ignored him. "I suggested to blow off some steam on the locals. What can you say? We both had the same tastes. Plus, they were just fucking Third World nothingness. Nobody would miss them."

"Is that why the local women were found raped?" Derrick stated.

"Yeah, a couple made it back," Stanton replied, almost too calmly. "Most didn't. That wasn't enough. Really, it was *his* idea to tape our fun."

"Creating videos of you raping and abusing female military officers?" Derrick's voice was raspy.

Positioning himself, Gavin raised his gun. He needed a clear shot. Stanton moved more to the right, but Gavin could not yet risk being seen.

"I really thought they'd be home videos," Stanton returned. "Little hallmarks. Little memories of good times. But then…" His voice trailed off.

"Then what?" Derrick purposely moved his body to face Stanton's direction.

"He fucking profited off of them!" Stanton exclaimed, sounding almost astonished. Now he stepped into view. "That weaselly fucker decided to sell them off! And never fucking told me! Can you believe that?! Never fucking said a word to me about it. Treated me like…"

"Taylor?" Derrick added.

"Yes!" Stanton pointed the knife at Derrick. "Fucking treated me like a little soldier. And I was the fucking idiot doing all the fucking grunt work. Getting the shipments, making the drop-offs, and all the bullshit. He just sat back and scooped up his share in all of it!"

Stanton stopped suddenly, and his body trembled slightly. The knife waved up in the air as if he were pointing at someone in the shadows. Then he pointed it back at Derrick.

"But, it was your dear little cunt wife," he stated, "who almost fucked everything. After you left, she treated Sills, Gable, and Carlton in the med clinic. And a couple of others. She recognized a pattern. Of course, she went to me because I was the senior staff member. Explained that a series of rapes were occurring on base. I dismissed it since she couldn't prove anything. With *his* help, they all went back to the States, discharged for mental distress. Then, she did something I didn't think would happen."

Stanton straightened up, squaring his back. He made a few quick strides toward Maria, only a yard from Gavin.

"Your little bitch wife," Stanton hissed, holding up his knife and laying the tip on her thigh. "She followed up with them and told them to put in a case file. To report it. What the fuck!" Instantly, the knife submerged into her leg.

"NO!" Derrick screamed out.

Stanton rushed over to Derrick and squatted near him. His voice lowered. "Do you know how much fucking bullshit *he* gave me? Because of your big-mouth cunt wife?!"

He held the knife up to Derrick's throat. Gavin silently winced when the blade grazed his partner's skin near his Adam's apple, causing a red smear of blood.

"Both of you have been a serious pain in my ass," Stanton snapped. "And he will see to that. When he receives his little goddamn community award, he's going to be kissing his own insides. That greedy fucking liar!"

Abruptly, Stanton kneed Derrick in his abdomen, making Derrick slump down. Stanton grabbed the back of Derrick's neck and stared him straight in the eye.

"And you, Sergeant, are finally going to pay for your insubordination," Stanton growled. "I want Maria to see you suffer, see the pain in your face when I fillet the skin off your body!"

Pointing his gun, Gavin slipped from behind the curtain and yelled, "Zachary! Put down the weapon!"

Stanton hunched over more and craned his neck to look over at

Gavin. The deep crevices in his face, the V-shape of his beard, and the dead green eyes made him appear more demonic than human.

"Gavin, stop!" Derrick yelled.

"I was wondering when you'd come out from the shadows and play," Stanton stated simply.

"Put down your weapon!" Gavin returned and stepped closer to him.

Stanton slowly stood up, turning his back to Derrick. "Think your little fucking police pistol can match my goddamn skills, asshole?"

"Stop!" Derrick warned angrily. His body became rigid.

Stanton opened up his palms. His left hand clung onto the barbaric knife with his thumb, and his right hand revealed a long cylindrical object with a red button on top.

"Come on, shoot me, Officer!" Stanton took a step forward. A sinister grin filled his face. "All it takes is one shot through the heart. A simple shot. In that shot, the dying nerves in my right thumb will press the button. And fucking goodbye to us all. So go ahead, fucker, shoot me!"

"Gavin, put down your weapon!" Derrick shouted.

"Your choice, fuckhead," Stanton added. His frame arched slightly, as if he were ready to strike.

"If I don't shoot you, we all die," Gavin returned. "If I do shoot you, again, we all die anyway. It's a win-win situation for you, Zachary."

"The only person called me Zachary was my mother," he replied. "Hated that old whore for naming me that."

"Guess you showed her. By setting her house on fire," Gavin said, gripping the gun tighter. "With her in it."

His wicked grin widened. "Should have heard her scream," he replied. "Absolutely fucking priceless."

"Don't Gavin, please," Derrick stated loudly. "For Maria."

"Yeah, listen to the sergeant, boy," Stanton mimicked. "For Maria. Help a cunt out."

"I can't lower it, Derrick," Gavin replied. He briefly looked at Derrick. "I just can't do that. For Maria's sake."

"Goddamn touching. Feels like a dyke Hallmark movie." Stanton stepped forward again.

Firmly, Gavin planted himself in his spot, readying himself. "Zachary," he began.

"What the fuck did I tell you about that," Stanton interrupted.

Alright. "Major," he said instead. "Why do you want to set off the bomb here?"

Slightly taken aback, Stanton seemed lost in thought, as if he were choosing the right words. Whatever it was, it gave Derrick the opportunity. Behind Stanton, Derrick lowered his hands slowly and began to rise to his feet.

"Boy scout," he answered sardonically, "I can't fill in all the fucking blanks for you."

Precisely at that moment, Derrick leapt toward Stanton and grabbed his right hand. In a quick jab, the sound of breaking bones pierced the empty space, and the detonator fell out of his hand. Yet, Stanton's other hand swung around, and he plunged the knife into Derrick's shoulder. As if he had not felt it, Derrick elbowed Stanton in the face with a resounding crack.

In a split second, Gavin lowered his gun and ran to Maria.

"Big fucking mistake, Williamson!" Stanton grunted.

Gavin saw Stanton's left hand extend. Using the knife as an extra limb, he cut through the rope like it was warm butter. Ahead of him, Maria's body jerked slowly and then slid down the stake. She groaned out a muttered scream.

"Maria!" Derrick called out behind him.

Gavin sprinted to Maria, and with the sounds of cracks and grunts, Derrick and Stanton fought as Gavin moved. He caught a glimpse of Stanton pivoting on his leg and side-kicking Derrick in the head. With a loud grunt, Derrick stumbled off balance as Stanton took off to the other end of the darkened hall.

Reaching Maria, Gavin lowered her to the ground. The needle of the stake was sticking out of her right clavicle, and blood was pouring out. The coppery scent of Maria's blood filled his senses as he pressed his hand against her flesh. He ripped off his button-down shirt, rolled it into a ball, and pressed down hard, hoping to stop the bleeding. His own hands trembled against her weak, almost limp body.

Next to him, Derrick stumbled near them, screaming his wife's name.

Facing Derrick and handing him his gun, he yelled, "Get that son of a bitch! I got Maria!"

An expression of complete fury took over Derrick, and he raced after Stanton with loud thumps echoing.

"Maria, shh," Gavin said. Blood gushed out in an endless river from her legs. "You're not dying on me, okay Maria? Listen."

Maria's eyes rolled back in her head. A stream of blood oozed out of the sides of her mouth.

"GAVIN!" Evelyn shouted behind him.

"Evelyn, quick!" he shouted back.

In that moment, Evelyn was right next to him. "Oh God!"

"Pressure here!" Gavin stood up. "I'm going after Derrick and Stanton!"

She got on the radio and yelled: "Medics, ASAP! I said now, GODDAMMIT!"

As he turned, Evelyn began reciting the same mantra as Gavin had, demanding that Maria stay with them. Somehow, he had to reach Derrick and help him bring Stanton down.

*****

Outside, the frigid raw wind cut through Gavin's thin t-shirt. The dim light brought forth long shadows at the end of the pier. Turning the corner and feeling the full brunt of icy air, Gavin saw Derrick's thick back moving over the edge of the cement wall and then disappearing. The dark churning waters of Lake Michigan roared against the rocks.

In a quick stride, Gavin sprinted toward the wall. The black ice caught his shoes here and there as huge snowflakes filled the air, whirling around in the wind.

"Stanton! There's no escape!" Derrick shouted from below.

Looking down, Gavin saw Derrick making his way over the ice-covered jagged rocks in pursuit of Stanton. Thanks to his black uniform, the man stood out against the snow. Stanton stopped at the end of the rocks—where could he possibly go?

Leaping over the icy cement barricade, Gavin fell a couple feet short of the rock and lurched forward. The sharp ice cut into his legs as he steadied himself. Looking over in the dim light, he saw Derrick was already halfway down the rocks, struggling to stay steady.

"You are going to pay for what you did!" Derrick yelled out.

Coming from the south, a CPD chopper headed toward him. Gavin steadied himself and made his way to Derrick. His hands were freezing from the bitter temperatures. The increasing snowflakes were making it harder to see Stanton, even in his black attire, but Gavin could make him out as he inched himself onto an ice shelf over the lake.

"Stanton!" Derrick shouted. "Give up!"

Instantly, the chopper's high intensity beam circled them and then zeroed in on Stanton, who now had a gun pointed at them. Gavin estimated, he was a good twenty yards out. Behind him, the frigid, murky waters of the lake churned.

Derrick gripped his gun and pointed it at Stanton. Gavin could see the blood trickling down Derrick's arm and onto the ice-covered rocks. He needed to get to Derrick before he made a mistake. They needed Stanton alive.

"Don't go any farther, Stanton!" Derrick shouted. He stepped onto the edge of the ice cap. "I'll shoot!"

Stanton was enveloped in light from the helicopter above.

"Sergeant, you ain't the kind of man to fuckin' kill your superior!" A wide grin stretched his mouth.

"You're going to pay for your crimes, Major!" Derrick eased farther out onto the ice.

"Don't do it, Derrick!" Gavin was several feet away.

"Should listen to your partner!" Stanton pointed the gun at Gavin. "Think I can hit him easily from here. Clean shot!"

Stopping, Gavin looked over at Derrick, who still had not turned around. "This isn't about him!" Derrick roared. "It's our fight!"

Shrugging his shoulders, the man said with a smile, "You're right! I have nothing to lose, Sergeant! See you in hell!"

At that moment, Stanton and Derrick fired their guns. Gavin heard Stanton's bullet hit a rock right by his feet. In the light, Gavin saw Derrick's bullet go straight into Stanton's forehead. The back of his head exploded, and his brain spewed over the white ice. As if in slow motion, the body fell backwards onto the ice, which cracked open instantly.

Stanton's body disappeared into the murky, silky depths of Lake Michigan.

"For Maria, motherfucker," Derrick said. He turned to face Gavin.

In the bright light of the chopper beam, both utter fury and deep sorrow washed over Derrick's dark eyes.

DERRICK

FORTY-TWO

Casually, Creighton lingered in the doorframe of the interview room, reporting that Officer Liminski was on her way with the guests. Not saying anything, Gavin straightened his tie in the mirror and sat down in the stiff metal chair. Before Creighton left to go in the other room to watch, he stated that if they needed any assistance, they only had to nod.

"Yes, Captain," Evelyn answered for him. She fiddled with the paperwork again, nervously double-checking it. The scar on her neck was healing, but she had still applied some makeup to further disguise the wound.

Gavin stared at the open door and the cement wall ahead. The faint sounds of the station floated into the sterile room like the dreary melody of a classical song. Behind him, in the observation room, the audience was not for Gavin, but for Creighton. It didn't seem right having only Evelyn next to him, yet it had to be done this way.

"Remember." He leaned in her direction and whispered, "For Derrick."

Stopping, she looked over at him. Her dark bloodshot eyes brimmed with tears, and she blinked them back.

"Yes, for Derrick," she said softly.

A few moments later, Mary's voice echoed off the hallway as two uniformed officers passed by the door. They leaned against the wall, and Mary thanked the young men for letting them pass. She entered the interview room with a false sincere expression. Her eyes were also bloodshot. Everyone was exhausted, including Gavin himself. So much work had been put into this moment.

Following Mary, a tall yet wide man in full military uniform came through the door. His bulbous body barely fit his tight uniform.

"General Norquist," Gavin stated and rose to his feet. Evelyn also stood up.

"Yes," he replied. "Such formality that y'all are showing me today.

Being ushered in by this pretty lady here." He nodded at Mary, who deflected his words with a pursed smile. "And you must be Detective Gavin Nolan, correct?"

"Yes, sir," he returned. "My partner, Detective Evelyn Lopez."

A syrupy smile formed above his thick jowls and he replied, "Why, you're something. Think I have to visit the Windy City more often. So many lovely ladies residing in the northern cities."

"If you would like to have a seat," Evelyn suggested.

"Thank you," the general stated. "It's refreshing to have such hospitality."

"Would you like anything else?" Mary inquired, standing at the door.

As if on cue, Larry Hewittson rounded the corner. He wore another dark expensive suit that was too tight for his thick midsection. His smile was placid as he nodded toward the general.

"No, that'll be all, Officer," Gavin said to Mary. "Thank you."

"My pleasure," Mary returned. As she turned, Gavin noticed the smile fall from her face as sadness washed over it.

"Mr. Hewittson," Evelyn said. "Funny to meet you here. Again."

"Have you all met before, Larry?" Norquist asked, settling himself in the chair.

Hewittson made a small production of taking off his overcoat, setting it over the back of his chair, and placing his laptop on the table with a thud.

"Yes," the lawyer replied to him halfheartedly. "A couple weeks ago."

"Such a small world," Gavin replied.

"Yes, indeed," Norquist returned, letting his subtle Carolinian accent grace his speech. "Not to be a bother, but about how long will this take? I'm already a day overdue to get back to the base."

"Yes," Evelyn piped in. "That gas leak down at Navy Pier on Tuesday. A major story on the news. Even a couple of days later, Nicor still can't figure out where the leak came from."

"You were here for the community awards ceremony that was rescheduled for the next day, right?" Gavin said, eyeing up the general.

A brief smile appeared on his thick face. "A fine dinner. A spectacular gala. The food was incredible."

"May I ask, General, how did you get that award?" Evelyn then added, "South Carolina is far from here. Why not in your own community?"

"Well, in my small, quaint town, I assist in various church-related charities," he replied. A lucid smile appeared on his thick lips. "I like to give back to a community. My donations to various local organizations help bring some hope to the ones in destitute situations. My father, God rest his soul, was a preacher, and I always remember him telling me that I must give to those who need the most. His words stick with me to this day."

A casual smirk lined Gavin's lip, and he barely managed to resist the urge to jump over the table and hit the man.

"I know Chicago needs a lot of assistance," the general stated, "from reading the paper and watching the news. I wanted to make monetary donations to a community that deserves and accepts the charity humbly. Please do not get me wrong, my church does a fine job in various programs. Over the years, I wanted to give back to a larger community where the need was greater." He paused. "Actually, accepting my award is one of my official last acts as a general. I will be retiring at the end of next week."

"Good for you." Gavin sat slightly straighter. "General, do you come to Chicago often?"

"Rarely," he replied. "But I do love your city. Big, fast, and energetic. Plus, the steakhouses are a close comparison to the ones in Texas." He glanced over at Hewittson. "Larry and I are going out for some thick steak dinner right after this, right? Probably Harry Caray's place."

"Mm-hmm," Hewittson replied softly, puttering with the laptop.

"That's nice," Evelyn responded, tapping her nails on the manila folder in front of her.

"I apologize, General," Gavin spoke up. "I would love to talk about your insights on our fine city, but we should begin. We don't want to keep you."

"Very well, then." He placed his hands flat on the table.

Casually, Gavin leaned forward on the table and propped his elbows on it. "How well did you know Zachary Stanton?"

"He was underneath me," Norquist began.

"Sorry, General," Gavin interrupted, putting a hand up and turning to Hewittson. "I was asking your lawyer."

Immediately, the man stopped typing and faced Gavin, a blank stare on his face. "I don't understand what you mean, Detective."

"Four years ago," Evelyn spoke up, opening her file and sliding over a piece of paper. "You became Mr. Stanton's personal representative in a divorce proceeding, which his wife, Jacquelyn Stanton, issued."

Without looking at it, Hewittson maintained his gaze on Gavin. "He was a client. We had done much of our communication through emails."

"In fact," Evelyn added, "you and your client, Mr. Stanton, processed several junctions against the proceedings, claiming that Stanton's work kept him abroad. One even claimed that the distress of the pending legal battle caused irrevocable mental illness on your client. Just seven months ago, the last one claimed that Mrs. Stanton was badgering your client in order to—"

"I know the motions." Hewittson puffed up his chest. "Mrs. Stanton was harassing my client to end their marriage. He wanted to reconcile. I don't understand what this has to do with anything."

"But you knew why Mrs. Stanton, I correct myself, Jacquelyn Lenard, truly wanted the divorce," Gavin stated.

"Client-lawyer privilege, Detective," he replied and glanced over at Norquist.

"Were you aware that Mrs. Stanton was being physically and mentally abused by your client?"

"I cannot describe any details of the case; you know that," Hewittson replied impatiently.

"In October of 2011," Evelyn stated, sliding out another piece of paper. "A filed report by the local village police described that Mr. Stanton held a knife to Mrs. Stanton's throat while she was unconscious after he beat her. Mrs. Stanton was in the hospital for twenty-eight days due to internal injuries."

Hewittson said nothing, folding his arms over his chest.

"Mrs. Stanton," Gavin continued, "filed an assault and battery charge on him with a restraining order. However, it never appeared in any court. Actually, we would never have found the report at all if we hadn't found the judge who actually proceeded over the case."

"If you continue speaking, Detective," Hewittson replied, nervously, "I will sue you and the department for slander."

"We did find the judge," Evelyn stated calmly. "Yesterday in fact. Circuit Court Judge Deidre. He didn't recall any incident about Mrs.

Stanton's request until we subpoenaed his records. Judge Deidre had buried the battery charges and petition."

"After some persuasive conversation," Gavin jumped in, "Deidre confessed about filing the order away, which is, as you well know, a felony charge. To my surprise, when asked why he'd buried it…"

"This is ludicrous," Hewittson stammered. "Do you hear this crap they're saying about me?" He turned to Norquist, who seemed much more reserved.

"Deidre claimed that you, Mr. Hewittson," Gavin continued on, "saw him privately that week of the incident. You said that if he made the case vanish, then he would be rewarded handsomely. Sure enough, he did as you requested. Three days later, you gave him a sizeable check for his efforts."

"Bullshit!" the lawyer exclaimed, appearing to be surprised.

Sliding over a paper, Evelyn stated, "Here's a copy of the check."

Hewittson's full face reddened. Then he stood up, grabbed his jacket, and declared, "You haven't heard the last of me. I'll have your goddamn badge numbers!"

"You realize bribing a judge is a federal offence," Gavin said, looking at the lawyer. "And you will be promptly disbarred."

As soon as Hewittson opened the door, Detective Rodgers was waiting on the other side. "Larry Hewittson, you have the right to remain—"

Trying to struggle against Rodgers's beefy frame, the lawyer yelled to Norquist, "Phillip, don't you say a word. They're wrong! Let go of me!"

Instantly the door closed, and the room was oddly quiet.

Gavin leaned back in the chair. Even in the stale disinfected air, a subtle hint of cheap pine cologne wafted off the general. Norquist's stone face was unwavering, as if he were not surprised.

"General Norquist," Gavin simply said. "Since I have your full attention, would you like to proceed with or without legal counsel?"

*****

General Norquist's light blue eyes flickered past Gavin's stare, possibly at the mirror behind him. His focus was oddly intense, and then his eyes drifted back to Gavin. Puckering his lips, the general sat straighter.

"General Norquist," Evelyn began.

"Major Zachary Stanton," he interrupted her, "was a disturbed individual for some time. As noted from the military psychologist's report, Stanton was a highly unstable person suffering from post-traumatic stress syndrome due to being stationed for an extended period of time in Afghanistan. Over the last five years of his service, I perceived the way he conducted himself to be both offensive and vulgar. After several severe reprimands, I had the unfortunate decision of forcing him into early retirement two years ago. Since then, I have not had any contact with Zachary Stanton."

An air of confidence settled over the general, as if he were pleased with his response.

A good dress rehearsal. Slipping a photo from the file in front of him, Gavin slid it across the table and then asked, "We will get to Mr. Stanton in a moment, sir. Have you ever met this man? A Fernando Guerillo?"

"No, it doesn't ring a bell," he replied.

"You didn't look at the picture." Gavin pushed it closer to him.

His eyes darted down quickly and then back up to Gavin. "No."

"Do you know the Sanford and Pierce Realty Group?" Evelyn inquired.

"Yes," he returned. "At an event years ago, I met Mitchell Pierce."

"Have you ever conducted business with Mr. Pierce?" Gavin asked.

"Do you mean do *I* own any property in the Midwest, Detective?" He smiled. "I can barely keep up with my house in Carolina. My wife has a honey-do list a mile long."

"General Norquist." Gavin leaned closer to him. "Have you heard of Zanders Holdings Group?"

Norquist cleared his throat slightly and shifted in his chair.

"Yes, I own some stock it that company," he stated simply.

"According to this report," Evelyn slid out a piece of paper from her file, "you are actually a board member of the company. In fact, *your* company has many facets of business, and it's a near half-a-billion-dollar enterprise. Quite impressive."

"There is nothing wrong with serving my country and being part of another business."

"Like a side job?" Evelyn retorted.

"Yes, Detective," the general replied.

"Most side gigs aren't multi-million-dollar positions."

"What can I say?" His voice was rooted with confidence. "The lord blessed me with a great job in the military, and a decent head for business."

"I repeat," Gavin asked, "did your company conduct any business with Sanford and Pierce Realty Group?"

"Not that I can recall," he replied quickly. "I'm not involved in the minutiae of the company's dealings."

Slippery words.

Evelyn shifted in her chair. "Did you know that Fernando Guerillo worked for Zanders Holdings Group?"

Shrugging his shoulders, he said, "Again, I don't really know all the people involved. I'm more or less a silent partner."

"Interestingly," Gavin spoke up, "the murders that Zachary Stanton perpetrated—"

"Such a sad individual," he interrupted patronizingly. "Tsk. Tsk. Such tragic deaths."

"The properties where the murders took place were connected to Zanders Holdings Group," Gavin continued. "According to the records provided by S and P, many locations were within the Chicago-Gary, Indiana area. Guerillo oversaw the sites."

"I'm not sure where this is going, Detective." The general's voice feigned naivety. "We have many locations across the country."

"Actually, no," Evelyn stated. "After a thorough check on additional properties, we've found that Zanders uses the Midwest as the main distribution hub." She slid another paper in front of him. "See? That even surprised me."

"Maybe you are confusing your other properties with your subsidiary company," Gavin added in. "Wet Valley Studios."

For a brief moment, Norquist's smile dipped down. His hands clasped onto the roundness of his stomach.

"As a silent partner," Gavin stated, "I would like to know where my investment is going. Here, I know I'm growing my pension through the county. But really, God only knows if I'll get it paid out because Illinois is so broke. On the side, I saved some money and began to invest here and there. You know, plan for the future. My bet is in technology."

"Mine is in new fuels," Evelyn said, looking over at Gavin. "And yours, General Norquist? Do you know where your money is going in your investment?"

The man said nothing.

"Adult entertainment," Gavin answered for him. "Don't get me wrong. It's a big business. Lots of merchandising, extracurricular fun for all, and, how should I say this? A plethora of various stimulants for both sexes. Not bad at all. Overall, pretty harmless. Nothing unlawful about that at all." He paused. "Do you know what kind of business Wet Valley Studios does for you?"

Still nothing from the general.

"Adult films," he said. "All kinds of them. In every shape and form. Which is fine if the actors are eighteen. Right?" Gavin slipped a paper out and handed it over to him. "Back in oh-seven, Wet Valley Studios was raided and charged with filming minors and then distributing the films within your centers. According to this affidavit, Zanders Holdings settled out of court and paid a whopping five-hundred-grand fine."

Norquist looked past Gavin, probably staring at the mirrored wall behind him again.

"What does this have to do with your locations and Guerillo, you ask?" Gavin questioned.

"In a property leased by Zanders Holdings Group," Evelyn jumped in, "we discovered an editing station. CIA discovered a large deposit of blood in the fibers of the main living room carpet, which was deliberately, and poorly, I might add, scrubbed away. Two days ago, we found that Guerillo's blood matched the blood in the carpet, because his body was discovered off the shore of Kenosha, Wisconsin. Three close range shots in the back and one in the head. Very professional."

"When I was on the scene," Gavin said calmly, "my partner noticed the tiles in the bathroom ceiling slightly askew. As if someone was hiding something up there. No one would have noticed, unless you looked really hard. We found a flash drive. With the help of our IT detective, we discovered a listing of barcodes on it. All of the films were under the Wet Valley Studios film group." Gavin leaned closer to him. "Do you know what these films were?"

Norquist's icy blue eyes locked on him.

"Sick, horrible amateur films." Gavin lowered his voice, almost to a whisper. "They depicted young women being assaulted by grown men, bestiality at its worst, hardcore bondage. But the worst were the endless films of children." He paused. "Imagine, General Norquist, your retirement money was made from pedophiles drooling over young kids getting sexually abused."

"I will personally look into it," the general said with false sincerity.

"No need, General." Leaning back, Gavin returned, "Don't worry, you won't have to. We gave a copy of the list to the United States District Attorney already." Casually, he looked up at the white clock locked in a steel cage. "About an hour ago, a cease and desist order was mandated over Zanders Holdings Group. As we speak, the FBI is raiding all locations where filming, production, and distribution is taking place. In fact, all the studio's related films are being pulled from shelves and disconnected from online distribution. They will no longer be available for purchase."

A slight reddening flushed over the general's cheeks. He placed his hands on the table, and his fingers began to tap.

"In fact," Gavin added, "because of the severity of said movies, they are reaching out to several other countries to assist in stopping the distribution of these awful films."

"All I have to say," Evelyn went on, "is if you have stock in your company, it'll be at half value by the end of the day today."

"Guess your investment just bottomed out, General," Gavin added with a slight grin. "Though we actually aren't here to discuss your business affairs. But your connection to Zachary Stanton."

FORTY-THREE

A dull, moaning creak from the metal chair filled the silent space as General Norquist shifted forward an inch. His large frame sat even more rigid than earlier. A stern and powerful disposition took over his face and darkness overshadowed his eyes, as if he were straining to keep from lashing out at either Gavin or Evelyn.

"As I stated before—" the general replied, his voice lowering.

"Yes, we remember," Gavin interrupted him quickly.

A look of subtle anger flashed over the general's round face.

You don't like it when people interrupt you. Gavin stated, "Your statement doesn't necessarily coincide with our information."

"According to recent records from Stanton's military file," Evelyn stated. Her strikingly scarlet nails flipped over a page in the manila envelope. "Under your command, Stanton rose in the ranks solely through your appraisal mandates and proper training. In fact, your words at the major's hearing were, and I quote, 'efficient, effective leader and strong military discipline,' end quote."

"Yes, he proved himself at the time," the bulbous man said. "Back then, he was a capable individual with the ability to take and give strategic orders for classified missions. His jacket had proven a solid history of successful missions. His dedication to protecting our country's interest was paramount."

"His jacket certainly proves it." Gavin leaned back in the chair and innocently asked, "What I find interesting—and maybe you can help me with this—why would Stanton be stationed in one location for such a long period of time? Especially an active area of conflict like Afghanistan?"

"Major Stanton was a crucial asset in keeping the sovereign state protected from the growing number of factions against the government," he explained, as if he were speaking to an inexperienced politician. "Through various missions, he and his squad went on several crucial operations to quell resistance and build an international foundation of peace."

"What kind of missions did he have to go on?" Gavin inquired, knowing he was treading on thin ice. He proceeded cautiously and added naively, "I mean, I watch the news. Did he ever go after that faction named the Qahhar, for instance?"

A subtle change in the general's face flashed suddenly and then quickly dissipated.

"I cannot divulge secret missions, Detective," Norquist said immediately. "All of his missions were classified. You and your department do not have the jurisdiction nor authority to question me about top-secret missions."

"Very well." Instinctively, he slid out several DMV pictures of Bauerman, Parker, Pope, and Taylor and set them askew in front of him. "Do you recognize any of these individuals?"

"I cannot recall." Norquist stared blankly at Gavin.

"Take a good look at them." Gavin pushed the papers closer.

The general's haunted-looking eyes briefly scanned the pictures before settling back on Gavin. "No, I cannot recall."

"They were soldiers under Stanton's command," Gavin stated. "Which meant your command as well."

No response. The general looked past Gavin.

Evelyn then spoke up. "Each of these men had a series of fatal accidents within the past year."

"About a year after Stanton was discharged from the military," Gavin said, "we discovered that he had roundtrip flights booked around the times of their deaths. We thought that was too much of a coincidence. Funny thing though. The credit card associated with Stanton was not a personal card. But a corporate card. Guess from what company?"

The general's fingers tapped against the table softly.

"Zanders Holdings Group." Evelyn produced another sheet of paper, showing a credit card statement with a purchase history and highlighted lines.

"General," Gavin asked softly. "Did you know that Stanton was on your payroll?"

"I don't understand where this is going," Norquist retorted

bitterly.

"After I got divorced," Gavin replied, ignoring him. "I received a lot of crap from my ex. Stuff I took by accident. As was the case in Jacquelyn's divorce. She happened to grab a box of Zachary's, not realizing it, and opened it one day. And guess what she discovered?"

"A series of old paychecks from Zanders, dating back to the early 2000s," Evelyn stated. "Many paycheck stubs."

"Detective," Norquist said softly. "I may recall a conversation with Stanton where I suggested Zanders Holdings Group as a possibility. He wanted to earn some extra income on the side to support his growing family. I gave out a fellow name, and what he did with it, I didn't know. Guess he was on the payroll after all."

He took the bait. Gavin resisted a smile.

"We'll touch base on that shortly, General," Evelyn said before Gavin could speak as she shifted the manila folders. She set out a series of military mugshots of Sills, Carlton, and Gable.

"Do you recognize any of these women?" Gavin said loosely.

Shaking his head, he replied softly, "No, I don't believe so."

"You didn't even look at them, Sir," Evelyn stated and pointed at the pictures.

Hesitantly, he looked over them and said, "No, I don't recognize these women at all."

"They were also soldiers under your command," Gavin stated.

"Detectives," Norquist said pompously. "Do y'all know how many soldiers are actually under my command? I have at least two dozen high-ranking officers. Below them, I have a hundred midrange officers. Below them, I have, shoot, five hundred or so low-ranking corporals. Underneath all of them, I have up to five thousand soldiers. Trying to remember everyone's face becomes a challenge."

Poor you. "Understandably challenging, Sir." Gavin shifted slightly in his chair. "We are asking if you recognize any of these women. Because Stanton killed these women specifically."

Saying nothing, Norquist looked again at the mirror, and then back to Gavin.

"Is this going to be much longer?" he stated, briefly checking his ostentatious silver Rolex. "I do have a flight to catch."

At that point, Gavin slid Mylo's laptop over and flipped open the top. The screen instantly came to life.

"Yes, you are busy," Gavin stated. "Really, only a couple more questions."

Next to him, Evelyn leaned back in her chair and casually finger-combed her hair back. In his peripheral vision, the look of discontent and even subtle frustration was clear on her face. Gavin realized that he could only detain Norquist for so long, and the general could walk at any time.

Derrick, I wish you were here for this.

*****

"On that flash drive found at Guerillo's apartment," Gavin said nonchalantly, "we found a corresponding movie related to one of the victims. Sills here." He causally pointed at her picture on the table.

Norquist's eyes remained still. His large, thick hands rested gently on the table, and he tapped his index fingers while his posture stayed obnoxiously rigid.

"What we could not figure out," Evelyn piped in, "is why Stanton had been leaving CDs on the women? Both Gable and Carlton were so badly burnt that bits of the CD were embedded in their skin. On the other hand, Sills was the only one with the entire piece intact. Our IT guy was able to scrub enough data to reveal footage from the film. The amateur movie showed how Stanton drugged, beat, and raped Sills continuously."

"However, this particular film was different," Gavin continued. "After a brief comparison from the marketed version to the evidence, we discovered that it was the unedited version. A director's cut, if you will."

The general's fingers stopped tapping.

"Fortunately, our IT detective found some additional footage that we had not seen," Gavin stated. He tapped on the computer and pulled up the film clip. "Imagine, to my surprise, what I saw. Shall we take a look?"

Instantly, the film opened, with the large older man striking Sills as Taylor entered the scene. Gavin let the scene play, up to the point where Stanton was holding the camera and shifting toward the nearby mirror. Pausing on that still, Gavin zoomed on the face in the mirror to reveal General Norquist himself.

"So tell me, General," Gavin repeated, his tone dark. "Do you recognize any of these women?"

The stone face cracked slightly, revealing a hint of both surprise and vehemence.

"I have a story for you, General," Gavin stated simply. "In the late nineties, you had the opportunity to invest in a small company and never really thought of its potential. Even though it sold adult merchandise, which was a comfortable profit margin, you had bigger dreams. A few years later, when the stock market took a dive, as an active board member you sought out to buy a small adult film studio and changed its name to Wet Valley Studios. It then became a proverbial shark and gobbled up even smaller adult studios. Because there was a dark, underground market for disgusting snuff films, the distribution of the films was unbelievably profitable, especially internationally. No investor would know the difference. Really. On paper, everything was legit and legal. No one questioned how you were fronting money to purchase small businesses."

The general blinked, but his face remained unreadable.

"Then in oh-three, you approached a very good work friend about being a partner in the business. In fact, you set up Zanders distribution hubs here in Chicago, where your friend lived, because eventually he would take over the business."

Evelyn produced a small packet from her folder and slid it over to him.

"Stanton kept the contract hidden away for a rainy day." Without looking, Gavin opened to the last page. "His signature is here. This is Hewittson, and this one is yours, General Norquist. We wondered why Stanton would be so interested in this deal, so we dug a little deeper."

Evelyn produced an Excel spreadsheet and slid it over near Norquist. His eyes did not waver.

"You had your eyes on a much bigger prize," Gavin continued. "Zanders Holdings Group was actually a front for something else, something much larger. On Guerillo's file was a list of bank accounts from several shell companies in the Middle East and the Caribbean. Checking into Stanton's accounts, several of them match large amounts of monies added to his bank account over several years. In fact, in the last year, three deposits of five hundred grand were added on top of his small fortune. The basic math does not add up, despite how successful Zanders was in the porn industry. Do you want to know what makes this much more interesting, General Norquist?"

The harsh light seemed to magnify the general's deep wrinkles and sunspots as he pursed his lips and chewed on the inside of his cheek. Still saying nothing, his eyes went from Gavin to the mirror.

"Why the shell companies?" Gavin questioned, propping his elbows on the table. "Because Stanton said something unusual. He said something about getting the shipments and making the drop-offs while he was in Afghanistan. He claimed he was doing all the heavy lifting while you just took in the money. And he was real pissed about it."

"Stanton lied," Norquist finally spoke. "He doesn't know what he's talking about."

Ignoring him, Gavin continued. "Three things that you did not account for. The first, one person from Stanton's squad, Dr. Colleen Sheridan, was snooping into your business. She was figuring out how you were making your money by supplying a local faction with weapons in exchange for distributing drugs. You used the Afghan war and its people as the backdrop. Because Stanton was involved in ordering product, your stooge—Taylor—discovered what Dr. Sheridan was up to. But you had a different way of taking care of her. She was the inspiration for your films, wasn't she? In fact, she was the first part of the series. Your first Desert Blossom film."

With that, he hit the computer screen, and an image of the film cover appeared. "There she is in the corner. No one would ever know. For a few years, you, Stanton, and Cory Taylor abused these soldiers. Taylor didn't mind being the poster child, did he? Because you paid him off for it. These movies were a form of celebration for your other money-making deal. Yet Stanton thought the films were supposed to be home movies. In your mind, you were invincible; nobody would know it was you in these films. You edited only Stanton and Taylor raping and beating the women, and you were left on the cutting-room floor, as it were. However, you didn't expect your voice to be on the movies, which we now know is a digital match."

The general's lips turned into a bitter frown.

"How did he come across the original films, you wonder?" Gavin continued. "Taylor had something to do with that. We received his laptop three days ago, and our IT specialist uncovered the unedited footage. Perhaps when Stanton showed up to kill him, under your orders, of course, Taylor pleaded with him and bartered those films for his life. Gave Stanton the actual hard copies, I would imagine."

"That's the reason why Stanton," Evelyn added in, "went on to kill Sills, Carlton, and Gable in Zanders Holdings locations. Someone knew it would lead back to you."

"The second thing you did not account for," Gavin stated promptly, "was a nurse in Afghanistan who discovered these women were being victimized. She even told Stanton about it, and Stanton told you. When no action was taken, the nurse then approached the women and told them to file grievances. What did you do? You pushed through for an early discharge for Sills, Gable, and Carlton. The cases were conveniently dropped and then redacted carefully under your orders. As far as the nurse was concerned, you also gave her an early discharge and hoped not to hear from her again. You even forgot about her, because you thought that you were still untouchable.

"You see, General," Gavin said, remaining calm. He stared directly into the general's eyes. "I spoke to that nurse about the case, and she happened to remember one of the victims. Then, seven days ago, she called someone she trusted once. She happened to inform him that her husband, a detective, was looking into the cases. But this is where the nurse's connection made a mistake and then phoned Stanton. Perhaps that's what motivated him to clean up that detail. Something he did not expect either. Stanton kidnapped her and attempted to kill her the exact same way he did the others. Do you remember her name?"

"Well, this is some story," the general croaked. "I know y'all detectives spend all day, every day theorizing on who the bad guy is and how to catch him. I must tell you, it's quite a bayou tale."

"Corporal Maria Dominquez, first medical division," Evelyn stated evenly.

"The last thing you did not count on," Gavin pressed on. "A staff sergeant you were not aware of. He was under Stanton's squad. Derrick Williamson. While your suspicions were correct about Dr. Sheridan, you didn't realize that Williamson was assisting her. He knew what you and Stanton and the others were doing. In fact, I made a small request two days ago about Taylor, Bauerman, Parker, and Pope's personal banking accounts. They too received monies from several accounts from Guerillo's list, from your shell companies. Williamson knew early on that they were on the take."

A small bead of sweat crawled down his forehead.

"Actually, Stanton hated Williamson from the start," Gavin continued. "He didn't even see that he was connected to Dr. Sheridan. He had to get rid of him. He trumped up charges on Williamson as the drug dealer, which took the heat off of you for distributing it. But the months before Williamson was discharged, he was actually gathering evidence on you and the so-called shipments. He never told Sheridan about the documents, only the random shipments he physically saw. Williamson decided to make two copies of them. One he sent to a PO Box in Chicago for backup. And one to his only true friend in the military."

"This is absurd," the general began.

"You may know him," Gavin added. "Colonel Coniston."

"Coniston?" Norquist's face flashed an expression of puzzling bewilderment. "What the fuck?"

"The people behind this mirror will have some questions for you about those shipments," Evelyn stated. "However, Maria Dominquez made a call to this number five days ago." She pressed send on her phone. Soon, the sound of a cell phone ringing came alive from inside Norquist's breast pocket. "Aren't you going to answer your phone, General?"

"We discovered Stanton's phone," Gavin stated, "attached to a similar bomb at Navy Pier on Tuesday night. The actual night of your award ceremony. His intention was to kill Maria, himself, and bring you and half the pier along for the ride. After a little digging, I discovered that in oh-seven, the Zanders Group donated a substantial dollar amount to the restoration of Navy Pier."

"Stanton's lying about this. All of this." Norquist stood up, wiping his chubby hands against his uniform.

"He can't be lying," Gavin explained. "Stanton was shot and killed on Tuesday."

"This absurd," the general stated bitterly. He stood then, walked toward the door, and opened it. Out in the hallway, a pair of menacing military police stood in the doorway.

"As far as proof about your drug dealings, selling American weapons, and connection with the Qahhar," Gavin stated blatantly, "these men are here to make sure you go to the Pentagon for your arraignment."

"This is all a mistake," the man blubbered as he was being

handcuffed.

"Once they are done with you," Gavin said, standing up, "you will be extradited back to Chicago, where you will be charged as the accomplice in murdering Janice Carlton, Donna Gable, and Rhonda Sills. Because on Stanton's phone records, several brief calls were made on the days that they were murdered to your phone number."

"This is a mistake!" Norquist yelled out.

"Above all," Gavin walked up to him, seeing the spittle on the general's chin. "You will be charged for secondary murder for Maria Dominquez, who died from her wounds on Tuesday evening on the way to the hospital. She was Derrick Williamson's, my partner's, wife. *You asshole.*"

The two men manhandled General Norquist, roughly dragging him down the hallway as he screamed in denial all the way.

*****

"I can't believe that it's over," Evelyn remarked, already gathering up the files and papers.

Gavin casually looked back at the mirrored wall. The last couple of days since Maria's death had been trying, even with the major support of the precinct.

"Detectives," Commissioner Ronin said as he entered the room. His tall, thick frame filled the small space, making it claustrophobic. Just behind him, Creighton hovered in the hallway with a huge grin.

"Yes, Commissioner," Gavin stated.

"Not a bad job in there, Nolan," Ronin said. His thick jowls giggled as his hazelnut brown eyes scrutinized Gavin. "Next time, tell us if you are going to pull something out of your ass before you speak. Using a cease and desist order wasn't bad, but the department cannot afford rabbit tricks to go to shit."

"Sorry, won't happen again." *Maybe.*

Ronin eyed Evelyn and said, "You're new to this."

"Yes, sir," she replied with a subtle nod.

"Very good research," he commented. Then he added, "But don't ever try to overstep your bounds again like you did with Captain Leger. You'll be a good fit here."

A half-smile graced her lips. "I won't, sir."

Then he looked back at Creighton, who automatically stepped

forward. "Quinn, is Nolan studying for his lieutenant's exam yet?"

"Not yet," Creighton replied, almost too obediently.

Turning to exit, Ronin stated, "Nolan, you'll make a fine lieutenant. It'd make your father proud."

"Yes, it would," he said simply. John Clariden's words echoed in his mind: *Your father hated Ronin.*

Without much more, Ronin rounded the corner, disappearing. Creighton nodded to both of them and followed the commissioner. Two other people passed in the doorway.

"Good work, Detectives," said District Attorney Chad Whalen, who wore a clean, expensive navy-blue suit and flashed an unusually bright white smile. Then he walked off.

"We'll talk about transfer of evidence in the coming weeks," said Britany Fry, the assistant attorney general. Her long frame hugged her power-red pants suit. "Another great job, Nolan. Better than the alderman case."

"Yeah, suppose," he replied.

She too disappeared.

As they gathered their items, another man came to the doorway. His tall, fit stature wore the military uniform snuggly and with ease. A warm, inviting smile sat pleasantly on his defined angular face.

"Detective Nolan. Detective Lopez." His soothing, distinguished voice filled the room.

"*General* Coniston?" Gavin inquired, already stepping around Evelyn to shake his hand.

"Yes, the one." The general's firm handshake was quick. "I apologize for not getting here right at the beginning."

"Chicago traffic, we get it," Evelyn stated after she let go of his hand.

"You folks were excellent," he commented. The soft wrinkles around his dark eyes were weathered.

"Doing our job," Gavin returned.

"Honestly," he said, lowering his voice. "We should have had this one, Detectives. Sometimes the government has its own pace. You could have avoided all of this."

"Well, we wouldn't have had the pleasure of meeting you," Evelyn returned and looked down at her phone. "Gavin, I have to get going. I promised to get back home. Need to get ready."

"No problem," Gavin said to her.

Quickly, she gathered up her paperwork. "Pleasure, General," she said and left.

"She's spunky," Coniston stated.

"Yes, she is."

Then his smile dropped and he said, "How's Derrick doing?"

"As well as can be expected," Gavin returned automatically. Truly, he did not know. Derrick had not answered any of his texts in the last couple of days. Then again, Gavin had been consumed with finding evidence on Norquist. No matter, Derrick needed his space and time to cope with Maria's death. "Are you coming to Maria's wake tonight?"

"Of course," he said softly. A tinge of sadness dusted his voice. "Derrick would appreciate it."

"Yes, he would." Gavin added, "May I ask one question? If you can answer it."

"I'm intrigued," the general said. "Go for it."

"Was Dr. Sheridan working with the CIA?" Gavin almost regretted asking it instantly.

Sighing heavily, the man's dark eyes darted up to the ceiling and back to Gavin. "To be frank," he said, "I can't say whether she was or not. One thing about government operatives. Their goals are never shared with all the branches." He paused, most likely choosing his words carefully. "From what Derrick explained to me, the possibility of Sheridan being with another organization is highly likely. What was her intended purpose? What were the mission's objectives? We will never know because it died with her."

"Fair enough," Gavin stated.

"I have to leave," the general said. "Have to make sure that son of a bitch is loaded on the plane."

The general ambled down the hallway, buttoning up his long black jacket.

Gavin's phone vibrated. Looking down, he read the text from Chad: *At your apartment. Coming soon?*

Maria's death had put a different perspective on his relationship with Chad. Despite what had happened between them, Gavin couldn't lose him. Not now.

Yes. On my way. Love you.

As he walked through the station, he noticed most of the desks were empty. The wake was going to be filled with many people. The lingering sadness that he'd suppressed the last couple of days slowly seeped into his system. Tears filled his eyes as he realized how much he would miss Maria.

And the grief Derrick must be enduring due to Zachary Stanton.

EPILOGUE

"How still,
How strangely still
The water is today,
It is not good
For water
To be so still that way."
    —Langston Hughes

"Anybody could've told you
Right from the start it's 'bout to fall apart
So rather than hold on to a broken dream
I'll just hold on to love…"
    —Alicia Keys

DERRICK

Angela opened the door without much of a word and let him in. A subtle yet obligatory smile fell on her satin pink lips and then quickly disappeared.

Derrick's house was stiflingly humid, a shock from the frosty air outside. Gavin shrugged off his long coat as he followed Maria's sister-in-law through the foyer and down the long corridor. As he passed by the dining room, a heavy floral perfume wafted around him. The funeral flower arrangements hugged just about every square inch of the space from on top of the table to the floor itself. The bouquets still looked fresh no doubt due to the administrations of the women of the house in memory of Maria's spirit. In the right corner and near the windows, Maria's picture remained on an easel. The sparkle in her cheerful, dark eyes begged for life.

And not for it to be taken by some maniac.

Throughout the funeral, Derrick's expression was eerily blank and unusually somber. The bloodshot eyes and the faint grimaces hinted at his grieving. During the wake, Derrick's composure was rigid and formal, as if his military discipline choked down the visitors' sympathetic words. While the church was packed, standing room only and even many hoovering on the outside of the place, Derrick was automatic in his gestures and responses, and he clung to his children and his mother-in-law. Even though Chad remarked how beautiful the ceremony had been, Derrick's eyes spoke of a silent anger and even despair. Even then, Gavin had said very little to him, understanding that Derrick needed space to cope.

Now, a week later, after the several attempts Gavin had made to contact him, Derrick finally requested he to stop by.

The soft noises of activity in the kitchen bounced off the hallway. Gavin glimpsed a young woman's back as she was busy creating a meal that smelled of cumin, chicken, and sweet onions. Beyond that, Lucinda's room was open. From this angle, it looked as if Maria's mother was resting on her bed. The house was unusually still and quiet.

Stopping at the doorway to the den, Angela simply said, "He's in here." Then she turned and walked away, wiping her eyes.

Derrick was sitting in the same chair he had been sitting in on Thanksgiving. The bright sunlight cascaded over his body, while a long shaft of shadows covered his face. As Gavin approached him, a bleak scowl was plastered on his partner's face. His reddened eyes met Gavin's gaze, and then he turned his attention to his half-filled glass of Scotch. Gavin noticed Derrick's son sleeping in the Pack 'n Play nearby.

"Hey Derrick," Gavin said, sitting on the davenport near him.

"Gavin." Derrick's deep, low voice sounded like a phantom beckoning him.

"How are you holding up?" Gavin leaned forward, propping his elbows on his knees.

Not saying a word, Derrick took a sip of his drink. Gavin was not going to point out that it was nine thirty in the morning.

"Did you read my text about the service?" Then Gavin added quickly, "It was beautiful. A lot of people at the station kept talking about it for days."

"Yes," he replied. "It was beautiful. Like her."

Silence fell between them. Shuffling footsteps echoed down the hallway. Then, Gavin heard the small, happy squeal of Derrick's older child fill the room for a brief moment.

"I wanted to tell you a couple of things," Gavin began. "Not sure if you want to hear them now."

Derrick said nothing. His reddened eyes shifted down to the Pack 'n Play.

"The young woman's body in that house fire," Gavin began. "It turned out that she was related to Stanton in some manner. Maybe his daughter. We'll never know."

The day after Maria's funeral, Stanton's body was discovered near Blue Island. Luckily, the body did not get swept up by Lake Michigan's churning winter currents and remained within the breakwater. Susan had taken blood samples and matched them to the young woman's body from the Ashland house fire. Speculating, Evelyn believed that Stanton found out he had an illegitimate daughter from one of his rapes, and he probably did not want any more responsibility. She thought he had even been embarrassed. The young woman's identification was still unknown. Working with the FBI and with Creighton's approval, Mary took it upon herself to keep searching international missing person's files.

Derrick nodded slowly.

"Another thing," Gavin said quietly. He did not want to overwhelm Derrick with news. "About Norquist."

"I know," he answered grimly.

"That he killed himself late last night?" Gavin sounded slightly surprised.

General Norquist could handle neither the media pressure nor the military inquiry. His wife had left him immediately, and his three sons were horrified over Norquist's crimes, making their disgust widely known in the press. Early this morning, a MP found Norquist hanging in his cell.

"John called me earlier," Derrick stated, emptying the glass and then refilling it. "Why I'm fucking celebrating."

"Glad that you, um, heard," Gavin retorted.

Another brief lapse of awkward stillness.

"So you wanted to see me?" Gavin questioned him.

"Yeah." Derrick slowly swiveled his head toward the window to look outside. "Out of respect, I want to tell you first. Before anyone else tells you."

"Alright," Gavin replied. He swallowed roughly, his mouth dry.

"I told Creighton that I'm not coming back to the force."

The floor felt as if it had slid under Gavin. "You mean just a long leave."

"No," he answered back. "I can't risk my life anymore. I have my kids to think about. I'm now a single, uh…" He paused. "I'm a single parent now."

"What about Maria's mother? Her family?"

"They are extremely supportive. I would not be able to get through this without them." A grin crept to his lips. "I appreciate them more than they probably understand. But I can't rely on them forever."

"We can make it work," Gavin started. "And I'm sure we can figure out something, daycare plan…"

"You're not listening, Gavin," he interrupted. "I'm leaving the force."

Utterly shocked, Gavin leaned back on the couch and stared at Derrick.

"And another thing, Gavin." Derrick cocked his head toward the ceiling. "I need to ask a question. Please answer truthfully."

"Alright." Gavin felt nausea.

"Why were you fighting with the captain in the men's room a couple of weeks ago?"

"Creighton was being an asshole." Gavin could hear his own lie.

"If anybody else was caught having a fist fight with their superior," Derrick commented, "their ass would be suspended, IA would come in and investigate, and so on. Get my goddamn point?"

"We were not seeing eye to eye," Gavin stated simply.

"Stop it, Gavin," Derrick interrupted. "For the years I was with you, I heard rumors from the others about you and Creighton. I ignored them. I just didn't want to believe it. It was all bullshit as far as I was concerned. Then you got lead detective after the alderman case. I was totally fine with that. You earned it."

He paused for a moment to take a large gulp of Scotch. "I heard that you are considering becoming lieutenant. Did you know that Diaz had wanted the lead detective position for a couple of years? He was pissed that you bypassed him. Now Garrison is supposed to be up for lieutenant. And you're getting it before him. He's not happy about it."

"I earned my rank," Gavin justified.

"They always said Creighton favored you," Derrick continued. "I noticed immediately that it worked for our cases. Fine with me. I thought it was an advantage." His eyes scanned Gavin menacingly and then shifted back to the ceiling. "Yeah, you and Creighton were once beat cops, he trained you and bullshit. I got it. You guys always had a weird fucking symbiotic connection. But I didn't realize it was more than that."

"What are you implying?" Gavin could not breathe.

"Listen, when you came out to me that really meant a lot." Derrick ignored his question. "I don't care if you like fucking men, Gavin. Honest. As long as you are happy. Seriously. Chad's an awesome guy."

"Derrick," Gavin began.

"I told you that day." Derrick looked at him, almost angrily. "I always knew you had a secret someone. I just didn't realize who it was until that fight."

"Derrick," Gavin tried to say.

"I heard the end of your fight," he stated matter-of-factly.

Gavin's heart thumped harder in his chest. Sweat was forming on his hands.

"How long have you been fucking the boss?" Derrick stared straight at him. "Be goddamn honest."

"It's not like that," Gavin began.

"Be honest, Gavin." Derrick's deep voice soaked into his skin. "I hate fucking liars."

"No, it's not like that," he repeated. "Quinn and I—"

"See, it's that *shit*," Derrick interjected, shaking his head. "Friends are friends. But being something else. Lovers? Or whatever the hell you want to call yourselves? You fucking lied to me, all this time."

"No, Derrick," Gavin pleaded.

"You're getting up in the ranks because you're fucking the boss," Derrick retorted simply. "And screwing everyone else in the department for your personal goddamn gain. Never thought you'd be one of those assholes."

"No, Derrick, it's not…not like that," Gavin stammered.

"Bullshit!" Derrick's voice boomed. "Motherfucker, stop lying to me!"

Gavin said nothing.

Derrick finished his Scotch and turned away from Gavin, still shaking his head.

"Derrick…" Gavin's voice was barely a whisper.

"Get the hell out of my house," Derrick demanded.

"What?" Gavin was in disbelief.

"I don't want any more contact with you, Gavin," he stated, still not looking at him. "Leave me and my family alone. Got it?"

"You don't mean that," Gavin returned.

Derrick turned his head, his glare falling upon Gavin.

"Get the fuck out of my house." He stopped, clenching his fist. "Or I'll fucking throw you out, you lying son of a bitch."

As if in a dream, Gavin nodded his head, gathered his coat, turned his back on Derrick, and left.

*****

For the next several weeks into the Christmas holiday, Gavin was not himself. At work, the surprise of Derrick not returning shocked people. Yet they understood quite well that Derrick needed time to cope with his loss. Despite this, Evelyn noted Gavin's somber attitude, occasionally questioning what was wrong with him. Shortly after, Creighton assigned Evelyn to be his partner.

As far as Chad was concerned, Gavin never questioned him about the video, nor did he disclose his moment of weakness with Quinn and the other man. Perhaps keeping secrets, as he had with Emily, was just a vicious cycle.

However, Chad surprised him the night after he left Derrick's house. Because Chad was promoted to area manager for his tech company, he'd purchased a little getaway for New Years in Turks and Caicos. With everything that had happened, Gavin needed a break. Needed to be with Chad.

On New Year's Eve, Gavin gazed at the dark midnight water and remained planted on the still warm sandy beach. Next him Chad came up to him as his unbuttoned shirt fluttered in the warm ocean breeze. He handed Gavin a glass of champagne.

"Here, honey," Chad said softly, wrapping his large arm around Gavin's waist.

"Perfect timing," Gavin said with a faint smile.

Nearby, other couples were standing on the beach as well. They too were clinging to each other and holding hands. The midnight chime was only seconds away. Some teenagers were dancing on the beach a few hundred yards away. The hotel behind them was lit up, and inside the ballroom, people were partying.

The announcer began to count down. In Gavin's ear, so did Chad.

When the midnight hour struck, the dark sky lit up with fireworks. Gavin kissed Chad deeply and passionately, realizing that he could never lose him.

"I love you," Gavin said as he was wrapped in Chad's arms.

"So do I," Chad returned, pressing his thick bare chest against Gavin.

At that moment, Gavin looked into Chad's beautiful dark eyes. His mind went back to that night with Quinn, a night that he could not fully remember. Derrick's words still stung his thoughts like angry scorpions, making him question his relationship with Quinn even more.

Gavin would have to tell Chad about Quinn.

Someday soon.

*****

Ernesto Santiago sat in the abandoned floor in the building across the street from his former partner's apartment and turned off the taping unit, though he was convinced Nolan's apartment still needed to be under surveillance. Since the end of June, most of the recordings consisted of random useless calls about cases, casual listless conversations with his lover, and even more disturbingly, the heated passion of their grunts.

So far, nothing.

Honestly, Santiago had to fast forward through most of those moments. Never had he realized that Nolan was gay. Was Nolan trying to get into his pants when they were partners? A shiver tingled throughout Santiago's body—the thought made him sick.

However, he'd received an order that recent recordings had to be confiscated by the government. While he had not reviewed them personally, it was apparent that Nolan's partner, Williamson, had divulged important classified military operations. As he pocketed the flash drive, a part of him wanted to listen to them. But he resisted the urge.

That was not his priority.

Quickly, the elevator opened and he slid into it. He took one last glance at the unfinished floor, which was filled with dark, ebbing shadows. The streams of plastic walls created subtle imaginary figures, but Santiago knew no one else was there. They made sure the floor would be under construction until the investigation was over.

As the elevator descended, he could not help thinking about his sister's conversation. Evelyn had told him excitedly that she was assigned as Nolan's partner. Yes, the move was good for her. Away from that prick, Leger. But her partner was Nolan. Deep down, Santiago felt that Nolan had nothing to do with what was going on. However, that past November, Nolan had gone to Creighton's apartment and stayed overnight.

Santiago questioned his gut instinct. What was even more puzzling was the other man who had left Creighton's apartment shortly after. And who kept visiting Creighton since then? On and off? What was Scott Ronin, the son of Commissioner Ronin, doing with Creighton?

The elevator doors opened to the parking garage below the building. Hearing the clicks of his shoes, he listened as the echoes reverberated back and forth in the nearly empty space. Faint sounds of the outside traffic buffered in here and there.

Santiago felt the flash drive bounce around in his front pants pocket. The investigation into Creighton was becoming messier. So many more questions were being asked than being answered. Since he had been following Creighton, the captain's behavior had changed. He was much more erratic, visited other men besides Scott Ronin, and now his new divorce. Santiago had also followed him to police archives several times. What had Creighton been doing there? Creighton's meetings with Commissioner Ronin were getting less and less frequent.

Not making any sense.

Captain Quinn Creighton was becoming much more enigmatic.

Even Santiago's partner, Harper, found it challenging to keep up with him. Actually, the last couple of nights, she'd done a couple of night surveillances on Creighton. Her reports also conveyed how different he had become. As if Creighton no longer cared. As if he had nothing to lose.

But Creighton was covering something. Or even someone. Santiago couldn't pin it down.

About a hundred yards away, the dark, unmarked car was parked near the ramp. Although she had her daughter's birthday party today, Harper had still come with him to the building. Oddly, she explained to him that she felt as if she were being followed while watching Creighton. She couldn't place it. She didn't have proof. Really, Santiago thought that she was overworked—not like he wasn't—and needed a little break. That was what they were discussing before they came here.

As he approached the car, Harper's head was leaning against the headrest. She was too hyper to ever rest. God only knew when she slept. Yet, the car was turned off. She always kept it idling when she waited for him.

Opening the passenger door, Santiago said, "Alright, got it. Let's go."

Looking over, he saw Harper's open, dead eyes staring back at him. He could see a thick red gash across her throat and blood all over the front seat. Immediately, he jumped out of the car. Her body slumped forward, and her head hit the steering wheel.

"Shit!" Santiago yipped, pulling out his gun. Pivoting on his heels, his eyes scanned the garage space. There were no other sounds.

He glanced back at Harper's body and noticed the droplets of blood on the cake she'd bought for her daughter's seventh birthday in the backseat.

Santiago's heart was racing. Was Harper right? Was someone following her?

"Sorry, Liz," he muttered. Instead of calling it in, he headed toward the stairway. He knew he could not be placed there, and he needed to leave. Someone else would call it in. Later, he would act surprised about the news of her death.

Deep down, Santiago's paranoia heightened, but his determination to dig further into Creighton only increased.

TO BE CONTINUED...

November 2018

DERRICK

Here's a preview of

Russell's

QUINN

The Final Installment

of the Gavin Nolan Series

PROLOGUE

She stood at the top of the stairs. Her breath caught in her throat at the thought of who she had left in the dilapidated old building and what she was about to do with him.

The woman hurried down the steel-framed stairs much like the scurrying rodents in the far corners, her boots thudding on each tread. The heavy echoes of her pounding footsteps dissipated into the surrounding midnight blackness most likely frightening them away. Above her, the scratching sound of the rat's claws across the wooden floor created an eerie, melodic tune within the unnerving silence.

How much she loved this place! Even though a pair of night vision goggles dangled around her thick neck, she instinctively recalled each and every nook and cranny of the vast playground. Many times, she'd strolled the immense areas of the factory in the dark, carefully and purposely, and opened up her other senses to guide her. Due to this, her memory helped her eyes adjust easily to the encompassing blackness, and she noticed the faint outlines of doorways, crumbled machinery in the distance, and the nothingness beyond. With the large foreboding signs plastered over the building's exterior, no one else would dare enter the place. It was the perfect place to conduct her business.

After all, it once belonged in the family.

Once she hit the next level, which had been a storage area, she crept forward as would a phantom, seemingly floating toward the faint light ahead. The woman was alone. Well, partially.

A few times, she had heard soft murmurs in the inky darkness. The whispers were taunting, reassuring, and even seemingly familiar as she wandered the passages through the evenings. Even when she slept here, the presence of others could be felt around her. One time, she swore she could see the faint outline of someone near the old camping cot. Other times, even recently, several bangs had occurred up on the main level. When she had inspected the suspicious noise, clutching her rifle in her hands, just in case it was someone trying to invade her sanctum: Nothing was there, naturally. She believed that the voices, sounds and shapes were not harmful. Perhaps, *they* were content she was there.

Tonight though, the place was unbelievably quiet.

Stepping over the rubble of the collapsing ceiling, she peered up. She could see straight through to the main section of the building. Above her, the long lead glass windowpanes glinted with the reflection of the shiny moonlight. None of that light could pierce the darkness.

Suddenly, a faint groan filled her ears. A wicked grin caressed her cracked lips.

As she shoved the nearby rusty door open, the hard squeal of hinges sounded much like the death of several swine. When she lived on the farm, she often had to kill the pigs for the coming winter; the haunting scream was the same sound they made when she slit their bellies open. As she entered the next room, an elongated orange glow filled the space that had once been an employee locker room. In its current state, the lockers were crusted in rust. Some were falling off their hinges, inked with gang symbols, or ripped off the wall. Gingerly, she stepped over the maze and inched her way toward the carroty glow.

Taking one glance behind her, she stepped into the next room. The auburn glow enveloped the area, exposing the decaying walls, falling tiles, broken glass, and metal pieces covering the floor. In the abandon employee shower room of the old factory, various shaped nozzles appeared to be dead mechanical skeletal fingers reaching out from behind the walls. Yet, in the center of it all, her eyes zeroed in on the prize, and her devilish smile widened.

A man was slumped over on his knees on the mound of debris. His long, muscular arms suspended in a Y formation above him. As she slowly approached him, his head bobbled up and down lackadaisically and rolled back and forth almost comically. She stifled the urge to laugh. In the light, the man's naked back arched to show off the nautical star tattoos covering one side of it. The markings disappeared into the narrow of his pants. How disgusting to have that many tattoos!

Slowly, the man turned his head, and his eyes rapidly blinked at her as she walked into the room.

"Pl... please," he grunted out. The man's once pretty face was swelling due to the blows she had inflicted earlier.

Saying nothing, the woman hastily advanced to her worktable. The man couldn't see it from his position. Touching the crude blades on several instruments, which were slightly crusted and stained with blood, her fingers wrapped around the end of her favorite tool. Her father had designed it: a long razor wire whip on a thin oak spindle. Her father would use it on the animals to keep them in line, shredding their skins until they learned to behave.

Closing her eyes and feeling her energy surge, she gripped it tightly.

"Let...me go, please," the man whined childishly.

Turning, she walked around the disintegrating pillar and took in the sight. The man's bare chest rose and fell as he breathed heavily, causing his tight oblique and defined abdominal muscles to retract and constrict continuously. His marvelously toned body made him appear as one of those cover sinful, nearly naked models in magazines, yet those tattooed stars marred his upper chest and ran down the side. Such a waste. His body contorted slightly as he tried weakly to pull at the chains. A whimper escaped from the man's lips as tiny streams of blood dripped down from his wrists.

For days, the woman had watched the man before she finally grabbed him. At his work in the clothing store, the man would hungrily prance around older, thicker men, flattering and even drooling over them. At the gym, he talked more on his phone than worked out, and took even longer in the locker room. He always seemed more exhausted when he came out. She had also let herself into his apartment—what a filthy dump! Then, she followed him to those seedy bars, where the other men were... like him. All of them just touching themselves, each other, kissing, and even—

Those filthy animals should be goddamn punished. Daddy's words echoed in her mind—

She had to follow him. When she had discovered the man coming out of *his* apartment building--the very one she'd been watching for weeks—the man had been there several times. So last night, she had seen him enter and patiently waited until he had to leave. All she had to do was sneak up behind him, grab him, and bring him back here. The man hardly even put up a fight. Well, she did have to strike him hard across the head several times, but…

Simple.

As if in slow motion, the man lifted his head, squinted at the light, and jerked slightly at the chains. Small flakes of dried blood dropped from his forehead and into his watery eyes. She could tell that he was trying to hold back tears. Oh, the poor thing had never been beaten up before!

As she ambled around him, the man looked at her not with anger (as she would have hoped), but with utter fear. Even at this distance, the fresh smell of urine invaded her nostrils, and she saw a new dark stain on his khaki pants.

So weak.

"What do… you want?" the man snorted out. His eyes rolled around in their sockets, trying to see what was in her hand.

God, she so loved this part! The crunching mesh of tile beneath her black boots echoed sharply in the space.

"Say something!" he barked out. His desperate voice was unusually low.

Rounding his body, she stepped behind him, and he nervously craned his head as far back as he could. She lowered the whip, and the thin wire scraped against the floor. It reminded her of sparklers on the Fourth of July when she raced around the dark backyard as Daddy watched from the porch.

"Please, please," he implored desperately. "My dad has money. Lots of money. He'll pay whatever you want."

How insulting of this deplorable human being—trying to buy his way out of his fate! Her hand clutched the rough wooden handle, and a burning sensation of rage filled her. He was not the one calling the shots. She was in charge.

Swiftly, her hand raised with the whip, and she snapped it at the man's back. The wires instantly shredded the upper portion of his back, tearing apart the constellation of inked stars and exposing the innards of his skin. Through the man's bucking and screams, the tendrils of blood oozed down from the fresh wound, the color of a sublimely wonderful scarlet hue. She stepped forward as the man quieted down, slumping further and straining at the ropes.

"Plah... plah-please," the man stammered. "What... do you want?"

Sighing heavily, she spoke softly, "To know one thing."

His head flicked back and forth. His watery eyes didn't hide the anguish covering his face; she couldn't care less.

"Wha... what?" he cried out.

"Why were you at *his* apartment?" she hissed.

"Who?"

"You know who," she heatedly answered.

"I don't—"

"Shut up!" she yelled.

She struck the man three more times with the whip as trickles of red matter splattered all over the place—even on her. The man thrashed and yelled with each stroke and screamed in agony. Stepping back, she admired the beauty in the freshly scared, torn back, dripping with blood and gore. As the man rounded his shoulders, a glimpse of his porcelain bones peeked out. How lovely! It was so easy to just tear him to shreds. She let out a long heavy breath to relax. The woman needed him alive for just a little longer.

She needed to know about *him.*

As she headed back to her table, the man begged in a raspy and winded voice, "Please, no more..."

"You need to tell me the truth." She spoke loudly.

"I... will." The man sobbed uncontrollably.

Looking at the delightfully cruel instruments that had once been displayed so proudly in Daddy's workshop, she lowered the whip, now glistening with fresh blood and flesh. Next to it, she selected her favorite tool and hid it behind her back from the man. Turning to face him, her grin increased even more.

"Why were you there?" Her stern voice reminded her of one of her old teachers in Catholic school—Sister Anne Marie. She never liked that old spinster.

Blood dripped from the corners of the man's mouth, as it did from the fresh scars across his upper body.

"You... mean," he began, and looked up at her, seemingly acknowledging who she was talking about.

"I asked you a question."

"What I... go there for," he said softly. The fear seemed to seep from every one of his pores.

"You're trying my patience," she scolded, and she grabbed him by the nape of his sweaty, bloody hair. "Don't!"

"We usually... do... coke," he said softly, choking.

Letting go of his head, she backhanded him several times suddenly. Then she grabbed at his hair again.

"Why are you protecting *him*?" she stated, getting inches from his face. "Tell me what you actually do with *him*."

Gulping, the man replied, "We... fuh... fuck."

"Good boy." The woman patted his cheek. "That's a real good boy."

Stepping back, she glared at him. "See," she said softly, almost too gently. "You're no better than the rest. *He* never cared about anything or anyone. You're just disposable. Like *she* had been to *him*. Like how *she* was with us. Like *he* was with me."

"No, no, no," the man replied in shock. "He loves me."

"You're as dumb as you are pretty," she retorted with a sneer. "He needs to pay for *his* actions. To be accountable—"

"I don't understand... what... talking about," the man rasped, his words jumbled.

Amused, she returned condescendingly, "You don't have to, darling." She paused, lowering her other hand to reveal the machete. "I'm going to make sure *he* understands."

Raising the weapon and gripping the handle with both hands, she made a quick, intense arcing motion with her arms and allowed the blade to do its work. The man screamed and then was quickly silenced. The well-sharpened tool swiftly sliced through his neck and took off his head with a single blow. It fell and rolled a foot away from the twitching body. The stump continued to ooze out blood, while the limbs trembled against the restraints for a few seconds. Soon, a coppery scent filled her mouth and lungs. What a beautiful spectacle!

Taking a step forward, she picked up the head with both hands and looked into the still blinking eyes. Leaning into it, she kissed the lips, tasted the fresh blood, and licked her own lips slowly.

"Trust me," she whispered. "*He* will pay."

Daddy would be so proud of her now. Maybe, he was looking down at her from heaven. Fresh tears formed in her eyes. A long-ago song came to her mind then, and she began humming it. The same one Daddy used to sing to her when she was a little girl. Casually, she placed the man's head under her arm, laid the machete next to the twitching body, and walked out of the shower room into the attached dark room. She had to store it with the other ones.

Her night's work was just beginning…

ABOUT THE AUTHOR

For nearly two decades, Russell was an executive chef in the restaurant industry, in which he created succulent entrees and managed various types of kitchen operations. In the last seven years, he began to teach future culinarians how to achieve their professional goals in hands-on classroom and lecture settings. With his recent graduate work in the field of sociology, his interests center on organizational behaviorism, social theory, and food insecurity.

Russell has been writing for the majority of his life. Slipping into alternative universes allows Russell to enjoy the process of creativity from the novel's conception to its final draft. Most importantly, inspiration is a continuous piece of his work and results from the world around him. Currently, he lives in Up State New York with his two children and several cats.

Please visit Russell on these social media platforms:

His Website
www.russelltheauthor.com

Facebook: Russell (The Author)
https://www.facebook.com/Russell.The.Author

Twitter: @Russell_Writer

Instagram: @Russell_Writer

REFERENCES

Books

Balwin, James. 1953. *Go Tell It on the Mountain.* Everyman's Library. 280 pp.

Butler, Ocatvia. 2003. *Kindred.* Beacon Press. 264 pp.

Ellison, Ralph. 1952. *The Invisible Man.* Vintage Press. 581 pp.

Hansberry, Loraine. 1959. *A Raisin in the Sun.* Vintage. 151 pp.

Hughes, Langston. 1926. *The Weary Blues.* Knopf. 128 pp.

Hurston, Zora Neale. 1978. *Their Eyes Were Watching God.* Harper. 219 pp.

Morrison, Toni. 2004. *Beloved.* Vintage. 321 pp.

Mosley, Walter. 2010. *Devil in a Blue Dress (Easy Rowlins #1).* Washington Square Press. 272 pp.

Walker, Alice. 1983. *The Color Purple.* Mariner Books. 304 pp.

Wright, Richard. 2008. *The Outsider.* Harper. 672 pp.

Song Lyrics

Aracia, Marcella, Babbs, Durrell, Boyd, Luke, et al. *This is How I Feel.* "This is How I Feel". Tank. Atlantic Records. 2012.

tank this is how i feel lyrics - Bing

Austin, Johnta, Blige, Mary J. & Cox Bryan-Michael. *The Breakthrough.* "Be Without You". Mary J. Blige. Matriach, Greffen Records. 2005

mary j. blige be without you lyrics - Bing

Bhasker, John, Augeullo-Cook, Alicia & Reynolds, Patrick. The Element of Freedom. "Try Sleeping with a Broken Heart". Alicia Keys. Sony Legacy. 2014.

Alicia Keys - Try Sleeping With A Broken Heart Lyrics | AZLyrics.com

Donaldson, Tyran, Carter, Lang & Rowe, Solana. *Ctrl.* "20 Something." SZA. Legacy Records. 2017

sza 20 something lyrics - Bing

Drake, Maskati, Majid & Ullman, Jordan. Nothing Was the Same. "Hold On, We're Going Home." Drake. Cash Money Records. Republic Records. 2013.

Drake – Hold On, We're Going Home Lyrics | Genius Lyrics

James, Leela & Kelly, Tim. *Fall for You.* "Set Me Free." Leela James. BMG Records. 2014

Leela James – Set me free Lyrics | Genius Lyrics

Miguel. *Kaleidoscope Dream.* "Adorn." Miguel. RCA Records. 2012.

Miguel – Adorn Lyrics | Genius Lyrics

Made in the USA
Las Vegas, NV
16 February 2025